CW01619398

About the Author

Ruth Ward is the younger, better looking sister of the author Mark Hayden. Until recently, she lived abroad and worked for a mysterious organisation whose name and purpose have never been clear.

When she returned to Britain, Ruth was at a loose end and volunteered to write a cosy mystery featuring some of the characters from her brother's King's Watch universe.

Ruth lives in north Lancashire with her cat, Wombat.

Also by Ruth Ward

The Caffè Milano English Village Mysteries
Featuring Bridget and Lucy
Available from Paw Press

Murder Within Tent
Extra Shot of Murder

Extra Shot of Murder

The Second Caffè Milano English Village Mystery

Ruth Ward

PAW PRESS

www.pawpress.co.uk

01 Edition 01 December 2024

Map of Byford by Josh Hinge.

www.katiebirks.co.uk

ISBN
ISBN-13: 978-1-914145-07-0
ISBN-10: 1-914145-07-0

***

To Vanessa & Dave

Without whom our village would not be the same.

Publisher's Note

If you would like to see more maps, character lists and other information about the world of Byford, they can be found on the Paw Press website. This book was written in 2024, but the action takes place some time between the Brexit Referendum and the Coronavirus Pandemic.

www.pawpress.co.uk

Extra Shot
Of
Murder

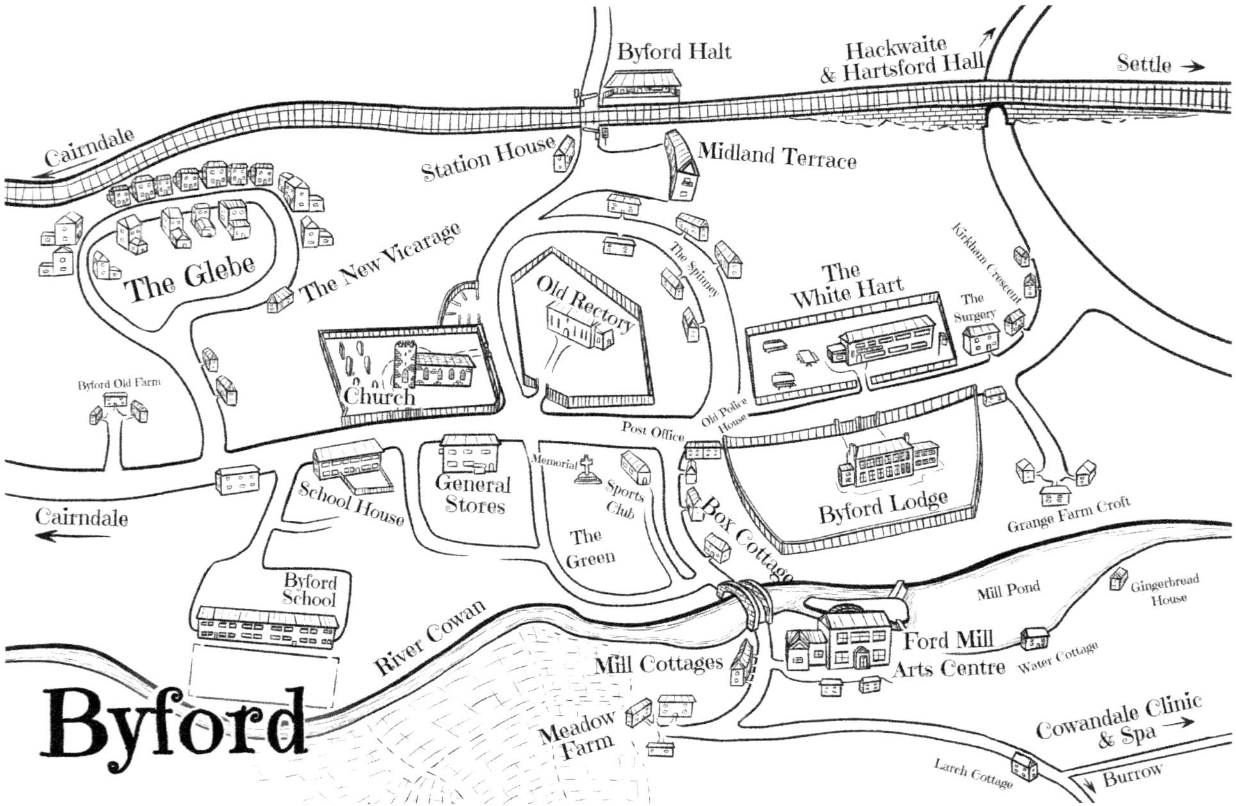
Byford
Byford Halt
Hackwaite & Hartsford Hall
Settle
Cairndale
Station House
Midland Terrace
The Glebe
The New Vicarage
Old Rectory
The Spinney
Kirkham Crescent
The White Hart
The Surgery
Church
Byford Old Farm
Post Office
Old Police House
Memorial
Sports Club
The Green
General Stores
School House
Box Cottage
Byford Lodge
Grange Farm Croft
Cairndale
Byford School
River Cowan
Mill Pond
Gingerbread House
Ford Mill Arts Centre
Water Cottage
Mill Cottages
Meadow Farm
Cowandale Clinic & Spa
Larch Cottage
Burrow

One

Some revelations come late in life, if thirty-six counts as late. Whatever. It didn't matter where she was on her journey because Bridget Gorrigan had discovered that after a lifetime of embracing the shadows and the darkness, she might, underneath it all, be a morning person. Who knew?

The sun was over the hills and the mini heatwave was due to continue for a few days yet. Another reason to seize the day. She passed two tractors on her way up the valley from Cairndale – the farmers were up and about, of course, even if the rest of the village was asleep. Oh yeah, and there was life in Byford General Stores.

She passed the turning that led to her new home and tried not to think of the unfinished unpacking. Instead of boxes, she focused on the idea of bringing her dad up to see where his little girl had landed – if he could survive being away from Liverpool for that long.

She crossed the bridge and drove into the Mill still full of the jokes and laughter that had foamed through his big birthday weekend like the head on his pints of Guinness, and how he'd talked her into staying one more night, even if that had meant leaving at half past bleeding five in the morning. *Best part of the day*, she told herself. *Yeah. Right.*

Thoughts of her uncle's rendition of "You'll Never Walk Alone" made her snort with laughter and miss the moment when she should have reversed up to the café's side door. She carried on past the mill building and into the empty overflow car park to do a U-turn. Only the car park wasn't empty. Oh. Add one more to the sunrise crew –

Anthony Carson was here. Well, it was a big day for him and the rest of Mini Magic Models. They were launching their online shopping channel at two o'clock this afternoon, and Anthony would be demonstrating how to build a replica railway station live on YouTube and Facebook.

Bridget's brain had its own junk filter, like her inbox, and when Tony had explained what he was doing, a lot of words had been caught in the mental mesh, including *Great Western, laser-cut, OO Gauge, pre-grouping …* and many, many more. The only thing which had made it through the filter and lodged in her head was that he was building a station out of wood live on TV. That was enough to cope with.

She drove back to the Caffè Milano door and unloaded the aromatic cakes and pastries from the van. She left them in the kitchen, then she started up the coffee machine, made herself an espresso and began preparing an Americano just the way Tony liked it: with two extra shots.

She slurped her coffee, popped a croissant on the tray with Tony's drink and took the customer lift. The TV studio was on the third floor of Ford Mill, above the craft village, above the Dukes Gallery and above the Cowan Theatre. Bridget had never been past the first floor and she was looking forward to seeing what was going on.

The lift opened and she emerged into a space which covered the whole of the main building, or it would do if someone hadn't thrown up a new divider. 'CARM yourself, girl,' she said with a smile. 'Railway modelling is not infectious.'

The top floor had been split 40/60 with the model railway club run by Tony's brother in the smaller "half" and the TV studio in the larger space beyond the engineered board of the partition.

The railway modellers had moved in over the weekend. They'd set up several trestle tables covered with dust sheets and they'd left a whole pile of stuff against the partition, barely leaving room for the rickety connecting door. She put the tray down on a stack of wood and tiptoed up to one of the trestles.

She lifted a corner of the dust sheet, expecting to be transported to a miniature wonderland. Oh. Fair enough. All she could see on the smooth board under the cloth were a whole pile of inverted plastic containers recycled from the kitchen and now labelled with stickers saying things like *Water Tower* and *FRC Down*.

Placeholders. Of course. These temporary structures were surrounded by pencil lines and annotations that she couldn't be bothered to read, so she carefully returned the dust sheet, hoping desperately that she hadn't moved the *WC Male* into the path of an oncoming express.

Bridget had rules about carrying trays: if you can't open the door using your hip, put the tray down. The dividing door to the studio had a handle, so she left the tray and went to see what the world of selly-telly looked like behind the scenes. Or smelled like, because there was something whiffy getting right up her nose.

The smell got worse when she opened the door, and she muttered, 'Please let him not be eating curry for breakfast. That's rank that is.'

The smell of ripe spices and something riper underneath pervaded the studio, or what little she could see of it as she came face to face with a whitewashed wall made of plywood. *Why would you fake antique brick when you're surrounded by the real thing?* She shook her head and listened to see if they were rehearsing or something. Silence. And the smell of curry wasn't dispersing.

'Morning, Tony! Got something for you.'

More silence. She peered cautiously round the plywood and her world heaved off its axis. She swayed, heat rashing her skin with fire. She staggered away from the sight in front of her and bumped into the solid, cold, all-too-real brick of Ford Mill.

TV cameras stood on high stands. A control panel blinked. Lights burned down from the gantry, illuminating a chair, shining on a workbench and picking out bloodstains all over this side of the plywood backdrop.

The body was on the floor next to an open and empty instrument case: the *City of Lancaster* was gone.

And someone had already given Anthony Carson his extra shot.

Two

The police found her outside the Mill, which is where the emergency operator had told her to go, 'In case there's someone in the building.'

Bridget had been reluctant to leave Tony on his own up there for someone else to see like that, but she'd done as she was told. The lingering chill in the shadow of the Mill had helped her see that the day was totally fucked. In every way. She'd sent a quick message to the extended WhatsApp group – *Serious incident @ Mill. Police on their way* – and then she'd shut down her phone. She could only cope with so much, and so she kept everything else at bay by addressing the trivia. *What am I gonna do with a day's bakery order? Should I move me van?*

There was only one officer in the patrol car that roared down the access road, and Bridget was relieved to see Police Sergeant Ryan Marsh, a fellow Scouser, emerge from the vehicle and stride over.

'You okay, kid? What's going on?'

She told Ryan what she'd seen and where she'd seen it. He told her to stay there and headed into the Mill. The next patrol car turned up five minutes later, and the whole circus arrived before half past eight, led by the ringmistress, Tracey Kenyon.

Tracey's van had the stripes and the markings, but not the bar of blue and red lights on top, because she was the crime scene manager, not a warranted police officer. She took the last of the vacant spots outside the front door and came over to see how Bridget was doing.

'How d'you think?' answered Bridget.

Tracey's meaty fist gave Bridget's shoulder a reassuring squeeze before she stepped back and surveyed the Mill. 'You've done this deliberately, haven't you?' declared Tracey.

'Eh?'

'Where am I gonna get coffee now?'

'I'll open the café. Give me something to do.'

Tracey's arms swept around the building. 'Maybe this afternoon. Probably not. Right now, the whole bloody thing is out of bounds.

Bloody typical.'

They took Bridget away to Cairndale police station shortly afterwards. As the patrol car drove down the lane, they passed a very worried Perry Lockwood and a shell-shocked Louis Young running up the road towards the Mill, and Bridget was sure the car abandoned in the lane by the gates was Hayley Horst's Audi.

At least they put her in the family room, not the stinky hole where suspects were interrogated. The youngest detective, Vicky Higham, brought Bridget a cup of tea and took a verbal statement, and then she disappeared. The next visitor, complete with witness statement forms, was one of the detective sergeants – Les Gartside.

'Are you okay?' he asked.

Bridget was about to say that he was the fifth person to ask that when Les pressed on. 'Need the loo or anything? I see you've already had a wash.'

Eh? What was he on about? 'How d'you reckon that, Les?'

He made a sweeping motion around his face. 'No black eyeliner or stuff.'

Since when did the bizzies care about witnesses' make-up? 'New, natural look for summer,' she told him, hoping he wouldn't go any further down that particular rabbit hole.

He didn't. 'Right. Sorry to keep you waiting, Bridget. And for the lack of decent coffee.' He tried a smile, and Bridget responded. Les was one of the good guys.

'Your tea's good,' she told him. 'Maybe it's the Sheriff's influence. Is he going to be allowed to take charge of the investigation? This has nothing to do with Lucy's business, I'm sure.'

Bridget's friend and boss, Lucy Berardi, had somehow ended up living with DCI Tom Morton, also known as *The Sheriff*. He had been barred from the last case Bridget had been involved in, but surely ...?

'What? No. Erm, haven't you heard? He's on secondment. From today. And today is also Liz's first day as the new DI.'

Bridget was stunned. Was this what Lucy had been planning to tell her at the meeting this afternoon? And why had it needed to wait? What was so secret that she couldn't have told her on Friday? Detective Sergeant Liz Swindlehurst's promotion must have been very sudden if word hadn't got round the coffee shops before this morning.

'Right,' Bridget said, trying to gather her thoughts. 'So is Liz in actual charge?'

'Sort of. The Commander has insisted on an old mate of his being the nominal senior, with himself as Liz's unofficial guardian angel.' There was a moment's pause while they both tried to assimilate the thought of the upright and immovable pillar of Commander Ross being any sort of angel. Les continued, 'But this is Liz's show.'

'Good for her. She deserves it.'

'She'll be along to see you later. When I've got your formal statement.' He clicked his pen. 'Right, Bridget. Tell me how you came to be delivering coffee to the top floor of the Mill at half past seven on a Monday morning?'

Bridget sat back and crossed her legs, tugging at her cream linen trousers. Why did they always crease as soon as you'd fastened the button? 'Did you know I've moved to Byford?'

'Not until Vicky told me.'

'Well, I suppose it started there,' she began.

Three

Ten Days Before Tony's Murder

Bridget was never late. For anything. At precisely ten twenty-five, she drove into Station Square and grabbed one of the empty spots in front of Byford Halt. The van containing all her worldly goods was due at eleven. She got out and leaned on the door to savour the moment, to enjoy the sunshine and to admire her new home.

The railway line ran above the village, so she was now effectively in the countryside. *Imagine that,* she told herself. *Bridget Gorrigan, Goth of Garston, moving into a proper English village.* Was the birdsong floating around her a welcoming committee? *Nah. Don't be daft. They're just doing what comes naturally. Unlike you.*

A clean but battered pickup rocked into the square, and her new landlord got out and waved. Now that summer was almost here, Perry Lockwood had discarded his waxed jacket and rolled up his sleeves. Bridget took out the extra-large coffee she'd made for herself and sauntered over to meet him at No 4 Midland Terrace, one of five built to house railway workers and now repurposed as desirable rental property for professional singles and couples. Bridget supposed that now she was a company director (on paper), she counted as a professional. Definitely single though.

'Morning,' said Perry. 'Are you ready for this?'

Bridget moved to stand in the shade, knowing that her life was not meant to be lived in the sunshine. Not often, anyway. 'Yeah, I'm ready. No. I dunno. I woke up at four o'clock and all I could think was that I was making a huge mistake.'

'I meant *are you ready to move in,* but if you want to have an existential crisis, don't let me stop you.' He grinned and took out a key to open the meter cupboard. 'Anyway, it wouldn't matter if you were making a mistake because you've signed a lease for six months and paid the deposit.'

'You didn't half pick the wrong career, you know. You're wasted as an estate manager, Perry. With empathy skills like that, you should have been a therapist. Thanks for letting me move in three days early.'

'No problem. The fitters signed off last night, and I know you'll be run off your feet with the bank holiday weekend.' He opened the cupboard and took pictures of the meters on his phone. 'Do you want a record?' he asked.

'I trust you.'

He took out two sets of keys and dangled them in the air. She held out her palm and he glanced at her arm, as he always did, looking for the skull-with-roses tattoo so that he could stare at it and fail to ask about it. It was covered up today, as it usually was when Bridget was due to meet someone new. Someone who might judge her. Like removal men.

'Let's do it,' she said.

He dropped the keys into her hand. She turned and unlocked the door, then stepped over the threshold, trying to quell the butterflies that had taken flight somewhere inside her. *No going back now.*

She walked down the narrow hall, turning almost sideways as she passed the staircase. She ignored the living room, because the real test was the kitchen. The first time she'd been here, when Feargal Hulme was in shock from Millie's murder, the kitchen was the only room she'd seen. She tried not to remember the disaster zone she'd encountered on that day and focused on the total renovation which Perry had promised.

She stepped around the dog-leg and into the rear of the house. *Sound* was her first thought. Then she looked down. 'Bloody hell, Perry. How come you've sprung for proper tiles not vinyl? And why are they green when the units are blue?'

He followed her down the passage, and his woody cologne wafted in front of her. It had been a long, long time since any man had stood behind her without making her turn round and step backwards and away to safety.

'You've answered your own question,' he told her. 'The tiles were left over from another job, so they were cheaper than vinyl. Easier to keep clean, too.'

Now she did flinch. Word of her ... *particular* approach to life had spread quickly from the Mill. She'd even had her own words quoted back to her in a TripAdvisor review: *Cleanliness isn't next to godliness at Ford Mill. Cleanliness IS godliness. Coffee's good as well, but a bit too strong for me.*

Bridget stepped into the galley kitchen, put down her full-strength coffee and started opening doors. Smooth action, well stocked with gleaming white crockery. No sawdust left over from the installation. Satisfactory.

She turned and found him leaning against the door jamb, a smile lighting up his face and making the lines round his eyes look like a life well lived and not a record of pain and loss. He brushed back his floppy sandy hair and straightened up. 'When is your stuff arriving? *How* is your stuff arriving? Are you going to collect it in your tasteful new vehicle?'

'Don't you start. Bloody Mina Desai. Or Mina Clarke-Desai as we're supposed to call her now.'

'I haven't met the woman yet, but the more you talk about her, the longer I can wait. What's Mina got to do with having your van painted bright red?'

'Because it's more tax efficient if it has *substantial branding* on it. Alright for her when her new husband owns a bleeding helicopter. You know I've been going to Southport?'

'I had heard. Kat told everyone that Lilianna is a much harsher mistress than you are. Southport's where you make the ice cream, right?'

'Correct. And where I lived for the past few years. I kept the lease on the flat there in case it didn't work out up here, so I had stuff in Southport and stuff in Cairndale. I packed up both lots and the removers are collecting them.' She checked her phone. 'Yep. They're on their way. Do I need to sign anything?'

'Just a quick one.'

He laid a document on the worktop and Bridget signed it without reading it. One of the first and hardest lessons of life in the countryside is that you have to trust the person you're dealing with because you'll bump into them most days. 'Thanks,' she told him. 'You off now?'

'I'll wait until the van gets here. No rush.' He sauntered back outside, and while he scanned the square, looking for her van presumably, she stuck to the shadows. She looked around, too, and then she remembered something that had been bugging her for a while.

The railway line and station formed one side of the square, the five houses of Midland Terrace another side, with the road down to Byford a third. The fourth side, the one directly opposite Midland Terrace, was a substantial Victorian villa with a high wall and nothing but the name *Station House* to tell of its place in the world. 'Who lives over there?'

'Not sure,' said Perry. 'I think it changed hands a couple of years ago and one of the directors in Dom Calvert's IT business bought it. One of the Angels, not that you'll find him singing in the choir. You should ask Jackie.'

At the bottom of the hill and in the heart of the village was Byford General Stores, proprietor Jackie Chester. There was very little going on in Byford that Jackie didn't know about and wouldn't happily share with anyone. 'I might just do that,' said Bridget. 'Or I might decide that it's best not to know, then I can imagine anyone I like living there.'

'Count Dracula, for example?'

'I'll take him for starters then work up from vampires to something more interesting. I find the fanged undead are a bit passé, don't you, Perry?'

She loved his smile. 'I defer to your expert knowledge. Just one thing, though. Don't sleepwalk over there and put a stake through anyone's heart.'

A breeze through the open front door wafted his cologne in her direction again. Had he put on more than normal today? It was also unusual of him to linger like this. She quite liked him lingering, and wanted to know what was on his mind, even if it was unlikely to be asking her for a date. Not that she wanted a date with Perry. No chance.

'Now that you're moving into the village, have you given any more thought to joining the quiz team?' he finally asked.

Oh. That again. She sighed. 'You've worn me down. I surrender. One condition, though: I get to choose the fourth member of the team.'

'So long as they're closely associated with the Mill, Fliss will have to like it or lump it.'

'I'll take Louis then.'

'Sorry. He's one of the Meadow Farm Magicians.'

'Hmph. I'll get back to you before Tuesday. Or was it Wednesday?'

'You've got an extra week. The quiz is postponed next Tuesday on account of the funeral and it being half-term. Are you sure you don't want to go to Millie's service?'

Bridget's first introduction to Byford had been the terrible murder of Millie Easterby, and Bridget had had a hand in tracking down the killer. That crash course in village life had been what convinced her she could live here, and Tuesday would be Millie's funeral.

'No, it's more that I can't go with it being half-term next week. We really need to get a move on with recruiting some new staff.'

'Where will Lucy be?'

'Would you believe she's going to a different funeral? Tom's granddad, over in Yorkshire.'

'Oh. I see. I'm sorry to ask this, but 3M3 are moving into the Mill Studio at ten on Tuesday, and that's when the service starts. If you could say hello and answer any obvious questions, I'd be grateful. Just until I get back.'

Her second lesson of life in the countryside had been that even a reserved man of few words like Perry would have no hesitation in asking a favour with the expectation of it being granted. She would have done it anyway. For Perry.

'Of course I will. Do you want me to put some "Welcome to Ford Mill" coffees and pastries on your tab?'

Lesson number three: if you don't ask, you won't get. Especially when it came to Perry. How could someone so generous be so tight at the same time?

'Twenty quid max,' he told her. 'And thanks. You can spend some quality time with your admirer after that.'

'Sod off. I am not going to be the object of anyone's admiration.'

He raised his eyebrows. 'I don't think the object has much choice in the matter.' Before she could have a real go at him, he pointed down the road. 'Here's your van, Bridget. Welcome to Byford.' He paused and shuffled away slightly, frowning and dropping his voice. 'Coming to Byford was the second-best decision I ever made. I hope you think the same. See you later.'

Presumably the best decision of Perry's life had been proposing to Lisa, or something equally romantic, like plucking up the courage to ask her out in the first place. He was leaving Bridget to work that out for herself.

Perry didn't shy away from Lisa's name. He often mentioned her.

But there are limits, and when Millie was laid to rest on Tuesday, the pall bearers would carry her coffin to the corner of the churchyard where all the Easterbys are laid, and on the way, they'd pass the grave of Lisa Lockwood, beloved daughter, sister and mother. And wife, too, of course.

Four

Six Days Before the Murder

It was quiet. Too quiet for a business with the overheads of Caffè Milano, but that was okay for today. Everyone had something better to do.

At five to ten, Bridget left the Spinning Room by the side door that opened directly onto the car park and allowed herself a daily moment of sunshine. Just enough to produce some Vitamin D but not enough to spoil the look. And then she thought, *Sod it. Why shouldn't I aspire to a healthy glow like any normal thirty-six-year-old woman?* The voice in her head said, *Because you're not normal.* This time she ignored it, just like she'd ignored it when she did her eye make-up this morning. Bronze, not black. Like a normal woman.

A shift in the gentle breeze blew the sounds from St Peter's Church up from the village as the community prepared itself for Millie's funeral. Instead of the joyous circling notes of the regular church bells (which Bridget quite liked), a single peal tolled out at an agonising interval, and it was still going on when a specialist removal van crossed the river and turned into Ford Mill, followed by two cars. Not the best omen for starting a new business.

Bridget waited until the van slowed down and then directed the crew round the back to where they could get easy access to the goods lift. The following cars parked close to the main entrance, and the team from 3M3 got out. Bridget pointed inside the Mill and went back to the café.

Ford Mill Arts Centre was a curious hybrid, with an empty space on the top floor which was supposed to be a TV studio, only no one wanted to make television in Byford. Until now. And was an online shopping channel *actually* television?

Perry Lockwood was effectively her landlord, but he was really the estate manager for the Byford Estate, and the Byford Estate was owned by Edwin and Felicia Duke, and the Mill was Felicia's baby. She had apparently been trying to get proper TV companies interested in the studio, but it was both too big and too small, and she had admitted defeat when Mini Magic Models made a firm offer.

They were known as 3M3 because, well there were three Ms in the company name and it was jointly owned by the three people walking through the archway into the café. Two of the three jostled to get to the counter first, and one hung back.

The jostlers were a woman who'd dressed expecting other people to be doing the heavy lifting today and a man who looked like his idea of heavy lifting was carrying a tray of beer from the bar. This was the man who Perry thought was Bridget's admirer. As if.

'Hello again,' said the woman, her elbows discouraging the man from getting any closer, and a perfectly manicured hand extending to be shaken. 'Such a shame about the funeral, and thanks for being here, Bridget.'

'Hi, Hayley. Welcome to Ford Mill.'

Hayley Horst was the face of 3M3. According to the internet, she'd had a patchy career as an actress, a presenter on bigger shopping channels and some work as a voice-over artist, including credits on all four series of *Space Fruit*. There were also two different opinions about her age, and Bridget was a firm believer that forty-three was the truth and thirty-seven a lie. Not that Hayley looked forty-three.

Hayley was about to say something, but she wasn't the only one with sharp elbows. Bridget herself leaned left and around her, then stretched out a hand to greet Anthony Carson. She was not going to miss a chance to feel those fingers.

Anthony looked every day of his forty-four years and didn't care that he was still dressing like a student on one of the geekier courses at a university no one had ever heard of. Bridget didn't care either, because those fingers … they were long, clean and moved with intent. She'd been dying to touch them since she first saw them. She'd even looked up whether finger fetish was a thing (it was, but it came bottom of a list where foot fetishes were at the top. Urgh).

Anthony put down an expensive-looking instrument case and returned her handshake. When she gripped his fingers, they didn't disappoint.

'Still got it, I see,' said Anthony, pointing to the back counter where an example of his craft was proudly on display.

Anthony Carson was a model maker in the same way that Fabergé was a jeweller. With nothing but his memory and a quick snap on his phone, Anthony had produced a perfect replica of the Caffè Milano counter, coffee machine and operations manager. There, under a glass dome, was a model of Bridget making coffee for … a giant strawberry. With arms and legs and a ray gun.

A few years ago, a children's cartoon had become a cult hit, and the man behind the models for *Space Fruit* was Anthony Carson. Sadly for children of all ages, the intergalactic fruit salad had completed their last mission and Anthony had switched to model railways. Oh the pain! Oh the waste! To think that these fingers were now turning themselves to engine sheds, shunting yards and whatever else sad men made in their attics.

Bridget was reluctant to let go of Tony's hand. She finally did, and was about to say something nice, when the third member of the triumvirate cut in with a gesture towards the model of Bridget and Captain Berry.

'I see he's captured your likeness. Especially the eyes.'

'Knock it off, Donna. It was a rush job,' said Anthony, with something more than irritation in his voice. *Closer to hurt,* Bridget thought.

Donna Ramsey had a microscopic footprint on the internet. She was listed as *Assistant Model Maker* on *Space Fruit,* and she was mentioned in several references to closed groups on social media focusing on doll's houses, and that was it. Bridget hadn't even been able to find out her age or marital status, and now that she was in front of her, she was going to guess at somewhere between Hayley's two parameters. And single.

Donna eased herself between her partners and shook hands. She had short, stylish hair and fair skin. Her fingers were also shapely but they did nothing for Bridget. 'Anthony has never mastered faces,' said Donna. 'That's why your head is down concentrating on the coffee machine and not on Captain Berry.' She released Bridget's hand. 'He can do fruit faces, but he struggles with real people, don't you, Tony?'

Ouch, thought Bridget. *Do you two have a history or what?* She was about to say that Anthony had done a remarkable job of capturing her ink when Hayley stepped in to change the subject. 'Is my sister here?' she asked. 'Laura Paige? The bookbinder?'

'I know who you mean, but I've never met her,' said Bridget. 'I haven't got round to doing a tour of the craft village on the second floor yet. I heard that most of the craft shops were closing for the funeral, including Laura and Shannon's.'

'Shannon?' said Anthony with a frown; Donna also perked up at the name, but her response was quickly smothered with a bland smile.

'Never mind,' said Hayley quickly. 'We'd better get on. The removers will be ready now.'

'Perry has put some money behind the bar for coffees. I can't bring them up because I'm on my own, but if you tell me what you want, I can put your order on a trolley. How about that?'

'You're a star,' said Hayley. 'That would be brilliant.'

'Give me your number,' said Anthony. 'I'll text you the order. We'd better include the removers or they'll drop the cameras.'

'Sod them dropping the cameras,' said Donna. 'They've got the Mini Mansion to move.'

'Yeah, well we'd actually miss the cameras,' said Anthony.

'Just a second,' said Bridget quickly. 'Here you go. No problem.'

She grabbed the order pad from her apron and fished out one of the business cards she kept tucked in the back. Look at her – professionally printed business cards. Her hand was extended with the card when she realised what she was doing. This was the first man in years she'd given her number to who wasn't a police officer. Perry had her number, of course, but Lucy had passed it on when they signed the lease on the Spinning Room. 'There you go, Tony. I look forward to seeing the studio.'

'Half a studio,' said Hayley abruptly, and then, 'Come on you two,' in a tone that must have come from her own childhood.

She swept out, leaving Tony and Donna to follow. When Donna turned round, Tony exclaimed loudly. 'Watch out!'

Donna made a face at Tony and stepped carefully over the case on the floor before striding off. Anthony leaned down and picked it up, then spoke to it. 'Soon be back home.'

'Is that the original Captain Berry in there?'

'What? God, no. Something much more valuable. See you soon. Mine's …'

'… A large Americano, two extra shots.'

'We have a great future together, you and me, coffee lady.'

She waited until he was out of earshot before she muttered, 'If you call me *coffee lady* again, we'll have no future of any description.'

Five

Bridget didn't see any of her new co-tenants after she'd prepared the trolley. Instead, one of the removal men came down and said that he was nipping outside for a smoke before taking their refreshments up in the customer lift.

When he'd departed, she got out her phone and sent her love to Lucy, currently getting ready for the later-starting funeral on the other side of the Pennines. Lucy replied straight away with two pictures and this message:

Hat or no hat??? Have 3M3 moved in? What's Tony really like? Have you got them to sign for an account? Make sure you get the business credit card number. LuX.

That was Lucy all over: a whirlwind mixture of gossip, hard-nosed business and insecurity. Bridget considered the two pictures and decided that anything which kept Lucy's hair in order was a better option.

Hat good. Leave the rest to me. Thinking of you. Love to Tom.

She put the phone away and went back to work. Two minutes later, she was replenishing the pastry display when footsteps clattered through the foyer, and Bridget's entire team of one gangly duckling dashed through the archway into the Spinning Room. The duckling started to unbutton the severe black blouse she'd obviously borrowed from her mother, and which was consequently too full in the bust and too short in the arms. The black skirt fitted better but was way too short for a funeral, even with the black tights. There was going to be a story in that outfit.

Katarina Chester – elder daughter of Jackie and Chris at the General Stores – was very tall, very young and very unlucky in love. Kat had worked at the old Miller's Rest Café, and when Caffè Milano took over, Kat had stayed on and taken Bridget as her role model, hence the *duckling* tag: Bridget had been the first adult to imprint herself on Katarina. With mixed results, it must be said, because Bridget was *not* someone who got undressed in front of customers.

Kat had reached halfway down the buttons of her blouse and was about to pull down her skirt when Bridget decided to step in. 'We are open, you know,' she told her duckling.

'Eh?'

Bridget gestured to a retired couple (who were trying not to be seen looking). 'You've got an audience, kid.'

'Oh my actual God! Why didn't you say?'

Kat dashed through to the kitchen, clutching her blouse together with one hand and carrying a tote bag with the other. Bridget sighed and reached into the fridge for an energy drink. It was a daily source of disappointment to her that Kat could spend six hours serving coffee and never touch a drop herself.

Bridget deposited the caffeinated chemical concoction on the kitchen sink, averting her eyes from Kat's enviably thin body. She couldn't resist what she did next. She stood up on her toes and peered out of the window. 'Hiya, Joe! Give him a wave, Kat.'

Kat paused, torn between ignoring Bridget and double-checking to see if Coffin Joe was indeed standing on the island in the mill race. 'I hate you,' she decided, then continued to don the bright red and black polo shirt of her Caffè Milano uniform and then struggle with her leggings.

Bridget turned around. 'How was it?'

Kat tied the strings of her half-apron. 'Alright, I suppose. You know what, you get more like my mother every day.'

To be more like Jackie Chester would involve having two children and a husband, an unlikely prospect in the immediate future. It was an intriguing idea, though. 'How do you reckon that?' Bridget asked.

'Because you're both wind-up merchants, that's why. I didn't believe it when Mum said everyone would be wearing bright colours at the church. I thought you had to wear black for funerals when there's been a violent death. I tried to run home when I saw everyone in orange and green and stuff, but Mum stopped me. It was *mortifying*.'

'And how was the service?'

'Yeah.' She shrugged. 'I could have borrowed your purple skirt. The one you wear with the red corset.'

'And you'd need the corset to hold the skirt up. No need to rub it in. And talking of skirts, is that your old school skirt?'

'It's Jasmine's. She was wearing her choir-thingy so she didn't notice.'

Jasmine Chester was six years younger than her sister and had the voice of an angel, according to the vicar, and talking of the vicar …

'How was Debs? It must have been so hard for her today.'

The Reverend Deborah Giddings had been Millie Easterby's adopted mother of sorts, and Debs had been the one who had made Millie's killer confess. Bridget had a soft spot for Deborah, despite what she stood for.

'She was on fire,' said Kat, rather inappropriately. 'She had the whole church in tears nearly. Great performance.' She slowed down and took a breath. 'Where are your skull earrings, Boss? I'd have thought they'd be nailed on for today. Those are bit … vanilla by your standards, and we know you don't do vanilla.'

'I do do vanilla. It's the espresso of ice cream: if you can't do vanilla, don't bother.'

Bridget sounded defensive because she was feeling defensive. She had chosen the earrings deliberately, trying to tone down her look for a change. Nothing to do with seeing Tony again. Nothing at all.

'Right,' said Kat. 'Ready for action.'

'You take a minute and have a drink. And catch up on your phone. And see if Brad Nicol has posted any pictures on the *Lancashire Mercury* website. He's bound to have been there.'

'No. He wouldn't …'

The next one back from the funeral was Perry. Bridget was already steaming the milk for his cappuccino when he approached the counter. He'd opted for a pink shirt and red trousers to honour the vicar's request for colour, and it looked like the trousers had been bought for him by someone else – given how big they were, possibly by Lisa. Bridget had seen pictures which showed a more comfortably padded estate manager when his wife was alive.

'How was it, Perry?' she asked. 'Must have been awful.'

He shrugged. 'It's over. Any problems with 3M3?'

'None. They're cracking on like they know what they're doing. I served refreshments, as offered. Here's the tab.'

'Good. Thank you for that. I'll nip up in a minute and see for myself, and I'm sorry we haven't caught up since Friday – I was on that mini tour of Gloucestershire with the boys. How have you settled into Midland Terrace?'

Perry had two sons, both of whom played rugby, and Perry had joined the Cairndale Juniors on tour. He was pretty much the definition of *responsible adult*. Behind him, two women joined the queue – mourners, if the one's yellow dress and the other's red leather jacket and bright green top were clues.

'I've settled in great, thanks,' Bridget replied with a smile, looking up from the milk thermometer. 'Considering how mad busy we were over the bank holiday weekend, not too bad. I've not unpacked much, but I've cleaned it from top to bottom. I've even got used to the noises.'

'I didn't think the railway was that busy.'

'Nah. It's the *birds*. Five o' bleedin' clock they start up. And then your boss's lorries start trundling through at half past six! Can you not give the drivers a lie-in or something? And can I borrow your shotgun for that bloody blackbird who thinks he owns the place.'

He grinned. 'Thankfully I'm not responsible for Edwin's quarries, just the Byford Estate. And the thing about blackbirds is that if you shoot one, there's always another waiting to take his place. It's a jungle out there, Bridget. Happy to give you lessons in potting the wildlife if you want, though.'

'I'll pass, thanks.'

'Good. Then you can focus on the quiz team. Who've you recruited?'

'Too busy for that. I might ask Donna or Anthony from Mini Models.'

Perry had moved aside as Bridget finished making his drink. He gestured to the two women behind him. 'Haven't you asked Laura and Shannon?'

'Oh. Right. Hello,' said Bridget, putting down the milk jug and stretching out a hand to the woman in the yellow dress. 'I'm Bridget.'

The mourner was in her thirties, with long brown hair and a pretty face. 'I'm Laura Paige. Pleased to meet you at last. We've heard so much about you.'

Bridget also shook hands with the other woman, who had black leather biker trousers to go with the red leather jacket. Both looked functional rather than fashionable, as did the short hair. Bridget wondered which of the two motorbikes regularly parked by the Mill were hers. Probably the big one. 'And you must be Shannon,' said Bridget. 'I've heard absolutely zero about you two, despite the fact that Katarina usually takes her lunch up there with you.'

Laura smiled and glanced at her taller, older partner from Turn the Paige. 'Kat comes to worship at the altar of Shannon's prints, doesn't she?'

Shannon looked uncomfortable. 'Well, you know. I'm not going to say no to discount coffee.'

Bridget raised her eyebrows. '*Discount* coffee?'

Shannon looked even more uncomfortable. 'Kat says that she gets so much staff discount a week, and because she doesn't drink coffee, she doesn't want it to go to waste. And she's not worshipping at anyone's feet, she's looking at what I do with a view to going back to uni. She should learn a trade … erm, not that there's anything wrong with being a barista, of course.'

'Glad to hear it. And can your barista be of service today?'

Shannon looked mortified. Good. Laura stepped in, saying, 'Two lattes, please, both full-fat, and we'll share a slice of the walnut cake.'

Perry coughed discreetly. 'Could I have my chocolate sprinkles, please, then I'll let you get on with it.'

It was Bridget's turn to blush. She *never* left a drink unfinished. Never usually. Maybe it was moving to the countryside. She flicked her wrist with the shaker over the stencil and a perfect coffee bean took shape on Perry's cappuccino. 'Sorry. And here you go – I saved you a croissant and it's on the bill for Mini Magic Models.'

Perry put his hand on his chest. 'Are you suggesting I cheat my employer of a pastry?'

Bridget grinned. 'No. It's my fee for lending the trolley to 3M3, and I gift it to you, Peregrine. There you go.'

Perry took his drink and croissant to his favourite table, and Bridget started on the lattes. Before she could make polite conversation, Shannon frowned again and said, 'Ice cream! Now I know where I've seen you before, Bridget. You had that stand at the Whitby Goth Festival. Couple of years ago, when I was going out with … never mind. The Hobgoblin Crunch was awesome. Were you there this year?'

'Not since I signed up with Team Lucy. And I'm getting a bit old for that now.'

'Rubbish,' said Shannon. 'Kat's shown me all the pictures. You totally rock the look, and the vibe.'

To hear someone of Shannon's years use *vibe* should have sounded wrong, but it didn't, and Shannon had more. 'You shouldn't lose sight of who you are just because you have to wear a different uniform during the day.' She snorted. 'It's what I did. And what's more, I would totally come here to buy a Vampire's Kiss 99 and be served by a Bride of Dracula.'

'Shame the lord of the undead hasn't proposed,' said Bridget, keen to close down the conversation and change the subject. 'How are you at quizzing? Either of you?'

Shannon pointed to Laura. 'She's the one you want. I swear that when she puts one of those books in her press, she squeezes out the knowledge and drinks it.'

Bridget poured milk. 'Why would you put a book in a press?'

'Holds everything together until the glue has set,' answered Laura. 'If this is about the quiz team, then Feargal tried it on ages ago. Sorry, I can't afford to waste babysitting vouchers on quizzing.'

'What's a *babysitting voucher* when it's at home?' asked Bridget.

'Spare time and money,' said Kat, emerging from the kitchen. Bridget had discovered that due to the peculiar acoustics of the Spinning Room, you could hide in the kitchen doorway and hear everything said at the counter (and vice versa). How long had Kat been listening, she wondered.

Her duckling moved past, ready to take the drinks order from the next customers, who were currently examining the salads, and Kat pointed to Laura. 'Loz says that any spare time and money left over at the end of the month is her *babysitting voucher*.'

'Loz?' said Bridget.

'Don't you start,' said Laura.

'And don't you duck out,' Shannon told her. 'Your kids are with their dad next week. There's no reason you shouldn't join the team. Do it once and see whether it's worth committing a voucher the week after.'

Laura glanced up as if it was an argument she'd had before, then she shook her head and said, 'Go on. Count me in. See you at the White Hart. How much do we owe you?'

Bridget put the walnut cake on the tray and completed the sale. 'Nice to meet you both. I am going to make a resolution to come up and see your place for myself.'

Six

Now that St Peter's had released the village to get on with its life, the café quickly got busy, and Bridget was well into the zone when a neatly dressed woman in early middle age with a gentle Scottish accent paid for her Americano and said, 'Are you still looking for new staff? I saw the advert outside.'

'Yes, we certainly are. We're having a round of interviews on Friday, but if you can't make it then, we'll fit you in. I'm Bridget Gorrigan, ops manager. Pleased to meet you.'

They shook hands. 'And I'm Wendy Sadler. I'd be looking for afternoons.'

'We're flexible. Have you got another job?'

'Oh yes. With Mini Magic Models. We've just moved in upstairs. You might have heard.'

'I thought there were only three of you.'

Wendy gave her a pained expression. 'There are three owners because I didn't have the money to invest in the company. No profits for me, just a wage.' She smiled conspiratorially. 'And employee discount, of course.'

'Trains or doll's houses?'

'Do I look like a railway modeller? And before you make some gender-neutral observation, just go and look at the pictures of their national convention. Donna Ramsey upstairs is the Gordon Ramsey of miniatures. Minus the swearing. I'm lucky to work with her.'

'Could you take a seat for a minute? I'll nip over in a second.'

'Sure.'

Bridget handed over the counter to Kat and grabbed a tray. She cleared two tables and joined Wendy, who had chosen a seat by the archway. Something had been bugging Bridget since she'd first heard of 3M3, but what with everything else it hadn't been a priority. She sat next to Wendy and said, 'It sounds like they've all made a big investment in this.'

'They have. To get the professional look on a craft channel you need HD cameras, lights on a rig, a mixing desk and radio mikes. And that's the minimum. Then there's the set, the workstations and goodness knows what else. That's their domain, though.' She smiled self-deprecatingly. 'This is not a face destined for TV.'

'I dunno. Don't run yourself down, Wendy.'

'I don't want it! For one thing, there's the clothes. You should see the wardrobe that Hayley made Donna buy. She's been moaning to me about it for days.'

Bridget gestured to her polo shirt. 'I get mine for nothing.'

'And very smart it is, too. Hayley even made Donna buy duplicates.'

'That doesn't make sense. I thought the idea was to have an infinite variety of outfits.'

'It is. Except that Hayley is going to intercut some pre-recorded scenes, so Donna – and Tony – need to have some outfits in duplicate. Hayley already had them from her FirstFashionTV days, and it's not going to bother Tony much.'

'Typical man.'

'Tell me about it.' Wendy leaned forwards a fraction. 'Discussions about Tony's wardrobe are ongoing, especially the choice of T-shirts.' She shook her head. 'The designs are funny, but this is supposed to be a business, not a meeting of the Sad Bachelors Club.'

That sounded like Tony. The women shared a knowing look which encompassed their mutual despair at the opposite sex. Bridget sat back and said, 'So if you're not in front of the screen …?'

'I might not be an IT guru, but I can update the online inventory and pack the orders. They might even let me go to the post office.'

'In other words, without you, there would be no orders shipped or satisfied customers.'

'You sound like me talking to my daughter when she got a job collecting glasses in the pub.'

'I have platitudes for all occasions, Wendy.'

'But no children, if I'm not mistaken?'

Was Bridget emitting a spinster pheromone all of a sudden? That was a topic which needed closing down. 'The world isn't ready for my offspring, Wendy. Look, no matter how magic they are, mini models don't sound like big business to me. Am I missing something?'

Wendy glanced at the clock. 'Maybe. They're still discussing the *third prong* of the offer. Apparently. I'd better go.'

Bridget passed her a business card. 'Email me your CV and contact details, and we'll see you on Friday.'

'I look forward to it.'

Seven

Bridget didn't see any of 3M3 again on the Tuesday, and the half-term madness continued on Wednesday, the sun bringing families out to pick their own strawberries (from Mike Mason's farm rather than the Intergalactic Fruit Force). After splurging on berries, they often popped into the Mill to check out the crafts and take refreshments at Caffè Milano. The weather was getting hotter, and by mid-afternoon on Wednesday Bridget had propped open the side door to the Spinning Room to get some air circulation.

When four o'clock rolled round, she was standing at the counter wondering whether their limited offer of ice cream at Ford Mill should be expanded, except that would mean arranging regular frozen transport from Southport. She shrugged and looked at the clock. Finally. She was done in and more than ready for her early finish – tomorrow was her day off.

She wafted her polo shirt away from her chest and blew out some hot air, and that was when Tony Carson appeared. He looked even hotter than her, and the sweat stains on his top were meeting in the middle. 'How's it going?' she asked.

'Good, thanks, but I need a break and a cold beer. Desperate. The removers have gone for today, so we're taking a break. I fancy a walk to the shop.'

Bridget was rarely impulsive. 'I'll come with you. It's home time for me.'

'What about your van?'

'Day off tomorrow to finish unpacking, and Lilianna from the Cairndale branch is borrowing it. She can pick it up from here as easily as from home. I'll just tell Kat that I'm off and get my bag.'

'Here,' said Kat, emerging from the kitchen. 'Enjoy your walk.'

I could strangle that girl, thought Bridget. *Sort your own love life out first before sticking your nose in mine.*

Out loud, she replied, 'Cheers, Kat. See you Friday.'

She slung her apron on the counter and her bag over her shoulder. She smiled at Tony and pointed to the door. 'Let's go.'

'Where do you live?' he asked when they'd got outside.

There was no point hiding it. If Tony Carson was a serial killer, or worse, he could track her down just by asking in the shop. 'By the station. How about you?'

'Do you know Marina Bay House?'

She did know it. Just down river from Cairndale town centre was a small marina with a gleamingly modern apartment building that mirrored the sunlight on the water. When it wasn't raining. Bridget was impressed, because if that was where he actually lived, then he was doing alright for himself. Unless he was about to tell her that he actually lived in a poky terraced house round the back.

'Yeah. I know the place. Never been inside, obviously. Well out of my league.'

He smiled for a second. 'Yeah, well I came into some money and I don't need a big place. Not now I've got a workshop here. I didn't want to say anything in front of the others yesterday, but I was talking about you with one of my neighbours.'

Bridget didn't like the sound of that. 'Oh yeah?'

'Abigail Tennant. The lawyer? She said you were not to be messed with.'

'I wouldn't mess with her, so that makes us even. Do you see her much?'

'Given that she goes running all the time and drinks green things by choice, no I don't. We've only spoken once, when I moved in. You know, we were just finding things in common, and one of them is you. In fact you're about all we do have in common.'

Abi Tennant was the sort of woman whom men call *pushy* because they feel threatened. As one of Cairndale's defence lawyers, Abi often rubbed the police up the wrong way, and Lucy's boyfriend was a policeman, not that Tom Morton felt threatened by Abi Tennant.

They had reached the bridge over the River Cowan, the flow of water a shadow of its winter size. Tony leaned on the northern parapet and looked over to the right, towards the Mill and the island formed by the mill race. Bridget looked to the left, towards the back of Byford Lodge, where Edwin and Fliss played at being lord and lady of the manor. Well, Fliss actually *was* Lady Felicia, and an actress to boot, so the role came naturally to her.

Bridget glanced down to admire Tony's fingers again. His elbows were on the parapet, the hands gently entwined, a love nest of digits.

Stop it! You're losing the plot, she told herself. She stood up straight and changed the subject, even if the subject was one which only existed in her head and which Tony knew nothing about. 'Is it right that you're from here originally?' she asked, picking up on an internet tidbit.

'I am. Many years ago.'

'Any family still around?'

'My brother. You might see him at the weekend when CARM move in.'

'Eh?'

He almost giggled. 'Great name isn't it? Cairndale and Aldhaven Railway Modellers. CARM. I'm sure you'll love them.'

'Sorry, Tony, I'll have to wait for that … pleasure. I'm off to Liverpool on Friday afternoon. My dad's seventieth birthday.'

'Nice.' He hesitated. 'My – our – dad passed away four years ago. Just me and Jonno now.'

He sounded more like an orphan than an adult when he spoke, and Bridget couldn't see a way into that conversation that wouldn't overtax her, so she picked up on the name. 'Jonno is the CARM guy?'

'Yep. All his life, really. They've got the other half of our studio. It was part of the deal with Perry, and I'll be working with them. Like the prodigal engineer.'

'You've lost me completely.'

He started walking again. 'I really have got a thirst and it really is a long story. The promo edit version is that I've got CARM's Ark of the Covenant in the case that Donna nearly tripped over yesterday. Remember?'

It had been a moment. A tiny second in a busy day. Tony must have seen that she'd noticed his interaction with Donna. 'I do remember. Before we get to the case, are you and Donna still an item?'

He snorted. 'No fucking chance.' He forced a smile. 'That came out wrong. We get along fine. Now I don't have to see her over the breakfast table.'

'Ouch.'

He hesitated, right outside the floral perfection of Jorie Lutworth's Rose Cottage. Thank goodness Jorie wasn't out watering her hanging baskets; that was a conversation Bridget didn't want today.

'My mum always loved Byford,' he said, apropos of nothing. 'She said Aldhaven was too steep and too close to the sea to have a proper garden. Shame she never got to live here.'

He glanced at Bridget, then left and up at the village green. 'The Shannon Turner who works with Laura. I think I might know her.'

'Tall? Rides a motorbike? Makes prints?' suggested Bridget. Surely he'd checked first.

'Yeah,' he said, 'I used to know her. The printing thing is new, because she used to do backdrops at Leyland Films.'

'Leyland Films?'

'Oh. I thought you knew. We – they – made *Space Fruit*. That's how we all met.'

'And did you date her as well as Donna?'

'No chance. She was married to a friend, for one thing.' He closed down the conversation by striding out again. For five steps. Then he slowed down and blew out his cheeks.

They were climbing up the hill from the bridge to Byford Green, and both of them were breathing heavily. *I must do this more often*, thought Bridget. Her biological clock didn't just tick off the moments of fertility: lately, she'd been starting to worry about Type 2 diabetes.

They paused by the war memorial. 'So, what's in the case that means so much to CARM?' she asked.

'The *City of Lancaster*. In streamlined LMS livery. It's a locomotive.'

'How come you've got it?'

He shook his head. 'That would be the very long story I'm too hot to tell you.' He looked to the east and pointed to the White Hart, just visible on the Hackthwaite road. 'What's it like in there?'

'Okay. Nice, really. Not too gastropub.'

'How about I tell you the story over a drink one night? In a few days, when the madness is over.'

'I'd like that.' She had a thought. 'Hey, you four should form a quiz team and take us on.'

He didn't even think about it. 'No thanks. Not my cup of tea. Like my coffee, I prefer an extra shot in my entertainment.'

She looked at the messy hair, the bulging belly under the T-shirt with *IRONIC* written over it, the Jeremy Clarkson jeans and the dirty trainers. *An extra shot in his entertainment?* Pull the other one.

'Maybe some other time,' she said. 'That's me up there.'

'Let me get you something from the shop. Something cold.'

She was about to walk away, as she usually did. Maybe it was the heat that stopped her. 'Go on. I'll have a rocket lolly.'

He put on a spurt again and jumped into the shop, appearing shortly after with a cardboard carrier containing four bottles and the promised rocket lolly. She pointed to the beers. 'Thirsty?'

'Peace offering. The girls are ganging up on me about the launch on Monday. Maybe when things settle down and they've untangled their knickers.'

'Is it only *girls* who get their knickers in a twist, Tony?'

'Sorry. That came out wrong, but they are ganging up on me. Here.'

His exquisite fingers held the stick of the rocket lolly out to her, and she brushed against them. Those fingers could excuse a lot. 'Thanks, Tony.'

'Take care, Bridget. See you tomorrow ... no, it's your day off isn't it? Have a good day, and I'll see you Friday.'

She waved goodbye and headed up Church Road.

Eight

Bridget was getting used to the blackbird who perched on her roof. She was getting used to the 06:40 to Leeds and its interminable list of stops broadcast to the still morning air, but she couldn't get used to the heat. With some reluctance, she put on a long skirt instead of her jeans when she left Midland Terrace on Friday morning. It was just too hot for denim. At least the heavy lifting would be done before the sun really started baking the Cowan Valley.

She collected the bakery order from Cairndale and drove into the Mill car park, reversing up to the side door. She ducked into the shade and walked along the wall to the main entrance, getting her keys out. As she approached the glass tunnel, the automatic doors swept open. 'Who's unlocked them?' she wondered aloud.

Even stranger, there was a customer waiting in the foyer, a good hour before opening, and she recognised him: one of the specialist removers working for 3M3. 'Morning,' he said cheerfully. 'Any chance of a brew? The ones you sent up on Tuesday and Wednesday were ace. Much better than yesterday's.'

'If you give me a hand with the trays, I'll see what I can do. This way.'

She had to go through the Spinning Room to open the other entrance from inside. On the way, she leaned over the counter and switched on the coffee machine and water boiler. She smiled at the remover and said, 'You're here early. Who let you in?'

'Boss said the Mill would be open and to crack on. The creatives are coming later. It's only stock we're delivering today.'

Bridget left him to bring the bakery trays inside and started making drinks, for which the remover was very grateful. 'And I'll take three of them sausage rolls 'n' all. It was torture carrying them in when they smell so fresh.'

Kat arrived on time at ten, but with it being half-term, they were soon full-on busy. Bridget's urge to interrogate Kat about Shannon's revelation would have to wait. It was so busy that Bridget was wondering how they were going to conduct the interviews for new staff, and where was Lucy anyway?

With ten minutes to go, and with two candidates already sitting in the theatre foyer, Lucy Berardi breezed into Ford Mill with her usual smile. 'Sorry I'm late. Traffic was terrible.'

Lucy had been in constant touch since the weekend – but only to talk about how the funerals had gone and to ask pointed questions about 3M3. Every time Bridget tried to ask about their *own* business – about the company Bridget was supposed to be operations manager of – Lucy changed the subject.

'How many have we got again?' asked Lucy, dumping her bag in the kitchen. 'I like the look of this Wendy Sadler you've found. Shame she doesn't have any barista experience.'

Bridget barred the way out of the kitchen. 'What's going on, Lucy?'

Lucy's hair was already escaping the clips she'd put in, and she fiddled with them for a second. Bridget folded her arms.

'Help!' said Kat from the servery. 'I think we've got a coach party coming in!'

Bridget wheeled around. 'Bugger me, she's right. Our first coach party. What are we gonna do, Lucy?'

Lucy pushed her in the back. 'You and Kat are going to serve our customers, and I'm going to do the interviews upstairs in the gallery, and don't worry, I'll tell all the candidates that this is a first interview. The final decision is yours. I'll pop down and clear the tables between sessions. You can do this.'

'We'll soon find out, won't we?'

It soon got worse. There had been an accident on the M6, north of Cairndale. Travel reps in need of a break were quickly Googling *Cafés near Cairndale* and Ford Mill was an attractive option, with the large car park out the back.

'We need more help,' said Bridget, and Kat summoned her sister on the promise of an extortionate bonus. Even with Jazz on tables and dishwasher, they barely survived, and Bridget had to bite her tongue so often it was bruised.

Eventually, the motorway reopened and the Spinning Room returned to something like normality. Bridget's eyes bulged at the amount in the tip jar, so at least there were some compensations. 'Where's Lucy?' she asked.

Jazz was also eyeing the tip jar. 'How much of that do I get? Most of the money was handed to me.'

'You get one third. Just because you're blonde and wearing a miniskirt doesn't give you special privileges. Has *anyone* seen Lucy?'

Jazz pouted, then slapped her forehead. 'Oh yeah, she asked me to pass on a message.'

Silence descended.

'Go on,' said Bridget. 'What was the message?'

'Dunno. I told her I don't do messages and she should WhatsApp you. If you actually had your phone on you like a normal person, you'd know.' She smiled like an angel and spun on her heel before heading to the kitchens.

Bridget followed and grabbed her phone from the isolation box. The screen said that Bridget had a voice note. She pressed Play and put it on speaker.

'Hi, Bridge. So sorry about today. You and Kat are amazing. Especially you.' There was a pause. 'Look, something's come up and I've had to dash. I'll explain it all on Monday afternoon. Mina's coming, and I won't know until then precisely what's going on. Wendy Sadler is exactly the sort of person we need, and I've told her she can have a week's trial starting Monday. I know, I know, but she'll either love it or leave of her own accord. You can re-interview the others when you've got time. Don't worry about it over the weekend. I'll be here making sure your standards are maintained, now go and enjoy your dad's birthday.'

Of course Lucy would finish the message with reference to Bridget's dad. It was probably unconscious, because Lucy was a good person, but she couldn't help implying that Bridget was lucky to have a father she could visit when she wanted and not one whose social calendar was governed by prison visiting rules.

Bridget stared out of the windows. She loved watching the mill wheel going round. It was the closest thing she had to meditation. Lucy was up to something. One hundred per cent. Just like Natalie had been up to something, and that something had ended with Natalie's death. Even Kat was up to something.

Bridget tried to empty her mind.

The wheel turned and turned again, then slowed down and stopped. Things would either work out or they wouldn't, and there was nothing she could do about it.

Nine

The Day of the Murder (or not, as it turns out)

Bridget declined Les Gartside's offer of a third cup of tea. She wouldn't have said no to a sausage roll, though, because she'd been up for eight hours and had nothing but a diet of caffeine since leaving Liverpool, and the vibe she was getting from the family interview room didn't help, either.

There was only so long she could stare at the stacked boxes of toys without being dragged back to the first time she'd been in a room like this, down in London. That had been a hot day, too, and the room there had been stifling, with no air to breathe. Or was that just how she'd been feeling?

It was cooler inside the Cairndale station, its unique design coming into its own. There was still a subcommittee somewhere trying to get to the bottom of how the Lancashire & Westmorland Constabulary had commissioned a Spanish architect to design their new building, and why no one had queried his specification of reflective steel cladding and passive internal cooling for the wettest police station in England.

Rumours that he'd mistaken the average rainfall figures in inches for millimetres were unproven but a very good story (and eighty-three inches is a *lot* of rain). Bridget smiled, both at the thought of the architecture and the fact that she was avoiding thinking about what had happened today.

The image of Tony Carson lying dead on the studio floor would never leave her. She knew that. It would join the others in her gallery of nightmares, the gallery she'd carefully constructed with help from the therapist, and the doc's words were just as vivid now as the last time she'd seen her. *If something bad happens in the future, don't deny it and don't get stuck in it.*

It was time to move. Okay, she wasn't going to walk out. Time to do *something*, because CID couldn't want to take a *fourth* statement, could they? She had her phone in her hand and was reaching for the power button when Liz Swindlehurst blew into the room.

The new ranking detective in Cairndale was fair, fortyish and formidable. There were authenticated pictures of a husband and children, but Liz hadn't joined the bizzies to explore her maternal side. That didn't stop her understanding people, and even though she had brought all her police paraphernalia with her into the room (topped with the inevitable packet of Haribo), Liz came over to the couch and dropped herself next to Bridget. 'It doesn't get any easier, does it?' she began. 'And I'm not talking about diets, but it's true about them as well.'

'Hello to you, too, Liz. No it doesn't,' said Bridget. 'I've heard that you're supposed to give up when they get harder.' She shuffled on the seat. 'Please don't tell me you want to interview me as well.'

'Not when Les did such a good job. And now it's been confirmed that you were in Garston when the incident happened, I've come to offer you a lift back to Byford.'

Bridget gave her a dark look. 'Please also tell me that I was never a suspect.'

'A suspect? No. Just routine. It really is.'

'I know.' Bridget was well acquainted with the processes of police work. She hesitated. 'Congratulations, by the way. This is all a bit quick, isn't it?'

'Tell me about it. I only took my Inspector's Board a week before the bank holiday, then all of a sudden I'm summoned to the Commander's office and told to take accrued leave at half-term, "Because you'll want to see your bairns while you can." I didn't think work-life balance is in our Commander's dictionary. I'm going back to see whether we can reopen more parts of the Mill, before Edwin Duke starts bending the chief constable's ear. Do you want that lift?'

'Yes, please.'

Liz marched Bridget through the building and out to the secure car park. She pointed to her Volvo 4x4 and unlocked the doors, then threw her stuff in the back. Except for the Haribo. They went into the cup holder. As soon as the vehicle had passed the barrier, she shocked Bridget with her first question. 'How well do you know Perry Lockwood?'

'Perry! He can't be a suspect.'

'He can, because he was out last night and he owns a shotgun. We're starting with all the licensed gun owners who knew the victim.'

'Not Perry. Even Lucy's more likely to kill someone.'

Liz glanced over and raised her eyebrows. 'I can believe that. What about Joseph Hayton of Water Cottage?'

'Who?'

'Owns Elysian Meadow Joinery.'

Bridget snorted. 'You mean Coffin Joe.'

'Do I?'

'You do. And no one I know knows anything about him. Not really.'

Bridget hadn't crossed her fingers when she spoke, but she had kept quiet about the rumours. They weren't even rumours, and she wouldn't dignify children's stories by passing them on to the police. Coffin Joe deserved his privacy as much as anyone else.

'Well, he's not at home,' said Liz. 'And before you say anything, we're checking everyone who lives at Byford Lodge, too. You won't catch me being deferential to the lord and lady of the manor.'

Bridget didn't need to imagine Edwin Duke with a shotgun because she'd seen him with one, striding over the fields at dawn, and the reality of someone she knew walking around with a deadly weapon drew her up short.

'Forget it, Liz,' she said. 'I'm not gonna grass on the village.'

Liz slowed down to pass through Byford. 'I trust you, Bridget, and no one in the village hears more than you do.'

Bridget pointed to the General Stores. 'Jackie does.'

'Fair point. Okay. No one hears more in *Ford Mill* than you do. I could really do with a pair of eyes and ears, Bridget. If Tracey doesn't find any forensic evidence, we'll be chasing our tails. *I'll* be chasing my tail. I'm ready for this, but I need all the help I can get.'

Shameless. An appeal from one sister to another. Not gonna work. 'I've got enough on my plate as it is. What the hell? What does that idiot think he's doing!'

Liz stopped by the village green as the air was filled with the roar of aircraft engines. Ahead of them, just beyond the bridge, a lurid yellow and black helicopter was manoeuvring above the millpond.

'Conrad Bloody Clarke,' said Liz.

It figured. Mina was supposed to be coming, wasn't she? And how else would a Rani travel? 'I thought his helicopter was blue. It was in all the hen party pictures.'

'The Smurf. That one was never his, but this one is. Behold the Wasp.'

The chopper swung its angry-looking tail around and descended on the island formed between the mill race and the river. Liz turned to Bridget again. 'Are you sure?'

'Positive. I want you to find who did this, Liz. It's awful, and I really liked Tony, but you'll have to do it without me.' She looked the inspector in the eye. 'If I hear something or see something which is going to help, then of course I'll tell you, but I won't go looking for it.'

'Fair enough.'

Liz drove slowly over the bridge towards the patrol car which was blocking the entrance to the Mill grounds. Bridget saw Perry walking down the drive and said, 'Let me out just past the barrier, Liz. I could do with some fresh air.'

The uniformed officer stood aside to let Liz drive past, then he returned to his main job: not talking to the press or the residents who were gathered in front of him. Liz pulled up, then put her hand on Bridget's arm. 'Try not to be alone for a day or so, Bridget. Sounds daft, I know, but you really have had a terrible shock.'

Bridget appreciated the gesture even if she didn't appreciate the physical contact. She opened the door and pulled gently away. 'I've survived worse, Liz. Good luck.'

The Volvo drove away and Bridget walked up to where Perry was waiting to talk to her.

Ten

'How are you feeling?' Perry asked, the worry plain on his face.

'I've been better, but I'm okay,' she replied.

He lifted his hands as if he wanted to hug her or something, and they fell back to his sides with a flop. 'I just can't believe it,' he said. 'Who would want to do this?'

'How about you, Perry? Liz has got you on her little list.'

He shook his head. 'Means nothing. They're just waiting for my alibi to confirm where I was.'

He was speaking like a cop show, as if he was avoiding the obvious. 'Your *alibi*? No one goes out for an *alibi*, Perry. They go out for a kebab, perhaps, or a pizza. Except the killer, obviously.'

He looked over her shoulder towards Mill Cottages, where he lived with his boys, who presumably had been left last night under the supervision of that well known babysitter *Call of Duty*.

'I was at the Fisherman's Arms,' he told her. 'Just for a drink.'

His face filled in the gaps. 'You were on a date!' she exclaimed.

His smile was rueful. 'Turns out that algorithms are dependent on input,' he replied. 'Specifically, dependent on people telling the truth about their attitude to other people's children.' He shook his head and sighed. 'It's you I'm bothered about, Bridget. That was a nasty shock this morning. Are you going to be okay?'

She looked at the outside of the Spinning Room ahead of her. 'If I'm not, it won't be Tony Carson's fault. Sorry, Perry, I need to see what's going on. Have we been allowed back into the Mill?'

'About half an hour ago. Tracey Kenyon declared that everywhere except the top floor and the service entrance had been processed. You – we – can't reopen to the public until tomorrow though.' He managed a genuine smile. 'Any suggestion that Tracey wanted Caffè Milano to make coffee for her team is a slander.'

'Thanks. I'd better get on.'

'Of course. You know where I am if you need anything.'

'I know. See you.'

The sun was burning her face. Not a cloud in the sky. She needed the shadows, and quickly. She hot-footed it towards the side door of the café, then stopped when she saw who – or what – was watching her.

A pair of mismatched eyes stared at her from the grass, one brown, one blue. They belonged to a stretched out black-and-white shape, an elongated missile of canine mischief. The Border collie stood up and a huge pink tongue lolled out of his mouth.

Bridget knew that dog. She didn't like dogs. At all. And this one was just plain *creepy*. It had studied her, considered her as a person and found her to be *boring*. It was a pretty brutal assessment of her life right now.

The dog licked his muzzle and let out a short bark.

'Arff!'

Then, duty done, he wandered round the corner of the Mill and started to slurp from the water bowl placed there to compensate for the fact that Caffè Milano had the strictest *no dogs* policies that Bridget could get away with. This dog was Scout, and where there was Scout, there was sure to be … ah, yes. The disgusting smell of burning tobacco.

Bridget followed the dog round the corner, just to make sure, and there he was: Conrad Bloody Clarke, all six feet four of him. As soon as she entered his peripheral vision, he looked up, frowned for a microsecond, then beamed at her. Then he remembered what had happened this morning and frowned again.

'Hello, Bridget. Didn't recognise you for a moment. Sorry to hear what you've been through.'

His voice was public school posh, his presence intimidating and his business was some deadly secret. Emphasis on the *deadly*. He was also unfailingly polite and was now married to Mina.

'Is it too late to congratulate you on the wedding?' she asked. 'I loved the pictures.'

'Thank you. Are you sure you're okay?' He moved away from the wall, wincing and stumbling slightly. A large chunk of his left leg was made of titanium.

'Do you want me to get a chair, Conrad? Normally we put one table outside for you lot, but what with one thing and another …'

'I'll take the hound for a walk. A few minutes of striding out and I'll be fine. What a lovely spot you have here.' He smiled and gestured to the helicopter resting on the other side of the mill race. 'And a superb landing zone. When it's dry.'

She frowned at the loudly painted helicopter. 'Where did you get that, eh? It can't be government issue decked out like that.'

He had the grace to look a little embarrassed. 'Some of my friends and colleagues chipped together to buy a stake in it. When I'm on official business, I can claim on expenses. But not today. Your taxes have not paid for this flying visit.'

'So you're not here to arrest Coffin Joe for being a mole?'

'What? Oh. That sort of mole. No, Bridget, I am here strictly as Mina's chauffeur. If I didn't have the Wasp, and you didn't have such a handy and safe LZ, she wouldn't be able to talk to you all face to face.' He looked at the end of the island. 'It could do with a proper bridge, though. I nearly fell in crossing the sluice gate gantry.'

'A bridge would be great on days like this,' she told him. 'I'd love to have tables out there. Coffin Joe is actually a joiner, but the clue's in the nickname: he makes coffins not bridges.'

'Get Liz's family on to it.'

'Liz Liz? As in DI Swindlehurst? I thought her husband ran a haulage business.'

'He does. It's her dad's family. Ask her to put you in touch with Skelwith Construction and tell them I sent you. They owe me a few favours. You could say.'

A quote from Liz ran through her mind. *May your troubles never be so bad that Conrad Clarke is the solution.* She shuddered. 'Thanks, Conrad, I'll bear that in mind.'

'There you are!' said Lucy from behind her. 'Liz said she'd brought you back, and I wondered where you'd got to. Come here.'

Lucy put down a coffee and opened her arms. Bridget had no choice but to hug her. Actually, it felt good. She hadn't realised how stiff she was from all the sitting in the police station. And from the early start. And from what she'd seen.

Lucy slowly disengaged herself and passed the coffee to Conrad. 'Come in and I'll make you a double-double. You'll need it.'

She did need it, but more than that, her stomach was rumbling like the end of the world was nigh. 'Food, Luce. I need at least three sausage rolls and a doorstop of black forest gateau.'

Lucy led her inside, and she was spared further hugs because Tracey Kenyon really had sent her team down to rest and recuperate, and Kat was busy serving them (and trying to work out if any of the younger ones were single, knowing Kat).

'We're in the kitchen,' said Lucy. 'Come on.'

Mina Desai was as much of a hugger as Lucy, but she read the room and confined herself to offering a sympathetic smile and brushing her fingers against Bridget's and giving them a tiny squeeze.

Bridget's breath caught in her throat. Mina Desai was tiny. Even smaller than Lucy, and Mina's fingers were light and delicate, like the rest of Mina. They were also adorned with bejewelled rings and more jewels glinted on bracelets. So far so Mina, but thinking of Mina's hands made her think of Tony and the fact that Tony's exquisite fingers would never touch her again.

She forced herself to focus on someone else. 'Warm enough for you, Mina?'

Despite growing up in West London, Mina had inherited the thermostat of her Indian heritage and moaned constantly from September to May (according to Lucy). Here in June, despite the sweltering temperatures outside, Mina had chosen a long-sleeved, high-necked dress that looked like it came from a kiddy's birthday range, together with red leggings and high-top Converse. Was that a baseball cap in the corner, too? And did it match the one Conrad had stuffed in his pocket?

Mina saw her looking and waved her hand over her outfit. 'I am helicopter ready, Bridget. The rotor wash and uneven landing grounds are no place for floaty dresses and heeled sandals.' She gave a smile. 'Plus there is the sun to think of. No girl from east of Suez ever exposes her skin to the sun if she can help it.'

Bridget didn't know what to make of that, so she tried a smile.

Mina touched her arm again. 'You have gone pale, and you look so different without the 101 foundation. Sit down. Come on. Before you fall down.'

She allowed herself to be drawn to the far corner of the kitchen, where an old table and chairs filled the empty space.

'Here,' said Lucy. 'As ordered. With sparkling water for now. I'll get Kat to bring the coffee in later.'

Mina excused herself and Lucy sat next to Bridget, who suddenly found that she wasn't really hungry.

'Eat,' said Lucy. 'Go on. Just try a bit.'

Bridget drank first, then took a bite of Tabor Bakery's finest sausage roll. Flaky goodness and peppery sausage hit her tongue. She *was* hungry. And by the time she'd made inroads into the gateau, she wasn't feeling faint any more. And then she saw the look on Mina's face as Caffè Milano's financial adviser carried a tray of coffees through from the counter.

Eleven

Bridget turned her shoulder away from Mina and towards her friend. 'Talk to me, Lucy.'

Lucy sighed. 'It's a long story, Bridge, with a big picture.' She smiled. 'That's how Tom described it.'

Tom Morton was famous for many things, and one of them was his ability to mix a metaphor at forty paces. *A long story with a big picture* is exactly what he would say, and talking of Tom Morton …

'Where is he, Lucy? And why did I only hear about his "secondment" from Les Gartside in the interview room and not from you, eh?'

'That's part of the story,' said Mina. 'It really isn't Lucy's fault at all. It's—'

'Do *not* say "complicated",' snapped Bridget.

Mina blinked. Her midnight-black hair was still long and luxurious, though six inches shorter than before the wedding. Another change was the ruby sparkling on the side of her long, pointed and previously unpierced nose. Mina hooked her hair behind her ears and kept eye contact with Bridget as she drank her coffee. 'What would you have me say? I could blame my new husband, but he was only doing his job, and this is Tom's idea.' Point made, she sat back. 'Just tell her, Lucy.'

Bridget's friend took a deep breath. 'We're arranging to buy out Tara Doyle's stake in Caffè Milano.'

'Why? And what does this have to do with Tom and Conrad?'

Lucy faltered again, and Mina took over. 'Tom has left CID in Cairndale to work with one of the courts which try cases in secret. It is no longer appropriate for Tara Doyle to have a stake in Lucy's business.'

'No!' said Bridget. 'Tom isn't the boss of you, Lucy. Tell him to fuck off. *You* built this business, not him. You can work with who you want, and what's wrong with Tara anyway?'

Not two months ago, the gutter rag *Celebrity Enquirer* had featured a big picture of Tara Doyle with her arms round Lucy and Mina at Mina's hen party, and Tara Doyle had led the Bollywood dancing at Mina's wedding to Conrad Bloody Clarke *in the grounds of Clarke's house*! Bridget had a soft spot for Tara – a fellow Scouser who'd stayed true to her roots, married a top footballer and carried on working after taking a break to have kids. What had changed?

'Come on, Mina. Spill,' ordered Bridget.

Mina looked at Lucy again, and Bridget got a tiny feeling that whatever was going on was ultimately rooted in something to do with Conrad Bloody Clarke. Rooted like Japanese knotweed, an invasive plant that was destroying the foundations of Bridget's carefully constructed new life.

'Tara Doyle is … blameless, really. As is her husband. What you see is what you get – a celebrity married to a professional footballer.' She sighed. 'Unfortunately, the same cannot be said of some of Tara's associates. The most charitable interpretation is that Tara does not know what they are getting up to.'

'Such as?'

Mina shook her head, letting her hair fall in front of her face. It was her signature way of taking a timeout from uncomfortable conversations.

Lucy looked close to tears. 'I am so sorry, Bridget, but I can't tell you. Really and truly I can't, but I've got to do it. For my sake as well as Tom's. It's why I had to rush off last week. It's all sorted now.'

Bridget knew when to move on. For now. She'd come back to this one day soon, though. 'Did you liquidate some of your trust?' she asked Lucy.

'No. I can't, and no one I know has two hundred and fifty grand lying around their bank accounts.'

'No one except Tara Doyle,' said Bridget. 'So who's buying in?'

'Remember Conrad's sister? Rachael? She *does* know people with that sort of money. I've sold Tara's shares to one of their holding companies with a six-month option to buy them back at cost. That gives us breathing space to find a proper investor.' Lucy let that sink in for a second, then looked down. 'That's not the worst news, though.'

Bridget breathed deeply through her unpierced nose. She'd thought about it during her high-Goth phase, then decided that piercings were just too unhygienic. 'Go on.'

Mina took over. 'Tara can be a vindictive bitch,' she said smoothly. 'And this is all deniable, of course. She has used her influence to work on Owain Marshall.'

The icy grip of winter took hold of Bridget's insides. That second sausage roll was not sitting comfortably. Owain Marshall was another stand up Scouser, a local boy who was now Merseyside United's veteran left back. He had also rescued the business of his childhood football coach: Giuseppi's Gelateria.

The ice cream parlour and café had been Bridget's sanctuary when she left the women's shelter; it had given her a job and a purpose, and it had led her to meet Natalie. And then Lucy, and Lucy had had the mad idea of starting a coffee shop chain.

'What?' said Bridget.

'We've been given notice on the Southport management agreement. Three months and we're out.'

Lucy was near to tears. What on earth for? It wasn't *her* life being shredded. Bridget was *not* going to be kicked around and used as anyone's football. Sod that.

'So am I,' she said. 'Three months should see this place up and running, and I'll be in touch with Owain to get me job back at Giuseppi's. No ice cream in Caffè Milano, no Bridget in Caffè Milano.'

'No!' said Lucy. 'You can't do that.'

'Why not? If you can sack Tara Doyle off, I can do the same.'

Mina was fishing around the back of her neck for something, and she finally pulled a necklace out. Dangling from the chain were a silver helicopter, some Celtic symbol and a little image of the elephant-headed god, Ganesh, and it was the god whom Mina held up in front of her. 'I am not suggesting you sacrifice to Ganesh, Bridget, but you should think about him. He is the god of doorways and doors, and he is opening the door for you to make your *own* ice cream.'

Bridget was going to snap a response, but Mina's quicksilver fingers had returned the charm and were waving at the empty half of the kitchen. 'This space is wasted. You could turn it round.'

'I'll turn your head round if you're not careful, Mina. Stop sticking your nose in my business, and yes, I meant that as an insult.' Bridget stood up and towered above Mina. She looked over Mina's head at Lucy and said, 'I'm going to help Kat, then I'm off home. Don't worry, I'll be here tomorrow, and I'll order extra from Tabor's, because we'll be rushed off our feet with rubberneckers and journalists. I'll put my notice in writing, too. Now, if you'll excuse me.'

Twelve

Should she tell Kat straight away? Bridget swept out of the kitchen and found her duckling struggling to cope with the third degree from Tracey Kenyon. Nah. Kat didn't need to have her world rocked twice in one day.

'How are we doing?' she said to the room at large.

Kat rushed up, whether that was out of concern for Bridget or to get away from Tracey's gimlet eye was open to question. Bridget gave her the benefit of the doubt when Kat tenderly picked up the snow globe of Bridget and Captain Berry and held it out as an offering. 'I'm so sorry,' she said.

Bridget took the offering and tilted it to peer upwards. Her miniature face was a blank, just like Donna had said it would be, merely a few lines in the clay. She tilted it back. How had he managed to reproduce her tattoo like that? Some sort of laser? Surely he hadn't painted it so small? She placed the globe back on the counter and smiled. 'Thanks, Kat. You take a break. I bet Lucy's been no use if she's been entertaining Rani Mina in there.'

Kat's eyes flicked to the kitchen doorway with concern. She didn't like conflict, especially as Lucy had worked flat out over the weekend to cover Bridget's trip to Liverpool. Kat just said, 'Thanks,' and disappeared. Unfortunately, the gimlet eye of Tracey Kenyon was still unsatisfied.

'Do you want anything, Tracey?'

'No thanks. Not coffee anyway. I see you've survived a close encounter with CID.'

'Apparently the key time was last night, and I was doing karaoke in Garston, so I'm off Liz's radar. Is that right? He was killed last night?'

'Doesn't take a forensic pathologist to tell you that rigor mortis was fully established by nine o'clock, so yeah. Look, can I ask you a question?'

Tracey Kenyon had a tremendous reputation – for grumpiness, for dissatisfaction with life and for meticulous attention to detail. Trainee technicians from UCLAN in Preston had been known to leave their course rather than take up a compulsory placement at Cairndale.

'Sorry,' said Bridget. 'I've already told Liz that I've laid down my knitting needles.'

Tracey squinted. 'You don't knit.'

'Which is why I'm not playing Miss Marple. I've made my statement, and that's that.'

'Come on, Bridget. Just one question. You know how I hate having a hole in my reports, and that's what I've got: a hole. I promise not to bother you again, and it might help CID.' She paused. 'Don't make me say *pretty please*.'

Tracey had chased her technicians back upstairs, and she had no drink in front of her, so this must be important. 'Go on then.'

'Thanks. Have a look at this.'

The crime scene manager picked up her phone and she'd clearly lined up the picture in advance. Bridget could see from a distance that it wasn't a picture of Tony, so she took the phone and peered closely. Then she pinched the screen to zoom out.

'It's Tony's instrument case. His special one.'

'I thought so,' said Tracey. 'There's loads of them, all stacked neatly and labelled, and we've matched every camera, lens and switch to the empty spaces in the foam. Except this one. There's nothing lying around that remotely fits.'

Bridget passed back the phone. 'In that case you can add theft to the charge sheet. Tony said that it was a rare model of a steam engine. The *City of Lancaster*. Talk to his brother. Jonathan. Might have been some sort of heirloom, either family or that modelling group.'

Tracey stared at the picture. 'You don't know how happy that makes me, Bridget. Of course it's a locomotive. And tender. And a couple of other things, from the size of the holes in the foam. Spot on. Cheers.'

She left with a wave, and Bridget grabbed a tray. She stacked it with empties then realised that she didn't want to see Lucy again. Or Mina. She put down the tray on the counter and picked up her bag. On a whim, she wrapped the snow globe in a clean cloth and placed it carefully in her bag. From the kitchen doorway Bridget shouted that she was off and walked out of the Spinning Room.

She took one look at her van and decided that she wanted nothing to do with it. Driving through the crowd by the entrance would let them know exactly who she was, and if she then parked it outside

Midland Terrace, she'd only have herself to blame when someone came knocking at her door. Sod it. She could do with the walk, and she headed through the outbuildings to take a shortcut to the road, avoiding the main entrance and allowing her to slip through a gate, over the lane and into Meadow Farm.

It wasn't quite time for afternoon milking, so there were no close encounters with the Jersey cows who supplied Mike Mason's "Magic Milk". She shuddered at the thought of the unpasteurised lactose and bacteria soup dispensed from the vending machine ahead of her. Proper gave her the heebie-jeebies that one.

She cut past the farmhouse and took the path towards the P-Y-O fields, then turned right, away from the visitors and down towards the meadows which gave the farm its name and which made a vivid green carpet on the southern banks of the river.

The cows were munching happily, and for once Bridget didn't care about getting her trainers dirty, because they were going to have a wash soon. Oh. Hang on. She might have escaped the angry villagers at the Mill gate, but her path to safety was blocked. There was nothing for it – she'd have to mount a frontal assault.

The village of Byford got its name because it was … by a ford! Who knew? Well, Bridget hadn't. Not until the day she crossed the Cowan using the submerged carter's stones where the river was widest, just down from the bridge. On that day she'd been on a mission, heedless of the water and hunting for a killer. Today she was exhausted and seeking sanctuary, and the water was just as cold, even though it barely topped her ankles. Brrr.

She splashed across the river and huffed up the path to accost the man sitting on a grassy knoll and smoking a cigarette with an amused expression on his face.

'Sod off, Conrad,' she told him. 'You're a bloody menace, you are. This is all your fault. Right mess you've made. You and Tom. Damn the both of you.'

Scout sat up when he heard her tone, and he bared his teeth. She backed away, and he stepped towards her.

'Arff!'

'Down,' said Clarke. 'He's just jealous. I won't let him go in the water because he'd want to cross over and herd the cows, and that rarely ends well.'

Was he just going to ignore her? 'Sod you,' she told him. 'And your bloody hellhound.'

With that, she squelched along the river bank and up the steep slope that led to the back of the General Stores. She passed the Chesters' garden and tried the side door to the stock room. Open. Good. She banged on the door and went in.

'Bridget!' said Jackie, guiltily putting her hands behind her back, then realising that there was no point denying it. She popped the rest of the Freddo Frog bar in her mouth and scrunched the wrapper into a ball before hiding it in her jeans. 'You okay? Is Kat okay?'

'Kat's fine. I'm not. Have—'

'Your feet! They're soaking.' Her eyes widened. 'Don't tell me you've been in the river again.'

'Whatever. Have you got any writing paper?'

'Erm. Hang on.'

Jackie dodged into the shop and was gone long enough for a small puddle to form around Bridget's trainers. Jackie reappeared with a pad of writing paper that could have come from the props box of an actual Miss Marple film. Jackie blew dust off it and offered it to Bridget. 'Here you go. One of the last items on sale that doesn't have a bar code. Or a price sticker. Shall we say one fifty?'

'Here.' Bridget passed the coins and added, 'I'll tell you about it tomorrow. There's not much I'll be able to add to what Kat will no doubt tell you tonight.'

Jackie shook her head, curls bouncing. 'You don't know her that well then. If it wasn't all over the news she wouldn't say a thing. When I see her tonight and ask if she's had a bad day, she'll say "Yes. I had to see Bradley Nicol again" and not mention the murder at all. You take care.'

Bridget put the pad in her bag, mindful of not bending the corners. She'd just have to hope that there were a couple of envelopes left in one of the boxes she was now *not* going to unpack because she would also write to Perry and give him notice on Midland Terrace. Once she'd had a bath.

Thirteen

Lucy got out a tissue and started to wipe her eyes when Bridget marched out of the kitchen. *It's so not fair* ran round her brain like a funfair train, and there was nothing she could do to stop it. Mina put her hand on Lucy's leg and squeezed, then got out her phone. The only thing that stopped the runaway thought train was the sight of Kat breezing through the doorway.

'Shit,' muttered Lucy. 'I don't think Bridget's told her.'

'Good,' said Mina. 'Gives Bridget a chance to think it over tonight.'

Kat came up and asked, 'Is Bridge okay? She looked proper spaced out.'

'She's been through a huge lot,' said Mina while Lucy composed herself. 'She is strong, and don't forget she started this morning at five o'clock.' She arched her eyebrows and Kat got the message.

They all heard Bridget shout goodbye from the café, and Kat said, 'I'll take my break out there in case anyone turns up. Anything you want me to do?'

Lucy cleared her throat. 'Could you do a big Tabor's order for tomorrow and subtract what we have left over from today? Then message Bridget and tell her it's been sorted.'

'Right.'

When Kat had mooched off, Lucy slumped her elbows onto the table and picked at crumbs. 'What am I gonna do, Mina? I can't cope without Bridget. I'd never have stared Caffè Milano without her. She's my rock.'

Mina put her hands flat on the table, thumbs touching. Anyone else might think that Mina were admiring her own jewellery (and to be fair, this wasn't unheard of). Lucy knew better. Lucy knew that one of

Mina's secret powers was the ability to shut the world out for a second while she gathered inner strength. Mina was still for a moment, then she looked Lucy in the eye. 'Bridget may not appreciate this, but it's true. Ganesh works for all of us, including you, Lucy. If he closes the door marked *Bridget* then he is opening another one. Perhaps it's marked *Lilianna*.'

Lucy lifted herself off the table, then flopped back in the chair. Mina meant well. She did. They had a lot in common – they'd both lost brothers to violence for one thing. And if you kept a tally of trauma, then Mina was way ahead: the micro-scars on her jaw from all the surgery told that tale. Not only that, Mina was right about getting rid of Tara Doyle, even if they couldn't give Bridget all the reasons. But Bridget was her *friend*. More than that, Lucy had a sneaking suspicion that Bridget needed her, too.

'What a mess, Mina.'

'It is.'

'Maybe the universe will sort it out,' suggested Lucy hopefully.

Mina's tiny fingers rapped Lucy's leg. 'That is *not* how it works. *You* will sort it out. What are you going to do first? What would be the biggest help to Bridget and to the business?'

Lucy stood up and brushed crumbs off her dress. 'PR. I know you hate it and Bridget thinks it's the work of the Devil, but someone has to remember we're open to the public.' She tried a smile, and Mina's eyebrows told her she needed more practice. 'I'm going to invite Bradley Nicol from the *Lancashire Mercury* to come up for an interview. Can you keep Kat amused for a bit?'

'Whatever for? And does anyone under sixty actually *read* that paper?'

'No, but he also posts on three Facebook Groups and contributes to umpteen Twitter accounts. God knows how he monetises it, but he does. And as for Kat, he dated her, two-timed her and dumped her. She didn't take it well.'

'He shouldn't be walking around.'

'Yeah, well after Bridget laid into him, he nearly wasn't able to walk around, and that's another reason for inviting him. If he knows Bridge isn't here, then he'll be more pliable.'

'And how am I supposed to entertain Katarina? I'm only seven years older than her, but I feel ancient.'

'Just tell her how Tom arrested you. That always goes down well.'

Before Mina could throw gateau at her, Lucy dodged into the Spinning Room and got out her phone.

'You can do this,' Bridget told herself the next morning when she removed the *Closed* sign from the archway. She would *not* miss the fact that the Spinning Room had no door to stop people wandering in from the foyer.

Bridget wouldn't be alone to face the hordes for long – Kat would be here in an hour, and Lucy was coming at lunchtime after she'd covered for Lilianna in Cairndale. It was only when the 09:20 train landed that Bridget was reminded of an unpleasant fact: the University of Lancashire Institute of Science and Technology had a media department.

Ten minutes after the decrepit excuse for transport had pulled into Byford Halt, more or less the whole undergraduate body breezed into Caffè Milano, upset the seniors (who had been very well behaved) and made two of the toddlers from the mother and baby group burst into tears. Bridget folded her arms and gave them the eye.

'This is a café. What can I get you?'

Their leader was a girl with flickable hair (who could be Hayley Horst's daughter). She was clutching an audio recorder with twin microphones. Probably thought she was going to be a podcaster. Maybe she already was. Urgh.

She held out the recorder. 'You're Bridget Gorrigan, right? I'm Ciara Davenport and we just wanted to—'

'What can I get you?' repeated Bridget. 'We have coffee, tea and soft drinks.'

A rat-faced boy came through the archway. 'The lift's out of action and there's a copper on the stairs. He says the craft village isn't open today and he won't let me go up unless I'm on his magic list.'

'Too bloody right they won't,' said a loud voice from the left. 'Now are you lot going to form an orderly queue like civilised people or are you going to leave?'

Blimey, she thought. *Who'd have pegged Allan as my knight in shining armour?*

The students turned to see who'd spoken, and they found an old man holding a tray and ready to use it as a weapon. Allan was a retired engineer, chairman of the Byford Artists Society and one of the people who could be relied on to turn up and support everything going on in the village. Whether he was invited or not.

A knot of the would-be internet stars split from the pack and headed for the foyer, and the rest of the group separated into singles and pairs, leaving Allan a clear run to the till.

'Usual?' said Bridget.

'Please.'

She got working, and Allan selected a scone from the display. He put his plate on the tray and said, 'So it's true, then? You found him?' He didn't give her a chance to get upset or angry, he nodded to himself and added, 'That must have been terrible. I hope Sheriff Morton makes a quick arrest.'

'It's not Tom,' said Bridget. 'He's on secondment. Do you know the new DI? Liz Swindlehurst?'

Allan considered this. 'If Ross thinks she's good enough, then she probably is. Here you are. Keep the change.' Allan always calculated his tip to exactly balance the Sunrise Senior Discount, and he always paid cash. Did he have a huge jar of change at home?

When Allan had gone to join the three senior ladies already in residence, the rat-faced boy edged back up to the counter. 'Latte, please, in a takeout cup,' he said with a flat Birmingham-ish accent.

'Coming up.'

He twisted himself, one foot rising off the floor of its own accord. Finally, he did it and blurted out, 'Can I buy you one? Or you could put it by for later.'

Bridget started steaming the milk. 'Oh yeah? Are you asking me on a date?'

The aerial leg twitched alarmingly and he almost hopped backwards. She took pity on him. 'No, kid, you're okay. I'm not old enough to be a cougar yet. And I can't be arsed anyway. You can have one question for free, and two if you buy me a cappuccino, but think on this: the bizzies are all good customers of ours, so I'll not be telling you that he was found naked or anything.'

His eyes lit up. 'Was he? … Oh. You're winding me up. Can I think about the questions?'

'You can. What's your name, by the way?'

'Jed. Jed Holmes.'

After he'd paid – did he wince at the price when he tapped his card? – she promoted him from rat-faced to ferret-faced. Bridget hated rats and mice above all things, even above dogs, but she'd once seen a fairly cute ferret. It was still a ferret, though.

If Jed was going to compete with Miss Twin-Microphones, he was going to need help, though of course he did have the biggest advantage of all: when he grew up, he was going to be a bloke.

Fourteen

Bridget had broken her own iron rule this morning by keeping her phone in her apron. Kat was a repeat offender in this, and if Bridget weren't about to hand in her notice, she'd be forced to introduce fines later. A message came in from Laura Paige. *Is it safe to come down? Dave the copper on duty says there are journalists everywhere.*

You can hide in the kitchen if you want. RUOK? Bridget replied. By way of an answer, Laura slipped through the arch two minutes later, with Kat hot on her heels. Her duckling went to get ready, and Bridget smiled at Laura. The bookbinder tried to smile back and failed. 'Can I have a hot chocolate? Madness, I know, with this weather.'

'One super-comforting hot chocolate coming up. No Shannon today?'

'I've only just come from the police station.' Laura looked down at her outfit of sky blue top and short denim dungarees. 'I didn't know I was going to be on camera when I left the house. Shannon's still there.' She blinked. 'So's Hayley.'

Bridget could have asked whether Laura had an alibi for Sunday night. She didn't. She was not going there. She dropped the chocolate portafilter in the sink and said, 'Did you say that your kids were with their dad this week?'

'Don't you start,' said Laura, the smile genuine this time.

'Start what?' said Bridget. 'I never go looking for trouble.'

Laura chuckled. 'Well, it's like this. You know she won't admit it, but Hayley's ten years older than me.'

'No comment. She might still be a customer.'

Laura pointed to one of the toddlers, a little girl with jam all over her face. 'When I was about that big, Mum got a new job and Hayley got landed with a lot of childcare.' Laura's voice was softer than her sister's, and they could have come from anywhere in England. 'Know what I mean?'

'I do, as it happens. I've got an older brother who ended up doing much the same job. He did a lot better when he became an actual father and not a surrogate one.'

'Ouch. No, I mean Hayley started channelling Mum. You know, *Put your coat on, Laura. Where's your school bag?* Well, she hasn't changed. I've had days of *Shouldn't your children be in school next week?* The answer is *None of your business*, because ... well, yeah. I'll tell you about my ex and his novelty girlfriend some other time.'

Bridget passed the assembled concoction over the counter. 'I look forward to hearing about it. All Millites get one free drink today. This is yours. And you get free advice: make sure you claim two days rent off Perry. Not your fault the building was closed.'

She laughed. 'I might just do that. Or better still, get Esmeralda to do it on our behalf. It's not just us other tenants who are scared of her. Perry is, too.'

Bridget swapped places with Kat and took five inside the kitchen. She had found two envelopes last night. Eventually. One was repurposed from a birthday card she'd bought but never sent, and the other was a plain window envelope which had contained a welcome message from the water company. She lined them up next to each other on the table and thought again about what they contained.

Staying here would be easy. Kat was lovely. Laura and the other craft makers seemed worth getting to know. Lucy was always around. And then there was Perry. She put the envelopes back in her bag. Staying would be easy, until Kat went off to college, Laura went bust and Perry got matched with someone on a dating app.

Leaving would be harder. Harder but healthier.

'Bridge?' said Kat. 'Guy here called Jed Holmes. Says you're expecting him.'

'Coming.'

Jed Holmes was trying to look like a confident and experienced reporter as he waited at the counter. The mangled and shredded takeout cup in his hands gave the lie to that. Bridget relieved him of the distressed cardboard and tossed it in the special recycling bin. 'Want anything else, Jed?'

'No. I'm good, thanks.'

'Kat. You can come out.' Her duckling slipped from behind the door with a frown. 'Jed's one of the media students at ULIST. He's bribed me to answer two questions.'

'Oh yeah,' said Kat, folding her arms.

Holmes nearly ran away. Nearly. He gripped the counter and said, 'If you're not going to talk, then who *should* I visit?'

'Good question, Jed. Do you want an honest answer?'

'I want whatever you're going to give me.'

'I'd work on that, if I were you. A simple "Yes, please" would have been better. Well, no one who knows anything in this village will talk to you. That's a given. Your best bet is to follow Bradley Nicol into the pub and buy him a pint. And tell him how awesome he is. You'll get everything then.'

Jed snorted. 'I thought you might say something like that. Seriously? No one?'

'No one worth talking to if you're after a story. Next question.' His nose twitched. 'Do NOT sneeze at the counter!' she told him.

He stepped back. 'Was it a burglary? Was anything taken?'

Damn him. He'd got her relaxed and feeling in control and hit her with a sucker punch, because her face told him straight away that he was on to something. What could she say to that?

Kat stepped forwards. 'The police believe that it was a targeted attack, not a random burglary. This was not opportunistic.'

Bridget wheeled right. 'What she said. Where did you get that from, Kat?'

Kat shrugged. 'True, though, innit?'

'Thanks, Kat,' said Jed. 'Now is that short for Katharine?'

'Errm …'

'It's Katarina Chester,' said Bridget. 'Her mum owns the General Stores. You can quote Kat, but if I see my name near yours online, I will hunt you down. Clear?'

Everyone was sweating today. It was getting *very* muggy in the Spinning Room. Jed took it to another level of moisture entirely, and he retreated with a nervous smile and a thank you.

'What did you have to tell him about Mum for—'

'Shh. Laura's coming over. Something's wrong.'

Laura was holding her phone to her ear as she sprinted over from the corner, and the entire room turned to watch. 'It's Cairndale custody room,' she hissed to Bridget. 'They've arrested Hayley.'

Fifteen

Laura was on the verge of going into shock. From the phone gripped in her white knuckles, a woman's voice said, 'Hello? Are you still there?'

Bridget didn't think about it. She acted. She prised the phone away and said, 'Hang on,' into the handset. She pressed mute and told Kat to take Laura into the kitchen, then followed behind them and stood in the doorway, watching to see if anyone came sneaking up on her.

She unmuted the phone and said, 'Is that Cheryl? This is Bridget.'

'Yeah. Hi. Is Ms Paige still there? I haven't finished the notification.'

American suspects get a phone call when they're arrested. At least they do on TV. In England, you have the right for someone "To be notified", and the senior custody officer will do it for you.

'I'll sort it,' said Bridget. 'Look, Cheryl, has Hayley got a lawyer?'

'My next job. She's asked for the duty solicitor.'

'Do us a favour, will you? Hang fire on that for a minute while I see what I can do.'

There was a long pause. 'You're not going to call Abi Tennant are you?'

'I might.'

'I want free coffee for a month.'

Bridget was asking Cheryl to bend the rules to the point where the Commander would take exception and CID would be furious. 'A week. And you have to collect from Ford Mill, not the Market Square.'

'Done. Ten minutes.'

Bridget disconnected and swapped to her own phone. Should she ring the landline number or the mobile? Abi could be with a client, so …

'McEwan and Company. Good morning. How can I help you?'

'Hi, this is Bridget from Caffè Milano. Is Abi free?'

'Let me check.' Bridget went to bite her thumbnail and held her hand up in shock because it wasn't black. She kept forgetting she'd changed colours. 'Putting you through.'

'Hiya, Bridget,' said Abi. 'What's up? Are you touting for business, because it's too hot for coffee right now.'

'Got a client for you. Hayley Horst has been arrested for the murder of Anthony Carson.'

'Ooh. Now you're talking. When?'

'Her sister's just had the custody notification. Get on the phone to Cheryl quick as you can.'

'Cheers, Bridget. I owe you one.'

Bridget breathed out. She had no idea what was going on here, but she'd done her duty to her fellow Mill worker – Hayley Horst now had the best criminal solicitor in Cairndale on her side. Bridget went over to the corner and put Laura's phone on the table. 'Kat, could you take over for a bit?'

Kat did not want to go. She was way too excited to serve coffee. Bridget put her hand on the back of a chair and stared out her duckling.

'Okay,' huffed Kat. 'Don't be too long. It's getting busier, and no one has cleared up for ages.'

Bridget sat down and told Laura what she'd done. Before she could retract her hands, Laura grabbed them and squeezed. 'Thank you *so* much, Bridget. You'll help out, won't you?'

Bridget tugged gently. Bookbinders must develop odd muscles, because Laura wasn't letting go. 'What do you want me to do? Phone your mum or something?'

The squeezing became almost painful. 'She's dead. No, I mean help clear Hayley's name.'

Bridget had muscles, too. Carrying a full tray is a workout on its own. She disengaged her fingers and wiped them discreetly on her apron. 'I'm sorry, Laura. I can't do that.'

'But it was *you* who found Millie's killer! Kat told Shannon all about it. Said you were implacable.'

'Did she? Only after she'd used an online thesaurus, I'll bet.'

'It's not a joke, Bridget.'

No, it was not a joke. Bridget knew it wasn't a joke, but how else was she going to deflect Laura? Play the sympathy card. 'This is different, Laura. Sticking your neb into police business is risky. Asking awkward questions is a one-way ticket to ostracisation, but turning over rocks looking for someone who uses a shotgun is downright flipping dangerous.'

'One of those doesn't matter, does it?' said Lucy from behind her. Had Lucy been taking lessons from her boyfriend on being sneaky or did Bridget need a hearing check? 'Being ostracised isn't a problem for someone who's leaving anyway. And Liz wants your help, so the police aren't a problem.'

The extra information was overloading Laura's brain. Damn Lucy.

'Still leaves the shotgun-wielding maniac,' said Bridget.

Lucy walked round the table. She'd swapped yesterday's summer dress for the proper uniform of red and black. If she wasn't short and didn't have a face made for fun, she might even have looked intimidating. She planted her feet and said, 'Just don't get too close. Safer that way.'

Bridget stood up and got her bag. She took out the letter addressed to Lucy and slapped it on the table. 'You can tell Kat what's going on while I take Laura upstairs and she tells me all about it.'

She hustled a bewildered Laura out of the kitchen and through to the foyer, where they almost ran into Perry. 'You go up and I'll see you in a minute,' said Bridget to Laura.

'Laura? What's wrong?' said Perry.

Laura shook her head and went past the bored constable to climb the stairs. Bridget got out the other envelope and said, 'Laura's sister has been arrested. Here.' She shoved her notice to quit into his hand and followed Laura. Slowly. No point in being out of breath.

Sixteen

The first floor of Ford Mill was home to Dukes Gallery, an exhibition space that doubled as a bar when there were performances at the Cowan Theatre. It was also home to Louis Young, the artistic director. Bridget would be heading his way soon enough, but first she had to climb up to the Ford Mill Craft Village.

She reached the second floor and couldn't go further because progress was barred by police tape. She shuddered at the memory of Tony Carson lying up there on Monday morning. No. It was not a joke. She pushed through the fire door into the craft zone. Oh. Laura was not alone.

The high, open space of the craft village had been partitioned and laid out like Disney's version of a Victorian shopping street. The eight small businesses had been given premises of varying sizes, each one with a shop front that didn't reach the ceiling, as if they were surplus stock from a theme park. The first two were in darkness, but where the walkway bent left, Bridget saw Laura talking to the most distinctive of the crafters, and the only one to reject that title, because Esther Thornfield was an *artist*, not a *crafter*.

It had been Louis who gave Esther the nickname *Esmeralda*. Cruel, Bridget knew, but somehow fitting. Esther was somewhere past sixty in age and was rarely seen without a paint-spattered smock. At least she was seen, and had become a regular patron of Caffè Milano, especially when the vicar was taking a break from her pastoral duties. An unlikely friendship, but there you go.

The one time of the day you *wouldn't* see Esmeralda was when the senior discount was in force, and not because she was pretending to be too young (like some of them did). No, it was because there was a near certain chance of her meeting some of the Byford Artists Society. According to Kat, who had it from Shannon Turner, Esther had dubbed them *The Byford Dabbers and Daubers Club*.

'Ah. There you are,' said Esther in her cut glass accent. 'Laura has been telling me that her sister has been arrested for the murder of that terrible man and that you are going to sort it out.'

The police tape on the staircase had reminded Bridget that a life had been cut short. 'Anthony Carson was not a terrible man.'

'Yes he was. An overgrown schoolboy who wasted what little talent he had and deserved everything he got.'

'Maybe he was,' said Laura, 'and maybe he wasn't. The important thing here is that Hayley didn't kill him.'

'Did the police find her in possession of a smoking gun?' asked Esther. 'No? Then your job is clear, Ms Gorrigan: show that Philistine woman Swindlehurst that she has no evidence. With a bit of luck they'll never find anything and it will go down as *unsolved*.'

'Don't underestimate Liz,' said Bridget. 'There's plenty who did that and had time to re-think their choices inside a cell.'

'You'll soon discover that plenty of people wanted Anthony Carson dead and plenty of people had the opportunity to rid the world of his presence.'

Where to start unpacking *that*? Bridget was still parsing Esther's statement when the artist said, 'Who's on the counter while you're up here with Laura?'

'Lucy and Kat.'

'Good. Lucinda makes superb coffee.'

That was too far. 'It's *Lucia* if you don't want to use her preferred name.'

'As you say. Now, if you'll excuse me, I shall drag my arthritic bones down the stairs and berate that dim-witted constable until he lets me come back up in the lift.'

Esther left them, and Laura pointed round the corner. 'This way.'

Turn the Paige had been given a space on the south side of the Mill, and hazy sunlight flooded a workshop with a complete split personality. Bridget had wondered what printmaking and bookbinding had in common, and the answer was a bit like her parents' union: a marriage of convenience.

Laura's zone could have been from a low-budget fantasy film, where they'd had to reuse the set of a sci-fi epic. A weird mixture of ancient tomes, stacks of leather, reams of paper and sterile work surfaces showed a degree of order that harmonised with Bridget's approach to life. The same could not be said for Shannon Turner.

'How do you work with that in front of you all day?' asked Bridget.

The eastern wall of Turn the Paige had been covered with a moonscape. Of sorts. If the moon in question was inhabited by talking fruit. And seen through a lens of LSD.

It was obviously a composite backdrop from *Space Fruit*, but the individual panels had been printed using a variety of inks. In some places the ground was purple, and in others the printmaker had turned outer space lemon yellow and supplied it with red stars. And Bridget hadn't watched every episode, but she was sure there had never been a *dog* in it, still less a dog which breathed fire. She couldn't help thinking of Clarke's dog, Scout, and what he might do at the full moon.

'Takes a bit of getting used to,' said Laura. 'I moved my bench so that I could turn my back on it when it gets too much. Have a seat.'

In front of the nightmare moonscape were Shannon's more mundane artefacts: ink-splattered tables. Silk screen frames. Bottles of pigment and plan chests covered with sticky labels. Esther was wrong about something – she wasn't the only *Artist* up here. And quite possibly she was a lot less bonkers than Shannon.

Bridget took a stool and turned to face the door. Laura would have the sun in her eyes, but neither of them would have to face the wall of psychedelic fruit.

'Tell me what you know,' Bridget began. 'Why have the bizzies picked on your sister?'

'Because she has no alibi, because she was at the Mill early yesterday and because of the contracts,' said Laura. 'And the video that was posted last night.'

Laura was getting agitated again, and Bridget felt herself being sucked in. Not good. 'Let's take it back a few steps. Presumably the police wanted to know your movements on Sunday night? Where were you?'

'They wanted to know my movements from twelve till twelve on Sunday. Simple. I was at home trying to get the kids' stuff packed until four, then I drove down to the motorway services on the M6 toll road to meet their father. He was late. There was an accident on the way back. I stopped for fuel at Lancaster Services around ten thirty and my neighbour saw me arrive home twenty minutes later. He was doing late-night watering. They even had my phone and checked the satnav.'

Bridget hadn't always had an instinct for when people were holding things back. She'd developed that after living with Natalie. 'What else, Laura?'

The bookbinder sighed. 'I didn't mention it yesterday, but they pushed me on it today. They wanted to know why I'd gone via Hayley's place.'

'Why had you?'

'I couldn't face going home to an empty house. I messaged her to say that I was coming, but she never replied and she wasn't at home. I tried denying it to Barney, but …'

When Laura trailed off into internal speculation, Bridget gently said, 'Did Hayley ever reply?'

'Not till eleven. Just said she was sorry she'd missed me and we'd catch up in the morning. When I asked her yesterday, she said she was shattered and had gone for a walk when it was cooler. The police kept going on about whether she'd told me she was coming back here on Sunday night! Why would she come back here after she'd been here all day?'

Why indeed? 'You said she'd turned up early yesterday or something?'

'She got to the Mill just after the police, and she said last night that they were asking her about it for some reason. They asked me, too, but I didn't know anything.'

Bridget made a mental note and moved on. 'What's this about contracts, Laura.'

Laura balled her hands into fists, and Bridget forced herself not to look at them. She did not want a reputation for fetishising fingers, even a reputation in her own head.

'If only she'd talked to me about it!' said Laura, venting her distress on a might-have-been. 'All I know is that there was some sort of summit meeting on Sunday about "the third prong". That's what Hayley called it. She said it was crucial for 3M3 to have it, but I don't know what it was.' She hung her head. 'And when Louis was holding court yesterday morning, I'm sure he said that there'd been a row.'

'That's another reason I need to talk to him,' said Bridget. 'You know I was in Liverpool all weekend, right? Who was here on Sunday that you know of. You don't normally work weekends, do you? I've never seen you here on a Sunday.'

'No. Not with the kids to look after. Shannon sometimes comes in and runs courses. She didn't have a course this weekend, but I'm sure someone said she was here. I also sell my stuff through Penny, and she's usually around.'

'What *does* a bookbinder sell?' Bridget asked.

Laura passed her an exquisite leather-bound journal. 'Most of my work is archival restoration. Old books needing new covers, but libraries and collections are always short of money, so the work's haphazard. I make these when I haven't got anyone in the sick bay.'

'Oh, you mean damaged books.' Her phone vibrated and she checked the message. *Getting Busy. LuX.*

Bridget gave the journal back and stood up. 'Is there anyone else here you can spend time with?'

Laura checked her phone. 'Shannon's on her way back.'

'Good. Where do you live?'

'Grange Farm Croft. Number three.'

'Where's that again?'

'Past the White Hart and it's on the right before the T junction.'

'Okay if I pop round later? And I haven't forgotten about the video you mentioned. Send me a link when you've got your head together. Here's my card, and I'd better go before there's a meltdown.'

Laura fanned herself with the journal. 'Bit late for that. I think everything's melting today.'

Seventeen

Bridget was miles away as she walked down the stairs, and that's why she nearly bumped into the middle-aged man on the first floor. Being British, he was the one who apologised.

'I'm sorry. I was miles away,' he said, blinking.

He looked like he *had* been in a dream. Or possibly a nightmare. 'No worries,' said Bridget. Then she remembered where she was and what was going on. 'Are you with CID?'

The man's suit, well made but rumpled, would certainly fit with a DI brought in from outside, and there was a depth to his eyes that spoke of understanding. He rubbed his face with a strong hand and said, 'Totally the opposite.' He looked at her properly for the first time, and being a man, that survey included a sweep of her chest, and there his eyes rested, but not on her assets.

Having peered at her badge, he said, 'Bridget of Caffè Milano.' His head jerked up. 'Are you the one who …?'

Bridget put together the eyes, the cheekbones and above all the fingers. It had to be. 'Jonathan Carson? Jonno?'

He nodded.

'Then I'm so sorry. So sorry.'

They were on the landing of the Dukes Gallery floor, and he'd either come from the gents or from Louis Young's office. Given that there were toilets on the ground floor and a constable guarding the stairs, he must have been to see Louis. There were a couple of chairs outside the firmly locked gallery, and Bridget pointed to them. 'Yeah. It was me.' She pulled the chairs apart and sat on one. Tony's brother followed and sat down as if he'd been on an overnight flight.

'I'm sorry,' she said again. 'I really liked Tony, and I'm afraid I can't say anything about yesterday morning.'

'Figures.' His accent was stronger than Tony's, his hair much greyer and neatly cut short. He sat up a little straighter. 'Tony talked about you. Said you were off his Christmas card list for going AWOL on their big weekend.' His eyes focused on Bridget's sweaty face. 'He made it sound like he knew you and really missed you. How long had you known him?'

'All of three days, Jonno … now I've met you, you don't seem like a *Jonno* to me. I guess you always were to your little brother.'

'When he was speaking to me, yes. Most people call me Jon. You must have made a big impression on him in a short time, Bridget.'

Bridget was not keen on her relationship with Tony Carson being the story. Not now she was on the case. 'I've got a brother. We didn't speak for a bit, and I hated it.'

'We didn't speak for a lot longer than *a bit*, and now …'

'Tony told me about CARM,' she suggested. 'It must have been good to be working on something together.'

Tears started forming in Jon's eyes, and he tried blinking them away, then got out a folded handkerchief. 'It's all so … *overwhelming*. I'm not cut out for this. I'd better go.'

'Hey, Jon. It's okay. No one is cut out for grief. We all deal with it differently, and we're all grieving different people. You've lost a brother, I lost a guy I quite liked. And then there's his friends, of course.'

'What friends?'

'Hayley and Donna.'

'They're not friends.' He thought about that. 'He never had any time for Hayley. Not really. I suppose there was Donna. A bit. In as much as he could use her to gang up on Hayley.' He messed with the handkerchief. 'We lost our dad four years ago. Did he mention that? Of course he didn't. And now I have to tell our mother before his name is all over the news.'

'I thought she was already … I mean, he told me she never got the chance to live here. I assumed she'd passed away, along with your dad.'

'No, she's in a nursing home at Aldhaven.'

'Didn't the police speak to her?'

'Not once I told them where she is and what's the matter with her. It's going to kill her.' He went quiet. 'Did your mum have a favourite?'

Bridget was not going to go there. No way. Not even Lucy knew the full story about her mother. 'It's different when it's a boy and a girl,' she told him. 'When there are two brothers, a mother has to choose, doesn't she? And she chose Tony. It's none of it fair, is it?'

'No, it isn't, Bridget, and Tony was many things, but he was never a bad son to her. Since he moved back here, he's been almost every day, and not just flying visits. He even popped in on Saturday night after spending all day up there.' His eyes pointed to the ceiling, then flicked to the gallery doors. 'And with no one visiting for three days now … I'd better go. There's no easy way to do this, is there? Thank you for listening.' He stood up and put the handkerchief roughly in his pocket.

She stood up, too. 'Don't bottle it up, Jon. Sounds like a cliché, but it isn't.'

'Isn't it? Thanks again.'

Bridget almost expected him to offer a handshake. Not quite. He nodded and left her to follow or stay put. She was tempted to try and see Louis, but she'd been away from the Spinning Room long enough now. She let him get ahead of her on the stairs, then followed him down.

Since walking up the stairs earlier, Bridget had picked up a whole basket of food for thought. There was the *Space Fruit* legacy and the history with Shannon. There was Esther Thornfield deliberately trying to muddy the waters, and then there was the brother …

Jon/Jonno Carson was clearly very upset, and very clearly hiding something. The conversation had been heading strongly in one direction until Jon had got on to the subject of visiting their mother.

If Tony had been so devoted, he would have messaged his brother about not going on Sunday night, it was safe to assume. And then Jon should have gone to the nursing home in his place, and when Jon's train of thought had arrived at the same station as Bridget, he'd clammed up and walked off. What was Jonathan Carson doing on Sunday night, then? Was he down the pub and feeling guilty about neglecting his mother or was he back in Byford with a shotgun and looking for his brother?

Bridget really didn't want to think about that. Not at all. Cain and Abel had never been her favourite Bible story.

Eighteen

It wasn't *that* busy down in the Spinning Room when Bridget peered through the archway. They could have waited. She was spotted by Lucy and waved over. 'What?' said Bridget.

'You need to speak to Kat before the coach party arrives.'

'What coach party? We can't be on the itinerary for murder tours yet. It was only yesterday and they won't have had time to sell tickets.'

Lucy blinked. 'Murder tours? Seriously?'

'Big money in the dead. And the undead.'

Eye-roll. 'No, Bridget. It's last Friday's coach to the bonny, bonny banks of Loch Lomond, and they're on their return journey. The courier says the old dears have been asking if they can come here on the way back.'

'Don't give her any money.'

'Who?'

'The courier. Or the driver.'

'Why … oh. Do they really ask for bribes?'

'Some of them, but that's usually for lunch, not coffee and comfort breaks. We did one to Cornwall when I was a kid, and I definitely saw money change hands. When are they due?'

'Ten minutes.'

'Fine.'

Bridget found Kat on her phone in the kitchen, which was a bit like saying she'd found the milk in the fridge; it was the kid's natural habitat after all. 'What's up Kat?'

'You're what's up. You can't leave so soon. It's not fair on me. I'm still in recovery after Feargal went bust. I can't be expected to cope with a new boss. Especially if they're Polish.'

'Hey! None of that. I expected better of you.'

'Now you're twisting my words. I meant her from Cairndale. I'm sure that not all Polish women are horrible.'

'Her name's Lilianna, and she's a hard worker. Like *all* the Polish people round here. Doesn't matter, because you'll soon be off anyway.'

'Off where?'

'I don't know. Shannon told me you wanted to go back to uni and do printmaking.'

'No I don't! Now *she's* twisting my words. You're all the same.'

Kat stretched herself to her considerable height and walked out of the kitchen in the highest of high dudgeons.

'That went well,' said Lucy, taking Kat's place by the sink. 'Is she really leaving? Shame. I've been thinking.'

'Last time you did that we ended up here, so I'd be careful. Oh. Wait. The last time you did some thinking, you decided to sack Tara Doyle off. That went well, too.' When Lucy didn't rise to the bait, Bridget leaned against the wall. 'Go on then.'

'I was thinking about ice cream. Obviously it's never been part of Caffè Milano's core business, so I don't know the numbers. It's basically cream, isn't it?'

'Clue's in the name, Lucinda.'

'Stop trying to distract me.' Pause. 'Who called me *Lucinda*?'

'Esmeralda. Go on.'

'That explains why she was so nice just now. I thought she must be up to something. So. Cream, yes?'

'Yes. Cream, full-fat milk and sugar. Everything else is optional.'

'Well, the dairy farm with the most awards for creamy milk is right there.' Lucy emphasised her dialectical point with a dramatic gesture aimed at the millpond. 'It's not over there, is it?'

'If you mean Meadow Farm, then no, it's that way. And if you think I am going to start an ice cream plant using *raw milk* you haven't been listening for the last two years.'

'Incoming!' shouted Kat.

They did not fold, but they did crease. Especially when the trippers discovered that there had been a murder on the premises. Two couples immediately returned to the coach and demanded that the driver let them in, and two more buttonholed Kat, demanding all the gory details, and if she couldn't supply the gory details, could she show them how to find the gory details on their phones, because they'd been told you could get news on there but never believed their grandson …

When Lucy got a call from her Uncle Paul, Bridget felt her knees going. 'Do you have to take that?' she demanded.

Uncle Paul was Lucy's godfather and unofficial legal adviser. 'Yes,' said Lucy.

'Who's that just come in?' asked Kat. 'And why is she putting on a

Caffè Milano apron?'

The new arrival smiled. 'Shall I start now instead of next Monday? Not as though I can do my other job, is it?'

'I could kiss you, Wendy Sadler,' said Bridget.

'Please don't. You look rather sweaty.'

'Story of my life. Look, Wendy, there's a big tray, a bottle of cleaning spray and a stack of microfibres by the dishwasher. Start clearing the tables at the back and work this way if you don't mind.'

'But watch out,' added Kat, skating past with a buttered tea cake (who ordered *that* in this weather?). 'She'll come and inspect your work.'

'Good,' said Wendy. 'I'd expect nothing less.'

When the trippers had been summoned back to their coach, Kat asked, 'Why did Lucy choose these polo shirts? It's like wearing a wet towel in the bath.'

'What would you suggest? I don't think a crop top would suit me, somehow.'

'Surely there must be something lightweight and wicking, and stop changing the subject.'

'Eh? What subject? You just asked me—'

'No. From before. You haven't told me why you're leaving. I—'

'Hold the fort, kid. I need to speak to Donna.'

The third member of 3M3 had wandered into the Spinning Room in a daze, carrying a can of Diet Pepsi. Bridget intercepted her and said, 'Would you like something on the house to replace that?'

Donna stared at the can, then shook herself. 'Do you do any iced coffees?'

Bridget sent a dark look towards the kitchen, where Lucy was taking Wendy's bank details and showing her how to load and run the dishwasher. 'Blame the Boss. She says they're "Not Italian".'

'Isn't *Frappuccino* Italian?'

'About as Italian as I am. No, it was invented and trademarked by Starbucks. Is your blood sugar low?' Donna nodded weakly. 'Hang fire.'

One minute later, Bridget slid a glass dish across Donna's table, filled with ice cream drenched in a double espresso. She placed a spoon and napkin next to it and said, 'I'm working on an ice cream-espresso martini combination to cover all bases, but this should do the trick for now.'

Donna stared at the dish. 'It's the best thing I've seen for days.'

'Good. Do you mind if I take the weight off for a minute? Thanks. Can I say that I'm really sorry about Tony. Whatever happened between you, he must have meant something once.'

'He still did.' Donna dug in her spoon and savoured the first mouthful. 'He really liked you, Bridget. He talked about you a lot.' Another mouthful. 'He said your coffee was all that stood between triumph and disaster for 3M3.' A third spoonful. 'I'd hang on to that endorsement if I were you, because if you'd actually started dating, you'd have a very different opinion of the man.' A fourth dripping scoop of black-streaked goodness. 'He was still special, though. Very special. We'll miss him.'

'What's going to happen now?'

'Is Wendy here? She said she was going to offer her services to you.'

'In the back, being inducted or something. Do you want me to call her?'

'Not yet. I just wanted to catch up on the gossip with her. The police were very tight-lipped, but is it true that Hayley has been arrested?'

'Yeah. About that. Do you know her sister?'

'We spoke for about two minutes last week. Has *she* been arrested, too?'

'No, but she has been on my case, and she wants me on Hayley's case.'

'I see,' said Donna with a frown. 'The police told me not to discuss things.'

'Have you lived in a village before, Donna?'

'No, and I still don't. I live in Penwortham, just south of Preston.'

'Well, you can't *not* discuss things in a village. Trust me on that, and if you were going to discuss them with Wendy … Well, I've said I'll help Laura find out what was going on, so just tell me what the row was about on Sunday. She knows there was one, but she has no clue what it was about.'

Donna scraped the last of the mixture onto her spoon and gave an *Mmm* of pleasure. 'If Hayley had stuck to presenting and voice-overs and not gone on that business start-up course, I think Tony would still be alive.'

Bridget was taken aback. 'Do you think she killed him?'

'I don't know. Tony and me stopped sharing personal things a while ago, so for all I know he seduced Fliss Duke and Edwin took revenge. It's easier to believe he died over an affair than over a piece of plastic fruit.'

Bridget didn't push it. Donna glanced at the kitchen. Still no Wendy. Donna moved the ice cream dish and leaned forwards. 'What do you know about *Space Fruit*?'

'That Lieutenant Lemon was my favourite character and that she was badly treated by Captain Berry. Sorry. I didn't mean to be flippant. All I know is that you all worked for Leyland Films and so did Shannon Turner.'

'Yes, and that's all you could prove in court. The rest is down to word of mouth, verbal contracts, divorce, reversionary rights, the law of probate and the validity of post facto licensing agreements. And you need to know the name *Andy Staton*.'

'Andy Staton. Right. Is he a suspect, too?'

'No. Andy took his own life two years ago, which was two years after Shannon kicked him out.'

Bridget sat back. Wow. She was tempted to get her order pad out and take notes. It was too hot to remember anything beyond *word of mouth*. Where was the Sheriff when you needed him? Even Mina would be on more solid ground with that memory of hers.

Wendy's voice echoed through the Spinning Room. 'Donna! You're here.' The woman herself followed and slid into the empty seat to give Donna a hug, which was only half returned. 'Are you okay?'

'Thanks to Bridget, yes, and thanks to Bridget, no. She has the secret of eternal youth in that elixir she gave me, but she wants to know about the Captain Berry clause.'

'So do I,' said Wendy. 'I have no idea what you're on about.'

Donna looked at Bridget. 'If you get me a pot of that Red Rose Tea, I'll tell both of you. If they can spare you behind the counter. I don't think your young girl is very happy about something.'

'She's never happy,' said Bridget. 'But you're right, I do need to check in with them. No problem about the tea, though. Coming right up.'

Nineteen

'We can cope,' said Lucy to Kat and Bridget. 'Tom would prefer to stay away from Cairndale for a couple of days, and I'd rather be here working than go back to an empty house. Not a problem, is it Kat?'

Bridget's duckling plonked an extra-large teapot on the tray. Water and tea leaves slopped out of the spout. 'I still want to see you after,' she told Bridget. 'And if another coach comes in, I'm not doing it on my own.'

'I wouldn't do that to you,' said Bridget. 'Pass me a bit of blue roll and three cups.'

Bridget had been watching Wendy and Donna out of the corner of her eye. Wendy's hand had been on Donna's for a short while, then Donna had shifted in her seat and got up, leaving the Spinning Room. She'd pointed to the toilets as she left, signalling that she'd be back.

Bridget cleaned the spillage from the tray and took it over, setting it down gently on the table. 'I know you're a fan, but how did you actually end up working for Donna?' she asked.

Wendy gave a bitter smile. 'For a while, I thought she might be working for *me*. I fangirled her on Facebook and said that I wanted to sell her stuff in my new online store. The one I was going to set up with my redundancy money.'

Bridget could see shame in Wendy's face, and she asked as gently as she could, 'I take it things didn't work out?'

'I should have listened to my son, not my daughter. She said I should follow my dream because anything was possible. He said it was money down the drain. The fact that he was getting married and wanted a handout made me a bit sceptical, I'm afraid.'

'Children, eh? What do they know?'

'Jack knows his mother is what he knows. It turns out that working for a bank is not good preparation for e-commerce.' Wendy forced a smile. 'I did listen to one thing he told me, though. I set up a limited company and pulled the plug when the bank – *my* bank – suggested a loan secured on the house.'

'I'm so sorry.'

Wendy shook her head. 'I'm happy here.' She glanced up. 'Donna's coming back. Shall I be mother?'

Donna had clearly taken time to freshen up, carving her hair back into its sharp parting and putting on some mascara. Wendy placed the first cup of tea in front of her idol and added milk without thinking. Clearly Wendy knew exactly how Donna liked her brew.

'I keep expecting things to re-set,' said Donna. 'You know, you go to the loo and you expect Tony to be waiting outside ready to be annoying.' She shivered. 'You … you saw him, didn't you, Bridget? You found him?'

Bridget nodded slowly.

'Was it … was it bad? No. Don't tell me.'

'I'd rather not, thanks. It did smell of curry for some weird reason. Not figured that out.'

'No weird reason,' said Donna. 'It was for the Sunday Night Summit, as no one was calling it except Hayley. She got the curry, too …'

Donna lapsed into silence. Wendy drank some tea and urged Donna to do the same, then Wendy said, 'We were flat out all afternoon, but by five o'clock we'd cracked it. Everything set up and tested ready for a final rehearsal on Monday morning and going live on Monday afternoon. We all split up and I walked down to the car with Hayley. She said she was going home, then picking up the takeaway from the Jewel in the Crown at seven. Do you know it?'

'I do,' said Bridget. 'Finest curry house in North Lancashire. You weren't at the summit then, Wendy?'

'No. My daughter came round to complain that she hadn't seen me for days and I ended up raiding the freezer for both of us.'

That put Wendy firmly in the clear, assuming her daughter stayed all evening. Bridget turned to Donna.

'What did you do?'

'I went to see Shann. Shannon Turner. She deserved to know what was going on.'

Bridget's brain was starting to bulge again. Shannon was part of the crew at Leyland Films, and had been married to Andy Staton, so …? Before she could formulate a question, Donna carried on, following her own internal thread.

'We talked, and I told her she had to be there, so I brought her back in my car.'

'She lives in Byford?'

'Yes. Sort of. She lives up the hill in an old cottage near the clinic.'

Bridget slotted the location into her mental map: it was where you ended up if you turned left out of the Mill and headed away from the village.

Wendy asked a question. 'How did Tony feel when he saw her? He was dropping enough hints about her all week.'

'Oh yes?' said Bridget. Maybe she'd enlist Wendy as her new assistant.

'Not happy,' said Donna. She made eye contact with Bridget. 'Tony blames Shann for what happened to Andy.'

'Blamed,' said Wendy gently.

Donna started blinking back tears. 'I can't believe he's gone, the great big … Oh, I don't know. I don't know anything, Bridget. He could have been the nicest man in the world if he'd grown up, and who'd want to shoot an overgrown schoolboy?'

'I could have slapped him a few times,' said Wendy, 'and I've only known him for a couple of weeks. Knew. I only knew him. This is hard. Are you sure you're okay, Donna?'

'I'll finish the tea and my story.' She took a deep breath. 'He made a joke of it at first, and he'd brought beers from the pub. Said it was the closest we'd get to a *Space Fruit* reunion. He even talked Hayley into doing Lulu Lemon.'

'Wait,' said Bridget urgently. '*Hayley* was Lieutenant Lemon?'

Donna managed a small laugh. 'I know. Weird or what. She was Pammy the pink grapefruit, too. In fact she was everyone except Captain Berry himself.'

Bridget had re-watched two episodes of the show last night – they were all available online. 'Who was he?'

'Milton somebody. A jobbing voice-over actor from LA. He went into a local studio over there and recorded his lines after everyone else. I only saw him once, when we video-conferenced at the end of season four. Big bloke.' She shrugged, running out of steam.

'What happened next?' said Bridget.

'Hayley told Tony that it was finally time to put the third prong in place and get his agreement for the licences.' She paused. 'We all knew that 3M3 couldn't turn a profit on trains and doll's houses, and Hayley had come up with a good idea. Well, I thought it was good. We would sell custom merch for cancelled shows. Niche stuff.'

Bridget was getting lost again. 'Take a step back, girl. What's *custom merch* when it's at home?'

'*Merch* is *merchandising*,' said Wendy.

'I know that,' said Bridget. 'I used to have loads of it. It's the *custom* part that gets me.'

Donna looked over towards the counter. 'Oh. It's gone. Your snow globe of *Barista with Strawberry*. That sort of custom. Have you still got it?'

'Of course. It's in a safe place, and I have no plans to cash in on it. Aren't merchandising contracts tied up tighter than the Bank of England?'

'They are, but shows get cancelled and rights can be reverted or bought for buttons. Hayley had already been in talks with the producers of a French show called *Sous Cosmos*. It's—'

'I've heard of that,' said Bridget, surprising herself. The French sci-fi show had featured on Conrad Bloody Clarke's stag weekend, of all things. 'I thought it was still running.'

Donna's eyes flicked around the room, and she lowered her voice. 'Don't tell anyone, but it's been cancelled. Especially don't tell the fans! They're real fan-atics.'

It was the closest Donna had come to forgetting what was going on. A tiny moment of the future. It didn't last long, because Bridget saw Donna following the thought back to the studio upstairs. 'Doesn't matter. Tony said no to licensing *Space Fruit*, but only after Shannon had shown him the Captain Berry clause, and don't ask me what that's all about because there was such a row then. I stood back and let them get on with it.'

'What happened?'

Donna finished her tea and put the cup neatly on the saucer before placing both equally neatly on the tray. 'Shannon stormed out in tears. Hayley started tearing Tony off a strip, and I went to find Shann, but she'd gone. I drove up to her house to try and catch her, but no sign. I went to the White Hart, but she wasn't there either. I had a drink, then realised I had to drive back to Cairndale, so I went for a walk around the village. It's nice.'

'Drive back to Cairndale? Not Preston?'

Donna shook her head. 'I stayed at the Red Rose Hotel on Sunday night. And last night.'

Wendy looked hurt. 'You know you could stay with me. I did offer, and the offer still stands.'

Donna stood up. 'And I'm grateful, Wendy, I really am. Sometimes you just need to zone out, and the last few days have been like that.' She looked at Bridget. 'I know you mean well, and it was good to talk about it, Bridget, but this isn't a game.'

Bridget tried to keep it light. 'That's usually my line, Donna. Take care, yeah?'

Donna nodded and picked up her bag, then took the side door.

Bridget and Wendy watched her go, and Wendy gave a great sigh. 'This is terrible. We're all victims. Trite but true.'

'Yeah.' Bridget paused, then stood up and gripped the tray. 'Come on, let's see how Lucy and Kat are getting on.'

Twenty

Lucy had been keeping her eye on Bridget, Wendy and Donna as they talked. It looked like Bridget had bought into the investigation in a big way, and Lucy needed to finesse the next element. Not that she would admit to interfering. As soon as Donna left, Lucy was in place and ready to intercept Bridget and Wendy when they returned to the counter.

'How's Donna?' Lucy asked when Bridget deposited the tray.

'Rough. Cut up.' Bridget checked her phone. 'Nothing from Laura, so Hayley must still be in custody.' She looked at the windows, like she always did when seeking inspiration. 'I could really do with talking to Shannon and Louis.'

That was music to Lucy's ears. 'Oh yeah? Where does Shannon live?'

'Up the hill towards the clinic somewhere.'

Perfect. Lucy executed a jeté towards the kitchen and grabbed Kat before she could escape. Bridget's right-hand woman was nearly a foot taller than Lucy and about as graceful as a collection of bent pipe cleaners, and she was stunned that Lucy had managed to fly through the air. Lucy used the element of surprise to drag her to the counter. 'You know where Shannon lives, right? Why don't you take Bridget there? I'll carry on showing Wendy the ropes.'

'I was going to—' began Wendy.

'Great,' said Lucy. 'Is it in walking distance?'

'Suppose,' said Kat.

'Right. Off you go.'

Bridget gave Lucy the *I know what you're doing and you'll pay for it later* look; it was one of Bridget's favourites, even though it didn't look nearly as scary without the Goth make-up and accessories. Bridget took off her apron and chucked it at Lucy, then said, 'C'mon, kid.'

Kat could strop for England when she wanted. *Mega mardy* didn't come close. At the same time, Kat was what Grandma White would have called "A well-brought-up young woman." Kat folded her apron and placed it neatly on the counter, then waddled off to catch up with Bridget.

'Right,' said Lucy breezily. 'You can serve our next customer.' A young lad who was trying and failing to grow a beard had been hanging around by the archway, and now that he wasn't outnumbered four to one by women, he edged over.

Wendy scooted round the counter and took up position. 'Hello there. What can I get you?'

Lucy picked up the tray which Bridget had left, added the two aprons and went into the kitchen, taking up a position by the doorway to see how Wendy got on with handling the order, not that Lucy would let her use the coffee machine yet.

'Hi,' said the lad. 'Can I have a … a J2O? No, I'll have a pot of tea, please.'

'Anything to eat?' asked Wendy as she reached for the teapot and tea bags. 'A scone would go nicely.'

Lucy smiled and winced to herself simultaneously. Wendy's manner was warm and welcoming, but that wasn't how it was done in Caffè Milano. You do not make food suggestions unless asked. She was thinking about that and almost missed the lad's response to the suggestion of a scone: he flinched back and blinked. Either he had suffered an unspecified scone-related trauma in childhood or he was very short of money.

'Erm, no thanks. Tea's fine.'

'Milk? If so, what sort?'

Again, almost perfect: you give them proper milk unless they ask for non-dairy.

'Regular.' He smiled at Wendy in a *most* inappropriate way. She was old enough to be his mother and have spare change. 'You must be new, right? No name badge or scary polo shirt.'

'My first day,' said Wendy, with a glance towards the doorway where Lucy was lurking. 'I'm allowed to dispense tea and sympathy, but not coffee. Yet. Nor do I have the first idea how to work this till. I do know my own name though: it's *Wendy*.'

'And I'm Jed. Jed Holmes. You must be Wendy Sadler, from 3M3?'

Wendy didn't miss a beat, and only the rise of half an octave in her voice gave her away. 'Oh yes? Didn't I see you hanging around with that influencer girl?'

'Ciara's only an influencer when she looks in the mirror,' said Jed with some venom. 'We're both on the media and journalism course at ULIST. Ciara's more on the media side, and I'm more of a journalist. I just wondered how this was affecting you?'

There was a pause, and Lucy was on tiptoe, ready to intervene, but Wendy was ready for him.

'You mean, *how has the brutal murder of your employer made you feel?* Really, Mister Holmes, how do you *think* I feel? And Donna and Hayley and Shannon and Laura will say the same, too. Here's your tea. Lucy!'

Lucy glided out of the kitchen and smiled at the lad. 'Bridget said there'd been a plague of fleas this morning. Not that I'm against the free press or anything, but, you know, Jed, there's a time and a place, and if people can't see their coffee shop as a haven and sanctuary, they won't go there, and I'll lose business.' She added a beam to the smile. 'Does that make sense?'

Jed looked around him, maybe even noticing the surroundings for the first time. A hot and bothered pair of grandparents pushing a puce-coloured infant in a purple buggy came through the archway. 'Excuse me, do you have baby changing facilities?' asked the grandfather.

'Just out there on the left.'

The grandmother started messing with the overstuffed baby bag hanging from the buggy, then wheeled the whole lot out of the café while her husband peered at the display.

'I see what you mean,' said Jed with a look Lucy remembered vividly from her student days: *I should have worked that out for myself.* 'Neutral territory,' he added.

'That's me. I'm positively Swiss-Italian.' He looked confused. 'Forget I said that and give me two pounds forty instead.'

While he fished in his pockets, Lucy got a plate and grabbed a box from under the counter. 'Thanks. These are from yesterday, but they're still good. Have one on the house.' She leaned forwards and put a plated pastry on Jed's tray. 'But don't tell anyone. Our secret.'

He smiled and walked off. Lucy accepted a bottle of formula from the grandfather and put it in the microwave, then gave Wendy her first lesson in *l'arte Italiana del caffè.*

The Spinning Room got busier as the after-school crowd drifted in – a few mothers, a couple of teachers and a girl in a garishly striped blazer which could have come from the Henley Regatta. Must be a private school somewhere nearby.

Lucy avoided the burning topic of the day when talking to Wendy because she wanted to get it from Bridget later. There was also training to undertake: Wendy's skills as a hostess were impeccable, but making coffee for her colleagues at the Morecambe branch of Praed's Bank was very different to life at Ford Mill.

'You're close to Bridget, aren't you?' said Wendy when the rush had died down. 'I could tell by the way you looked at each other.'

'Sorry?'

'There were three conversations today that you had with Bridget when no words were exchanged.'

'That's very … Zen, Wendy.'

'No. It was one of my unofficial tests for mortgage applicants: if the couple didn't communicate non-verbally, I always dug deeper.'

Lucy laughed. 'You'll get on well with Mina in that case.'

Wendy smiled. Briefly. Then she retrieved her phone from her bag and said, 'If Bridget is serious about trying to clear Hayley, then she needs to see this.'

Lucy had already swapped numbers with Wendy, and a few seconds later a link to the website of a corporate bonding venue came through, and a video began to play. A striking woman in tweeds turned to face the camera and slid her hair behind her ear. Lucy paused the video. 'What's this?'

'That's Hayley. Keep watching.'

Lucy fiddled to get the sound on as Hayley's lips moved silently, her eyes flirting and blinking with the camera. She finished saying her piece just as Lucy got the volume up.

'When the pressure's on, who's going to keep their nerve?' asked Hayley with an aristocratic voice.

Then the camera backed away and showed that Hayley was standing next to a rack of shotguns. She took one as casually as Lucy would grab a portafilter and strode up to a marker.

'Pull,' said Hayley, and the video cut to a clay pigeon trap.

The operator yanked the lever and a pair of clays flew into the sky. The video cut back to Hayley tracking their flight and then two loud blasts rang out around the Spinning Room. One of the mothers at the nearest table let out a small cry.

'Oops!' said Lucy. She raised her voice. 'Sorry about that.'

A beaming Hayley turned to face the camera, and whatever she said was buried by the mute button.

'She's a natural, isn't she?' said Wendy.

'Mmm,' said Lucy. There was no point denying it. Whether or not Hayley had hit the clays, there was no denying that she had handled the gun – and the powerful recoil – as if to the manner born.

Lucy was stunned. Very few ordinary people ever use firearms in this country. She was still digesting the video when Jed Holmes returned his empty tray. 'You've seen it, then?' he said nonchalantly.

Lucy locked her phone and gave him a bright smile. 'Anything else I can get you?'

'No thanks.' His face scrunched up in something approaching a smile, and his nose gave a little twitch. 'You've been very generous.' He turned to Wendy. 'And thanks for the tip about Laura Paige and Shannon Turner, Ms Sadler. I had no idea they were involved until you mentioned their names. Don't worry, I won't stalk them in here.'

'Damn and blast,' said Wendy when he'd gone. 'Me and my big mouth. How do you deal with the press so … naturally, Lucy?'

Lucy sighed. 'Years of practice, I'm afraid. Let's go and clean up.'

Twenty-One

Bridget huffed up the lane. 'Walking distance my arse,' she muttered.

Kat put on a spurt and drew level. 'What's the rush? My feet don't like this.'

Bridget came to an abrupt halt. 'You're wearing Jazz's trainers again, aren't you?'

Kat looked down at her feet. 'Well mine are like boats, and now it's so *hot*, I can't cope.'

The kid had a point about the heat. And about her shoes. Bridget sighed. 'Too late to go back now … Whoa!'

A Lycra clad missile came round the bend on two wheels, mirror shades gleaming. Kat gave a squeal and jumped out of the way. Into Bridget.

'Owww!' said Bridget when she hit the verge. 'Oof!' she added as Kat landed on top of her. 'Oh, shit. Now look what you've done. I'll have stains all down these jeans and they were clean on this morning.'

'Look what *you've* done,' said Kat, disentangling herself. 'You're running out on me and you won't say why.'

Bridget considered changing the subject, but as that would mean getting up, she carried on sitting where she was. It really was too hot to be walking around the countryside. And what was that gooey stuff on the grass? Eurgh.

'I'm sorry, Kat, but Lucy left me with no choice. We're getting kicked out of Giuseppi's in Southport, and no contract with Giuseppi's means no ice cream. I built up that business, and I'm not gonna let it melt away.'

Kat brushed sticky green stuff off her jeans, then looked up. 'Was that a joke? *Melting away*. You're worse than my dad, and it's not funny. Do you have, like shares or something in this Giuseppi's thingy?'

'No, but I have invested years of my life in it.'

Kat folded her arms and towered over her seated mentor. Not that Bridget was feeling particularly like a responsible adult at the moment. Kat stared down and said, 'And you've invested even more in Caffè Milano. What about that? What about me?'

'It's not all about you, kid. And Shannon told me you were applying to go back to uni anyway.'

Kat had once started a course in criminology at a university in Cheshire only to run back home during the first year. She shook her head. 'Well, yeah, but only part-time on the foundation course at the College of Art in Lancaster. Shann says I should explore my talents, and the part-time course is, like, *two years*.'

Bridget held up her hand, and it took Kat a moment to twig that she was supposed to help Bridget up. 'No comments about me being a dead weight,' said Bridget when she was vertical again. 'How much further is it?'

'Just round the bend, which is appropriate. Can we get a lift back?'

'Let's see if we arrive alive first. Come on.'

Larch Cottage *was* just round the bend. And down a short track, where Shannon's imposing motorcycle sat on guard in the middle of the drive. 'Lucy would approve,' said Bridget.

'Why? I didn't know she was a biker.'

'It's a Moto Guzzi, and Lucy approves of everything Italian on principle, even if the German version is twice as good and half the price. And don't get her started on all things Japanese.' Bridget edged past the bike and rang the doorbell.

The gleaming Moto Guzzi was the most impressive thing about Larch Cottage. It might be nestling in the countryside, but the grey render and small windows of a 1930s bungalow were anything but quaint. There were nicer cottages in Speke, Bridget reckoned.

A cacophonous chime echoed from the house when her finger left the bell, followed quickly by a shout of, 'Round the back,' that came from beyond a concrete garage which was even uglier than the cottage. The same could not be said for the garden – now that *was* quaint.

'Over here,' said Shannon from behind some bushes.

They found the printmaker reclining on a lounger in a bower formed of low hanging trees, looking cool in a vest and shorts.

'Oh. It's you.'

'Who were you expecting?' asked Bridget.

Shannon sat up and said, 'Do you realise how intimidating you look with the red and black uniforms?' She paused. 'Perhaps not today.'

Bridget thought about Kat's description of the shirts as wet towels. About right. 'Sorry to bother you, Shannon, and I'm so sorry about what happened to Tony.'

'Laura said you might want to talk to me. Didn't expect you to show up so quickly.' She looked around. 'I'd offer you a seat, but I only have the one. You look like you need a drink, too, and I only have one glass out here.'

Bridget was expecting that declaration to be a prelude to dismissal, but no. Shannon pointed to a mature fir tree and said, 'Park yourselves in the shade and I'll get you some lemonade.'

Bridget and Kat collapsed onto the grass and leaned against the tree trunk, glad to be out of the sun. Bridget closed her eyes for a second, and when she opened them, Kat was pulling off her borrowed trainers. 'Don't do that. You'll never get them back on again.'

'Yes, Mum,' said Kat, yanking her right foot free and peeling off the sock. 'You have no idea how good that feels,' she added, before starting on the other shoe.

Shannon returned and gave them both a glass of home-made lemonade stacked high with ice. Bridget felt the acid cut through the gunge in her mouth and strip her throat. That was *so* good, and then the sugar hit her bloodstream. *Even better*. 'Cheers for this. We may need to find a local supplier if this heatwave carries on.'

'Pleasure.'

Shannon sat on the edge of her lounger and looked Bridget in the eye. 'Are you here for Hayley or Tony?'

'I'm here for Laura, mostly. She needs to know there's someone on Hayley's side who's got the energy to ask awkward questions. Not that I've got much energy left right now.'

'I thought the police were asking enough awkward questions without needing your help.'

'I'm sure DI Swindlehurst is doing a great job.' Bridget drank more lemonade, then found a flat spot to rest the glass and let the ice melt a little. 'You're Laura's business partner, right? And Hayley is Laura's sister. So why did Tony look surprised when I mentioned your name the other week? Didn't he know you were here?'

'Bloody Hayley. She deserves time in custody for that alone, never mind the rest. Yes, you're right: she told Tony about Laura's business, but not about me being her partner. And Laura never mentioned it, either. It was *very* awkward when we met up again. Tony thought he was being set up.'

Bridget decided to let that one pass for now. 'I don't want to touch a raw nerve, Shannon, but can you tell me about Andy Staton and *Space Fruit*? Donna said it was mostly his baby.'

Shannon gave a little snort of pain and blinked rapidly. Her chilled exterior was cracking, and she looked away, over the trees and into another time and place. Bridget watched her struggle for a moment, then give in and lift up her vest to wipe her eyes.

'Sorry,' said Shannon. 'You never know when it's going to bite you in the arse. Even after years, the word *baby* can be a vicious little bugger.'

'Oh, Shann, are you okay?' asked Kat, in some distress.

'Yeah, fine.' Shannon looked down and breathed in and out. 'I spent eight years with Andy Staton convincing myself that there was plenty of time to get pregnant, and when we tried, it turned out that there wasn't. We spent the next eight years trying. On and off. When he could face it and when he wasn't down the mines.'

Bridget and Kat glanced at each other, and Bridget gave a tiny shake of her head. When Shannon showed no signs of continuing, Bridget said quietly, 'How did you meet? I didn't think there were any mines left. Not in this country.'

Shannon grimaced. 'There's plenty of mines in the *Depths of Mythranor*.'

'Uh?' said Kat.

'Fantasy RPG,' said Bridget. 'Before your time. He worked on that?'

'We both did. It's how we met. He was lead designer and I was lead landscape artist. Not that there was much actual *landscape* under the Blasted Plains of Mygrithil.'

'So how come you all ended up at Leyland Films?'

'The mines were all "worked out" when I got pregnant for the second time. Andy was brilliant that time. Unlike the first. I really thought we were going to become a family.'

There was a micro-pause that Bridget nearly filled, until Shannon pressed on. 'When I lost Emily, Andy tried to cheer me up by showing me the book he'd written while I was in hospital. Stupid man had no idea that there's a fairly large gap between birth and literacy.'

This time the pause was longer. 'I'm so sorry, Shannon. Really sorry.'

'Thanks. At first I didn't want a reminder stuck in my face, but he'd dedicated it to Emily, and I'd rather have a book as a reminder than an empty cot. Helped me think about what she might have been. I have no idea why I'm telling you all this.'

'Because I'm guessing you've not told anyone for years.'

'More lemonade?'

'No thanks. We're fine. What about the book?'

'Andy couldn't draw to save his life. One day when he was in Mothercare, he saw some plastic fruit shapes next to some outer space nursery furnishings. You know, planetary curtains and asteroid duvet covers. You probably don't know, do you?'

'I can guess, and I can guess that's how *Space Fruit* was born.'

'To be exact, it was how *Emily and the Space Fruit Rangers* was born. Created. Not *born*. One of my old art school friends came round to see me when I was in a really bad place, and she saw the book. She loved it, and she was assistant creative director at Leyland Films.'

'And the rest is history,' said Kat decisively, as if she were minting the expression for the first time. 'Come on, Chief, we need to get back.'

'Chief! Where did that come from? And I haven't finished me lemonade.'

Kat's whisper was very much of the *stage* variety when she said, 'Poor Shannon's been through a lot.'

So have I, thought Bridget. She was about to press on when the silence of the English countryside was interrupted by clashing *tings* and *brrps* from Bridget and Shannon's phones.

'Why do old people never set their phones to silent?' said Kat.

Bridget unlocked the screen. 'Because we are all sad and don't receive sixty messages an hour.' She read the message, as did Shannon, and they looked up at each other.'

'What!' said Kat. 'What's going on?'

'It's Laura. Hayley's been released on police bail until Thursday morning. She says not to bother her tonight.' Bridget thought for a moment. If she pushed Shannon even closer to the edge now, she might get shut out, and there was still time to grab someone else. If she had the energy. 'Thanks for seeing us, Shannon. I'm sorry for bringing it all up.'

'You don't know the half of it,' said Shannon, more to herself than Bridget.

Bridget took a healthy swig of lemonade and rolled over to push herself upright. When she looked down at Kat, Bridget saw she couldn't even get her bruised toes through the opening of her trainer, never mind all the way to the end. 'What am I going to do?' she quacked.

'I'll give you a piggyback,' said Bridget.

'Will you?'

Shannon gave a snort of laughter, and Bridget said witheringly, 'Don't be daft. Of course I won't. It should be you giving them to us *old people*.'

'I could do with some supplies,' said Shannon, pointing to her bike. 'Sorry, Bridget, but there's only room on the back for one.'

'I'll survive. Make sure you tell Jackie that you've had to bring her home because she can't go back to work like this.'

'Hey! You can't do that,' spluttered Kat.

'We old people stick together,' said Shannon. 'Don't we, Bridget?'

Twenty-Two

Bridget was hot, sticky, sore and grumpy when she cut through the meadow to Ford Mill. Her hair was rat's tails and there was definitely chafing. In more than one place. She emerged from the trees by the estate office, and of course that's when Perry appeared.

'Hello,' he said. 'You look … glowing.'

Bridget lifted a finger and pointed it firmly at his barely creased shirt. 'Don't you even *think* about making another comment.' She looked up at the old building where the estate office occupied the first floor. Around the side, she spotted the telltale sign of a heat exchanger. 'You've got aircon in there!' she said accusingly. 'That is *so* not fair! When are we gonna get it in the Spinning Room?'

'You've got it.'

Bridget's eyes bulged out. 'Whaaa?'

'Well, you had it. The condensers are still mounted outside, and the plumbing's still there, but Feargal sold the cassettes when he got in trouble. I can give you the name of a local firm if you like.'

Feargal Hulme had left plenty of mess behind him when he'd abandoned his café at the Mill. Most villagers still thought of him as a lovable rogue, a description which covered a multitude of sins. 'And to think that I was once sorry for him,' declared Bridget. 'Bastard.'

Perry stepped closer. 'Apart from heat, are you okay? I hear you've taken up arms on Hayley's behalf. Or should I say that you've taken up *knitting needles* on Hayley's behalf, Miss Marple?'

He cared about her. She could see it in his eyes. 'Yeah. No. I don't know, Perry. It's too hot for this, I know that much.'

'I don't know how you do it, Bridget. I wouldn't know where to start with an investigation like yours. Look, I was coming to see you anyway.' He had slipped on his waxed jacket before coming out (a sure sign of overworked air conditioning upstairs), and from the pocket he took Bridget's envelope. The one with the notice to quit. He showed it to her and said, 'What's going on?'

That was too much. She couldn't cope with explaining herself again, and the thought of the chilled ice cream room in Southport was akin to paradise right now. 'I'm leaving,' she said as gently as she could. 'Ask Lucy about it. She's half Italian.'

'I know she's half Italian. Everyone knows. It's the second thing you learn about her after, you know, what happened to her brother. What's her heritage got to do with anything?'

'She copes with the heat better. Sorry, but I need to catch Louis.'

'Too late. He's been summoned back to Cairndale to give another statement about the murder. I think he passed Joe Hayton coming out. Have you heard?'

'Damn. I really needed to see Louis. What were they talking to Joe for?'

'That's a very good question. I'm on my way there right now to find out. Fancy coming with me?'

That was possibly the least enticing offer since a bloke at Layla's Piano Bar had offered to show her his collection of *Star Wars* figures. Not that there's anything wrong with *Star Wars*. 'I think I've had enough for today. Thanks for telling me.'

He waved the envelope with her notice once more before putting it back in his pocket. 'I'm not going to accept this until we've had a talk.'

'Whatever.' She closed her eyes. 'Sorry. I didn't mean to come over all Katarina Chester.' She breathed out. 'It's a lovely gesture, but I've given you the notice, Perry, and I won't be changing my mind.' There was a movement behind his shoulder. Someone had been earwigging, and the shifty form of Jed Holmes scurried away from the building. Bridget raised her voice. 'Oi! What you think you're doing?'

Jed froze like he'd been speared, and he turned round nervously. 'Nothing.'

Perry was frowning at the young student, but as ever, he let Bridget do the heavy lifting when it came to confrontation. 'Doing nothing? Pull the other one, Jed,' she told him. 'What are you doing lurking around here and listening to private conversations?'

He shuffled on the spot and tried to retreat, but he had his back to the rotting doors of the ground floor store room. Bridget stepped away from Perry to block Jed's escape sideways. She asked herself what a young ferret was called. A poult? A cob? Never mind. 'I asked you a question. Why are you listening to private conversations?'

'Lucy told me I had to lay off asking questions in the café 'cos it's neutral territory.'

'Correct. It's Switzerland as far as the bizzies and the press are concerned.'

Jed's Birmingham accent was more pronounced now that he was nervous. 'Yeah. She said that, too. I had to Google why Switzerland was neutral. Anyway, it's a public place out here. I thought if I hung around, I might catch Laura Paige or Shannon Turner.'

How had he made *that* connection? 'I'll save you the bother. They're both at home, and that's where you should be going. I'll tell you this, Jed, if you doorstep Laura or Hayley tonight, you'll have me on your case, and you don't want that.'

Jed brightened considerably. 'Oh! Hayley's been released? Thanks for the tip-off.'

Bridget closed her eyes and started counting to ten. She'd got as far as three when Perry intervened.

'I don't know who you are, but I'm guessing *journalist* of some sort. Am I right?'

'Jed Holmes,' he replied confidently. 'More of a podcaster.'

'Well, Mr Holmes, I'm sure you know who I am.' Perry paused and waited until Jed had nodded. 'If you need a statement, you can find me. Perhaps you should take Ms Gorrigan's advice and head home.'

Jed nodded. 'I think I'll head to the White Hart, actually. Brad Nicol's the actual journalist, and there's only room for one of those round here, and I'm sure that what I've learnt is worth a couple of pints. Plus of course the fact that Byford's own sleuth is working herself into a right lather on Hayley Horst's behalf.'

'You little …'

'Too late,' said Perry, as Jed slipped past the Bridget blockade and quickstepped down the drive.

She turned to face him. 'You'll know this, being a countryman. What do you call a young ferret?'

He tried not to laugh. 'We called ours *Jonesie* after one of the boys' teachers, but the official word is *kit*. As in *kitten* presumably.'

'You had a pet ferret,' she stated.

'Rescue ferret rather than pet. We passed him on to Joe Hayton when he'd recovered. You're not suggesting a comparison between Mr Holmes and a young ferret are you?'

'You know what, Perry? Right now if you told me that Coffin Joe was dating Taylor Swift, I'd believe you. I am going inside to catch up with Lucy, and then I'm going home for a bath seeing as how I've *worked myself into a lather*. Arsehole.'

Twenty-Three

Inside the Spinning Room, Lucy had almost finished putting the café to bed. Bridget made her way to the kitchen and flopped into a chair. 'Where's Wendy?'

'I sent her home. You look shattered.'

'I am. How come you look fresh as a daisy? Is there any way we can get a summer uniform, Luce? These shirts are like sweat boxes.'

'Lightweight wicking fabrics cost a fortune, but you're right. I'll look into it.'

Bridget lifted a warning finger. 'Do *not* tell Mina. Yet. Get me an iced water and tell me what I've missed.'

Lucy bounced around the kitchen, served the life-saving water and told Bridget that there was nothing new except that Wendy showed great promise as a barista and was a bit put out that it hadn't been her who went with Bridget to see Shannon. Lucy got her own drink and sat next to Bridget. 'How did you get on?'

Bridget was about to tell her when she got a message from Jackie Chester that began with four open-mouthed shock emojis alternating with three crying-laughing ones and which continued like this: *OMG! Chris is taking Kat to miner injuries unit. Thinks she might have broken a toe!!!!!!!!!!!!!!!*

Bridget was still staring at the screen when a two-word follow-up arrived: *Miner=Minor*. Good to know that Kat's mother had her priorities in the right order.

'You know what, Lucy, I think I'm too sane to carry on living here.' She passed her phone to Lucy and took a long swig of water.

'Whaaa?' said Lucy. 'What have you done to her?'

'Long story. So is the one about Shannon Turner and *Space Fruit*. I haven't even told you the one about meeting Tony's brother on the staircase.'

The refurbishment of No 4 Midland Terrace had gone beyond the bare minimum, but not too far (except for the kitchen floor, of course). In the bathroom there was a decent shower over the bath, which Bridget enjoyed in the mornings, but after a day like today, she needed a *long* soak.

It was still way too hot to dry her hair when she got out, so she wrapped a black towel around it and tucked in the ends. Not only did the black prevent stains from the top-up dye, it fitted her image. Or it used to. She wasn't so sure any more. She threw on the bare minimum of clothes and headed to the kitchen in search of a cold drink. She had just reached the bottom of the stairs when there was a confident knock on the door which spoke of someone with *way* too much energy for a heatwave.

'Shit,' she announced to the hallway. 'Who the hell's dat?'

The front of the property had a four foot "garden" separating her house from the square, which was just enough for her to peer through the curtains (closed against the sun) and see who was trying to disturb her peace. If it was Jed Holmes, she'd plead temporary insanity when the bizzies came to arrest her. Thankfully for Bridget (and Jed), it was a woman. A very unexpected woman. 'What in God's name does *she* want?' muttered Bridget into the curtains.

A sixth sense must have told the visitor that she was being watched, and Abi Tennant held up a bottle of Prosecco and waved it with a smile. Bridget sighed and opened the door.

'Come in, quick, before anyone sees you,' she told her visitor.

Abi didn't come in quick. She raised her eyebrows and took in Bridget's taupe sweats and the towel on her head and said, 'Before anyone sees *me*?'

Abi was dressed for a run, with navy capri leggings, hi-tech sandals and her hair sticking out the back of a baseball cap. The make-up and lack of sweat stains showed that she hadn't *actually* run all the way to Byford from Cairndale Marina, but Bridget wondered if the woman's wardrobe contained anything except running gear and suits from Zara.

Bridget stepped well back from the door. 'Some of us have our reputations to consider. If any of me mates at Cairndale Division know I've been talking to you, we'll lose half our customers at the Market Square. You do know that Lucy lives with Sheriff Morton?'

Abi finally stepped over the threshold. 'The polis aren't my enemy, Bridget. We work together in the interests of justice.'

Abi was from Glasgow, and she'd delivered her line about the cops with as much sincerity as a politician saying he understood the plight of single mothers. Bridget closed the door. 'Tell that to

Commander Ross.'

'I mean it, and I've told him maself. My job is to help them out by making sure their evidence is solid and legally gathered.' She added a bright smile. 'If it wasnae for me, they'd be off to court half-cocked. Through here?'

'No …'

It was too late. Abi had gone into the front room and found the Leaning Tower of Boxes, all still unpacked from Southport. 'Wow, Bridget. Why do you have two boxes labelled *Skulls*? On second thoughts, don't tell me. I can't represent someone who's made a confession.'

Bridget stomped down the hall into the kitchen, relishing the change to cool ceramics under her feet when she got there. She turned and leaned against the sink, waiting for Abi to follow in her own good time.

The lawyer put the Prosecco on the counter and gestured towards it. 'A thank you for pointing Hayley in my direction. She's taken me on as a private client, which is good for both of us.'

Bridget peered at the bottle. There was no condensation, so it clearly hadn't been chilled. She took it and put it in the fridge, swapping it for two bottles of Peroni; she used to drink San Miguel until she met Lucy. 'You look like you plan on stopping,' she said, offering a bottle to Abi. 'Even with your negative BMI, one bottle shouldn't put you over the limit.'

'I took the train.'

The question which had struck Bridget the moment she saw Abi at her door returned to the front of her brain. 'How on earth did you know where I live?'

'I asked Barney Rubble, and he said you'd moved into Feargal's old house as well as his café, and as Ferg was briefly my client, I knew exactly where to find you.'

Bridget shook her head and passed Abi the bottle opener. 'Let's go outside. Sun's off the back and you can almost breathe out there.'

Abi opened the bottle and took a drink. 'Would you mind if we didn't? I want a wee chat about something, and these houses are awfy close. Don't want the neighbours leaning over the garden fence.'

Bridget had been hoping to empty her mind with some brain-draining TV, not talk about Tony's murder. 'This way.'

The back room of No 4 had been laid out just as Bridget wanted it: sofa, coffee table, TV and Bluetooth speaker, and nothing else except the two ornaments on the fireplace. Much easier to keep clean, and as she wasn't staying …

'I love the minimalist look,' said Abi. 'As there's no chair, which is your end of the couch?'

By way of an answer, Bridget collapsed onto the end of the sofa with the best view of the telly. Then she got up again and rummaged in one of the two removal boxes she'd brought through. When she found a second coaster, she passed it to Abi and collapsed again.

Abi looked at the coaster. It was black, with a skull and cabalistic symbols etched in white, as was its fraternal twin already under Bridget's drink. 'Don't tell me I'm your first visitor since you moved in.'

'I prefer to socialise out of the house. Much less messy,' said Bridget. She was getting quite hot again, and it wouldn't take much for her to visit the same fate on Abi Tennant that she'd planned for Jed Holmes.

Abi shrugged and sat down, placing her rugged runner's rucksack carefully on the floor. 'To be fair, I've no' had any more visitors than you in the last month. Pot and kettle as ma Ma would say.'

'How's Hayley?'

'Exhausted. Frightened. In shock.' Abi centred her beer on the coaster and turned to point her knobbly knees at Bridget. *That girl's just skin and bone,* Bridget thought. Abi carefully took off the baseball cap and settled her ponytail. 'I cannae talk about Hayley's statements, nor what DI Swindlehurst told me in confidence, but Hayley's said that you're taking an interest, as it were.'

'I am. For Laura's sake, mostly.'

Abi nodded enthusiastically. 'Good, good. Well, it's like this. Hayley's due back in custody at ten on Thursday morning. Tracey Kenyon will have more forensic tests completed by then, and judging by the look on Swindlehurst's face, she's expecting to spring a surprise on us. Unfortunately, judging by the look on *Hayley's* face, there's something she's not telling me either.' She held up her hands. 'I cannae talk about that. I'm here for a different favour.'

'You don't get much of a favour for half a bottle of Prosecco.'

'Half?'

'You've already drunk the equivalent in Peroni.'

Abi laughed. 'Fair point. How about this?'

Abi loosened the bungee cords on her rucksack and pulled out first a bottle of champagne, then a MacBook, both of which she placed on the table. 'The champagne's yours if you help me out with the CCTV. I need to know who's who, and Hayley wasnae in a fit state to sit through it after a day in the cells.'

Mentally, Bridget rubbed her hands. Access to the CCTV was what she'd wanted to see Louis about, and having it delivered on a plate like this was a real bonus, even if she wasn't going to let Abi see that. She sighed theatrically and said, 'Go on then. I hope we're not going to sit through hours of nothing for five minutes of blurred shadows.'

'No, thank God. Your man Edwin Duke didnae stint on the CCTV system.'

'Perry. It was Perry Lockwood who specified the CCTV.'

Abi raised her eyebrows. 'If you say so. Still Duke who paid for it. Either way, it records ninety seconds of nothing then continuously wipes the footage unless the motion sensors are triggered. Expensive to buy, but saves loads on storage. At least for the inside stuff.'

Bridget heaved herself upright as Abi opened the MacBook and brought it to life. 'Who's that?' she asked as Abi's screensaver flashed briefly. It showed Abi with a slightly older man and a teenage girl, all of them dressed in that half fancy dress that serious runners do when they're trying to show they have a sense of humour – a tutu and tiara for Abi, reindeer antlers and a Rudolf nose for the man, and an elf costume for the girl. Then Bridget saw through the disguise. 'Isn't that Nicholas Webb from your rivals?'

Abi was the senior (and only) solicitor in the Cairndale branch of McEwan & Co, a regional practice based in Carlisle, and their office was above a ladies' fashion boutique on the Market Square. Across the square, in a Victorian building with its name carved in stone, was the firm of Carter, Webb & Carter. It was no surprise that Carters were the solicitors to the Earl of Morecambe Bay and Abi Tennant handled most of the local drug dealers.

Abi kept her gaze on the screen. 'Law Society fun-run last Christmas. I don't do selfies, so this was one of the few pictures of maself I've ever had. Right. Here we go.'

Bridget would *love* to know if Suzanne Webb was aware that Abi had her husband's picture as a screensaver. Some other time. 'One sec, yeah?'

She stood up and took the towel off her hair, went to get her bag and found a brush. Ugh. *Not using that.* It had been through her sweaty hair all day (and all yesterday). She tossed it in the sink and plodded upstairs to get a replacement. And then two more beers and the bottle opener. Watching TV was thirsty work.

Twenty-Four

'I had the junior paralegal do the donkey work,' said Abi. 'He's good at it. Do you know where the cameras are at the Mill?'

'Lucy says they're very straight about it – only the public areas and the car parks. You can't see into the Spinning Room, for example. Lucy says we should have one; I'm not so sure.'

'Mmm. Well, she's right about the Mill. It's a trip and snatch setup, which means the cameras are mostly there to stop people pretending that they slipped on a patch of wet floor and claiming on the insurance, and to provide evidence if there's any funny business in the car parks when they're open to the public.'

Abi sipped her beer and tipped her head to the side. 'You know, Bridget, you'd almost think that the estate didnae want everything covered for a reason. You'll soon see that there's a glaring hole in the coverage. Right, here we go. Just pretend that I don't know who anybody is except Hayley and tick them off. Just to make life easier, ma boy even did stills.'

The time stamp on the still image said that it was 15:00 on Sunday afternoon and showed the very top of the main staircase, and coming out of the lift was the Caffè Milano trolley pushed by … 'Wendy Sadler,' said Bridget.

'She's the part-time employee at 3M3, right?'

'And for us as well, though she might have to go full-time now that her other job's on hold. Hang on a sec.'

'Sorry? There's no more here.'

'Look at the trolley, girl. How many cups are on it?'

'Oh. I see what you mean. There's seven, I think.'

'I think you're right. That's three for 3M3, one for Wendy and I'm guessing the others are for CARM. The model railway children.'

'Thanks. I couldn't comment on the mental age of railway modellers, but that fits with what happens next.'

'This is a good quality image,' observed Bridget. 'You can tell that Kat did the chocolate sprinkles on the cappuccino.'

'Can you? Right. Here are the boys.'

The time stamp jumped to 16:15 and three men were leaving the studio space. 'Jon Carson,' said Bridget. 'On the right. Don't know the others.'

As well as Jonathan Carson, Bridget saw a man around sixty with a rucksack and one around thirty pushing the Caffè Milano trolley. Abi's fingers flew over the trackpad and keyboard, making a note of Jonno's possible identity and trying to find any clues about the other two men. Nothing. 'I've found something on Jonathan,' said Abi. 'You'll see what I mean in a minute. Oh, and we both know the next guy.'

Bridget let out a gasp when Perry's head appeared on the stairs, then she saw the time: 16:58. 'He must have been on duty,' she murmured. 'Locking up.'

'What is there to lock?'

'It varies, but usually it's just putting down the roller shutter on the main entrance. Then there are rules about who locks and checks the goods door. There's a security alarm on the whole building, and that's set by whoever does the final check. It's a bit of a mess, to be honest.'

When Abi did her sour face, it would curdle milk. Good job they were on beer not tea. 'I don't suppose you know who that would ha' been on Sunday?'

'Nope. I was doing karaoke on Sunday night. Good question though.'

'I won't ask you what you were singing. It might be a terrible let-down.'

Bridget gave her some serious side-eye. 'I'm glad you think enough of me for that to be a let-down, Abi. Last I heard, the bizzies don't rate witnesses on their karaoke choices.'

The lawyer did a most Mina-like head dance. 'I think mebbe they should. Moving swiftly on, talk me through the back areas. They're a bit confusing.'

'Have you ever been to the Mill?'

'No. On my to-do list for tomorrow.'

'Well, you'll see that Caffè Milano is in an extension to the south-west, right next to the front entrance; we have a side door to the small car park, too. The whole of the main building is between us and the goods entrance.'

'Can anyone use the goods entrance?'

Bridget pulled a face and tried to work out how to describe

something she'd only seen once, when Louis gave her the full guided tour of the entrances and exits and made her sign a form to say that she knew what she was doing.

Strangely, in Bridget's experience, signing a form rarely meant that you knew what you were doing. The health and safety protocol at the lab in London was a case in point, and she wondered if Joshua's hair had ever grown back.

'Why are you making that face?' said Abi with more than a little concern in her voice.

'Sorry. I was thinking about thioglycolic acid. Crops up where you least expect it. Erm, okay. Right. We'll start at the top. The studio and the craft village are on the two upper floors, and they have an external metal fire escape at the back.'

'What sort of doors?' asked Abi briskly, as if Bridget were her consultant and not a naked-faced part-time Goth in chav loungewear and no bra, and who was now regretting the lack of support. Abi raised an eyebrow, and Bridget rushed to answer the question before she started burbling about her boobs.

'There are locks on the doors so you need a key to open them from the outside, but you can *always* open them from the inside with a lever or else they wouldn't be much use in a fire.'

'Gotcha.'

'The next floor down is similar, but that fire door *can* be locked from the inside because it's only accessible from the Cowan Theatre, and that only needs a second exit when it's open to the public. Then it starts to get complicated.'

'How?'

'It would be so much easier if I could show you. When you go through the main doors you're level with the café, the foyer and the middle of the theatre. We call that the ground floor, but there's another floor below it that's called the ground floor on the plans, but it's not really because most of it's underground.'

Abi groaned and took another drink. 'Why?'

'The site slopes away towards the millpond, and that's where the goods entrance is. That one's a bit more complicated.'

'Go on. I thought you might say that.'

'There's actually *two* doors there. One's a fire escape door like the others, but it's tucked away. The other one is a big slidey thing and it locks from inside and out. From the sliding door you can get to the scene dock of the theatre, the theatre staircase and the goods lift. Both theatre access points are locked.'

Abi checked her notes. 'And something called *Elysian Meadow Joinery*?'

'Coffin Joe.'

'You what?'

'Joseph Hayton, joiner and coffin maker. If he actually exists. I've been here a month and not met him yet.'

Abi sat back, her gaze unfocusing and presumably thinking back to the interview room. 'DS Gartside asked a few questions about Joseph Hayton and Water Cottage. Hayley said they'd done no more than exchange greetings and that she'd never been to his house. Seemed dismayed that they might think that she had. I take it you don't fancy talking to him on Hayley's behalf?'

Bridget raised her bottle. 'Nope. That's one you can handle yourself.'

Twenty-Five

Bridget opened the second Peroni and Abi showed more still images, this time from the goods entrance. At 17:03, Donna Ramsey left the Mill, appearing by magic from off the right edge of the screen and striding confidently to the fire door then out into the car park. Bridget identified Donna for the record, and the screen switched back to the top floor.

At 17:04, Wendy and Hayley left the studio together, just as Wendy had said they did, followed a few seconds later by Perry. Bridget updated Abi and said that it was likely that Perry would have locked the main doors on his way out.

'Really? That *is* interesting.' Abi made a note while the screen returned to the service entrance and showed Tony leaving at half past five and returning thirty minutes later, presumably after his drink at the White Hart. What was shown next matched Wendy's description: Hayley arriving with takeout bags stamped Jewel in the Crown, Donna arriving with Shannon, then later, a blurred picture of Shannon running out in distress, followed by Donna and then Hayley.

'This is when it gets *really* interesting,' said Abi. 'Oh, and I've just remembered something Tony said the one time we met.'

'According to him, you talked about me,' said Bridget innocently.

'We did.' She frowned. 'He was most keen to let me know that he knew you, and talking of *keen*, I think he was keen on you.'

Bridget tried not to blink or move her head. 'He was. He'd asked me on a date but we hadn't fixed anything up.'

Abi leaned out her hand and almost rubbed Bridget's foot, changing her mind at the last second and giving Bridget's calf a squeeze instead. Thank God for that. 'Sorry, hen. I really am.'

Partly to get away from further physical contact, Bridget got up and took the snow globe from the mantelpiece. She placed it on the coffee table and resumed her seat. 'As love-notes go, this one's a first,' she said lightly.

Abi examined the artefact carefully. 'Wow. I had no idea he was so good. The level of detail is phenomenal, and that painting of your tattoo is superb.'

Bridget did blink now, and turned her body to hide the tears. 'You said you'd remembered something.'

'I did. He mentioned the family business.' Abi buried herself in the internet for a second, emerging with a picture of Jonathan Carson and a slightly younger woman with someone who was clearly their daughter and who was clearly graduating from university. Abi pointed to the girl. 'The future Doctor Carson.' She looked at Bridget. 'I said the video gets interesting. Watch this.'

At nine o'clock, Jonathan Carson came in via the basement fire door, carrying a large holdall. 'He must have a key,' said Abi, 'and there is no trace of him leaving, so I'm guessing down the fire escape. I wonder why?'

'And if he has a key, then who else does?'

'Mmm. This is the *really* interesting bit: there's no more interior CCTV. Zip. Zero. Nada. I'm told that the next time it's triggered is when you arrive in the morning, but they didn't disclose that footage.'

'Hang on. Didn't it show who unlocked the doors before me?'

'If it did, they didn't mention it, and to be fair, anything *remotely* relevant and they'd tell me.'

'Hmph,' said Bridget sitting back. 'What about the car park?'

'Another dog that doesnae bark in the night, more's the pity. Did you know it doesn't run all the time?'

'Sorry? I thought you said it was on a motion sensor.'

'They only work in confined spaces. Unless you've a government-sized budget, of course. The car park cameras only record from nine to five, except when there's an event in the theatre. They shut down at five on the dot, and that was before Hayley, Donna and Wendy left.'

Bridget sat up again. 'What about Jonathan Carson? He comes in carrying a shotgun-sized bag and there's no pictures of him leaving. Please tell me the police spoke to him.'

'They told me they'd seen him even before they gave me this footage. DS Gartside said that a man had been interviewed under caution.' The milk-curdling face returned for a moment. 'But they didnae *arrest* him, and that's what makes me think they've a surprise up their sleeve for Hayley on Thursday.'

Bridget sat back and finished her beer. 'Do you think that Prosecco will be cold enough now?' she suggested.

Abi glanced at her smartwatch. 'I'd better head off. I've no right to ask this, but it would be a big help to Hayley – and Laura – if you could ask around about the keys to they fire doors. I've blocked out the afternoon to see the place for myself, so we can catch up then, eh?'

'Have you any idea when Tracey will be finished?'

'Oh, her. Not my favourite person. I think you're lucky you even got to open the café today. They won't let the public into the craft village until Thursday at the earliest.'

Bridget wondered what Abi had against Tracey. From the look on her guest's face, it was more than just professional friction. She stood up and said, 'Will you be alright getting back on your own? I wouldn't catch a train at this time of night.'

'Night? The sun's still up. I survived growing up in Govan, so I think I'll be okay.'

Bridget physically bit the tip of her tongue to stop herself speaking out. It was Abi's choice, and she'd lived here a lot longer than Bridget.

Her visitor drained her bottle and put her MacBook into her rucksack. 'I'll leave you in peace. Maybe you can unpack one of your boxes of skulls.'

Perhaps it was the second beer that loosened her slightly sore tongue. 'No chance. Not now I'm leaving in a few weeks.'

Abi's head whipped up. 'You what? You've no been here five minutes.'

'Change of circumstances. I'm quitting Caffè Milano and heading back to the ice cream parlour in Southport. Don't worry, I'm on three months' notice, so I'll be around to ferret out anything that'll help Hayley.'

Abi stood up and swung the rucksack onto her shoulder. She looked around the room and even went to the window to peer at the paved yard at the rear. 'How much is the rent?'

'You what? Apart from being a bit presumptuous, why would you swap Marina Bay House for this?'

'Because the rent on that flat is killing me.'

Bridget was dumbstruck. 'I thought you owned it!'

Abi looked down and fiddled with the seam on her leggings. 'Associate solicitors don't earn much. Especially when you're on a profit-share and most of your clients are Legal Aid. Government pays us for that in washers.' She looked up and put on a brave face that made her look vulnerable for once. 'If I do well enough, they'll offer me a partnership, but you have to buy into that, and ma savings are nowhere near the partnership level yet. Thanks for the beer, Bridget. I'll see maself out.'

Bridget let her pass and followed her into the hall. Abi looked back for a moment, her hand on the open door. 'If you ever need a local lawyer, you know where I am. I'll take part payment in coffee if it's served before nine in the morning.'

Bridget flicked a smile. 'Take care. And text me when you're home, yeah?'

'Yes, Auntie B.'

Abi left the door open behind her, and Bridget watched her jog towards the station, just as the arrival of her train was announced to the evening air, rudely interrupting the avian answer to Luciano Pavarotti who was currently serenading Byford from atop the telegraph pole outside No 5.

Bridget watched Abi bounce up the station steps like a Duracell bunny and closed the door. Back in the kitchen, she put the kettle on and started texting Lucy and Kat with the news about the CCTV.

L: *We'll have a good look at the back of the mill in the am.*

B: *Good idea.*

K: *Then U cn talk to Perry*

B: *I think that would be better coming from Lucky.*

K: *Ohno. Defo you B.*

B: *Bloody predictive text. Can you stop it turning Lucy into Lucky????*

L: *Bridget should definitely talk to Perry.*

B: *No.*

They were still arguing the toss when a picture of the sunset over Morecambe Bay arrived on Bridget's phone, and it was only when she knew that Abi was safe that Bridget realised just how much her shoulders had knotted up. So much for a relaxing evening.

Twenty-Six

Lucy and Lilianna surveyed the back of Lucy's Mini Countryman. It wasn't all going to fit in, was it?

'Why you do this?' asked Lili, a deliciously moist coffee and walnut cake cradled delicately in her arms.

'Because I had my mind on higher things,' said Lucy. 'The more important question is why Bridget didn't remind me that there was extra on the order.'

'Because she is not stupid and she gets more time in bed.'

Lucy opened the passenger door. 'Put it in the footwell. There.'

'No. I have seen your driving and there will be cream all over the car. I will not waste cake.'

Lucy remembered her old car and the smell. She'd had *higher things* on her mind that day, too, and completely forgotten the ice cream under the blanket in the boot until the smell ballooned out and filled the whole interior like a noxious airbag.

Lili shut the passenger door with her hip. 'I take this and all the rest you have no room for. My husband bring it later with beans and milk.' She adjusted the cake and headed inside. Lucy got into the driving seat and fired up the engine.

She waited until the display informed her that her phone was bonded, then she told the system to *Call Tom*. She put the car in Drive and pulled out of the Market Square just as the love of her life took the call. 'Hiya. Just passing your favourite post-modernist building,' she told him.

'If you're talking about Divisional HQ, then it's not post-modern, it's contemporary.'

Tom's fluid tones, not quite posh and not quite Yorkshire, always got to her, especially when she hadn't spent the night next to him. No day could be a bad day when she'd heard him discuss the niceties of architectural styles. To keep the conversation going, she said, 'So what happens when we're old and grey? It won't be contemporary then, will it?'

He chuckled. 'I can't imagine you going grey, love. Should that day ever dawn, we will no doubt have passed through post-contemporary, modern revival and be deep into neo-contemporary. And who knows, maybe the weather in Cairndale will be warm enough by then to justify the passive cooling features. Or maybe it will have rusted away. Are you on your way to Byford?'

Lucy had already cut through the Rivers Estate and was heading into the countryside. 'Where else would I be going with a car full of bread, cakes and pastries. I … Whoa!'

The line went silent for a moment. 'You okay, love?'

'Yeah. Fine,' said Lucy, as breezily as she could.

'You forgot the humpback bridge again, didn't you? How much damage?'

Lucy stopped the car and looked behind her, very grateful to Lilianna for hanging on to the cake. *Not too bad,* she thought. *So long as I can put everything back before I have company.*

'Talking of humpbacked Bridgets,' she said, 'I am going to do everything in my power to make sure she gets fully engaged in this case. If I can get her *actually* engaged to Perry Lockwood, so much the better.'

'He seemed like a nice man to me. What's he done to deserve that?'

'I thought you liked her.'

'I did, until she upset you. People who upset you go onto my naughty list.'

Lucy grinned. Having a protector was a wonderful feeling. She headed off again, trying to remember which of the upcoming bends concealed the farm with the aggressive tractor. 'What you up to today?'

'Same as yesterday and the day before: sacrificing my will to live on the altar of that case in the secret court. Reading the draft judgement may send me back to uniform duty, because after three days of wrestling with the legal basis of fiat currency, the thought of a Friday night punch-up outside the kebab shop seems quite attractive.'

'You love it really.'

'I'll get back to you on that one.' There was one of Tom's pauses. The one where he worked out how to approach a difficult subject. Lucy had been terrified of them at first – partly because he was interviewing her about her brother's murder and partly because she quite fancied him from the day he walked into her shop. She was used to them now, or thought she was.

'Commander Ross begged a favour off me last night. I thought you should know.'

Lucy waved her hand dramatically. It wasn't her fault that this was a voice call. 'I should know that Allister gave you a job? So what? Tell me something new. Actually, tell me what the job was.'

'Liz has got her team looking at the regular bank records, but Ross wanted someone with a bit more experience to take a look at 3M3. Limited companies can be tricky to follow, and as it hasn't been trading long, he reckoned I could dash it off.'

Tom had done his stint as a uniformed police officer in the City of London. A brief stint, but a stint nonetheless, followed by a transfer to CID in the fraud squad, or Economic Crimes or whatever they called it now. Lots of spreadsheets. Lucy wasn't surprised that the accounts had landed in Tom's lap. Again, though, that wasn't the main thing.

'What did you find?'

'Mmm. Bit tricky that one.'

'But you did find *something*.'

'I did.'

'And you're not going to tell me.'

'No, I'm not.'

Damn him. Damn him and his honesty. Lucy grinned. 'I wouldn't have it any other way. Just one thing, though. Why have you told me something that you can't tell me? If you'd never mentioned it, I'd be none the wiser.'

'Because you'd see it in my face. This way, you can finish getting angry while I'm on the other side of the Pennines.'

She laughed. 'I don't bother getting angry with people who aren't there. I have enough to get angry about with the people in front of me.'

'Which is why we all learnt how to swear in Italian. Talking of the people in front of you, what's your next move now that you're flying the family flag for detection?'

Family. It was easy for him to say. Lucy had had an amazing time at Conrad and Mina's wedding in the spring. It had been *epic*, but it wasn't *her* wedding.

Yes, Tom was still missing his granddad, and there would be no nuptials in the near future, but that shouldn't stop him *proposing*, should it? He needed to get a wiggle on, did Thomas Alexander Morton, or Lucy might find herself being the one to set her cap at Perry Lockwood. Perhaps not. Too old. She'd leave him to Bridget.

'Like I said last night, we're going to try and sort out who had what keys, and see if you can get into the Mill without being caught on camera.'

'Good luck.'

'That's if we don't melt first. I am *so* going to look for lightweight uniforms today. When is this weather going to break?'

'You're asking the wrong man. Try Conrad Bloody Clarke. I think he has a hotline to the weather gods.'

Lucy had passed through Byford and turned into the grounds of Ford Mill. 'Got to go, love. I need to put the bread tray back together before Bridget gets here.'

'Let me guess. If she thinks the goods have hit your upholstery, they'll be for the skip.'

Lucy went from shivering at the sound of Tom's voice to shuddering at the thought of Bridget consigning a day's order to the food waste bin. She did a quick reverse up to the side door. 'Love you.'

'Love you, too.'

She was desperately trying to get crumbs out of the boot carpet as Bridget's bright red van skirted the Pothole of Doom and headed for the rear car park. When the woman herself appeared round the corner of the Mill, Lucy had stashed the trays safely inside the Spinning Room.

Lucy smiled and then frowned. 'You do know that the skirt you're wearing is the perfect shade of magenta to clash with your Caffè Milano top?'

'Colour me indifferent,' said Bridget. 'It was the only loose skirt I had left that was clean. And why are you wearing an eighties peasant blouse?'

'I left my shirt in the kitchen last night. I'll change in a minute.'

Bridget looked stunned; Lucy tried to get past her, but no luck.

'You can *not* wear that shirt two days running. I won't have it. Let me guess: you still can't work the washing machine.' She shook her head mournfully. 'As a penance, you'll have to wear one of the spares.'

'But we've only got XL left! Wendy took the last small ones, and I'll drown in fabric!'

'As I said, it's penance. Shall we get set up, then go for a walk round the back?'

They stacked, sorted and removed the veg from the chiller ready to start prepping the salads. Bridget switched on the coffee machine and held out the XL Caffè Milano shirt. 'I seem to remember someone saying that we should be *on brand* all the time. I wonder who that could be?'

Lucy snatched the shirt, glanced through the door and swapped it for her blouse. There was two seconds of relief as the cold cotton hit her skin, then the temperature started climbing. Not only that, the damn thing was long enough to wear as a dress on her XS frame, like when she wore Tom's shirts sometimes … 'Stop it,' she told herself.

And Bridget.

'Stop what?'

'Never mind. Let's go.'

Twenty-Seven

Lucy and Bridget left the Spinning Room and turned left towards the lower car park. Lucy asked, 'What's she like? Abi, I mean. I've heard bits about her.'

Bridget shrugged. 'Intense. My gran would have called her *highly strung*. Abigail Tennant thinks she's faced the worst that life can throw at her and come out on top. She's got a big shock coming one day.'

And that was one of the many things Lucy loved about Bridget: no matter how positive the situation, she could always see the dark side. It helped Lucy count her blessings.

While Lucy was wondering what Abi Tennant was *really* like, Bridget had been surveying the buildings and broke into Lucy's reverie with a slap to the head and an 'Of course!'

'Of course what?'

'The public footpath.'

'What public footpath?'

Bridget swished off towards the estate office building and pointed down the side and through the trees. 'That public footpath. It comes out above Meadow Farm. A real shortcut. Someone could have walked through there.'

'How did you know about it?'

'I saw Amos go up there one day and decided to see where it went.' Bridget shrugged. 'Then again, with no CCTV on the car park after five o'clock, why not just drive in?'

'Because the entrance is right in front of Mill Cottages. It's worth bearing in mind. We'd better hurry up, or Wendy will be here.'

'She's not due for ages yet. No need to work up an extra sweat on top of the one I've already got.'

They headed down the slope and round the corner. There were no police vehicles here – yet. Lucy stopped and stared, really examining the far side of the building properly for the first time. On every other occasion she'd been out here, she'd looked at the trees, the millpond, the river, and above all the elegant shape of Byford Lodge across the water. She glanced over because it wasn't that she had total house envy or anything. Not really. To be envious, you'd have to believe that you *might* live in the beautifully re-built and refurbished Georgian gentleman's residence over the water.

'Hey! We're here to look at the fire escapes, not moon over Fliss's house,' snapped Bridget.

Oops. Lucy really had meant to check out the Mill, but the Lodge looked so *peaceful* in the morning light. Cool and chic and … 'Sorry, Bridge. I was just wondering if they had a good line of sight across the river.'

'That's an excellent point, or it would be if you weren't trying to decide whether to change the curtains when you move in. As it happens, they do have line of sight.'

Lucy felt Bridget take her arm and gently but firmly turn her away from the Lodge and towards the black iron of the Mill's emergency exits. From the top, three blank doors led onto three landings as the stairs zig-zagged down the wall. After the Dukes Gallery/theatre circle exit, the stairs were less steep and ended up at the water end of the lowest floor. Bridget was right. Anyone climbing or descending those stairs would be in full view of the Lodge.

Lucy turned round, towards the trees that screened Water Cottage, home of Coffin Joe. He wouldn't have seen anything, and it sounded like he wasn't there anyway.

'Come on,' said Bridget, pointing to the staircase. 'Unless you don't like heights.' She tightened her scrunchy, as if it were a battle harness. 'I can't believe how long I've known you and never had a conversation about heights. Did you know that acrophobia is the second most common phobia after creepy crawlies?'

Lucy gave an eye-roll. 'And where does yours come then?'

'Mysophobia comes after claustrophobia, agoraphobia, fear of flying and fear of the dentist, since you're asking.'

As far as Lucy knew, she wasn't afraid of any of those, and she was about to march up to the staircase when Bridget gave a bright-eyed smile that bordered on manic and declared, 'Anyway, I don't have mysophobia, because my concern with cleanliness is entirely rational. The shrink said that it didn't negatively impact my normal life, so it wasn't a medical condition.'

Lucy had seen the inside of Bridget's flat in Cairndale *and* the one in Southport; the jury was still out on whether her friend's life had been *negatively impacted*. That was for another day, and she smiled a friendly agreement. Bridget, though, was in no mood for friendly agreement. 'Unlike *your* phobia,' she announced.

Lucy felt herself doing the frightened rabbit thing with her eyes, so she squeezed them closed. 'What phobia?'

'*Forosophobia*,' announced Bridget. 'Come on, what are you waiting for?' And with that, Bridget's stout boots clanged onto the first iron step.

Lucy's jaw dropped. 'What's *foroso*—'

'Look it up.'

Lucy's little legs rushed to catch up with Bridget. There was just enough room for them to walk side-by-side, and they did so in silence until they reached the very top. Okay, it wasn't so silent after the second turn of the staircase because Bridget was starting to wheeze. Just a bit.

Bridget took a deep breath. 'Looks like Tracey's been here. See? Fingerprint powder all over.'

Lucy peered at the railings and the grey door. There was powder everywhere. She took a tissue out of her pocket and tried the handle. Not only was it locked, it was very stiff. She rattled and twisted the handle, then gave it a good tug, and then screamed when it opened from inside, pushing her back into Bridget and pushing Bridget into the railings. There was a *creak* and a *ping* from the iron, then Bridget pushed her back and she slammed her face into a man's chest.

'Eurgh!' she mumbled, desperate not to breathe through her nose, because the owner of the shirt had not washed it for a *long* time.

'Are you girls alright?' he said. 'You want to be careful up here.'

Bridget pushed Lucy aside, trapping her in the corner of the landing, with nothing between her and the unyielding stone of the car park except thin railings and fresh air. Twenty-eight is not too old to develop acrophobia.

'We are not *girls*,' snapped Bridget, going to poke the man's chest then changing her mind when she caught a whiff. 'And what the hell are you doing here?'

'I could ask you the same question,' said the man, affronted. '*I'm* here to guard the crime scene, and I thought you were my relief. What are *you* doing up here?'

Lucy forced herself to focus on the man's epaulettes. *BGS* they said.

Bay Gate Security. Of course, the police wouldn't have a warranted constable wasting his time guarding a locked building.

'We'd better go,' she said to Bridget. 'After you.'

Bridget looked like she wanted to exit via the TV studio until she realised that the guard was taking his job (if not his laundry) seriously. 'It's you who wants to watch out,' she told him with a parting shot, then clumped down the stairs with both hands firmly on the railings.

'We run the café,' Lucy told the guard. 'On the ground floor. Feel free to drop in.'

His face was slightly bloated and soft. One of those that only a mother would love, until it split into an open smile. 'Coffee Milanese? Ooh! I like the sound of that.' His enthusiasm dropped. 'Are you actually open?'

A rare gust of wind blew Lucy's curls over her eyes. There hadn't been a breath of wind for days. She turned her head away from the breeze and couldn't help but look down again. The ground seemed to move up to meet her, like it was calling her to step closer to the edge. 'We'll call it a worker's special,' she mumbled to the guard, then shuffled to the steps and grabbed the rail. One of them. Her arms weren't long enough to reach both.

She clung to the handrail next the wall and resolutely stared at her feet, only there were gaps in the treads. She gritted her teeth and promised herself the reward of a glimpse of the Lodge from the next landing. She made it, now ten feet closer to safety, and the Lodge looked even more achingly beautiful from up here than it did from Mother Earth. The morning sun sparkled from windows, and something tickled at the back of her mind.

She set off again and tried to work it out, and when she got to the last step, it made sense. Not only that, she'd forgotten about the height. Acrophobia? What acrophobia? 'Hey, Bridget, come back here a sec.'

Bridget's clashing combo had almost disappeared round the corner, and she swivelled to look back. 'What?' she demanded. Lucy stood her ground and beckoned with her hand. Bridget sighed and clumped back. Those boots must be like sweat boxes in this weather, never mind the polo shirts.

'Look,' said Lucy. 'We're in the sun here, right?'

'Durr. Yeah.'

'You need to come back at nine o'clock tonight and see it again. This side of the Mill will be in the shade, and I reckon that the setting sun will be on the Lodge.'

Bridget was about to object. Then she thought about it. 'You're right. Not sure how us being here is gonna help figure anything out.'

'It won't,' said Lucy with a smile. '*You'll* be here. I'll be at the Lodge, looking out.'

Bridget's eyes narrowed. Lucy could see her working through the moves, like a chess game, the thoughts tracking over face. *If we swap places, I'll have to be nice to Fliss.* When she spoke, it was with a grunt. 'We'll see.'

Lucy reached out and touched Bridget's arm, right on the skull tattoo. 'I'm not going to let you go without a fight, Bridge. You're special. Always will be.'

Bridget's new beauty regime might be more comfortable in the heatwave, but it meant the colour was instantly visible in her cheeks. 'And you, Luce.' She drew her arm away. 'Did I hear you offering to open up for that security guard? Well, you can serve him. I am not getting within ten feet of that bloke without a face mask. I hope you now realise why mastering the washing machine is an important skill.'

Lucy saw that Perry Lockwood's pickup was already parked outside the estate office. 'Just tell Mister Whiffy that you'll bring it to his table.'

'Eh? You what?'

'I'm going to see Perry.' She turned and walked backwards for a few steps, looking Bridget in the eye. 'Unless, of course, you'd prefer to see Perry yourself?'

Bridget pushed past her and stomped towards the Spinning Room. Lucy whipped out her phone and did a quick search. 'I am *not* afraid of the taxman!' she shouted at Bridget's back. 'I do *not* have forosophobia!'

A faint mutter from Bridget might have been *Yeah, right.*

Twenty-Eight

Lucy tried to adjust her outfit. The skirt was too short to go with the oversized top, and without the apron to tidy things away, she felt off balance. Never mind. Perry was a man, so he wouldn't notice.

She pressed the buzzer on the door, and Perry's voice crackled out of the intercom. 'Hello?'

'Only me!' said Lucy.

The door buzzed open, and she stood for a moment at the foot of the stairs, luxuriating in the cold air. *If the Devil ever offers to trade my soul for a lifetime's aircon, he's got a deal.* She breathed out and climbed up to the modern, open plan office upstairs, with three desks and a meeting table which stuck out like a sore thumb because it didn't belong here. Literally didn't belong, as in was made of reclaimed wood and recycled steel and matched the others in the Spinning Room. Perry allegedly took it from Feargal in lieu of rent, but Lucy wasn't so sure. Her money was on a losing bet. Did that work as an image? Sod it. Too hot to worry.

'Morning, Perry. Could I have a quick word? Sorry, but I haven't brought you a drink. Not quite open yet.'

'Bit early for your rocket fuel, Lucy,' he replied from behind his desk, then he stood up, collected a folder and came round, pointing to the table. He waited until Lucy had made herself comfortable and joined her, waving the folder and placing it carefully on the wood. 'I'm prepared. What is it now?'

She shook her head and felt the aircon drying the sweat on her neck. Her hair would have exploded by now and be untameable until she could get a shower. 'You're off the hook today,' she told him, sliding the folder away and out of their eyeline. Inside its manila cover was an annotated copy of the Caffè Milano lease of the Spinning Room, along with several amendments, each one dissected at this table and the entrails studied for omens. Lucy blinked. Where had *that* image come from? Eurgh.

When it came to interpretation of some clauses in the lease, both sides' analysis could be robust. Lucy and Perry had never come to blows, but that was mostly because he was a true gentleman. 'If not the lease, then what can I do for you?' he asked. 'I was actually coming over later to see you and Bridget, so this saves me a trip. You first, though.'

'It's about Hayley,' she began. 'You know Bridget's on her side, right?'

He touched the folder, as if arguments over cleaning schedules were a safer topic. 'I think it's more than that,' he said uncomfortably. 'I think it's more about *Tony* than Hayley.'

Lucy took a breath. 'So long as she's doing some good, does it matter?'

'Mmm,' he said. He said that a lot. 'You don't know Joseph Hayton very well, do you? And please don't use his nickname.'

'No. I mean, yes. I mean … What's up with Coff—' She cringed. 'After you.'

Perry's eyebrows did the talking for a moment, then he looked down. 'He's a very private man, is Joseph. Having said that, he's quite happy for me to share this with you and for you to pass it on.' He flashed a smile. 'Joe was away on Sunday and Monday. Didn't get home until very late and went straight to bed. First thing yesterday morning he went down and into the scullery, where he found that someone had broken into Water Cottage and stolen his shotgun.'

'Oh,' said Lucy because something always came out of her mouth, whether it was intelligent or not. Then what he'd said really sank in. 'Oh my God! How? I mean …'

'Mmm.' He took a breath. 'When I say they "broke into the cottage", what I actually mean is that they hunted around the back garden until they found the spare key under a plant pot.'

'Ouch. What about the gun cupboard …?'

This was a much more serious matter: leaving a key to the back door under a flowerpot would invalidate his insurance; leaving a gun cupboard unsecured and even inadvertently supplying a murder weapon would mean prosecution.

'They used one of his firewood chopping axes.'

Lucy's eyes bulged. 'They took an *axe* to the gun cupboard? Hang on, you said *one* of his axes. How many does he have?'

'Two. One big one and one huge one. They used the big one.'

'And the gun?'

'The police aren't saying. They clearly haven't found it yet or they'd be on to him for confirmation.'

Lucy sat back and reached for her coffee. Oh. No coffee. 'I think you should tell Bridget this yourself. I'll make you a free coffee!'

'It's not my birthday. And it's definitely not Christmas, unless you're Australian.'

'Why Australian?'

'It's summer. They have Christmas in the summer.'

'But … Whatever. Do you want this coffee or not?'

'Yes please. When we've talked about this.'

He opened the folder and took out an envelope. From the envelope he took a letter and showed it to Lucy from a distance. She recognised Bridget's handwriting straight away. 'What's going on?' he asked. 'Bridget wouldn't talk to me about it.' He made a great fuss of putting the letter away so that he didn't have to look at her. 'I'm not owed an explanation, of course, but something must have happened.'

So he *did* care about her. Lucy was even more determined to make Bridget stay. Didn't change the fact that Tara Doyle had to go, though. In fact, as of yesterday, Tara Doyle was history. 'I had to buy out one of my investors,' she said. 'She didn't take it well, and she got us kicked out of Giuseppi's Gelateria, and ice cream will always be Bridget's first love.'

'That's … chilling. Sorry. Not funny. Why—'

She held up a hand. 'I can't go into details, Perry, so don't ask.'

'A big investor?'

Her face told him it was.

'Who's taken over?'

She squirmed. He knew enough about her business to pick the answer out of her accounts if she lied, so she gave a version of the truth. 'We've taken a venture bridging loan until the new investor comes on board.'

'You have one lined up?'

Next to the murder of Tony Carson, the finances of Caffè Milano were a footnote, and Lucy desperately needed that coffee. She stood up and said, 'We soon will have. You coming?'

He put the folder back on his desk, grabbed his phone and followed her down the stairs. 'How are you going to do it?' he asked.

'I know people who have a lot of money. One of them will be

interested.'

'I'm sure they will. I was talking about Bridget. How will you get her to stay?'

Lucy put her hand on the door. 'How well do you *really* know her, Perry?'

'Put like that, not really.'

'The cleanliness? The war on bacteria?'

'I think everyone knows that. I heard Jackie Chester talking about it once.'

'Grrnh! Is *nothing* private round here?' She took a calming breath. 'My plan is to start making ice cream in the Spinning Room kitchen, using Mike's Magic Milk, and before you say anything, I know about her aversion to raw milk.'

'Aversion? That's like saying vampires have an aversion to garlic and crosses.'

'No such things as vampires,' said Lucy automatically. Oops. 'I mean, yeah, I get your point. But haven't you seen the change in her recently?'

'She's dialled back the Goth look a bit, but she's still Bridget.'

'And she's using less of the chemical spray. I saw her shake hands with someone last week and not run straight for the sanitiser.'

'I think you're being a bit optimistic, Lucy.'

'I'm *always* optimistic, Perry.'

Lucy pushed open the door and returned to the reality of sticky weather and the sticky smell of the undergrowth which lined the footpath she'd only just realised was there. She made a mental note to follow it up later.

'Is this how Italians cope with the heat?' he asked, waving his hand vaguely at her.

'You've lost me.'

'Wearing extra baggy shirts.'

So maybe he did notice things. 'Laundry crisis,' she told him. 'Let's go and talk shotguns.'

Twenty-Nine

It was still early when Bridget got to the café, despite the shenanigans with the fire escape. Fire escape? More like a lucky escape after that soft lad had nearly pushed them to their deaths. She shuddered.

'You okay?' came the gentle voice of Wendy Sadler from the kitchen doorway. 'You look like you've seen a ghost.'

Bridget flinched back. 'Oh. Hi, Wendy. You're early.'

Wendy gave her a thin smile. 'I know. I think I was in shock on Monday, and yesterday it all hit home. Seeing Donna like that made me realise just what a shitty mess everything is.'

'You're not wrong there.'

The main doors behind Bridget opened, and she turned to see a thickset woman walk through, carrying a rucksack and wearing the same uniform as the man on the top floor. The relief guard nodded to Bridget and headed for the lift. Bridget would have to act quickly …

'Look, Wendy, I need to freshen up. If a guy turns up saying he was promised early service, take his order and tell him to sit down. Won't be long.'

Bridget took her time in the ladies, and the security guard had been and gone when she emerged. 'He wanted a takeout, and it was tea, not coffee, so I served him,' said Wendy. She pursed her lips. 'You weren't avoiding him were you?'

'Who? Me?'

'Hmph. Where's Lucy? Her car's here.'

'Talking to Perry. She won't be long.' Her phone pinged from somewhere inside her loose skirt. 'Hang on,' she told Wendy and went to grab her apron and check the message. It was Laura.

Hayley wants to talk but won't go near mill. Can you come here.

Bridget tapped out *Yeah. No probs. Will come when Kat arrives.*

She fastened the apron, dropped the phone in its pouch and started showing Wendy how to make up the morning display. She was dusting crumbs off her hands when Lucy returned, with Perry in tow. What now?

'I need coffee,' declared Lucy. 'Why don't I carry on showing Wendy the ropes while Perry tells you about the Water Cottage connection? I'll bring it over in a sec.'

They were due to open to the public shortly, and if not the public, then the police would certainly be here. A short break would be good. 'Sound.'

She headed for her favourite table, the one with the view of the wheel and the millpond.

'Are you okay?' asked Perry.

Bridget brushed him off. 'Yeah. Fine. What's this about Joe's place?'

He told her about the break-in, and Bridget was stunned. It was like playing a card game and a new rule being announced halfway through. How had the murderer known about the shotgun? And the axe? She was digesting this when a movement out of the window caught her eye.

'Police!' she said, pointing upstream to the millpond. 'Looks like divers, too.'

Perry craned his neck around and stared. 'Not that they need divers with the water level this low. I'd better go and see what's going on in case they decide to open the sluice gates.'

He hurried to the counter, where Lucy was just about to bring over a tray, having sent Wendy into the kitchen for something.

Bridget followed him, and he said, 'Sorry, but could I have that to go? I need to avert an environmental disaster.'

'Of course, but I need to ask you about keys.'

She held on to his drink, and he quickly said, 'What about them?'

'Who has outside keys to the fire escape doors, and are they easy to duplicate?'

'You can't get them copied in the market, I know that much. You need to order them from the manufacturer. As for who has them, you'll need to ask Louis: he's in charge of those doors. Could I have my coffee, please?'

Lucy decanted the drink into a takeout cup and passed it over.

'Thanks, Perry. See you later.'

Bridget was about to say something, but Lucy was looking at the entrance and went slightly pale. 'They're for you, I think,' she muttered and vanished. Bridget turned around, and there was DI Liz Swindlehurst, along with a man who was definitely not a copper.

'Morning, Bridget,' said Liz. 'This is my distant cousin, Simpson. Any chance of a coffee?'

Bridget made her way behind the counter and sized up the newcomer. Size being the operative word – he was shorter than Bridget and built like an outhouse. 'What can I get you?'

'Tea, please. Nice to meet you.'

He stretched out a hand and Bridget felt the callouses of manual labour and the strength of a weightlifter. She couldn't imagine a bigger contrast to Tony's handshake (and fingers) if she tried. 'Hi. Won't be a sec. What brings you to Ford Mill? Are you here to help the divers?' She looked at Liz. 'Perry's just told me about the break-in at Water Cottage.'

Liz grunted, and Simpson (First name? Last name?) looked confused.

'We'll talk outside, shall we?' said Liz.

'If we must. I do have a business to run.'

'That's why I'm here,' said Simpson.

What on earth was going on? Bridget made the drinks in mugs, took the one Lucy had prepared for her and pointed to the side door. 'Shall we?' On the way across the Spinning Room, she looked over her shoulder and saw Lucy grinning at her from the kitchen. There would be a reckoning for this.

Once outside, Simpson turned right and stood by the railing that stopped customers from plunging into the mill race. Further off, Perry was talking to two men who were donning wetsuits.

'I hear you want a bridge, Bridget,' said Simpson.

'Oh yeah? And how did you hear that?'

'Do you or don't you?'

'I don't want anything.' She looked at Liz. 'Did Lucy put you up to this?'

'Who's Lucy?' said Simpson. 'I got a call from the Dragonslayer.'

Liz's hand shot out and grabbed Simpson's arm. 'You mean *Conrad Clarke*, don't you?'

'That's what I said. Do you want a bridge over to the island or not? I've got a hole to dig if you don't.'

'Please,' said Liz to Bridget. 'Now he's come out, at least let him have a look at the job.'

Simpson did not look like a man who gave you two chances, and *someone* would be running the café in three months, even if it wasn't Bridget. 'Sorry. Crossed wires. Yes, please, my boss would like a price for a simple footbridge from here to the island, preferably made from sustainable materials.'

Simpson turned slowly round on his heel and surveyed the landscape. He took out his phone (thoroughly battered and with a crack in the screen), and from some magic pocket he found a notebook and pencil. 'I'll have a look, then.'

Liz jerked her head away from the Mill and wandered along the river bank. Bridget sighed and followed her. 'What?' she said.

Liz sipped her coffee and gave an *Mmm*. 'Thanks for this. I had a word with … with Abigail Tennant yesterday.'

It was clear that Liz had wanted to use some pejorative nickname and had bitten her tongue. Bridget wasn't going to make this easy. 'Oh yeah?'

'Yes. She says you're looking into things for Hayley. Have you found anything?'

'I don't have a major incident team working for me, Liz, I have a duckling. Other than discovering that Shannon Turner is involved and that Jonathan Carson has questions to answer, I've barely passed first base. Oh, Abi did share the CCTV footage with me.'

Liz grunted and took out a packet of Haribo. 'There's been a few developments, Bridget. I thought I should let you know.'

'Thanks for nothing, Liz, because you won't tell me what they are, will you?'

Liz shook her head and chewed on the sweets. 'You know I can't. And we really do have an open mind, you know. We follow the evidence.'

'Yeah, so I've heard. We'll see, shall we?' She checked the time. 'We're opening for business in a minute.'

'And they look like your first customers.'

Walking up the drive at a leisurely pace were the kit ferret Jed Holmes and Ciara Davenport of the flickable hair. 'Oh no. I can do without them, I really can.'

Liz popped another Haribo. 'Aren't they from ULIST? I've seen them hanging around the station. Not together, though.'

'Yeah. Call themselves "Podcasters". Lucy warned them off pestering people in the café.'

A car rolled up the drive behind them, a battered estate with a rattly diesel engine from the days before everyone drove a 4x4. It was muddy dark blue in colour and was big enough to fit a large canvas in the rear, a fact which Bridget knew because she'd seen Esther Thornfield loading it up a few times. The car closed the gap with the students, and Esther put her hand on the horn.

The kids must have heard it coming and either didn't care or thought they owned the road. Jed and his classmate almost jumped out of their skins, and Ciara skidded in the dust, then collapsed in a heap. Esther roared past her, and Jed ran to see if she was okay.

'Better go,' said Bridget to Liz. She looked at Simpson, still absorbed in his notebook (and where had the tape measure come from?). She raised her voice. 'Excuse me, erm, Simpson. Sorry. I'll be inside when you're done.'

He lifted a hand in acknowledgement, and Bridget strode over the grass. The girl was being helped to her feet by Jed, and there was a nasty-looking graze on her leg. Blood mixed with dirt was not Bridget's favourite combination, and a cold shiver gripped her chest then squirmed down her spine to somewhere deep and low inside her. *Breathe, girl,* she told herself. 'You okay?' she asked.

'Maniac!' said Ciara. 'What the absolute *fuck*? And would you look at my sandals! One of the straps is broken!' Jed went to put his arm on Ciara, and she pushed him roughly away, then brandished a wedge-heeled sandal in his face. 'See?'

Bridget swivelled and ran to the side door. She stuck her head in and shouted, 'Lucy! First aid needed out here!' She walked back to Ciara, now testing her ankle. A flash of genuine pain cut through the outrage, and she winced. 'Someone's coming,' said Bridget soothingly. 'Lucy's a qualified first-aider.'

'I don't need a first-aider, I need the police. Whoever was driving that car needs arresting for dangerous driving.'

'You're in luck,' said Bridget. 'DI Swindlehurst saw the whole thing.'

'Where is he?'

'She,' said Jed abruptly. 'And she walked off because Est— I mean the driver didn't hit you, and this isn't a public road. And she's got a murder to investigate.' He looked at Bridget. 'Are those *divers* up there by the lake?'

Lucy appeared, carrying the first aid kit. 'What's up? Oh. That looks nasty.'

'I think she might have twisted her ankle,' said Bridget, turning away from the sight of blood. And dirt in the wound. Dirt from outside.

'Hey! Still here!' said Ciara.

Bridget turned back to apologise and saw that Jed had slipped away. *Little git.* 'Lucy will sort you out,' she told Ciara, then hot-footed it round the Mill to see what Jed was up to and why he'd kept Esther's name from Ciara.

Thirty

Bridget was already hot and bothered – well on the way to working up a lather, in fact – and putting on a spurt to catch the little ferret was above and beyond, it really was.

She arrived as Jed intercepted Esther Thornfield's car near the estate office. Esther got out the driver's side, and there was a passenger, too, but they stayed inside the car, and Bridget couldn't see who it was from this angle.

Jed already had his phone out. 'Hi, I'm Jed Holmes,' he said, then pressed the screen. 'I'm talking to Esther Thornfield, the renowned local artist. Ms Thornf—'

'You are *not* talking to me, you little pest. Put that thing away and go and bother someone your own age. The primary school is just down the road, back the way you came.'

Jed flinched, but he didn't give up. 'How did you feel when you saw the post on your Facebook page this morning? Have you any idea who did it or where they got the image from?'

Esther was thrown, as if Jed had started to talk in ferret and not just look like one. Esther had gone for her oldest clothes this morning, and Bridget couldn't help feel relieved that Jed wasn't video recording, because there was something going on here.

'What are you wittering about?' said the artist. 'Move out of my way. Now.'

Jed held his ground. 'It's not very flattering, is it?'

The passenger door creaked open, and a woman's voice spoke up. 'Esther, you *must* get this seat belt fixed.'

The interruption threw Jed off his stride, and he stabbed his phone, presumably to pause the recording; Esther took the chance to march past him as he watched the Reverend Deborah Giddings swing herself out of the car and smile at everyone. Jed looked uncertain, possibly because Deborah wasn't wearing a dog collar, and the disjunct between her confident voice and her unremarkable presence wasn't something he'd seen before. Poor lad. He'd learn.

'Bridget, hi,' said Rev Deb. 'Is that girl alright? I saw her take a tumble after we passed. I do hope she's okay.'

Bridget was a lapsed Catholic (and a lapsed *Liverpool* Catholic at that). She'd been brought up to look down on the Church of England as the heretical lapdog of the ruling class, and she'd been quite surprised by the way that Debs handled both herself and her parish. 'She's fine, Deborah. No bones broken. Lucy's looking after her.' She turned to Jed. 'Do you want a tip?'

Jed looked at the two women, and it was to his credit that he didn't try to man it over them. It was going to save him a lot of grief, too. Bridget wasn't sure about his sense of humour, though, because he said, 'If your *tip* is telling me to switch courses, then you're too late.'

'No, soft lad, my tip is to get your skinny arse round to the millpond, because I reckon they're going to find the murder weapon fairly soon.'

'How ...?'

Deborah shut her door with a creak and a bang, and followed Esther into the Mill.

Jed nodded. 'Thanks for the tip, Bridget.' He tried to square his shoulders and look assertive. Didn't work. 'Is Kat in?'

Really? That was unexpected. 'She won't be long. I won't tell her you're asking after her.'

'Why not?'

'Because she hates journalists on principle. See you later, kitten.'

She left him looking confused and put a little sashay into her exit. Just for fun.

When she reached the shade of the Spinning Room, she found Wendy sending out distress signals from behind the counter. Esther can have that effect on you. 'I'll sort it,' Bridget said, swerving to get back in place. 'Usual, Esther?'

Esmeralda, though, wasn't finished. 'You shouldn't leave her alone if she doesn't know what she's doing,' she said.

That wasn't on. A successful woman like Esther shouldn't take it out on the sisterhood. 'We all have to learn,' Bridget told her. 'And I'm sure you'd rather wait than be served a substandard coffee. I'll bring them over.'

'And I'll pay,' said Debs. 'My treat, Esther.'

The artist looked suspicious for a moment, as if there was something going on, then sniffed and left them alone. Bridget paused a second before starting the machine and cocked an ear. A screechy warble from the kitchen was either a distressed wading bird or Ciara Davenport having her graze cleaned. Bridget pushed the button, and as soon as the pump got going, Deborah leaned forwards for a confidential whisper.

'I turned up at Esther's this morning to distract her and break the news.'

'What news, Debs?'

'That boy must have been stalking Esther's "socials" or something. Or he did it.' She registered Bridget's blank look. 'Haven't you seen it? Here. Quick.'

Bridget started the milk and accepted Deborah's phone, open at the Facebook page of *Esther Thornfield Artist*.

First she saw the name of the poster, then she saw the image. 'You're joking,' she said. 'How is that even possible?'

'I have no idea,' said Deborah, swapping her phone for a ten-pound note.

Bridget cashed up and gave the vicar her change, her head still spinning at what she'd just seen. It *couldn't* be Tony, could it?

'I'll take the tray, shall I?' said Debs.

'What? Oh yeah. Thanks.'

Wendy had gone outside to escape Esther, and she returned with two empty mugs and a message. 'A gentleman called Simpson said that our tea is a tribute to Mother Nature and that he'll be in touch about the bridge. What bridge?'

'Thanks, Wendy. Could you pass the message on to Lucy. She'll explain the bridge. I need another look at something and I'll cover here.'

'Fine.'

Bridget got out her phone and was still searching for Esther's Facebook page when Kat arrived.

'It's *so* not fair,' grumbled her duckling. 'You and Lucy are *always* on your phones and you're *always* on my back for doing the same thing.'

'I'd complain to the HR manager if I were you,' said Bridget without looking up. 'How's your toes today?'

'I shouldn't be here. I tried to get a note from Dad, but he's gone to work and Mum laughed at me.'

'That's because you're twenty-two, not twelve, and it serves you right for being vain.'

'She said that, too. Are you her secret long-lost sister or something? Who's the HR manager? I didn't think we had one.'

'Mina Clarke-Desai can be HR manager. She charges enough to be financial adviser, so she can do HR as well.' Bridget finally found the place and whistled. 'Wow.'

'Wow what? Let me see.'

'I'll AirDrop it to you. Hang on.'

Bridget pinged over the page and continued staring. It still didn't make sense.

Esther Thornfield – Artist was not the most well-curated page on the internet, but it was updated fairly regularly, and there was a post from last week showing a dark canvas with one source of light and titled *Saint Peter's Church XIII – Easter Revisited*. Bridget was intrigued by the picture, but she was brought up short by the comment and the image posted underneath.

The user ID was *SpaceFruitTony*, and the profile picture showed a grinning Captain Berry. Anyone could have created that, but only the real, living Tony Carson could have created the diorama posted with the words *And so they worship*.

Bridget had to pinch and zoom to get the full impact. In some sort of cavern, a witch, complete with cartoon warty nose and pointed hat, was sticking a big knife into an obviously male figure on a stone slab. Behind the witch, a cauldron bubbled, and as Bridget scrolled, the camera angle changed, bringing into view a collection of female figures, all prostrate before the altar and holding up an offering.

'The witch. It's Esther!' said Kat, shock running through her voice and pitching it up into a squeak.

'Yup. No realistic face, as usual, but there's only one person who wears smocks like that.'

They both pinched and zoomed their own copies of the image. A few seconds later, Kat spoke up. 'If that's Esther, then who … Oh my God, that's Shannon and Laura! The biker jacket and the hairband are a giveaway, so who's the other one?'

Bridget considered the figure. 'It's Donna. Look at the hair. And the microscopic house she's holding out like an offering. Shannon's holding a strawberry, Laura's got a book, so who else could it be?'

'You're right. That's so … mean. It's horrid.'

Bridget looked up as a group of seniors arrived. 'It's more than horrid, kid, it's childish and spiteful. But who posted it?'

'And when,' added Kat.

'When? It's new this morning.'

'But it could have been scheduled at any time.'

'Damn.' Bridget put her phone in her apron. 'Go and get changed and see how Cinderella's doing back there.'

'Who?'

'You'll see. If she's giving Lucy a hard time, tell her that Byford's all out of Prince Charmings.'

'Whaaa?' said Kat.

'Shoo.' Bridget put on her smile. 'Morning, Allan.'

'Morning, Dark Lady.' He peered at her. 'Not so dark, these days.'

'I'm finding that there's plenty of darkness around without me adding to it. Americano with warm milk on the side?'

'Too hot for that. I'll have a pot of tea, please.'

Bridget turned her back, and didn't see what happened next. She heard it, though. A loud scrape of wood on wood, then a thud, then a voice. She stopped the flow of boiling water and turned round.

At the other end of the Spinning Room, Esther was standing next to her upturned chair and clutching Deb's phone as if she wanted to smash it. 'Well, if you can't do it, then I'll have to!' she shouted. She tossed the phone casually onto the table, where it landed on the tray and sent a cup flying and cascaded milky coffee into the air. The cup teetered for a second, then fell off the edge and smashed onto the floor.

Deborah was torn between picking up the pieces and rescuing her phone from a latte lake. Esther didn't notice. She was already out of the door.

Thirty-One

'I'll give the vicar a hand,' said Allan. 'You get a dustpan and brush.'

'Thanks.'

Bridget rarely delegated incidental cleaning (except cleaning of wounds – Lucy was welcome to that). Bridget liked to show that she was one of the team, and when it came to hygiene, she was a firm believer that if you want a job doing properly, then you need to do it yourself.

In the kitchen, Wendy was already getting the cleaning materials together and Lucy was finishing her repairs to Ciara Davenport's leg; Kat, of course, was on her phone and trying to be inconspicuous.

Bridget held out her hands to Wendy. 'I'll sort that. You finish Allan's order.' The newest team member handed over the cleaning trug and propped the long-handled dustpan and brush set against the worktop.

'When you've got a sec,' said Lucy, with a warning tone.

'Yep. One minute.'

Bridget bustled out and found that Allan had already organised things ready for her to finish the job, and Debs was checking that her phone was undamaged. 'Here,' said Bridget. 'Give it a spray and wipe with this. It's only water.' She passed a spray bottle and microfibre and started to deploy the dustpan. 'Thanks, Allan. Lifesaver. Wendy's got your order covered.'

'No bother. What's up with Esther?'

'She's been trolled,' said Bridget. 'Someone pretending to be Tony Carson put a nasty picture on her Facebook page. I'm surprised you haven't seen it.'

Allan shook his head. 'I leave all that sort of thing to the wife. Was it one of these pornographic things? No, don't tell me. Ignorance is bliss when it comes to the internet.'

He headed for the counter, and Bridget swept up the cup. 'I'll need to mop this. Do you want another?'

'No thanks,' said the vicar. 'I'd better get on. I only came here to let

Esther down gently.'

'You're a good friend to her, Debs. Why did she rush off like that?'

'Obviously she wants to delete the posting, but she doesn't have Facebook on her phone and I can't do it. She's gone home to use her laptop.'

Deborah gave Bridget one of her measured looks, the sort the doctor gives you before deciding what treatment is necessary. 'I'll need to see her again later, Bridget.' She put her phone in the pocket of her practical skirt. 'When I showed her the image, she said, "How did that get there?" She'd seen it before, and I didn't get a chance to ask where. I'll see you later, and sorry about the mess.'

'Wasn't your fault. Look, I'm off to see Hayley Horst in a minute. Do you know anything about her?'

'I'm the vicar, not the owner of the village shop, Bridget. Why don't you call round to St Peter's before choir practice tonight? It starts at seven thirty, and I'll be there from seven.'

'I might just do that. Cheers, Debs.'

Bridget headed back, thanking Allan on the way and then turfing Kat out of the kitchen to go and help Wendy. She returned the cleaning things, washed her hands and finally went to see why Lucy had been sending out distress signals.

The nasty graze on Ciara's leg was much less nasty now that it had been cleaned and covered with antiseptic gunk, but that wasn't the issue. 'Ciara might have damaged her ankle,' said Lucy.

'I've definitely damaged my espadrille,' said the victim. 'These are *Gucci*. Do you know how much they cost? Who's going to pay for them?'

'Your dad,' said Lucy somewhat abruptly. 'Turns out that our fathers know each other. Ciara's dad is in the image business.'

'They *knew* each other,' said Ciara. 'Emphasis on the past tense.' She turned to Bridget. 'Where's Jed? Why did he run off and leave me?'

'He could see you were in good hands,' said Bridget. Jed Holmes was annoying, yes, but he didn't deserve to be thrown under a bus driven by Ciara Davenport. 'He went to follow the story. Probably best to let him get on with it and he can share it with you later.'

Ciara huffed. 'Share it with Bradley Nicol more like.'

'You're heading out, right, Bridget?' said Lucy, thankfully concealing her destination. 'Could you nip into Cairndale and drop

Ciara at the station? She can get a taxi to Lancaster Royal Infirmary. If we order one here, it could take ages.'

'And cost a fortune.' The girl considered her options. 'Would you really take me into Cairndale?'

'I would,' said Bridget. It was a twenty-minute round trip, but if it got Little Miss Podcast out of Lucy's hair, then the sacrifice was worth it.

Ciara was cradling the wedge sandal like a wounded animal. On closer inspection it *could* be described as an espadrille. She looked up. 'I was talking to the tall girl. Katharine, is it? Whatever. She said that her dad's a lecturer in physiotherapy at the college. They have a sports injury clinic run by the trainee physios under supervision. All I need to know is whether my ankle's broken.'

'Her name's Katarina, and taking you there's no problem. Can you make it to the side door? I'll bring the van round.'

'I'll give it a go,' said Ciara bravely. She stood up and tried taking the weight on her ankle.

Bridget looked down, and Lucy was right: there was swelling there. Probably nothing. Then again, no matter how good Lucy's skills with the first aid kit, she was not an orthopaedic surgeon. Better safe than sorry.

'You'll need to take the other shoe off,' said Lucy, standing up and packing away the kit. 'I'll give you a shoulder.'

Bridget left them to it and swapped her apron for her bag. Outside, she found Jed lurking in the shadows by the estate office. 'If you don't want Ciara to rip you apart with her false nails, I'd disappear for a minute.'

'Why? What have I done?'

'Abandoned her. I'd abandon her, too, but I've got to take her to get her ankle checked.' She winked. 'When I've gone, Kat will be at your mercy. Just tell her you're a friend of Brad's and she'll be putty in your hands.'

Jed snorted. 'Nice try, miss. Brad told me what happened when they split up.'

Miss? *Miss? What am I now? A teacher? Give me strength.* 'They didn't split up. He two-timed her. Now scoot.'

He did scoot. Bridget moved the van and watched Ciara limp theatrically towards the passenger door, which would have been very moving if she hadn't trodden on a stone with her good foot and swapped her limp to the other side. *Kids, eh?*

Because the van was intended for food transport, it had the divine gift of air conditioning. Ciara perked up no end when she realised. 'Might help slow the swelling,' she said innocently.

Bridget headed off, and when they were out of the village she said lightly, 'So what is it with you and Jed? Classmates? Collaborators? Frenemies?'

'God, no. To be a frenemy you have to act like an *actual* friend. When I saw that he'd got a *credit* on one of Brad's articles, I couldn't believe it. Yeah, it was only *Loco Lancs Online*, but there it was on the byline: Bradley Nicol with Jed Holmes.'

'There's no money in that, right?'

'Not to Jed, but that's not the point. I went to see him last night and told him we should collaborate.'

'Was there anything in it for him? Did you find out anything to trade with him yesterday?'

Ciara held her face towards the air vent and lifted her hair away from her neck to dry it. 'That's not the point,' she said, not quite admitting that her investigation had been a bust. 'I said he needed someone the audience can relate to?'

Ciara had finished the last sentence with a rising inflection. It was a habit Bridget found intensely annoying. She pushed a little harder. 'Why can't they relate to Jed?'

'Oh they can,' Ciara gushed. 'Absolutely they can. It's just that I can focus on the *interpretation*? What the listener hears and the viewer looks at? I'm their medium to the message.'

'I see,' said Bridget. 'Where are we going?'

'Oh. Yeah. D'you know the Rivers Estate? Good. Take the old bridge road and then you can get round the back of the Millhouse and avoid the A6.'

'I think I know the way.'

The home of Caffè Milano, Byford, was of course *Ford Mill*. Just to make life really confusing, the University of Lancashire Institute of Science and Technology had its heart in another mill, this one a much larger cotton mill, known as the Millhouse. That building fronted the main road in Cairndale, and the university college sprawled out behind the imposing brick relic, with low-rise teaching blocks, gyms and all-weather pitches for the sports science students.

Bridget had never been this far back, and one mystery was solved: Spice Ireland. Kat had told her it was where the Goths hung out, and now Bridget knew why she'd never been there – the pub was a long way from Market Square. She slowed down. 'Give us a clue, Ciara.'

'Sorry?'

'Where's the sports injury place?'

'Oh. Down to the right, then pull in next to the Shepherd Building.'

Bridget drove cautiously over speedbumps and through students as oblivious to vehicles as Ciara had been when she twisted her ankle. 'Any relation to Colonel Shepherd?' she asked when she saw a small, modern building next to the Cowan Sports Hall.

'Who?'

'Never mind. Did Jed give you any clue as to why he was interested in Esther?'

Ciara frowned. 'I'm not sure. When I saw him last night, he asked if he could check the archive.'

'Sorry?'

Ciara waved a hand as if it were nothing. 'I have a subscription to the Newstower digital archive. Jed got me to enter a multi-term search and invert the date order, and that's when he saw something.'

Bridget waited. And waited. Two enormous lads with rippling muscles passed in front of her van. When they saw Ciara, one of them waved, and she waved back.

'What?' said Bridget.

'Jayden. Well fit, but he's Australian. We dated, like, once or twice?'

'Give me strength,' Bridget muttered. 'The news archive. What did Jed find?'

'Oh, it was something to do with art schools. Here – he made me save it.'

Throughout the entire journey, Ciara had asked and answered every single one of Bridget's questions with one eye on her phone. Bridget re-doubled her commitment to enforcing the ban at Caffè Milano. Just as soon as she'd sorted this business out. Ciara swiped an app and handed over her phone.

Bridget saw a headline: *Visiting Judge Honour for Local Artist.* She opened the article and saw a picture of a much younger but still spiky and idiosyncratic Esther Thornfield standing in front of a pair of canvases. The text reported that the Thames School of Fine Art had asked Esther to judge their undergraduate show, only she wasn't Esther Thornfield then – she was Esther Makepeace. Hmm. So what? It must have meant *something* to Jed, though it clearly didn't to Ciara.

'Go ahead,' said Ciara. 'I don't mind. It's faster than yours.'

Oops. Bridget had started looking for the *Lancashire Mercury* pieces – using Ciara's phone. She passed it back. 'Thanks. Did Jed say what the link was?'

'No. His eyes lit up when he saw it, though. I'm sure his nose twitched as well, you know. Like a bunny.'

'Ferret,' said Bridget. Oops. That came out without a filter. Perhaps she was seeing too much of Jackie Chester.

'What's a ferret?' said Ciara. 'Look, thanks for the lift, Bridget. This is really starting to hurt now.'

'Pleasure, Ciara. And don't worry, I won't tell Jed what you said about him.'

'I didn't say anything!'

'Yes you did. You said he was ugly and had a boring voice. I hope they can sort your ankle.'

Ciara lifted her nose and turned to get out of the car. She hobbled to the Shepherd Building with a martyred expression, and Bridget engaged Drive. It was time to see what Hayley's story might be. Though maybe she'd stop off at the shop on the way and get one of those chilled energy drinks. Suddenly, they seemed quite inviting.

Thirty-Two

When confronted by the reality of the chiller cabinet, Bridget couldn't help herself. She picked up the lime green concoction that was Kat's favourite and checked the ingredients. 'Bloody hell! Three of those shouldn't be in cattle feed, never mind human food.'

'I know.'

'Bleeding hell, Jackie, will you stop *doing* that!'

'What? Talking to my customers?'

'No! Creeping up on people. It's … unnerving. That's what it is.'

'How else am I going to see what they're up to? Especially when they're on their phones. Do you know what I caught the acting headteacher looking at the other day?' Jackie shook her head mournfully. 'And it's supposed to be a church school, too.' She blinked. 'Kat drinks that stuff. I let her buy it by the case at cost.'

Bridget put the radioactive bottle back in the chiller. 'You're an enabler, and that stuff is toxic. From tomorrow, I'm gonna ban her from drinking it. Maybe I'll get her on to tea. As a gateway drug to espresso.'

'Good luck with that.' Jackie frowned, as if she'd just solved a complex mathematical problem. 'I love your custom, but why are you looking at this stuff. Don't you work in a café or something?'

'Ha bleeding ha, Jackie. I'm off on a mission and it's so hot I need something refreshing.' She picked up the old standby, Vimto. Yes, there were a couple of preservatives (and a tooth-rotting level of sugar), but her kidneys would thank her for it. She took it to the till and got out her purse.

'That's got additives,' said Jackie.

'I know. I'll risk it.'

Jackie kept a straight face when she said, 'You know what's got *no* additives? Mike's Magic Milk. You should try some.'

'And you should try minding your own business and we'll see who cracks first, shall we?'

'I always mind my own business,' said Jackie with a voice that came from the top of the moral high ground. 'It's not my fault if my business is universal.'

Bridget considered this. She had a point.

'What you up to?' said Jackie. 'I hear you're on the case again.'

'For me sins.'

'Anything you want to know?'

'You didn't take your dog for a walk on Sunday night did you?'

Jackie looked with misty-eyed fondness at the door through to the accommodation. 'If Chris would let me have a dog, I would *definitely* have walked it on Sunday, and we'd definitely have gone past the Mill at the right moment to see Esmeralda sneaking in with a shotgun.'

Bridget paused with a five-pound note in her hand. 'Why her? Why not Hayley or Donna or Shannon or Jonathan?'

Jackie plucked the note from Bridget's fingers and punched a button on the till. 'I dunno who Jonathan is, but Esther Thornfield was once arrested for assaulting her ex-husband.'

'Oh. Right. Cheers, Jackie.'

'No problem. Here's your change.'

Bridget walked out of the shop with her mind on higher things and climbed into her van. In a moment of environmental dereliction, she turned on the engine and whacked up the air conditioning, counted to ten, then turned it off again. That would give her a window of five minutes before she melted.

Once she'd slaked her thirst with Vimto, she got on to her phone. There was no Google reference to an arrest for Esther Thornfield *or* Esther Makepeace, but an article posted by Bradley Nicol did answer one question: Tony Carson had enrolled at the Thames School of Fine Art the year before Esther had been made a visiting judge. Bridget went onto the Newstower website and discovered that it was a combined archive for both a national newspaper and all of the local titles in the group. When Bridget saw how much a subscription cost, her eyebrows shot up.

Ciara clearly wasn't making full use of something which had cost *someone* a lot of money. Given that her father knew Lucy's father, Bridget was guessing that Daddy was paying. As sweat began running down her back, Bridget started the engine and drove slowly to the end of the village in search of Grange Farm Croft.

Byford is not huge. Even so, Bridget had simply never had to go beyond the White Hart before. She passed the pub on the left, then the high wall surrounding Byford Lodge on her right. There was an imposing building next to the inn, but she didn't have time to look because a turning on the right had a modern sign telling her that she had arrived at her destination, and all without needing a satnav. She turned into the Croft and looked for number three.

Around a dozen new houses were interspersed between conversions of old buildings, with the original farmhouse as the queen bee of the development. Number three was a narrow, detached property tucked into a corner. Hayley's car was on the drive, and Bridget had to park on the pavement to leave room. She took another drink, then regretted it because Laura was sure to offer refreshments. Never mind.

The front door opened before she could get there, and Laura waved her in. Despite the heat, Laura looked clean and comfortable in a vest and shorts. As soon as Bridget had levered off her boots, Laura told her why.

'My ex-husband has agreed to keep the kids for another couple of days so that I can be there for Hayley. Could be expensive, but worth it.'

'Expensive? Does he charge for looking after his own children or something?'

Laura laughed. 'Far from it. It's just that they may need therapy, and that's not cheap, you know.'

Bridget did know, and – like *Fight Club* – the first rule of therapy is that you don't talk about it. 'Good luck with that.' She lowered her voice. 'How is she?'

'In the kitchen.'

'I said *how*—'

'This way.'

Laura's kitchen could have come from an interiors magazine illustrating *perfect family spaces*. If you used a wide-angle lens. What it lacked in size, it made up for in bright colours, neatly stacked boxes and educational toys. Opposite the door, a wall-mounted whiteboard was adorned with children's drawings and paintings. Start them young seemed to be the motto round here. There was even a child-sized table in one corner, squeezed next to an adult version, and that's where Hayley Horst was sitting.

In the past seventy-two hours, Hayley's business model had come off the rails, one of her partners had been murdered and she'd been arrested for it. You wouldn't know it to look at her. Then again, why should she go to pieces just because she's a woman? She had as much right to front it out as any man.

'How are you?' Bridget asked, squeezing herself into a chair opposite Hayley while Laura put the kettle on.

Hayley looked down at her hands, and they showed the turmoil that her casually expensive dress was hiding. Apart from the fact that her fingers did nothing for Bridget, she noticed that Hayley's nails had been immaculate last week. Not any more, and there was no way she'd be appearing on camera without an emergency visit to the Bridge Street nail bar, and that made Bridget wonder about the future of 3M3, if there was one. She closed that thought down and filed it under *not relevant*.

'I'm in limbo,' said Hayley. 'It's like sitting under the sword of Damocles waiting for the other shoe to drop. I'm not allowed to see anyone, talk to anyone or go anywhere. I'm surprised the cops didn't put your name on the list.'

'I'm too useful to be off limits. I'm here to help, Hayley. Totally.'

'Thank you, Bridget.' She breathed in and out. 'It means a lot, and Abigail said I shouldn't hold anything back.'

'Good. Why don't you start with the easy stuff? Did you both grow up here?'

Hayley blinked, as if it were a trick question, and it was Laura who answered. 'Bridget's just being nice. She doesn't care about the police statement. Not everyone's having a dig at you, Hayles.'

'What statement?' asked Bridget.

Laura brought over a proper teapot, an old brown family heirloom teapot, which no doubt had a tannin lining thick enough to keep you warm in winter. Unless Laura had bought it from a junk shop, of course. Laura went back for mugs and said, 'You know what the cops are like at this stage: they give nothing away, but their press statement did say that *A forty-five-year-old woman has been arrested*. Hayley doesn't like people knowing her real age, do you? Worrying about that helps her stop thinking about the other stuff.'

Hayley tried to smile. 'I suppose this is payback for when I used to act the big sister, isn't it?'

'Karma's a bitch,' said Bridget. 'Unless you speak to our financial controller, in which case karma is a force of the universe. Anyway, where *do* you two come from?'

Laura dropped a cottage-shaped tea cosy onto the teapot. 'Do you know Byford Old Road, right in the middle of town?'

'Yeah, I know it. Big Victorian houses, mostly. Has a dead end at the A6.'

Laura continued, 'We grew up there. Dad was a lecturer at ULIST and Mum was a librarian.' Laura put her arm round Hayley and gave her a squeeze. 'Dad died when I was little. I can't really remember him.'

Bridget had mostly grown up with one parent, too. 'I'm sorry. It's hard. Is that where you live now, Hayley?'

'God, no. Mum sold up when she retired. She bought a cottage in Scotland and split the rest with us.' Hayley looked around Laura's kitchen. 'I guess I inherited the period features bug from Dad. I live in one of the railway houses by Midland Station.' She blinked. 'Don't you live in one of the ones by Byford Halt?'

'I do.'

'Nice. Lovely spot. The ones in town are a bit bigger, I think, but nowhere near as good a location. Sorry, got distracted. I've been there twelve years, and before that I lived in London.' She gave a half-smile. 'I came back up north with my tail between my legs.'

Bridget had to gamble: was that relevant to Tony's murder? The timescale didn't fit, but she had to be sure. 'Did you know Shannon or Andy Staton when you were down south?'

'London is a big place,' said Hayley with just a hint of the patronising git voice that had rubbed Bridget up the wrong way when they first met. 'No, the first time I met them was when they waltzed into Leyland Films.'

Bridget was glad she'd asked. There was nothing in Hayley's body language to suggest this was a lie or half-truth, so she pressed on. 'Were you involved in *Space Fruit* from the beginning?'

'I could tell they were onto something right away.' The self-deprecating half-smile was back. 'Until Lieutenant Lemon came along, I was very much a part-time voice artist at Leyland Films, so I made myself indispensable to the post-production team's office manager. He knew his way around a mixing desk, but not a spreadsheet, so I topped up my hours with work as his admin assistant, and that's how I got to see the *Space Fruit* storyboards. I was there the day they first brought them in, before Tony had worked his magic on them.'

Bridget smiled encouragingly and nodded at Hayley.

'Andy and Shannon came up for a long weekend, and they were

going out for dinner with Shannon's old friend on the Saturday. I loved the concept, and when I saw Tony's eyes light up at the drawings, I knew I had one chance to get a foot in the door. I said we should go to this little Italian place on the Friday night – Shannon and Andy, Tony and Donna. And me.' She shook her head.

'Tell her,' urged Laura. 'It was your idea.'

While Laura poured three mugs of tea, Hayley sat upright and wiggled her bum to adjust her dress. Bridget knew a party piece when she saw one coming.

'It was all very different in the first sketches,' Hayley began. 'I think Andy was trying to show his feminist credentials, but the original version had Captain Berry as female and Lemon as male, and it was all very … *heroic*. I said they should swap genders and that Captain Berry should be a bit of a liability and always need rescuing.'

'Because that's never been done before, has it?' said Bridget rather tartly. Laura cringed as Bridget continued, 'What the galaxy needs is yet another loser man who gets bailed out by a woman on half his pay.'

'You've been speaking to Donna,' said Hayley.

'No, I'm stating the bleeding obvious. Donna said almost nothing about the Leyland Film days. Did she object at the time?'

Hayley made a face. Briefly. 'You could say that.'

'What did the others think?'

'Tony was all over it, and Andy looked like I'd unlocked the secret of the universe. Shannon was on the fence. You have to remember that we were on our third bottle of Chianti, and then I did this.' Hayley sat even straighter and lifted her head. '*Captain Berry! Don't use the ray gun in here, you'll burst the … Oh no!*' She sat back. 'Shannon loved it.'

Bridget blinked. The woman approaching early middle age and sitting in a suburban kitchen had vanished for a moment and been replaced by an earnest and dedicated yet impish and carefree slice of citrus fruit in a galaxy far, far away. Wow.

'And the rest is history,' said Laura. 'Fancy a biscuit? I do.'

Laura got up and started rummaging, and Bridget smiled gently at Hayley. 'So how did you get from the Italian restaurant to a massive bust-up over the *Captain Berry clause*?'

'Do we have to?' said Hayley.

'Yes.'

Thirty-Three

Laura found the biscuits on a shelf high enough to be out of her kids' reach and brought them over. 'I normally have chocolate ones, but not in this weather. Hobnobs it is.'

Bridget took one and was wondering whether she could dunk without ruining her image. While she hesitated, Hayley took a delicate nibble and started chewing very, very slowly. Laura watched her for a second and then took over the story.

'Andy had been burned before, right when he started out in the gaming industry. He knew all about IPR.'

Bridget had been brought up in a world where video games were played by boys who needed to get out more. She'd heard that the majority of gamers were now women (because playing *Candy Crush* on your phone counts as gaming, apparently), but she still struggled to believe that there was actually an *industry* responsible for this collective descent into mindlessness. 'I'm starting to sound like Esther,' she muttered.

'Sorry?' said Laura, clearly possessed of a young mother's hearing.

Bridget pretended she hadn't said anything and pressed on. 'Andy might have known about *IPR*, but I don't. Giz a clue, Laura.'

'Intellectual Property Rights. He kept most of them when he signed with Leyland Films; they made him buy a five per cent stake in the company, instead. Anyway, when he split up with Shannon, it got very messy. The designs of the *Space Fruit* characters were absolutely his, so he could do what he wanted with them, but Shannon was entitled to *something*.'

She looked at her sister, and Bridget could imagine Laura sitting in the headteacher's office and giving the same look to one of her kids: *You have to tell the story, Hayley*. Her sister got the message.

'When everything was going well, it wasn't an issue,' Hayley began, looking anywhere except Bridget. 'When Andy got ill, he became a bit ... unpredictable. At the end, he went round to his solicitors and signed over a share of the royalties to Shannon in one document and left the rest of the rights to Tony in a new will.' She put down the half-eaten hobnob and brushed crumbs off fingers that were starting to shake. Guilt? Shock? Shame? 'Andy booked into a hotel in the Lake

District three days later and took his own life. They found him at dawn hanging from a tree in the grounds. Such a *waste* of a life.'

Natalie hadn't taken her own life. Not technically. Her system simply wasn't used to the pure stuff. That's what the coroner said, and that's what everyone kept telling Bridget. Bollocks.

Laura shocked her out of the moment with a soft, 'Things got a bit nasty after that.'

'*Nasty?* Were they not bad enough before?'

Hayley shook her head. Laura said, 'Shannon was distraught, as you can imagine. Her selfish bastard of a lawyer caught her on the raw and applied to the court for the new will to be set aside on the basis that Andy wasn't in his right mind. The lawyer saw pound signs in fees, of course. He *said* he was doing it so that Shannon got all of the royalties, like she did in the original will.'

'Whoa,' said Bridget. 'That *is* nasty. What happened?'

'The inquest ruled a straightforward suicide,' said Hayley suddenly. 'No mention of the balance of his mind being disturbed. It should have ended there.'

'Didn't it?' asked Bridget.

'No,' said Laura. 'The will is a separate legal issue. Thankfully, Donna got to Shannon before it was too late. Donna made Shannon ask her lawyer how much it would cost to go to court. When she found out, she told him to drop it.'

Bridget weighed it up. 'Have I got this right? When you formed 3M3, Tony had nearly all the rights, but Shannon had a share? No one else?'

'It's a bit more complicated than that,' said Laura. 'Tony held the licence for the *models* from Leyland Films, and he'd inherited Andy's five per cent shareholding along with ninety per cent of the character rights. Shannon didn't have much of a stake, but Tony needed her signature on any contract with 3M3. Or a court order or something.'

'I see. Is that why Shannon was there on Sunday?'

'Blame Donna,' said Hayley savagely. 'I'd been working on Tony for weeks, and he was ready to agree. If Donna hadn't dragged Shannon along, he'd have given in, then I could have got Shannon's signature later. She needs the money.'

Laura raised an eyebrow but said nothing. Bridget felt her way forwards. 'So it all kicked off between Tony and Shannon, did it?'

'Something like that,' said Hayley.

'You have to tell her,' said Laura. 'She needs to know.'

Bridget bit her tongue and didn't say that *she* was the cat's mother. So long as Hayley coughed up whatever fur ball was lodged in her throat …

Hayley drank some tea and made a face. She put the mug aside. 'Tony and Andy became very close, just like Donna and Shannon did. Tony blames Shannon for what happened to Andy, and he said as much on Sunday. When he said, "That bitch won't see a penny of Andy's money," the night was over.'

Bridget sat back, stunned. That was heavy. Vicious and heavy. She tried to reconcile the Tony Carson who'd made the snow globe and bought her an ice lolly with a man who could say something like that. She tried and failed.

'I am so sorry, Hayley,' she said. 'I won't keep you much longer, but just so I know, what did you do after you left?

'It's a cliché, but I just drove around. I went home, got changed, then went out again. I thought about trying to track Tony down, then realised what a *fool* I'd been. I shouldn't have dreamed of having that meeting the night before we were due to go live. Another week would have done. I was on my way to Tony's place, then thought better of it, so I drove to Cowan Sands and parked up and went for a walk to clear my head.'

Like most of the places nearby, Bridget had heard of Cowan Sands but not been there. 'That's out beyond the golf club, isn't it?'

Hayley nodded. 'Yes. Right on Morecambe Bay. It can feel like the end of the world when it's quiet. I didn't want to go home because I'd seen Laura's messages and I knew she'd want to know what happened.' She turned to her sister. 'If only I'd got drunk at home instead of trying to be healthy, I wouldn't be in this mess.'

Bridget needed one more answer before she left. 'Have you seen what was posted on Esther's Facebook this morning?'

Laura looked immediately guilty. She knew, alright.

Hayley, on the other hand, looked nonplussed. 'No. What was it?'

Laura sent her eyebrows into a frantic dance and nodded her head towards the patio doors.

Bridget improvised. 'Something about the Thames School of Fine Art? I think Esther was going to delete it.'

Hayley frowned. 'What's that got to do with anything?'

Laura's eyebrows were now doing the can-can, and she twisted her shoulder away from Hayley.

'Never mind,' said Bridget. She stood up and added, 'Abi Tennant's coming to the Mill this afternoon. I take it you won't be seeing her there.'

'I'm not allowed to,' said Hayley. 'Condition of police bail. She's coming round here afterwards. I doubt she'll stop long, though.'

Laura stood up. 'I'll show you out, Bridget. Thank you so much for coming. It means a lot.'

Bridget extricated herself from the furniture and headed for the front door, followed by Laura. When she bent down to pick up her boots, Laura pointed outside and waited until they were both on the front step before closing the door behind her. Bridget wasn't happy about this, because she'd get grit in her socks. It was in a good cause, though.

Bridget struggled to brush her socks, hold her skirt back and get her foot in her boot. It didn't help that she kept overbalancing, and when she put her foot down, she had to start again. Sod it. She sat on the step and looked up. 'So what's going on?' she asked.

'Look, I don't want to upset Hayley with too much detail, but that model? It's the Witch's Lair from *Depths of Mythranor*.'

'The video game that Shannon and Andy worked on?'

'Yes.'

'Then how ...?'

'Shannon inherited it from Andy, I think. He had it from some tabletop spin-off convention thing, and then Tony made the models.'

'Not *those* models, surely?'

'Oh no. The original ones were game characters. Shannon kept the whole thing in a cupboard, and she took it out the other day when she'd heard that Tony was here.'

This wasn't making sense to Bridget, and there was something Laura wasn't telling her. 'Go on, Laura. Spill.'

Laura passed Bridget her other boot, which had seemingly jumped off the step of its own accord. 'Hayley came down to see me a couple of times last week. One day, Shannon wrapped Tony's figures in tissue paper and asked Hayles to give them back. She said that he'd made them for Andy, not her, and he should have them back.'

'And then?'

'And then on Saturday morning, Shannon went into the Mill and found the Witch's Lair sitting on her table with the new figures in it.'

'Bloody hell. That's almost as bad as a horse's head.'

Laura looked affronted. 'It wasn't *that* bad! Not like actually killing something. Or someone.'

'If you say so. I reckon if I found that on the counter in the café I'd know someone had declared war. What did Shannon say?'

'Nothing, and I didn't find out until Monday, after Tony was dead. You'd have to ask her.'

Bridget's shoulders slumped. Every time she found one answer, it came wrapped in five questions. 'What about the Facebook post?'

'That wasn't Tony's regular account, I can tell you that much.'

'Then who the effing hell was it, Laura?'

'It wasn't me.'

'Great help you are.' Bridget looked at the image again, but all the background had been cropped out. It could have been taken anywhere. It was good, though, and you could see all the details. She sighed and locked her phone. 'One more thing, Laura. Keys. Specifically fire escape keys. Who has them?'

Laura opened the door and stepped back inside her house. 'Hayley said the police asked the same thing. I've got one, and so did she, but as for the rest …'

'Ask Louis. Yeah. I've got that message loud and clear. Thanks for the tea, and take care of Hayley.'

Laura gripped the door and looked down. 'I can't believe she did it, Bridget. I really can't. Can you?'

'I don't know what to believe, Laura, I really don't I do know that there's something she's not telling me.' She paused and waited for Laura to lift her head. 'Has she told you?'

'I don't know what you mean.'

Thirty-Four

From most perspectives, Lucy had a led a charmed life. She knew that. Rich parents, private schools, a leg up to start her first business. That didn't stop her being unlucky, though. She wasn't clumsy or careless or anything that could be cited as *contributory*. Not in her opinion, anyway. The fact that her boyfriend sometimes gave her a look was just Tom being Tom. He couldn't help being a copper, could he?

It wasn't her fault that her last car had ended up in the Manchester Ship Canal, was it? Nor the business at Aintree when *Celebrity Enquirer* announced to the internet that she was getting married. It's just that since Tom Morton moved up north, Karma had been paying her back for getting together with him. She paused and wiped sweat off the back of her neck. Was Karma a goddess or was that Kali? Whatever. The fact remained that ten minutes after Bridget headed off to take Ciara to the clinic, they were given a five-minute warning of a coach party.

'Should we get Bridget back?' Wendy asked. 'Once she's dropped that snotty girl off at hospital?'

'I think Ciara's brave,' said Kat. 'The way she's trying to make an impact.' Point made, she turned to Lucy. 'So long as you don't slope off too, Boss, we'll be fine.'

'Don't call me *Boss*! How many times!'

'But Bridget said we had to. And you are the Boss.'

'This isn't the armed services, Kat.'

Lucy didn't want this. Not now. Perhaps Bridget was winding up the troops behind her back. *Troops? Why did I call them that?* As if reading her mind, Kat plucked at the Caffè Milano logo on her shirt and said, 'Looks like a uniform to me, Boss.'

Thinking of the shirt and its colours gave Lucy a moment of

inspiration. 'We're a team, Kat! A great team.'

Kat's long face split in half with a big grin. 'Right, Coach!'

'I'll start prepping the toasted sandwiches, shall I?' said Wendy innocently. 'They seem to be our best seller with *coach* parties.'

'Not you, too. Yes. Go!' She hesitated. 'Any chance of swapping shirts?'

'No, Coach.'

'I need the loo,' said Lucy. She was on her way back, drying her hands on a paper towel, when a diesel engine in need of a new exhaust shook the windows, and Lucy's team jumped to it.

Ten minutes later, Kat swooped past with a loaded tray of empties and returned with, yes, two toasted sandwiches. She paused to collect a couple of napkins and said, 'We can cope with three people, but we can't make money the rest of the time with three, can we? Or am I missing something, Coach?'

She didn't wait for an answer, nor did Lucy offer one until the queue had disappeared, along with a plumber who'd seen how long he'd have to wait and gone off, possibly to fill Jackie Chester's coffers. In the midst of the panic, Lucy had had a message and needed to tread carefully, so she bided her time.

Kat finished a cappuccino with a flourish of chocolate sprinkles and passed it over. Lucy held up the card reader, and when the customer had paid and gone, she said, 'Is there a chocolate art competition? If there is, you'd win it no question. No, you're right, we can't be doing this on a regular basis. What was it like on Friday when the craft village was open to distract them?'

'Hard to say. It was our first time and there were two coaches in quick succession.'

'We'll have to see. Look, Bridget's been in touch. Can I have my break first and go see Louis? It's to do with the case.'

'Of course, Clarice.'

'What?'

Kat took a step closer, forcing Lucy to look right up. The girl really did tower over her. Kat lowered her voice. 'If Boss Bridget is Miss Marple, I reckon you're Clarice Starling, you know. She's a real powerhouse.'

Powerhouse. It was tall person's code for "short with attitude". Lucy had heard it before. A lot. 'What does that make you, then? Don't tell me, I'll work it out.' She took off her apron and the shirt flopped around her. She grabbed her water bottle, her phone and her blouse and headed for the first floor.

The manager of Ford Mill Arts Centre didn't have an office, he had a *den*. Opposite the entrance to the Dukes Gallery, a plain door hid a cosy gentleman's snug, complete with leather chairs, bookcases and a tasteful Farrow & Ball meadow green colour scheme that was totally at odds with Louis Young's taste in shirts, none of which could be described as Hawaiian. No, they were firmly rooted in the camp florals of the 1950s, and camp was a word you couldn't avoid when Louis was around. How on *earth* had he ended up marrying a cowman? Whatever.

The man himself, resplendent in a pale blue number, was sitting behind the desk staring at his laptop. Lucy hadn't been in here that often, and not on her own before. She couldn't resist it, and trailed her fingers along the frame of a watercolour scene of Byford Lodge, as painted from Ford Mill. No dust. Bridget would approve. 'Tell me something, Louis,' she began. 'Is this room a reflection of your inner nature?'

He snorted and pointed to his shirt. 'Darling, *this* is my inner spirit: colourful, in your face and skin deep. I did *not* design this office. Nice chairs, though. What can I do for my *favourite* barista today, hmm?'

After opening day, Bridget hadn't talked much about Louis. Perry, yes, and the Dukes, but not the man with the office upstairs. What had Bridge done to upset him? Lucy crossed the den and stood in front of the desk. Her bum was at the right height, so she rested it on the back of a chesterfield, glad to take a little weight off her feet. 'Bridget's gone to see Hayley Horst.'

Louis grimaced. 'How nice for both of them.'

'She's just trying to help. So am I.'

He sighed. 'I know you are, and I don't want a miscarriage of justice any more than you do. It's just that, well, you know Hayley.'

'No I don't. Never met her.'

'Lucky you. I hear she's got the Terma … the Terminator on her side as well. Abi. You know the one.'

'Again, not so much, Louis. What is it with you and Hayley? And you and Bridget, come to that?' The look on his face said that there was something, and that something was likely to remain unsaid. She took a risk. 'You can drop the act, Louis. I went to uni in Manchester. I know a camp front when I see one.'

He was not happy. 'As I said, colourful, in your face and skin deep. I have hidden shallows, Lucinda.'

'Fine. Just tell me all about the keys to the fire escape: who has them, where they come from, and are any of them missing?'

He went still. His eyes narrowed. He blinked. 'Are you here on your own account or someone else's?'

She breathed in, ready to answer, then stopped. She'd touched a nerve, but *which* nerve? For no reason she could articulate, her answer to his question was carrying a shedload more weight than she'd expected. 'Bridget's my friend. One of my best friends. That doesn't mean we share everything, though. Nothing you tell me will go any further. I'll give her an outline and that's that.'

He shut the lid on his laptop and opened a drawer. He fished around and pulled out enough keys to lock up HMP Cairndale. 'It's not Bridget's fault. Or Perry's, really, and I love Fliss to bits, so that only leaves Edwin. You know *him*. The Squire of Byford, as we don't call him to his face.'

Edwin Duke was a hefty man with a hefty portfolio of businesses. On the few occasions they'd met, Lucy had quite liked him. 'So?'

Mock horror twisted Louis's face. 'Those *quarries* that Duke owns, Lucy. Perfect place to dispose of your enemies. I bet his brother's in one of them, and I have no desire to join him. I am *not* going to say or think a bad word about our lord and master.'

On most days, Lucy could carry several ideas in her head. It's one of the things that gave her an edge in negotiations. Maybe it was the heat. 'Louis, you've lost me completely. What on earth are you on about?'

He swept his hand towards the keys. 'Everyone calls me the manager here. I am not. Look at the door on your way out. I am the *artistic director* of Ford Mill Arts Centre, which is a tenant of the Byford Estate, and Perry is the estate manager. Sadly, he has Edwin's ear, and much as Edwin loves to indulge Lady Felicia, he won't spring for a proper building manager, so it gets fudged and I find myself dealing with people I was never meant to deal with. I also find myself in charge of this lot.'

'Aah. I see.' She did see. 'Now I know why Bridget is kicking up a fuss about a caretaker.'

This time the angry face had nothing camp about it. Lucy had finally reached the real *Lucas Young* underneath the floral shirt. Oh yes, she knew all about him and his name change.

'Kicking up a fuss is right,' he spat. 'Bridget has put a list of demands to Perry and they're heading in my direction like a cannonball rolling down a chute.'

Lucy shrugged. 'I'm sorry, Louis, and don't hate me, but I'm as much behind that list as Bridget. Well, me and Mina Desai. The three of us went through the lease and put it together. I hope it doesn't all land in your lap.'

He looked at her for a moment. 'You don't actually care, do you?'

She shrugged. 'I do care. Of course I care. I also have customers and staff to think about, especially Bridget. I don't want to put you in an impossible position, but …'

'You're running a business. Feargal was *so* much easier to manipulate. I suppose that's one of the reasons he went bust.'

'That and the fraud, but yes, he worked on favours rather than contracts.'

'That's not such a bad way to operate. Not when it's people's lives you're talking about, and no, I'm not being a drama queen. You don't know about the cottage, do you?'

'No.'

'Mill Cottages, ours and Perry's, are gorgeous. Lovely. Who would live anywhere else? Unfortunately, they're also *Edwin's* cottages. He owns them, and no job, no cottage.'

Lucy had a basic grasp of the law, and frowned as she tried to figure out who worked for whom. 'Is it a tied cottage?'

Louis got busy with the air quotes. 'If you mean "Is it a secure agricultural tenancy?" for Amos, then no, it isn't, because it's me who's the tenant, so it's a "service tenancy". If I quit, I can't be evicted, but the landlord can set a fair market rent. You don't want to know how much that is. I couldn't do that to Amos.'

It was something Lucy hadn't thought about. Something she hadn't needed to think about. 'That's terrible, Louis. I'm sorry, and I'm glad you've told me.'

'Hmm. You did say this was confidential?'

'Of course.'

He pointed to the keys. 'What did you want to know?'

'Two things. First, just so we know, where were you and Amos on Sunday night?'

Louis let his eyebrows do the talking.

'Sorry,' she spluttered. 'I mean, did you see or hear *anything*?'

'Not from the Wheatsheaf. I took pity on Amos and drove us out there so we could have a quiet drink in peace. He doesn't often get the chance to unwind like that. We were away from Byford all evening. What was the second thing?'

'Fire escape keys. How many and who has them?'

He stared at the keys. 'I can't believe I'm doing this for Hayley. Laura's lovely, but as for her sister …' He looked up. 'Only the police know this, but the answers to your questions are *lots* and *everyone*. Satisfied?'

Lucy met his gaze. 'Thank you, Louis. Because I didn't have one, I assumed that they were restricted.'

Louis took an envelope from the drawer and took out two shiny keys that looked like something from science fiction, all pits and bumps. 'Allow me to rectify that. One for you and one for the Dark Angel.' He slid the keys over. '*Though they hide in plain sight, Angels will reveal themselves in glory.*'

Lucy frowned. 'Should I recognise that?'

'No, because I just made it up.' He looked into the distance. 'And I think it might go in this year's pantomime. As might Bridget. Now there's a thought.'

Lucy's eyes bulged and she tried not to think of Bridget in panto. Or someone playing Bridget in panto, which was even more alarming. She stood up and pocketed the keys. 'So who did design this office?'

'Lisa and Fliss. For Perry. Long story.'

Lucy took another look at the den and left Ford Mill's artistic director in peace. On the way down the stairs, she promised herself that she'd re-think Caffè Milano's caretaker petition. Maybe. If she could convince Bridget to stay.

Thirty-Five

When Bridget got back to the Mill, she drove into the overflow car park, noticed that there was much less police activity than when she had left, and then turned the van to face the back wall and its fire escapes. Would Lucy forget her intention to force her up there tonight? She sighed. Probably not. Just to prove she wasn't afraid, she clanged her way up the iron treads. Or most of the way up.

When she got to the craft village floor, she stopped, winded. *I really must get out more.* She forced herself to tread lightly up the last flight: she didn't want another close encounter with the security guard, either. Once at the top, she gripped the railings and looked out.

'I don't like it, but I am *not* going to be scared,' she announced to the view of rolling hills, millpond and Byford Lodge. She took two more breaths and started her descent, and if her legs were a bit wobbly, she blamed that on the unexpected exercise.

Back in the Spinning Room, the lunchtime trade was looking good. She waved to Lucy on the counter, then scanned the crowd. There, in the least popular corner, was Jed Holmes. She headed over and pointed to the empty chair. 'May I?'

He locked his phone and turned it face down. 'Yeah. Great.'

Bridget sat down and said, 'I thought you might want to know what happened to Ciara.' She pointed to his phone. 'Judging by the way she called you out, I'm guessing she hasn't been in touch.'

He looked shifty. Then again, that seemed to be his resting face. 'You all scooped her up like a bird that's fallen out of the nest. There was nothing I could do to help.'

That was a more poetic image than Bridget had been expecting. 'And besides,' she told him. 'There was a story to pursue.'

'I know! I got pictures of the divers before they put the cordon up, *and* I got pictures of the evidence bag with the gun in it.' He fished in his messenger bag and pulled out an attachment for his phone. 'Who needs long lenses when you can get these?' He put it down and leaned forwards. 'And I've sold *both* sets of pictures. For money.'

The pride on his face was wholly inappropriate for the circumstances and Bridget knew then that he really did have what it takes to be a journalist. 'Well done, Jed.'

'Thanks. I thought I'd celebrate in here. Not too much, because it takes weeks for the cash to come through.'

'I'm honoured you chose to spend it at Caffè Milano,' she said, and he smiled. *My God,* she thought, *kids really don't get irony, do they?* 'And you still haven't asked about Ciara.'

'Oh. Right. Was she complaining about not being able to wear skirts with those cuts on her leg? That's about her level.'

'Actually, she damaged her ankle, Jed. I had to take her to the sports injury clinic.'

'Oh. That's a bummer. I'll message her in a minute.'

Bridget nodded her approval. 'It was definitely a shotgun in the evidence bag?'

'Yeah. They were only in the water a few minutes. I wonder why the killer threw it away like that?'

Jed didn't know about the break-in at Water Cottage, and Bridget wasn't about to tell him, so she changed the subject. 'How did you get on with Kat?'

His face dropped. 'She's on lunch and nowhere to be seen. And your friend Lucy treats me like I'm a wild animal. At least you talk to me like I'm a person.' His eyes flicked behind Bridget. 'Ooh! Here comes my treat.'

Wendy Sadler approached with a professional smile and a cheese toastie. Bridget stood up.

'Enjoy,' she told Jed, then walked back to the counter with Wendy, casually asking, 'If Kat's on lunch, who made the toastie?'

'I did. Not had any complaints so far, and I shifted a whole load to the coach party that turned up after you left.'

Bridget forced a smile. 'Sorry about that. Well done. Could you cover the counter while I drag Lucy away for a sec? There aren't any orders outstanding are there?'

'Not at the moment. No problem.'

Bridget beckoned to her Boss and marched right to the end of the kitchen before turning round and folding her arms. This was not a conversation she wanted overheard. 'I've warned you before,' she announced.

Lucy flinched back. 'About what!'

'About putting people on food prep when they don't have a hygiene certificate.'

Lucy started to apologise, then changed her mind. 'Wendy brought up two children and is almost as OCD as you are about cleaning. She knows what she's about and we had forty hungry pensioners to feed. What else was I going to do?'

'Turn them away. Or get Kat to make them.'

'No. Kat has *two* certificates, Bridge, but anything more than a peanut butter sandwich is beyond her. Would you *really* have turned them away?'

'I— I don't know, Lucy. Clearly I'm not cut out for management.'

They stared at each other. It wasn't the first time they'd fallen out, but this felt different. Who was going to blink first?

'Two cappuccinos needed!' said Wendy from the doorway.

'I'm sorry,' said Lucy. 'You do not have OCD, and I know you don't. This weather is making me very grumpy. As is this shirt.'

Bridget nodded. 'Would you rather I took the counter or carried on in here?'

'You're the face of Ford Mill,' said Lucy.

'And you're incorrigible,' said Bridget, grabbing her apron.

'I know,' said Lucy sweetly. 'That's why you love me.'

Around two o'clock, they held their breath. When no more coach parties were announced, Bridget and Lucy took a break. Outside.

'Why have you dragged me out here into the sun,' moaned Bridget.

'So you can explain this,' responded Lucy, waving a page from her order pad. Or someone's order pad, because Lucy had never been known to write in green ink.

'If that's the reason, then I'm going back in, because I have no idea what you're on about.' Bridget looked again, and on second glance, the writing was incredibly neat (so Kat *or* Wendy) and quite large (Kat then). 'Why don't you ask the person who wrote it. And how come you get a piece of paper when all she ever does with me is send a voice note or a text?'

'Because I'm the Coach.'

Reflexively, Bridget checked the drive for passenger vehicles. 'Eh?'

'Never mind. It's a note about a man called Simpson, saying to expect his quote for the bridge and do we have a preference for stone or iron on the island? What the hell is this?'

Bridget's jaw loosened and dropped slightly. 'Don't you know?'

'Do I look like I know?'

Fair enough. 'Your friend Conrad Clarke sent one of Liz Swindlehurst's relatives to give us a quote for building a bridge to the island. Think of the business we could do over there. I mean *you* could do over there.'

Lucy stared at the note, then turned to look at the island, then the note again. 'Oh. That's a really good idea. Has anyone thought to ask whether the estate will pay, because a bridge will last a lot longer than our lease?'

'None of my business.'

Lucy shoved the note in her pocket. 'Later. How did … Oh.' She raised her voice. 'Hi, Liz.'

The detective inspector was looking even hotter and more bothered than Bridget and Lucy put together, and her fair skin had been outside way too long already. 'Is there no shade here?' she asked.

Lucy dodged past the dog bowl (which needed filling) and round the corner, where blessed shade prevailed.

'I was gonna send Barney with a message,' began Liz, 'but I was told that a personal visit to everyone involved was in order.'

'That sounds ominous,' said Lucy. 'Commander Ross?'

'I couldn't possibly comment. I've already seen Mr Lockwood and Mr Young. Ms Ramsey had to make do with a phone call as she's in Preston, and the Bartons with a voicemail. As of this afternoon, we have released the western half of the top floor. The other half – the TV studio – will be released at four o'clock. I also gave Ms Ramsey the name of two specialist cleaning services.'

Bridget and Lucy shared a look. *Blood.* Eurch.

'And I'm afraid I can't say any more than that,' concluded Liz.

'Who are the Bartons?' asked Bridget, even though she could guess.

'Geoff and Darren from the railway modellers. I didn't want to bother Mr Carson directly.'

'Thanks, Liz,' said Lucy. 'And tell, erm, Simpson that I'm grateful for him coming out.'

'You can tell him yourself. Right. I'll leave you in peace,' she concluded, then moved off, at a fraction of her normal express pace.

Lucy turned around again, her gaze lingering on the island (or on Byford Lodge – hard to tell). 'Look, Bridget, if I promise to do the bakery run tomorrow morning, can I stay at yours tonight? After I've nipped home to Garstang?'

Bridget had been looking forward to some peace, especially after her visit from Abi Tennant last night. On the other hand, they had a lot to catch up on. She was about to agree when something struck her. 'When you go to Garstang, that wouldn't be to collect the washing would it?'

'And if it was?' said Lucy, turning slightly red.

'I am *not* your mother. When are you gonna learn how to use a washing machine?'

'If you had been my mother, I might know what I'm doing. Mama always had people to do her laundry. I *do* know how to use a washing machine, just not *that* washing machine. I'll bring some grappa …'

'You will not. You will bring a case of Peroni.'

'Deal.'

'And have you forgotten that it's Thursday tomorrow?' Bridget paused and watched Lucy's mental cogs turning as suspicion grew.

'No,' Lucy answered in a slow drawl.

'It's my day off, so you'd have been doing the bakery run anyway.'

Lucy's hand flew to her mouth. 'I'm so sorry. I'll go home and get on to YouTube. There's bound to be a video on how to use the washing machine.'

Bridget sometimes despaired of the younger generation, even if Lucy was only eight years younger; she tried not to think about what would happen when Kat's peers were running the world. 'Nah. I won't be able to rest with all this going on. We'll stick to plan A.'

Thirty-Six

The early afternoon in the Spinning Room was busy, but not busy enough to warrant four staff. Lucy was making good progress inducting Wendy into the mysteries of the coffee machine, so Bridget barely hesitated when she saw two figures approaching. She hadn't seen them in the flesh before, but she'd seen their images on Abi Tennant's CCTV pictures. She strode towards the archway, where they were hesitating, and gave them a smile.

'Hi, I'm Bridget, and you must be Geoff and Darren Barton.'

The father smiled back, an open and slightly relieved expression on his face, and he went to shake hands. His son did not, and took a step back.

Geoff Barton was in a suit, but minus the jacket and tie. He must be around sixty, stocky and strong, with sleeves rolled up and hairy arms. His son looked like he'd inherited his father's build but none of the power. Darren was wearing a T-shirt with one of the most bizarre designs Bridget had ever seen: a flock of men in kilts with wings. Whatever. The T-shirt tried its best but couldn't hide the fact that Darren was XXL all over. Even the tent Lucy was wearing today would barely have covered him.

Geoff shook hands. 'Now that's what I call a personal greeting, Bridget. We were just wondering if it would be rude to ask for takeout cups when we're only going upstairs?'

Sometimes the gods smile on you, and Bridget passed the smile on to Geoff. 'That is not a problem at all. I've been hoping to have a word, and whatever you want, I'll bring it up for you.'

'That's very kind, Bridget. Very kind. Shall I pay now?' He turned slightly. 'You head up, Darren, and I'll see you shortly.'

His son escaped without having spoken or shaken hands, and Bridget took an order for a cappuccino and a caramel latte. She made the drinks, added a couple of scones on the house and headed for the lift.

Meeting new people, brewing the coffee and sorting the tray had taken her mind off it, but when the lift rose smoothly to the top floor,

Bridget was dragged down and back to Monday morning when she'd taken a tray up to Tony. She breathed in and out, and forced herself to look straight ahead, right at the partition.

Nothing had changed. The CARM space was exactly as she'd found it two days ago. Geoff saw her and rushed to take the tray off her hands. She was about to protest until she realised that her hands were shaking. Just a bit.

His powerful forearms hefted the tray and placed it on the pile of boards next to the partition. Exactly where she'd put Tony's tray on Monday. For that alone, she was very grateful. 'Thanks, Geoff.'

'No, thank *you*, Bridget.' He stepped away from the tray, and his expression changed. The polite old-fashioned gentleman was still there, but he was on guard now. 'You said you wanted a word?'

Bridget knew nothing about this man other than that he had a socially awkward son and an interest in model railways. Start with what you *do* know. She looked at the dividing wall and took a deep breath. 'Did you know Tony well?'

'Did *you*, Bridget?'

She jumped slightly when Geoff's question was answered from beyond a trestle table by the quiet but penetrating voice of Darren. 'Bridget's the Dark Lady of the Lake. Remember?'

Bridget was busy going red, and Geoff Barton was busy joining the dots, especially when he registered her tattoos. 'Of course. I'm sorry. We got served by Lucy at the weekend, and I thought Tony meant the tall girl who was always scuttling about. Tony talked about you, but I got the impression you were more … alternative.'

Her brain had supplied an *alternative* of its own. When Geoff had said, *I got the impression you were more …*, Bridget's subconscious had supplied the answer *attractive*. The more she'd learned about Tony, the more she began to realise just how little she'd known him. She opted for a safe step forwards. 'Not much of a lake out there.'

'No,' said Geoff. 'He said that *Dark Lady of the Mill* was a bit too like *The Lady in Black*, and no one wants to be named after a homicidal ghost, do they?'

That was a bit too far. 'I'm named after me granny and an Irish saint. In that order.'

'Of course. Sorry, St Bridget. Hearing about Tony has knocked me off my stride a bit.'

She offered a conversational trading token. 'I only knew him a few days. I wanted to get to know him better, and now I never will. Except through his friends and family. Had you known him long?'

'Years. Decades. I joined CARM when I was a lad, when Tony's grandfather ran it, so I knew them all: grandfather, father and both boys. Tony came himself for a bit, then dropped out. I heard about him after that, of course. Didn't we, Darren?'

Darren had been trying (and failing) to remove the dust sheets from the trestle tables without disturbing the mock-ups underneath. Finally, he gave up and swept them off, then with some difficulty, bent down and picked up the yogurt pots and takeaway containers.

Geoff kept his face turned to Darren. 'Jon used to tell us about him, didn't he?'

Darren had gone onto one knee and looked for a solid support to cling to. When he saw only trestles, he heaved himself slowly upright by using his knee like a car jack. 'Yeah. I couldn't believe it when he turned up. I thought he'd look more like a piece of fruit in person. Citrus fruit, of course.'

Darren had delivered his verdict without making eye contact. It must have been progress of some sort, because Geoff smiled and turned back to Bridget. 'Three years ago, when their mum had her stroke, he was coming up from Preston every day nearly. And then he moves into the Marina and starts coming to CARM meetings.'

'You made me look up the Parable of the Prodigal Son,' said Darren. 'Did we label the parts of the Millhouse?'

'No. They were all ice cream cartons. Double Jersey,' Geoff replied, and then to Bridget, 'All this was Tony's idea. First of all at the Civic Hall in Cairndale, then here.'

'And what is this, exactly?' asked Bridget.

Geoff spread his arms. 'Welcome to Carsondale, our tribute to the late Anthony Carson, senior.' He dropped his arms as it hit home. 'Both Anthonys now, I suppose. If we go ahead.'

'Carsondale?' said Bridget. 'I take it that's a pun on *Cairndale*?'

'It is. It was. It shall be again. That depends on whether we're allowed to stay here. We might have to scale back.' He looked up and smiled. 'As it were.'

'You've lost me,' said Bridget.

'It was one of Dad's daddier jokes,' said Darren, addressing an empty box of chocolates. 'It was a pun on *scale back*. As in *scale models*. You should ask him for the tour.'

'There's nothing to see, yet,' said Geoff modestly. 'Nothing of any interest.'

'It was of interest to Tony,' said Bridget, way more enthusiastically than she felt. 'If he cared about it, I'd love to know more.'

Geoff weighed her up. 'One of the apprentices at work keeps going on about *mansplaining*, you know. Do you know *anything* about model railways or miniatures, Bridget?'

'Not a thing.'

'One second.'

Geoff went to one of the stacks and started rummaging around. He took items from different chests and put them into a shoebox. He took the box and his drink to a table and beckoned Bridget over. She approached with as sunny a smile as she could manage. Now that she'd been in here for a while, the lingering odour of Sunday night's curry and the other smells was making her feel queasy.

Geoff pulled out two bits of model track, one large and one small. 'I'm sure you know that out there, just over the river, the very real Midland spur is four feet, eight and one half inches wide. That's standard gauge.' He slurped some cappuccino. 'Mmm. That's good.' He held up the large piece of track. 'This is thirty-two millimetres.' Then the small one. 'This is sixteen mil. The big one is called *O* Gauge, and the little one *double O* Gauge.' He paused to take another drink. 'Scuse me. Long day. Now look at this.'

He took out two carriages, both in a dark red, and Bridget's internal calculator started whirring in the background of her brain. In human terms, one carriage looked like a toy and one looked like an ornamental model. You'd play with one and put the other on a shelf or something. Geoff placed the carriages on their respective track sections. The O Gauge unit dwarfed its counterpart as the inexorable logic of ratios worked themselves out.

'I never thought it would happen,' said Geoff wistfully. 'It's always been a dream: to have enough space to build Cairndale junction and engine sheds in O Gauge.'

'Wow,' said Bridget. Her internal calculator clicked to a halt. 'Even this is too small. I mean, how …?'

'It's big enough for the track sections,' said Darren, who'd picked up his own drink and come nearer. 'The town and the Millhouse can be built separately.'

'That's right, Darren.' Geoff raised his mug. 'You haven't asked *why*, Bridget. Most folk do, and I'll save you the bother. We were – we might still – take the whole thing in sections to the NEC for the national exhibition next spring.'

The lines and drawings on the trestle tables came to life in Bridget's imagination. She'd used Cairndale station enough times to know about the mainline to London and Scotland, the branch to Barrow-in-Furness and of course the tiny line that delivered people to Byford. She saw part of them on this tabletop, and where the station buildings would be. 'It's huge. Do you think you'll still do it?'

Geoff put his mug down. 'It depends on Jon. Without him … well, there's no point. No Carsons, no heart. Literally.'

'Eh?'

Darren let his caramel latte slide down his throat like a pint of beer. He used the empty mug to point towards the partition. 'The heart of the railway is the fire in the locomotive,' he said. 'And the heart of this layout is the *City of Lancaster*.'

'Aah,' said Bridget. 'I see your problem.'

'Yes,' said Geoff. 'It could take months for probate and what have you. Assuming Tony left it to Jon in the first place.' He glanced up and noticed Bridget's face. 'What? What's going on, Bridget?'

She squeezed her eyes closed and offered a silent prayer to the police gods. *I've got no choice.* 'I am so sorry, Geoff. I think – and the police think – that it was stolen on Sunday night.'

The police gods gave Bridget immediate payback because that was the moment when Jonathan Carson walked in.

'Stolen! What do you mean, *stolen*?'

Thirty-Seven

Lucy loved Bridget in ways that Bridget might never understand. Not *those* ways, of course. Bridget wouldn't be Lucy's type if she were that way inclined. What Lucy loved was Bridget's way of seeing something about people which defined them instantly. When Bridget had told her that Abigail Tennant was *enthusiastically predatory with mousy highlights,* she had described the woman who walked into the Spinning Room to a T.

The smile that Abigail put on to approach the counter lacked only canine teeth, and Lucy had to force herself not to step back into the coffee grinder.

'Hello, I'm Abigail Tennant, and you must be Lucy.' They shook hands, and Abigail continued with, 'I've heard a lot about you, Lucy. And I'm sure you've heard a lot about me from your friends and customers. One friend in particular, of course.'

Lucy resisted the urge to wipe her hand on her apron. 'I'm sorry, Abigail, but if you mean Tom, then no,' she said sweetly and truthfully. 'Your name has never passed his lips.'

In her head, Tom's voice echoed with the words *That woman gives the legal profession a bad name.* No names, no pack drill, as Conrad liked to say, not that Lucy had any idea what *pack drill* might be. Anyway. 'It's a pleasure to meet you.'

'Likewise. Let me guess: your other customers are no so backwards in coming forwards about me. Ach, who cares? And please, call me *Abi*. Is Bridget around?'

'She's upstairs talking to the railway modellers. I'll show you the way if you like, or if there's anything I can help with?'

Abi looked a little uncomfortable. 'Well, it's a bit different with you,

Lucy.'

'We have strict Chinese walls in our house,' she told her firmly. 'So I'm as keen to get to the truth as Bridget. Just to prove it, when I spoke to Tom this morning, he told me he'd been set to look at the 3M3 accounts, but I have no idea why or what he found out. Just as he has no idea that I've spoken to Louis Young and discovered that I may be the only person in Ford Mill who *didn't* have a fire escape key last Sunday night. I've got one now.'

'Now that *is* interesting. Okay, would you mind showing me the outside ... including somewhere called *Water Cottage*. And if Bridget's not done when we're finished, we'll go and rescue her from the boys, shall we?'

'This way.'

Bridget's words bounced off Jonathan Carson like a Teflon ball hitting a trampoline. He blinked and shook his head and came further into the room; clearly his brain couldn't process the idea of someone stealing the *City of Lancaster*. He was carrying a Caffè Milano takeout cup; he lifted it and said, 'Lucy said you were up here, Bridget.'

'Jonathan!' said Geoff Barton. 'I know I said it on the phone, but I'm so sorry about Tony. I can't believe it.'

Something had changed in Jon Carson since yesterday, and the way he was looking at Bridget more than Geoff hinted that he had something to say to her. Propriety, however, won out. 'Thanks, Geoff. It's still sinking in.'

Unfortunately for Bridget, Geoff's brain had no problem processing her announcement. He gave Jonathan a sympathetic smile. 'And now this. Are you certain about the *City* being stolen, Bridget?'

'The police thought so on Monday. I haven't heard anything since.'

'And you do talk to the police, don't you,' said Jonathan with a sharp edge to his voice. He looked at Geoff. 'According to Donna Ramsey, Bridget is subcontracting, either for DI Swindlehurst or this Tennant woman who's representing Hayley Horst.'

'Eh?' said Geoff, not unreasonably. It was his turn to *non comprende*.

'She did it for Millie Easterby,' announced Darren. 'It was in *Loco Lancs Online* that she and Lucy were involved in tracking down the guy who did it.'

'I see,' said his father, drawing back.

It was time to make a stand. 'I'm not *subcontracting* for anyone,' Bridget told them. 'I'm asking questions about Tony because I care about what happened to him. The fact that I have Liz Swindlehurst's number is just a way of making sure the truth is heard.'

'Well, I'm sure we all want that,' said Geoff with an attempt at a pacifying smile.

When Jonathan didn't respond, Bridget looked into his eyes and she could see that he knew. He knew that she had questions about why he was here on the Sunday night, and she could see that he wasn't going to answer them. Not here, not now and maybe never. What she couldn't see was whether that was because he'd killed his brother.

Geoff Barton took Jon's silence differently. 'You shouldn't be here, Jon. You don't need to worry about anything. We've got it all under control, haven't we, Darren?'

'Not without the engine,' said Darren unhelpfully. 'We'd be better off doing Carlisle Citadel if we haven't got the *City of Lancaster*.'

'Why is this one particular model so important?' asked Bridget.

'Well, it's Jonathan's story, really,' said Geoff.

'You were there when it started. I wasn't,' replied Jon, memories clearly stirred. His obvious fondness for Geoff had made his reply deferential rather than defensive. 'You tell her.'

'I definitely wasn't there,' said Darren, abandoning the safety of the trestles and edging his way round to the stack of boards. He sat down and started buttering one of the scones Bridget had brought.

'I'd love to know,' said Bridget to Geoff, who was looking fondly at his son, as if eating in front of people was a bigger triumph than the faux pas of stuffing his face in front of a grieving brother (or murderer).

'Right,' said Geoff. 'Does LMS mean anything to you, Bridget?'

'Something to do with railways.' Inspiration struck her. 'Does the *M* stand for *Midland*? As in Cairndale Midland Station and the Midland Railway who built my house?'

'Spot on. LMS was the London, Midland and Scottish Railway. It was put together in 1923 because … well, it just was. For the first time, one company owned all the track, stations and everything round here. It's *ours* in a way, even though it's gone now. In the nineteen thirties, they produced a series of engines to rival what they were doing on t'other side.'

Bridget didn't need an explanation for that. Bridget was a Scouser first and foremost, but Liverpool lies in the royal county of Lancashire, ancient rivals to the larger but less fortunate county of Yorkshire, located on *t'other* side of the Pennines. 'Quite right,' she told Geoff with a smile.

He grinned. 'Our rivals – the London and North Eastern – they had the Mallard locomotives, and before that, the *Flying Scotsman* of course,' he said, pointing to Darren.

Even Bridget had heard of the mighty *Flying Scotsman,* and the winged kilt wearers on Darren's T-shirt now made sense. She decided not to ask about the Mallard. 'So the *City* was a winner was it? She? He?'

'Most definitely a *she,* and yes, the Coronation class engines were the most powerful steam locomotives ever built in Britain. Unfortunately, they were just starting to roll them out properly when the war began.' He shrugged. 'That's why we're doing "Carsondale".'

'You've lost me again.'

Darren had demolished his scone, butter and jam with the same ruthless efficiency he'd applied to his caramel latte. He wiped his lips and said, 'Black paint, no lights, everything back to basics. We're doing Cairndale junction in 1937, celebrating George the Sixth's coronation, but the *City of Lancaster* wasn't built until 1940. Dad, do you want this other scone?'

'No, you're alright, son. Help yourself.'

Bridget was watching Jonathan. His eyes had closed down during the history lesson, and when Geoff looked at him, they stayed blank.

Geoff accepted this as a sign of grief and carried on talking to Bridget, with a nod to Jonathan. 'The model of the *City* was handcrafted by Tony and Jonathan's granddad. It was the locomotive as she never was, in gleaming crimson lake and yellow, the LMS colours. Not only that, it had the most amazing interchangeable front, so you could have it streamlined or naked. I think we've got a picture somewhere.'

'I don't want to disturb you any longer,' said Bridget.

'It's not a problem, and I still can't believe that someone *stole* such a beautiful thing. I mean, it'd be worth a bob or two if you sold it, but there's no black market in railway models. Did they take anything else? Computers? Cameras? They had a lot of expensive kit in there.'

Geoff picked up a big folder, and Jonathan took two steps backwards. 'I think you were right, Geoff,' he announced. 'It's too soon for me to be here. You two sort out what you can, and I'll be in touch. Once I've spoken to the police.'

Bridget was torn between being rude to Geoff and missing her chance to get Jonathan on his own. When Geoff offered her a laminated picture, she knew the moment had gone. She forced herself to look at the badly photocopied pair of elderly snapshots and recalibrated her priorities. That model was something to be looked at.

In one picture, you could see the cylindrical boiler of the engine, exposed at the front but with blinkers at the side like a horse. In the other picture, all of the workings were hidden behind a smooth, streamlined shell. She'd seen something like that before, but in blue; this was in the same deep red as the carriages still sitting on the table, and with three yellow go-faster stripes meeting at the front. 'She's a picture, alright.'

'She is.' Geoff took the laminated images back and tucked them into the folder. 'It would be such a shame if the model were lost. It's our symbol. Mascot, if you like.'

'How did Tony come to have it?'

'Well, as I remember it, Tony used to spend a lot of time with his granddad after the old man retired, down in the shed at the bottom of the garden, and Jonny had gone away to university and left the group by then. Their granddad got very ill very quickly, and he left the *City of Lancaster* directly to Tony in his will.' Geoff shook his head. 'You won't believe this, but Anthony senior said that he didn't want his own son to have to choose who to leave it to, so he decided for him. The week after the funeral, Tony didn't turn up to the meeting and didn't come again until his mum was ill, like I told you.'

'How did Jonathan feel about that?'

'About what?'

'Anthony senior leaving the engine to Tony.'

Geoff gave her a funny look. 'It's a model engine, Bridget, not the crown jewels. Jonathan got ninety per cent of the family business, so what would he want with a train?'

'Carson Metrics,' said Bridget.

'That's right. Founded by their granddad after the war to make steam gauges for trains and boilers. Adaptable, though. Nowadays they make the business end of all sorts of sensors. I bet there's a Carson Metric in your coffee machine downstairs. We use them, too.'

'We?'

'I work at BAE Systems down the road. Multi-role combat aircraft.'

'And I've probably used Carson Metrics sensors at the lab in London.'

'I did hear there was more to you than coffee,' said Geoff.

'The once and future Dairy Queen, that's me. What about you, Darren?'

'Remote server support. It keeps me off the streets.'

Bridget had had a couple of messages, and now seemed the moment to check them. The most recent was from Lucy. *Abi tenent is here. Do you need rescuing?*

'Thank you so much for the tour, Geoff. I've learnt a lot today, and not just about railways.'

'Don't you want our alibis?' said Darren, putting all the crockery neatly on the tray.

'If you're offering.'

Darren stood back and let his father pick up the tray. Geoff brought it to Bridget and said, 'My wife, Darren and me were at home, watching the new episode of *Midsomer Murders*. You can't beat it. I'm surprised they haven't done an episode about model railways.'

'They've done one about doll's houses,' said Darren.

'Yeah, but this isn't TV,' said Bridget. 'Thanks for putting the tray together.'

'No, thank you, Dark Lady.'

'Not so dark, any more. I'm thinking of going mainstream.'

'Now that would be a shame,' said Geoff. 'I hope to see you around.'

Bridget didn't say that she was leaving Byford. Not that she didn't want to tell them, more that her arms didn't want to carry that tray any longer than they had to. She smiled and headed for the lift.

Thirty-Eight

As she descended through the Mill, Bridget's brain fizzed with what she'd learned, and it wasn't the relative size of model railway gauges that was strobing like a police beacon. No, it was her complete disagreement with Geoff about inheritance.

It might be different on Planet Barton (which was definitely alien to her), but in Bridget's World, a handmade symbol of commitment and emotional attachment was worth more than any amount of shares in a precision engineering company, especially one which had nearly gone bust twice in recent years and had to seek a white knight investor.

Back in the Spinning Room, things were ticking along, and Kat was peering over Wendy's shoulder at the coffee machine. 'Coach is round the back,' said Kat without looking up.

'Coach?'

'Lucy.'

Bridget dumped the tray and headed out into the heat again, and before she could reach the sanctuary of the lower car park, she was *ferreted out*. 'Hi, Jed,' she sighed. 'What now?'

'Who were those two guys who went upstairs? I saw you taking them coffee, so they must be connected to the case.'

She couldn't be bothered. Not any more. 'Cairndale and Aldhaven Railway Modellers. CARM. Now go away.'

Jed blinked. Then he backed off. 'If you're looking for that woman, she's gone.'

Suddenly, Bridget could be bothered again. '*That woman?* You wanna watch yourself, Jed. There's women *everywhere* these days.'

Lucy was in the shade, staring across the millpond at Byford Lodge. Surprise, surprise. 'Where's Abi?' asked Bridget.

'Her meter's running, and when I said you might be a while, she left. I told her what you told me – that Hayley's hiding something.' She shrugged. 'Has Jed gone?'

'If he knows what's good for him. How come you're *Coach* all of a sudden?'

'Because Kat is trying to wind me up. How did you get on with the model railway guys?'

'Frustrating. Jonathan Carson escaped before I could get him on his own. Not only is he not telling us something, he's positively hiding it.' She thought about what the Bartons had told her and said, 'Can you ask Mina to look into something?'

'Yeah. Course. I don't think she'll find much to discover about 3M3. Not with it being so new, and unlike Tom, she doesn't have the accounts. I can't ask him to pass them over. Sorry.'

'I wouldn't ask him to pass them over. Whatever he's discovered will come out sooner or later. No, I was thinking of Carson Metrics.'

'Who?'

'In science, measurement is crucial. A lot of science only advances because engineers build better measuring devices.'

'I'll take your word for it.' Lucy fanned the oversize shirt away from her body. 'It's too hot for a science lesson. Never was my favourite subject. You can't persuade an experiment to change its behaviour.'

Now that was a novel approach to human knowledge. Bridget filed it for another day. 'Carson Metrics is the family business. Jonno and Tony's family. They make very, very accurate sensors. We used to use them in the lab until less accurate but digitally integrated models came along, and they nearly went bust. That was actually news in the science world.'

'I can see why you switched to ice cream.'

Bridget had switched to ice cream for reasons that had nothing to do with science, and Lucy knew that. Lucy was also right about it being too hot for science. 'Can you get Mina to look into the corporate history of Carson Metrics? Tony inherited shares. How does that change things?'

'Okay. Now that *is* something Mina can do. I'll message her later.'

'Great. What did Abi think of the fire escapes?'

'She thanked me for showing them to her and gave nothing away.'

'A bit of a theme today, that. Why don't you get off to Garstang and I'll finish here? I'm going to see Rev Deb at seven. Do you think you'll be back by then?'

'Yes. Probably. I should nip into the Garstang branch and see how the new counter looks. Would you mind seeing the vicar on your own? I'd really like to FaceTime Tom.'

'Of course. After I've shown you how to use the washing machine. Coach.'

Lucy fully intended to visit the Caffè Milano outpost in Garstang. After all, she was supposed to be the Boss, and not just player-manager to the hospitality industry's weirdest four-a-side team. She fully intended to go there. Once she'd explored another avenue of proactive human resource management.

She turned left instead of right at the end of the drive, and then right instead of left to get into the yard of Meadow Farm, home to Mike Mason, his herd of Jersey cows and several small businesses which made Mike (in his own modest words) "Byford's leading rural entrepreneur."

The man himself was leaning against the shaded wall of a metal-sided building, the inside of which echoed to the gentle lowing and louder calls of the beasts. He glanced up from his phone, then looked up properly when Lucy got out of her car. Urgh. The *smell*. 'Hi, Mike! Any chance of a quick word?'

'It'll have to be quick, Lucy. Amos needs me to look at a couple of the heifers.'

Lucy looked longingly at the four-square, odour-free farmhouse. Never mind. She tried holding her nose mentally and discovered that it was no substitute for a clothes peg. 'How's things?' she asked.

'Alright. Been lucky with the weather for once. So long as this heatwave doesn't drag on, then we'll be in trouble.'

'You and me both. Doesn't do much for coffee sales, and don't tell me I need a better offer of iced drinks, because I know that. It's on my to-do list.'

'Along with finding a replacement for Bridget, or so I've heard.'

Of course he'd heard. Once the Kat was out of the bag, her mother would know, and once Jackie knew, then the whole village knew.

'Yeah. That's a tough one.'

He put his phone away. 'Can you actually replace someone as unique as Bridget? Where would you even start?'

'By trying not to lose her in the first place. You don't have to answer this, but where does your milk actually go?'

'No secret. I sell as much as I can through the vending machine, obviously.' He accompanied the statement with a wave at the raw milk dispenser sitting at the end of the yard. People came from miles around to get their milk unpasteurised, whole, and free from the homogenising process. He waved at the back end of a cow, visible through the railings further down the cowshed. 'But these girls produce a lot more than that. The rest goes to a paneer cheese factory in Preston. Trouble is, I don't get much of a premium. This isn't the only Jersey herd in Lancashire.'

'Do you have a separator?'

Mike's entrepreneurial antennae started quivering. 'Not at the moment. No need for one. Why do you ask?'

A milk separator was once found in the dairy of every farm with even one cow on it, and without one you can't separate the cream to make butter. Or other things. 'It's no secret, Mike, but Caffè Milano is losing its connection to Giuseppi's Gelateria in Southport. I'm thinking of starting something up here. Using raw milk.'

'Cowandale Creamery!' he exclaimed. 'I registered the name ages ago, and I was beginning to think I'd never use it.'

'I'd prefer something more Italian. You know, given the whole *Caffè Milano* thing?'

His head caught up with his heart. 'Are you serious, or are you just flying a kite?'

'I've got a lot of space in the Ford Mill kitchens. Way more than I need for the Spinning Room. I've got to work it somehow.'

'What does Bridget think?'

'She doesn't know yet. Would you invest in a separator if we went ahead?'

'If you were offering a minimum order and a one-year contract, then yes.'

'Of course. Keep it between you and me for now, if that's okay.'

'No problem.'

When Lucy got back into her car, she discovered exactly what that little button with the circular arrow did: it stopped the smell of ripe cow shit getting into your air conditioning. Euw. Gross.

Thirty-Nine

'I don't know why we had to walk,' moaned Lucy as they descended Church Road at sunset. 'I'm going to get sweaty in no time.'

'Because we both need to get out more,' answered Bridget. 'And it's alright for you. You don't have to go climbing fire escapes. Just think how good that cold beer will taste when we get back. Look out!'

Bridget pulled Lucy back to avoid a silver convertible, top down and obviously immune to the speed limit. 'Stupid git,' she shouted at the disappearing exhausts.

'Who was that?' said Lucy. They had been walking down the shady side of the road, the side without a footpath. Even so.

'Dunno,' said Bridget, stepping back into the road and brushing moss off her skirt. She'd seen the car before a couple of times. It was quite striking, and this was the second time it had roared up towards Byford Halt. Perhaps it belonged to the mysterious owner of Station House, in which case her neighbour was a proper bell end with a midlife crisis and a bald patch.

Lucy huffed and moaned again. 'Could we not have had one of those nice, cold beers – which I provided at great expense – *before* we came out?'

'Again: not before climbing up the side of a building.'

'You don't have to be Spider-Woman. There is a staircase, Bridge.'

'Wanna swap?'

Lucy shook her head. She did not want to swap. Not only would that mean testing her potential acrophobia again, Bridget could tell that she was desperate to get a foot in the door at Byford Lodge.

Bridget had set off from No 4 at a cracking pace, which she was now regretting. They reached the kissing gate at the north-east corner of the churchyard, and Bridget stopped. She held up a finger. Birds. A distant tractor. There it was – the choir of St Peter's, Byford.

'They're good, aren't they?' observed Lucy. 'I shall have to tell Tom. You know he loves choral music.'

They took a moment to listen to the voices running through "Love Divine, All Loves Excelling". 'It's wedding season,' said Lucy wistfully. 'One day, they'll be singing it for me.'

Bridget baulked at that. 'You'd have a Proddy dog hymn when you were brought up a good Catholic?'

'I've told you before, when your future in-laws are a judge and a cog in the wheel of the Archdiocese of York, you get married in the Minster.' Lucy saw the look in Bridget's eyes and changed the subject. 'Did Debs say anything useful?'

Bridget tipped her head to the side in thought. 'A few things. She came straight out and told me that Esther Thornfield is a friend and she wasn't going to share any confidences. She confirmed that Esther saw the diorama of the cave and witches in Shannon's workshop, so that needs to go into the mix.'

'Does it?'

'The diorama was left before the murder, so yes it does.'

'If you say so. Go on.'

'Debs also told me that *Esmeralda* must have known Tony for a lot longer than we thought. Esther's exact words were "*He hasn't changed*" and then Debs told me not to ask for details.'

'That needs looking into.'

'Along with everything else. The one thing she volunteered to me was that Esther had sounded off to someone at one point when Chris Chester was in the church.'

'So you'd hear it sooner or later from Jackie. What did she say?'

'According to Debs, Esther said that the world was a better place without Anthony Carson in it, and that whoever did it should get a medal.'

'Wow.'

'I know. It's what she didn't say that made the most noise. Our vicar is definitely worried about Esther. Come on, it's nearly dark now, and choir practice is over. Talking of which, how's Tom?'

Lucy broke into a grin, then frowned. 'He's great. Busy. Look, I might have to go over to York earlier than I thought. Something to do with his distant relatives. It might not be this weekend, but he's said it's important that I go if I can, and, you know, it's been difficult for him. Personally.'

'We can cope, now Wendy's on board. Might have to pass on the coach parties, though. Let's get moving.'

They reached the main road and turned left. 'So where are we?' asked Lucy.

'Too many suspects, not enough alibis and no physical evidence.'

'The murderer has to be local, right?'

'Local-ish,' said Bridget. 'They had to know about Coffin Joe's shotgun, so that rules out a complete stranger. I have no idea how Jonathan Carson might have found out about Water Cottage, but he could have overheard something at the weekend.'

'So, if we eliminate outsiders, who does that leave?'

'I reckon it could be Hayley, Donna, Shannon or Jonathan, and I'm gonna add Esther Thornfield until I have a reason not to.' They passed the war memorial, and Bridget got ready to turn down the lane to the river.

'Who are you going to see next?' asked Lucy.

'Donna Ramsey. Tomorrow morning. I must be mad doing this. Right, off you go, and I'll message you from the bottom of the fire escape.'

Bridget had worried about sending Abi Tennant off at sunset to catch her train last night, but she didn't worry about going to the Mill after dark for some reason. Even the older satellite buildings, some of which were quite creepy, didn't make her feel threatened. The same could not be said for the fire escape.

This side of the Mill faced north-east, and although there was quite a glow on the other side, round here it was close to darkness. She messaged Lucy, gripped the railings and put her foot on the first step. The fact that they were painted black did not help at all.

Bridget had deliberately chosen dark colours for tonight, though she hadn't gone as far as a balaclava. She also forced herself to tread lightly, sliding one foot up before using her arms to lift her body. When she got to the top, she leaned against the brick rather than the railing.

Taking it more slowly meant she wasn't quite so out of breath, so she had more energy to look around, and the first thing that struck her was how much Water Cottage stood out from up here. Anyone who had used the fire escape couldn't miss it, nor could you miss the chopping block and the embedded axe. You could even see the plant pot where Coffin Joe had hidden his key.

Her phone buzzed. *When you going up???*

She replied, *Am on top landing already.*

To which Lucy responded, *!!!! Can't see you at all. Come down and meet @war memorial.*

Going down in the dark was not good. Bridget took it very, *very* slowly, and Lucy was already waiting for her by the village green. Just to wind her up, Bridget leaned in as if for a kiss and gave a big sniff.

'Yeuch. What was that about?' said Lucy.

'Just checking to see if you smelled of Pimms.'

Lucy looked genuinely disappointed, and set off to walk back to Midland Terrace. 'I didn't even get over the threshold. It's not fair, Bridget.'

'You're right. It isn't. You totally deserve to see Byford Lodge's honey-coloured interiors lit by twilight.'

'Sod off.'

'What happened?'

'I rang the bell and Duke answered. He said that Fliss was dealing with a bath-time emergency and walked me through the gardens, which are very nice by the way.'

'And you really couldn't see me?'

'No. From the moment you messaged, neither Duke nor me could see a thing. Pitch black with the sun in our eyes. He also confirmed that the family were all indoors at the time of the murder.'

Bridget sighed. It had been worth it just to be sure. She was going to change the subject when she saw something in Lucy's face. 'What's up?'

'Duke was weird.'

Bridget's fight/flight response kicked in. The thought of her friend being alone in the dark with a much larger man was not good. 'What happened, Luce?'

Lucy stopped and put a calming hand on Bridget's arm. 'Me and my big mouth. Nothing like that. At all. He kept a professional distance at all times. No, it was more like he was fishing for something about the business. Honestly. He was mostly charming until he asked about the freehold on the Market Square branch.'

'Ohhhkay. Why is it that Church Road looks like Church Hill when you have to go up it?'

'Think of the Peroni in the fridge. And was that champagne I saw lurking?'

'No comment. I shall think of Italian beer and you getting up an hour earlier than me tomorrow morning.'

Lucy groaned. 'Did I really suggest that?'

'You did. And before you can open your beer, I need to check that you've passed your tumble dryer exam.'

Forty

Donna Ramsey was hours ahead of her appointment with the crime scene cleaners. Bridget had only just removed the *We Are Closed* sign from the archway when Wendy Sadler let out a cry of, 'Donna! How are you?'

The newest member of the Ford Mill team ran to give her idol a hug, and unlike Tuesday, Donna returned it with interest. Bridget reminded herself that Wendy had lost her dream job this week and cut her some slack. She shouted over a query, and Donna asked for a strong coffee and croissant.

'We don't really do anything but strong coffee,' said Wendy. I couldn't get to sleep for the first two nights.'

'Tell me about it,' said Donna, moving out of earshot and taking a seat.

Bridget started the machine and told Wendy to take five. By the time she'd finished and plated up, the women were deep in conversation. She picked up the tray and took a good look at Donna Ramsey on the way over.

The doll's house creator seemed a lot better today The sharp edge was back to her hair, and she was looking stylish in a loose blouse and looser jeans. If Bridget wore jeans like those she'd look like a bag lady, not a well put together expert in magical miniatures. 'There you go. First one's on the house, Donna.'

'Thanks, Bridget. I need this. Are you sure you don't mind coming up with me?'

Bridget had been in touch by email and said that she wanted to talk, and did Donna need any company when the police handed over the studio? Donna had said that, yes, she did.

'I'll go if you like,' offered Wendy. 'I know where everything is, after all.'

Bridget was quick to put her foot down. 'Only if Donna's happy to wait until Kat gets here. I don't want to leave Lucy on her own.'

'Coach can cope. I'll be back soon,' said Wendy.

'Coach?' asked Donna. 'Is there a coach party on the way?'

'No there isn't,' said Bridget. She was not happy with Lucy being *Coach*. For one thing, it made Caffè Milano sound like an American high school. Now was not the time for that battle, though. 'The craft village reopens to the public today,' she reminded Donna. 'And with the usual senior discount customers, we're going to be busy. Let's wait until Kat gets here, shall we?'

'Of course.'

Donna sighed. 'If you've got two minutes, Wendy, could you help me with this?' She waved a set of paperclipped documents adorned with the Lancashire & Westmorland Police logo. 'They've given me a list of everything taken into evidence, but I can't make head nor tail of it. Whoever wrote it down isn't an expert in TV gear or miniatures crafting. And I think a lot of it was Tony's anyway.'

Bridget bit her lip. Allan and an unknown but clearly long-suffering woman had just arrived, and they were two swallows who definitely made a summer. 'If you can do the tables, Wendy, then help Donna in between?'

'Of course.'

Bridget backed off and left them to it. 'Morning, Allan. Are you going to introduce me to your lovely wife?'

'I would, but she's not here today. This is my sister, and she's not lovely at all.'

'I was,' she replied tartly. 'And then you were born. It's been downhill ever since.'

Bridget laughed. 'You know what, Allan, my brother says exactly the same about me. Welcome to Ford Mill ...?'

'Sue,' said the woman. 'It doesn't help that his wife is also called Sue. Can I have a large Americano with hot milk in a jug?'

'Coming right up,' said Bridget.

'I thought Thursday was your day off,' said Allan. 'Where's Lucy?'

It took a bit of getting used to: the seniors of Byford treated the village like they were its grandparents. No question was too intrusive and no issue was none of their business. 'She's been and gone and coming back. She got the coffee roasters in Warrington to send up a sample of beans for cold drinks.'

'Whatever for?'

Bridget would miss this. The quality of banter in Byford wasn't as sharp as Liverpool (is anywhere?), but it was delivered with a velvet glove sleight of hand that often caught her off guard. When Kat rocked up half an hour later, Bridget was still having four different conversations about the merits of cold coffee in three different parts of the Spinning Room, as well as the merits of the supply teacher covering for Millie Easterby, and should teachers really wear skirts that short?

'Let's get it over with,' said Donna when Bridget asked if she wanted a third coffee. They gathered their things, Bridget double checked that Wendy could be spared, and the three women headed for the lift, until one of them backed off.

'I'll take the stairs. This lift is a bit cosy,' Wendy announced.

'It is a bit,' said Bridget. 'I've never used the service one. Is that any better?'

'If you don't mind travelling on Lancashire's slowest theme park ride,' said Donna. 'It is much bigger, and it saves picking the lock on the partition.'

'Why would you need to pick the lock?' said Bridget, confused. 'It's always been open.'

'I was joking,' said Donna, with no trace of humour in her voice. 'The conspiracy theorists have even infiltrated our Group,' she added, gesturing to Wendy and turning towards the main entrance to head for the service lift.

'You do right to take a break from Facebook,' said Wendy supportively.

'You've lost me,' said Bridget.

Wendy slowed right down, allowing Donna to get ahead. 'I blame that horrible girl, Ciara Daventry. There are comments all over the internet, and Ciara's friends are saying things like "Donna works with miniatures, so she must know how to pick locks." Of course she doesn't!'

'And given that everyone involved seems to have a spare key, it's not relevant,' said Bridget.

'Are you sure that *everyone* has a key?' said Wendy. 'I mean really, really sure?'

'I'm not sure of very much,' said Bridget. She saw the sliding door to the service entrance propped open and wondered if they'd find Jed Holmes lurking inside. Presumably Coffin Joe had left the door open to get some air circulating.

She stopped on the threshold and looked around. Stairs and a steep ramp gave access to the Cowan Theatre's scene dock and backstage area. A (closed) door led to Elysian Meadow Joinery. The fire escape door was right opposite the CCTV camera, as she'd guessed when she watched the video, and that left the lift.

Donna pushed the button, and the doors lurched open. 'I asked Perry about this, and he assured me it's been serviced regularly and that all old lifts jerk a bit. Come on.'

Not only did the lift jerk, it also juddered, rattled and shook alarmingly. Bridget ended up in the far corner, braced against the walls, and the lift was so slow that it might have been steam driven.

They finally arrived at the top floor, and after a moment to get its breath back, the lift shuddered its doors open. Bridget took a deep breath of her own and stepped out, straight into the studio.

She had barely registered anything of the room on Monday morning. Now that she had time to absorb the layout, she realised that she'd only been aware of a fraction of the setup. Metal racks blocked out all but the two windows overlooking the millpond, and the shelves were filled with packets and boxes which looked like 3M3's retail offering, as well as instrument cases and secure packaging for the TV equipment. A couple of desks were littered with more boxes, and scaffolding structures held TV lights which blocked Bridget's view of the heart of the studio: the set.

No, scratch that. *Sets*. Plural. On Monday, she had come in round the back of one set, and that's where she'd seen Tony. The three women had moved silently away from the lift, spreading out, and Bridget headed to the centre so that she could see both sets together.

As she faced them, Tony's last resting place had been on the left, and it looked like it had been gutted by the police and crime scene investigators. The chair was gone, the workbench was clear, and they'd even taken out one of the flats which made up the faux brick backdrop. She took a deep breath and looked at the other set. Donna's set.

Pride of place here had been given to an epic doll's house on its own table, complete with a stately home frontage of pillars and canopies. On a matching workbench to Tony's, components, tools and notes were neatly laid out, presumably ahead of the launch which never happened.

'What a mess,' sighed Donna. 'What a complete shitty mess.'

Forty-One

Wendy moved to console Donna, putting an arm around her shoulder and leading her away from the studio area towards a couple of chairs near the unobstructed windows. Bridget stepped forwards and took their place in front of Tony's workspace and froze to the spot. There was blood and unidentifiable matter *everywhere.* She shuddered and followed the other women away from the sight.

The first thing Bridget did was open the windows. For obvious safety reasons, only the top of the lights was functional, but this room needed as much air blowing through it as possible. She took the third chair and waited for Donna to stop crying, because the tears were flowing freely now.

Wendy sat patiently, leaning into Donna and ready to supply a replacement tissue. Bridget tried to still herself and not think about what she'd seen behind her. It was Wendy who spoke first.

'You don't have to do anything today. Let me show the cleaners round. You don't mind, do you, Bridget?'

'Of course not. Whatever you need.'

'No,' said Donna. 'We need to pack some of the stuff away.' Her smile was as unsteady as the goods lift. 'It's alright for you, Wendy. You've got a nice new job. I've got sod all unless I get some of my gear home and try to figure out what to do next. And there's Hayley to think of.'

The trio fell silent. Hayley had reported to Cairndale Division HQ at ten o'clock, and since then, none of them had heard anything.

'Where shall we start?' said Wendy. 'The Mini Magic Mansion?'

Donna shook her head firmly. 'That monstrosity belongs to 3M3. I want nothing to do with it.'

Bridget pointed to the stately home. 'Is that what you mean, 'cos you'd need a van to take it anyway.'

'Yes,' said Donna. 'Hayley came up with the idea of working through a stately home in different periods, starting with a Jane Austen ballroom.'

'Was Tony doing something similar?'

'Yes. Can you remember, Wendy?'

'A Cornish village station on the Great Western Railway, I think.

Poldark Halt Hayley called it. I told her she'd get in trouble about copyright, but she wouldn't listen.'

'Sounds about right,' said Donna, standing up. 'Can you get my case, Wendy? We'll start with the tools.'

Wendy headed into a corner, and Bridget followed Donna to the workbench. 'Is there anything I can do to help?' asked Bridget.

'Do you know anything about this lot?' said Donna, waving towards the lights and cameras and monitors.

'Not really. Not at all. I know me way round a laboratory, but this is a bit niche.'

Donna picked up what Bridget assumed was a hot glue gun and moved it to a corner of the table, then she picked up some craft knives and put them down again. 'Wendy was telling me that you're taking this private investigation very seriously.'

'I am. For Laura. For Hayley. For Tony.'

'He deserves that, I suppose.'

'Why wouldn't he?'

Donna shook her head. 'That didn't come out right.'

Wendy arrived with a tool chest full of lift out sections and labelled drawers. Donna looked at Wendy and said, 'Tony was having problems, wasn't he? Ever since Hayley got the monitor working.'

'I don't know about that,' said Wendy, looking down at the toolbox rather than meeting Donna's eye.

Donna turned back to Bridget. 'We did rehearsals in Cairndale Civic Hall a couple of weeks ago. Tony was not happy when he saw what he looked like in front of the camera. He did a load of demos on YouTube, but they were all shot from a single angle looking at his hands. 3M3 had three cameras, including a portrait one. That one there. He kept saying that customers would be distracted. I told him to try being a woman.'

Bridget was struggling to keep up. The thought that there were videos out there of Tony's hands at work had momentarily disturbed her equilibrium. 'Sorry? The world would be a better place if all men had to take their turns at being a woman, but I don't get you here.'

'Same as everywhere,' said Donna. 'He could go in front of the camera in any old T-shirt. Hayley and I had to be perfect, and have a wardrobe to match. No bed hair for us.'

Bridget was inclined to agree. Tony was no oil painting, and the few times that Bridget had been caught on HD cameras, she knew how merciless they were. And the banks of lights wouldn't help. On the other hand, she couldn't help but feel she was being distracted. Tony might have been grumpy about his self-image, but that hadn't got him killed. She decided to come at Donna from a different angle.

'Are you sure there's nothing I can do?' she began.

Wendy was more engaged than Donna and pointed to a very rickety set of shelves that could have come from a dystopian drama. 'See all that stuff on the bottom shelf? Could you take it and put it in a couple of those jumbo carriers over there? Then put the carriers by the lift? It's all Donna's personal property. You don't want it here, do you, Donna?'

Donna shook her head and swapped places with Wendy, taking tools from her and slotting them away. Bridget went to the shelves and found herself looking at a whole junk room's worth of online shopping. There were Amazon parcels aplenty, but also a complete index of mid-range fashion brands. Donna was clearly keeping her work wardrobe here. It would be private enough to get changed, she supposed.

Bridget collected a few packets and started placing them in a plastic carrier, like the ones you get in IKEA but woven into a gingham pattern. They crinkled loudly, and she had to stop filling to ask her question. 'Did you see much of the boys next door over the weekend? Tony's brother and the other two?'

To Bridget's annoyance, it was Wendy who answered. 'Not really. We said hello when they first arrived, and Geoff was very accommodating about access. They had to move all their timber through on sack barrows, and he didn't want to get in our way. Once they'd done the heavy stuff, they brought the rest up in the other lift. Jonathan didn't appear until Sunday.' She turned to Donna. 'Didn't he take Tony for a coffee?'

Donna looked up, as if she hadn't been listening. 'What? Oh yes. Jonno came and stared at the case with the engine in it, then when Tony wouldn't show him the locomotive, Jonathan offered to buy him a drink, but Hayley put her foot down, so they went for coffee instead. I'm sure Lucy will remember them.'

Bridget had already checked. No one from 3M3 had spent longer in the Spinning Room than it took to place and collect a takeout order. So where did they go? She filed that away for later, and having filled the first carrier, she took it to the lift. 'There's something you might know, Donna. I've been hearing weird things about Tony and Esther Thornfield. You know about the diorama, yeah?'

This time, Wendy held her tongue. Donna shrugged. 'Not Tony's finest hour. It was cruel, and that diorama was special to Shannon. It reminded her of Andy.'

'And Esther? Did he ever talk about her?'

'No.'

'Yes he did,' said Wendy. 'Don't you remember? The first time we worked late, there was that noise. Hayley said that maybe the Mill was haunted, and Tony said that there were enough witches and vampires, so a few ghosts would fit right in.'

'Oh yes?' said Bridget. This was getting interesting.

'Yes. When I asked what he meant, he said ... what was it now? That's right. "I always said Esther would end up looking like a witch because that's what she is on the inside, and you can take your pick of bloodsuckers." I never got to ask him what he meant because you sent me to get the part-made library.'

'Did you know what he meant by "bloodsuckers", Donna?' asked Bridget casually.

'Coffin Joe and Perry, I guess. The rent on this place wasn't cheap. Isn't cheap. That's another thing to worry about.'

'And did he ever mention Esther in any other way? Or before, when you were together?'

Donna flinched. 'The Tony I lived with ended up as the Tony you met, Bridget, but he wasn't always like that. And no, he didn't dwell on the past. Not until Andy and Shannon split up, and he never mentioned Esther.'

Bridget took a moment to put a large Seasalt package into the second carrier. 'Sorry to ask this, Donna, but just so's I know, where exactly did you go after the summit ended on Sunday?'

Wendy frowned and shook her head, but said nothing. Donna blinked and sighed. 'I went to see if Shannon had got home okay. She asked me in for a drink, but I said no. It had been a long day and it was going to be even worse on the Monday. Don't forget, Bridget, we were totally focused on launching the channel, weren't we, Wendy?'

Wendy looked puzzled. 'I was. You three were pretty distracted with your *third prong*. I could tell. You're right about one thing, though. On Sunday night none of us were thinking about going to the police station on Monday morning.'

Wendy's comment was something Bridget took on board. An entire project, an entire business had been carefully constructed. A ship of commerce had been waiting at the top of the slipway, ready to launch. And then it had blown up. Bridget toted the second carrier, then realised that Donna still hadn't finished answering her question. 'And after Shannon's house?' she asked. 'Where did you go then?'

'What?' said Donna. 'I went for a quick drink in the White Hart, walked around the war memorial to clear my head, then drove back to my room at the Red Rose Hotel and gave thanks that I'd paid extra for one of the new rooms. The ones at the back of the car park.'

'Why's that?'

'Individual aircon.'

Bridget chuckled. 'You're not wrong there, Donna.' The shelf she'd been asked to empty was clear, and Donna was closing the tool case – a really posh one, with wheels and a handle. When the last clip had fastened with a decisive *snap*, she wheeled it towards the lift.

Bridget wandered over to the display table and looked at the mansion. 'Is there anything in it?'

'Let me show you,' said Wendy with a burst of enthusiasm. She reached for the latch holding the front secure and released it, just as Donna realised what they were doing.

'No. Please,' said Donna. Bridget heard her, but Wendy was either medically or selectively deaf to the pleading.

'Here,' said Wendy, pulling back the entire front of the mansion. 'She's a genius.'

Bridget stared. 'You're not wrong.'

As soon as Wendy had revealed the interior of the doll's house, Bridget's eye had naturally been drawn to the darkest space, a room on the middle of three floors. She got a glimpse of books, of a desk with an inlaid leather top and a globe on a stand to the side. And seated at the desk, a beautifully bewhiskered Victorian gentleman.

'Please,' said Donna. 'I'd rather not. This is all the property of 3M3 now, and I'd rather not think about what's going to happen to months of hard work.' She gently removed Wendy's hand from the frontage and started to close it.

Wendy wasn't upset. She was fired up. 'This won't go to waste, Donna. I won't let it. The Mini Magic Mansion is too good to be auctioned off as an asset.' She gripped the left side of her top with her right hand, and her voice projected belief and determination. Seeing her, Bridget remembered that *fan* is short for *fanatic*. Would she have to check Wendy's alibi as well? No. DC Barney Rubble would have been round and seen Wendy's daughter already. And probably her neighbours, too.

As Donna was closing the mansion, Bridget had scanned her eyes over the other rooms – a kitchen, a sumptuous dining room, a bedroom, a parlour, even a bathroom. The largest room had been chosen for Donna's debut in front of the cameras. On the ground floor, an elegant ballroom, with LED chandeliers, a fireplace, a buffet table and delicate chairs, was laid out, the whole event watched over by ancestral portraits.

'Thanks, both of you,' said Donna. 'Getting busy has made a huge difference.' She breathed out and fixed on a smile. 'I'm ready for the cleaners, now. Bridget, can I borrow Wendy again in future? When we know what we're doing?'

'So long as you pay her,' said Bridget. 'Or someone does.'

'Of course.'

'Shall we go back in the twenty-first century lift?' said Bridget.

'You can,' said Wendy. 'I'll take the Hell-evator and put the bags in your car, if you like, Donna?'

'Leave the bags for now,' said Donna. 'If you could take the toolbox and that stack of high-density card down, that would be great. Here's the keys.'

Bridget left them to it and went round the back of the room the long way so that she could avoid looking at Tony's set. As she headed for the partition, something struck her about the Mini Magic Mansion.

The Victorian gentleman hadn't been the only figure on display. Maids in aprons were hard at work in the kitchen, two women in 1960s tweed skirts and twinsets were taking tea in the drawing room, and a maid in a knee-length dress was holding up a towel to hide the modesty of an Art Deco beauty in the gilded bathtub. So where were the dancers? A ballroom of that scale needed at least a dozen empire line frocks and a few Mr Darcys. So where were they?

Forty-Two

The door in the partition was open, and the key was in the studio side of the lock. Through the door, she saw that the Bartons had been busy after she left last night.

As well as the trestles with the layouts of *Carsondale,* one of the sheets of plywood had been moved from the stack and was in the process of being turned into a seriously large display table. Right now, it was an upside-down table, with clamps holding a frame and extra-long legs in position, presumably while the glue dried. When turned upright, it would be almost chest height to Bridget, which must be the right height for a display, even if it would be a pain to work on.

She passed through and was about to call the lift when her phone rang. An actual call. Must be someone over thirty. She checked that there was no one around then looked at the screen. It was Laura.

'Hi. What's happened?'

There was a ragged inhalation at the other end. The sweat which had been a steady trickle down Bridget's back in the studio broke out in other places. She closed her eyes and focused on listening.

'They've let her go,' began Laura, then she stopped and there was a loud sniffle. 'They've let her go, Bridge, but she's been released under investigation. They think she did it and they're waiting to get more proof before they charge her. I can't believe it! Hayley is *not* a killer. No way.'

'Take it easy, Laura. It's okay. Where are you?'

'At Hayley's house in town. She's getting changed upstairs. I had to call someone who believes in her.'

The one thing Bridget believed right now was that Hayley Horst was a better actress than the *Malvern Observer* had given her credit for in the only online review available to Google. 'What's happened?'

'I don't know. I really don't know. I think she's ashamed to tell me. Look, is there any chance you could come round? I know it's a lot to ask, but I've got to head off and pick up the kids from Stafford services. Apparently they've had enough of Daddy and someone told them there's a school trip tomorrow. I think my daughter has a future as a revolutionary.' There was another pause, another ragged breath.

'I'm sorry. Now I'm rambling.'

'Not surprised, Laura. I'd rather you rambled at me than bottled it up. I'm on me way down to the Spinning Room right now, and if there's no coach party on the horizon, I'll get straight over. Can you hang on for twenty minutes?'

'Yes. Thank you so much, Bridget.'

'Hold tight, girl.'

Bridget took the first staircase two at a time, then slowed down. 'No point in melting,' she told a disapproving Easterby, watching her from the landing. Then she backed up. Not just any Easterby – Donna Ramsey had reproduced this exact portrait in one of the rooms of the Mini Magic Mansion. Was there no end to the woman's talents?

Back in the Spinning Room, Bridget breezed past a growing queue of customers and buttonholed Lucy. 'Something's come up. It looks like Liz Swindlehurst is gunning for Hayley, and I need to get over to Cairndale.'

Lucy's eyes bulged. 'Where's Wendy? Kat's gone on her break.'

Bridget turned round. 'There. Right behind me. See you later.'

There was no parking outside Hayley's house. Not with a proper railway station round the corner. Bridget circled the war memorial in Midland Square a couple of times and tried driving up towards the old goods yard. In the end, she drove into one of the drop off/pick up spots outside the station and set a thirty-minute timer on her phone.

The drive down from Byford had done little more than dry the sweat on her back, and hadn't reached the other bits, especially her boobs. This bra needed to go. It really did. There wasn't even a shady side of the street to walk up, so she tried to be zen about the weather and pretend she was on holiday. Didn't work.

Hayley's house was in the north-eastern corner of the square, one of a row of houses built for the stationmaster and other traitors to the working class who'd taken the management shilling and left the real workers to find rooms in the slum cottages. Bridget shook her grandfather's lecture out of her ears and almost missed who was lurking down the alley.

Her pet ferret was hiding there, just out of sight and taking advantage of the shade. She pivoted away from Hayley's front door and marched round the corner. 'Oy, Jed. What in God's name are you playing at?'

'Just keeping an eye on things,' he said. As usual, there was a mixture of guilt and defiance on his face. If he was successful in his chosen career, would there be a showdown between the two? 'The police statement said she'd been released under investigation, so she's still the prime suspect. Just keeping an eye on who comes and goes. Like you've just done.'

'How did you even find her address?'

He shrugged. 'Company directors have to list their address, if you know where to look and have the right subscriptions.'

Jed's mission was hot, tiring and probably extremely boring, not to mention risky. He was right about Hayley being the prime suspect, though. In which case, where was the alpha ferret? 'Why are you doing this and not Bradley Nicol?'

'Brad doesn't want to get in trouble by naming a suspect before they're charged. That ogre Swindlehurst has already warned him off.'

Bridget had already nudged Jed backwards so that she could get out of the sun. She took another step towards him. 'Do you have a problem with all women, Jed, or just assertive ones?'

He went as red as the baking bricks out on the square. 'Doesn't she scare you?'

'No, because I haven't done anything wrong and because I'm happy to leave the crappy jobs to her and get on with making coffee in peace.'

Bridget had been about to say *Because I'm happy being who I am*, but she'd changed her mind. Right here in this dirty alleyway, confronting a junior sexist, she wasn't happy being who she was at all. There was something wrong inside her, and Jed Holmes wasn't helping her figure it out. 'The world's changed, Jed. You can get with the programme and realise that women can be detective inspectors and run businesses, or you can join the dark side. The *real* dark side, not the one I get tagged with, 'cos there's a big difference.'

He blinked. If he had somewhere to go, he might have run. He blinked again. 'I know that.'

'Good. So why *are* you here if you can't write about her?'

'If they do charge Hayley and it goes to trial, the more background we can pursue the better.'

It made sense. 'She won't be having any more visitors after me, and you're not getting paid, are you? If you're not gonna doorstep her, I'd get back to lectures if I were you.'

'Thanks. Good idea.'

She left him to reflect on his place in the pecking order and went round to knock on Hayley's door.

Laura ushered her in and shut the door, then leaned in to whisper. 'Thanks for coming, Bridget. I need to go, and she's still not told me what's going on.'

Bridget nodded, and Laura squeezed past Bridget to get away. 'In here,' came Hayley's voice from the back.

This house was a good ten per cent bigger than No 4 Midland Terrace in all directions, and the back had been extended recently to give the inside-outside space that everyone seemed to crave these days. Most of the time, a north-facing extension would be disappointing, but not today. Right now it was a blessed relief.

Hayley, wearing a plain maxi dress, was sitting on a well-padded chair next to a bistro table with a jug of fresh lemonade. Or freshly decanted lemonade. She didn't make the effort to get up, and pointed to the matching chair. Bridget sat down and Hayley poured her a drink.

As well as the plain dress, Hayley was sporting giant sunglasses. When she'd served the lemonade, the black lenses settled on Bridget's face, unmoving and alien. The eyes behind the disguise must have seen what they were looking for, and Hayley took the glasses off.

'Sorry,' said Hayley. 'I look a total mess and I think I'm beyond caring.'

Her eyes were red raw, from crying, from exhaustion and from fear. If she'd put on her warpaint to face the police, it had all gone now.

'You've got to get your priorities right,' said Bridget. 'I won't ask how you're bearing up, because I can see that for myself. They haven't charged you, right?'

Hayley shook her head. 'Not yet. But they will. And if they don't, it will only be because of lack of evidence, not because they think I'm innocent.'

In a big city, when you lived and moved through communities where a visit to the cops was routine, this was no big deal. You shrug, you move on. Not here. Not in Cairndale and definitely not in Byford:

once tagged as the prime suspect, you would remain guilty until proven innocent.

Forty-Three

Bridget was loving the patio furniture, if nothing else. The arms on the chair were wide enough to move around without bruising her hips and the cushion had some weird filling that took all the pressure off her bum. She tried not to think about whether to source some for the Mill and focused on the woman in front of her. 'Talk me through what happened, Hayley.'

'They gave me a chance, you know. Before the interview, DS Gartside had a meeting with Abi. He told her that they had new information, and did I want to change my statement? I made a big mistake. I said no. And then he slowly ripped me apart while that kid, DC Higham, looked on. She kept shoving the box of tissues at me, pushing me to break down and pretending to be sympathetic. That bitch Swindlehurst was in the observation room, sending Gartside messages. He barely looked at me and kept reading things from his iPad.' She closed her eyes and tried to breathe normally. It wasn't working.

'What did they say?' asked Bridget gently. 'You only have to tell me once, and I'll tell Laura if you like.'

Hayley shook her head. 'If only I'd called them on Sunday.'

Alarm bells were ringing in Bridget's head. 'Why's that?'

Hayley forced herself to sit up straight, and she spoke to the climbing plant behind Bridget's shoulder. 'First they hit me with the key worker insurance policy I'd taken out on Friday. They had a recording of my conversation with the broker, asking about sudden death payouts. It was to protect us, Bridget! I was looking after *all* of our interests.'

'Lucy's got one, too. I know that because I had to fill in a questionnaire. It's no biggie. What about Sunday?'

'I went back. Late. I saw the lights on in the studio and went up to see him, but I was too late. He was already dead. There was nothing I could do.'

A cloud moved over the sun, only it didn't because there wasn't a cloud in the sky. Whatever the weather, the courtyard was now plunged in darkness, and Bridget's sweat was crystallising into ice.

'Hayley! Tell me you didn't. Tell me they can't prove it.'

Hayley shook her head, and more tears came. Her voice was a hoarse whisper. 'I wish I could, Bridget. I wish I could say that I didn't go up there and that I didn't leave a size seven footprint in the blood.' She looked up and made eye contact. 'I wish I could hold it against you, Bridget, I really do. It's your fault I'm in this mess.'

Bridget bit back a sarcastic response and let her silence do the talking, along with the most open and sympathetic expression she could muster.

Hayley shivered and slurped half a glass of lemonade so quickly that some went down the wrong way and she broke into a coughing fit. Bridget instinctively put a hand onto her shoulder, and the physical contact made Hayley jump, turning the coughs into sobs. Bridget withdrew her hand and waited.

Hayley found a clean tissue in a hidden pocket of her dress and blew her nose several times, pausing to examine the tissue. Yeuch. Who does *that*? Apart from men, obviously.

Finally, Hayley seemed to be lapsing into silence, and Bridget said, 'Go on. Finish it off, Hayley.'

'I went into the Mill very early on Monday, but not early enough. You'd beaten me to it and called the police. If you hadn't stopped over in Liverpool, I would have been the one to "find" him, and I could have left fingerprints and footprints and DNA all over the studio and no one would have questioned it.'

Bridget didn't really want the lemonade. It cut her throat without really quenching her thirst, and left a sugary aftertaste. She passed Hayley a clean tissue from her bag and took a few sips to give herself some thinking time.

Hayley didn't need to act scared and broken because she was clearly both of those things. But was she also guilty of murder? Bridget looked up, and without the sun in her line of sight to blind her, the sky was a perfect blue. What she'd just heard had changed everything. Hayley might still be innocent, or she might be a monster. Either way, Bridget wasn't working for Laura any more. She was working one hundred per cent for the memory of Anthony Carson.

She put down her glass, grateful at least for its rehydrating properties. 'Why didn't you call the police on Sunday, Hayley? Why did you leave him there and what did you really do?'

There was a flick of the eyes around the yard. Hayley was about to lie or to miss something out. 'I had to check, Bridget. Once, in Leyland, he set up a complete crime scene in the store room. Life size with a realistic mannequin. Poor Shannon thought it was Andy. She screamed the place down and wet herself. It was beyond humiliating. I had to get closer to see whether he'd done the same.'

Bridget had seen her share of cinematic gore, and the best was beyond realistic. No wonder Hayley hadn't been sure. 'How close did you get?'

'Close enough for the smell to hit me. You can't fake that. You know what I mean.'

She did. What had hit her nostrils on Monday morning was not something you could spray out of a can. 'Then what?'

'It was beyond scary, Bridget. I ran out of the studio and down that fire escape like, I don't know, like there was a shotgun-wielding maniac on the loose. I can't believe I didn't break my neck, because then I'd have been found without the gun.'

Even though it was perverse, Bridget could see the thought behind it. *I'd rather be dead and innocent than alive and everyone pointing the guilty finger.*

Before she could go any further, Hayley continued. 'I genuinely think I had a … *fugue*. That's what Abi called it. A fugue. The next thing I knew, I was in the car and driving out of the village. There was a minibus coming too fast in the opposite direction, and I had to do an emergency stop. That was when I came to.'

'Okay, Hayley. I get that. You're sitting in your car in the middle of nowhere and your brain suddenly kicks in. Must have been awful.'

'You've no … I suppose you do. Only you called the police, and I didn't.'

Hayley was struggling. She was hiding something. 'Why was that? Why didn't you call them?'

'Because I still wasn't thinking straight, that's why. Oh, Bridget, I wish I had called them, but I didn't. Instead, I came up with the idea of arriving early on Monday. He was dead. There was nothing I could do.'

Bridget accepted that for now. 'What happened next?'

'Like I told you, I drove out of Cairndale and down to Cowan Sands. I knew there would have been parties on a warm night like that, and I was right. There were still a couple of fires alight on the beach, waiting for the tide to come in. I took my clothes off and burnt them.'

'You did what?'

'Took my clothes off. Fed them into the fire. Good job I try to wear natural fibres.'

Bridget felt her eyes bulging. She'd never heard something so bizarre in her life. Apart from when she found Son Ji in the lab, naked and wrapped in cling film, "No fibres!" was all he said to her. He had a bit more to say to the disciplinary board, but that was after Bridget had left.

'Let me get this right,' she told Hayley. 'It's almost midnight, and you're standing on a beach getting naked with who knows who lurking in the sand dunes?'

Hayley gave her a half-sneer, the one that says *You what?* 'Of course not. I had my gym bag in the car. The only problem was the shoes. You'd think that leather would burn. It was stupid, but there I was worrying about leaving melted plastic soles and charred leather. The rest all went up in smoke.'

'Then what did you do?'

'I went for a run along the beach.'

It was a good job Bridget didn't have any lemonade in her mouth or she'd have snorted it all over the table. 'A run?'

'Nature's way of repurposing adrenaline. I ran until I was exhausted, then I went home and collapsed on the couch until the alarm went off. If I hadn't had that shower, I still might have beaten you to the Mill.'

Forty-Four

Bridget sat back and tried to digest what she'd just heard, and more importantly, what she'd not heard, and in that moment of reflection, something struck her about where she was, so naturally she blurted it out. 'Your yard's quite noisy, isn't it?'

'I'm sorry?' said Hayley, who'd also gone off into a world of her own.

'Your yard. You can hear the road and other stuff.'

Hayley looked at the back wall, made from the cheapest brick available to the Victorian builders and not in the best of health. 'I suppose you can. In the evenings, you can hear the through trains as well. Almost as loud as an aeroplane.' She put her lemonade down. 'Is that like a clue or something?'

It wasn't a clue – or not a clue in this mystery, anyway. It was the realisation that No 4 Midland Terrace in Byford was free of continuous road noise. Before Bridget could think of a suitably sphinx-like response, the front doorbell echoed from the house. 'I'll get that. Could be a ferret.'

'A ferret …?'

Bridget was up and striding through the kitchen. There was no glass in Hayley's front door to spy on the visitor, so she put the chain on and cracked it open a fraction. 'Oh, it's you.'

'I could say the same,' said Abi Tennant. 'Come on then, let me in.'

Why are those door chains always so much easier to put on than get off, especially after the sunlight bouncing off the cars had dazzled her and when Hayley's hallway was so dark? Job done, Bridget opened the door and Abi slipped in.

'Has she told you about the shitshow this morning?' asked the lawyer, shaking her head. 'It's not often I want to slap ma private clients. Legal Aid ones, yes, but I thought she'd have had more sense than keep something like that back from me.' She sighed, and Bridget could see that the day had taken its toll even on the younger, hyper-fit woman.

'She told me about the insurance policy and about going back to the studio on Sunday night,' said Bridget. 'And there's more, isn't there?'

Abi put down her knapsack and unbuttoned the jacket of her trouser suit. She put her hands round the back and looked like she was lifting the fabric of her blouse away from sweaty skin. Bridget *really* hated hot weather. After a grimace, Abi's face settled into an interview-room blank mask. 'I don't know what you mean, Bridget.'

So that was how Abi was going to play it. Fair enough. 'You'll be wanting to speak to your *client* alone, then. I'll just grab me bag and ask to use the loo.'

Before she knew what was happening, Abi's hand had shot out like a snake and snatched Bridget's arm, right on the skull tattoo. 'I need everything you've got—'

Bridget broke the grip without thinking about it, just like she'd been taught, and she used the momentum to slam Abigail Tennant into the front door. 'Don't you *ever* do that again.'

Abi was in shock. And rattled. She might be fit, but there was nothing of her, and she'd had the full force of Bridget's shoulders propelling her.

'What the—' she began, but Bridget was in her face.

'No one touches me like that. Not even Lucy. Understand?'

'I … I'm sorry, Bridget. It was unprofessional.'

'Sod that. It was just plain *wrong*, Abi.' She backed away. 'If I hear anything that might help Hayley out, you'll be the first to know about it, but right now, it doesn't look good from where I'm standing.' She paused, then took another step backwards. 'You okay?'

'Aye. Nae bother.'

Bridget nodded and went for her bag. Out in the yard, Hayley hadn't moved and either hadn't heard the confrontation or didn't care. 'I'll be in touch,' said Bridget. 'You take care, yeah?'

Hayley looked utterly miserable, like all the goodness had been bleached out of her life and left her white and fraying at the edges. Bridget headed upstairs and couldn't help peeking in the main bedroom. *So they* have *been here*, she thought. The downstairs was clean, ordered and a beacon of middle-class taste. Up here it was different.

Tracey Kenyon might be careful, but when it came to a property search, she was nothing if not meticulous. Even the false front to the old fire had been removed and placed neatly to the side. They hadn't found the gun there, though, had they? No. It had been chucked into the millpond. Bridget managed not to disturb the detached bath panel and enjoyed a moment of cool relief. Who next? She got up, flushed and started washing her hands.

She flapped them dry (there being no paper towels to use) and checked her phone. *Shit*. Only two minutes left on the car – and it was market day, so there would be a full team of traffic wardens up from Lancaster. There was also a message from Lucy.

She slipped downstairs and out of the house without saying any further goodbyes and read Lucy's message as she crossed Midland Square. Or tried to read it. The shady yard and dark interior had lulled her into forgetting that it was proper scorchio outside. Squinting, she ducked behind the war memorial and just about made out the words. *Lili is shorthanded. We're good. Can you go to MSq for an hour? LX.* She reached the van just as a warden appeared up Bridge Street. Phew.

The journey from Midland Square to Market Square was three minutes on foot, four if you paused to admire the view down the river. The old bridge had been closed to motor vehicles for years now, and Bridget headed in the opposite direction to work her way round to the A6. As soon as her phone had bonded with the car, she called Lucy.

'Who's in the Mill today?' she demanded.

'How's Hayley?' came straight back at her.

'In bits and looking guilty. Who's in the Mill?'

Lucy told her, and Bridget announced, 'Well, if I'm being exiled to Market Square, you'll have to talk to them.'

Lucy's voice quivered. 'Me?'

'Yes you. I'll message when the lunchtime rush is over.'

The lights turned green, and Bridget turned onto the main road, heading for the modern bridge and passing Divisional HQ on the way. At least Hayley hadn't had far to walk after being released by the bizzies. Scant comfort.

'What's up, Coach?' said Kat as she shot past with a toastie (handmade by Wendy, loved by the customers and technically in breach of the food hygiene regulations).

'Stop calling me ... never mind,' responded Lucy to Katarina's disappearing back. She looked down at the call she'd just ended with Bridget and the screen went dark without giving her a reprieve. As soon as the rush was over, she'd have to do it. After all, it was her who had pushed Bridget into investigating Tony's murder, so she couldn't really complain, could she?

'You okay, Luce?' said the next customer. 'I'd tell you that worse things happen at sea, but I guess that's not true.'

'Sod off, Mike,' said Lucy cheerfully. 'What can I get you? Oh, hang on, I know what I can get you.'

Lucy went to the till and stabbed her way through the onscreen options until the printer woke up and dispensed a good six inches of paper. When the built in guillotine had cut off the mini document, Lucy snatched it and presented it to Mike Mason. 'Your overdue account. How's that for starters?'

'Sorry, Lucy, you know what it's like. I don't carry cash and the business credit card is sitting on the kitchen table at home.'

'Ah. What a terrible shame.'

Kat breezed back carrying some empties, her long legs making the apron flap. 'You trying to get Mike to pay his bill? Good luck with that.' She carried on into the kitchen and Lucy felt like sticking her tongue out. How Bridget had the patience, she didn't know.

At some point in the past, when Feargal Hulme had done some refurbishments during his tenure of the café, he'd had a new counter put in, one that suited his and Katarina's height. It was not working for Lucy at all. If Mina Clarke-Desai ever decided to get her hands dirty in the business, she'd need stilts or a personal walkway behind the coffee machine. Lucy hitched herself up and leaned forwards. 'It's terrible, isn't it, the way that technology rushes past you older people.'

Mike knew he was being wound up, like a man standing in a desert who's been shot at but doesn't know where the sniper is. Would he object to being described as old or being characterised as a technophobe? Vanity won out in the end. 'I'm not old!'

'Really? Because your memory must be slipping. I saw you in the General Stores this morning, paying for your sandwiches using your phone. It's time you settled your bill, Mike. Just bite the bullet.'

'But that's my personal account!'

'Which is a good job, because none of what you've spent here is a legitimate business expense. I'll just get the card reader.'

Mike laughed and took out his phone. As the transaction went through, he said, 'I rang a guy I know from Young Farmers. He tried going into home-made butter but his wife left him. Serves him right for playing away with a pharmacist. I mean, what's he gonna get from that? Free Viagra? He should have gone with a vet. Saved himself a fortune then.'

Early in her relationship with Tom, Lucy had discovered that there was a piece of his heart buried at Rooksnest Farm. No, not buried, *planted* there and watered with childhood memories. There had been a lot of running wild with his cousins and a lot of hard work, too. Despite him growing up in York, that made Tom a hybrid, and Lucy was very much a city girl. She suspected that she'd *never* understand farmers.

'You've lost me,' she told Mike as she got his order ready. 'What has his fling with a pharmacist got to do with him making butter?'

Mike looked like she'd suddenly broken into Italian. He shook his head and replied, 'He wasn't going to make the butter, was he? That was his wife's job. Anyway, he's out of dairy altogether now. Thinking of going into holiday lodges or glamping.' A misty-eyed look took him away from Byford for a moment. 'Nah. Never get planning permission here. Right. He's selling a proper milk separator. Perfect for ice cream. Have you spoken to the Dark Angel yet?'

'I'll get back to you on that, Mike. While you've got your phone out, how about paying for your order now?'

A look of horror came over him. 'When I can get credit? Never. Put them on my account and don't leave it too long before you talk to Bridget.'

Being a farmer, Mike was also early, and the lunchtime rush followed him. Not that it compared with the Cairndale branch, where office workers made lunchtime the busiest part of the day, and with today being market day, Lucy had had no option but send Bridget to help Lilianna out. Or she could have gone herself. Given her next job, she was beginning to regret her choices. When Wendy came back from her break, and the rush was definitely over, Lucy reluctantly took off her apron and told them she was heading upstairs. 'Wish me luck,' she told Kat.

'Good luck, Coach. What for?'

Lucy didn't tell her and took the stairs as another way of postponing the inevitable.

She worked her way through the craft village, including the dark and shuttered frontage of Turn the Paige. Around the corner and tucked in next to the fire escape she stopped in front of Esther Thornfield's studio and took a deep breath. You got a measure of the owner from the notice on the door.

Esther Thornfield RA
Artist
Commissions considered.
No Portraits.
Works for sale are in the windows.
Knock if serious.

Lucy knocked.

Forty-Five

'Oh good. She's out,' Lucy said to herself.

A voice from behind made her jump. 'No I'm not. I'm here, and why would you come up to see someone and be glad they're not around? Hmm? You know, Lucinda, you really do remind me of Alice, and not just because of the pictures.'

On her first proper night out in Southport, Lucy had been talked into wearing an Alice costume. Well, not so much *talked into* as plied with grappa until she thought it was a good idea. It was also pretty much a metaphor for her life since walking into Giuseppi's Gelateria for an interview and meeting the ultimate Mad Hatter: Bridget Gorrigan.

'Occupational hazard,' said Lucy, with no real idea what she was talking about. Resembling fairy story characters was not remotely an occupational hazard of espresso making. Except at Halloween. She took a deep breath and forced herself to smile. And not in a Cheshire Cat way.

'Missed you in the café today,' she announced, stepping aside to let Esther get to the door.

'That's because I'm doing precisely what you think I'm doing: avoiding Bridget. I suppose she's sent you in her place.'

Lucy had already ignored one insult (being called *Lucinda*). This was too much. 'We're in this together, and I can't see why you'd avoid us. Bridget's gone to see Hayley, as it happens. Have you heard the news?'

Esther's default expression was a mixture of unhappiness and disappointment with how she found the world. Her problem, not Lucy's. Today's blend of bile was slightly different – it had an undercurrent of worry seasoned with trouble. 'If you mean that Hayley is still Swindlehurst's prime suspect, then yes. It's taken a terrible toll on poor Laura, I've heard. That's what Shannon says.'

A couple of seniors who really should wear their hearing aids had arrived at the furniture upcycling workshop and were complaining about the prices. Esther looked at the corner, around which they might appear at any second. She took out a key and opened the door. 'You'd better come in.'

Esther's studio had been carved out to take advantage of two windows, something the overall square footage didn't merit. It gave her access to lots of light, and Lucy knew enough about painting to appreciate that artists prefer to have north-facing illumination. Funny how it rarely manifested in Esther's work. While Esther took her coat off (why a coat in this weather?) and put the kettle on, Lucy looked around.

The image she'd seen on her phone, the one about Easter in St Peter's, didn't do justice to the size or impact of Esther's output. The one online had been numbered *XIII*, and there were half a dozen others hanging in the studio. None of them showed the effect of the brilliant stained glass on the intricate stonework. Maybe Esther had only been allowed to paint at night.

'I don't suppose you want tea?' said the artist.

'No thanks. It's good of you to come down and buy your drinks when you've got a kettle. Not everyone does.'

'Very diplomatic, Lucy. Not only can I afford your prices, I actually like your coffee. It gets up your nose and slaps your brain around.'

'That's a very original endorsement. I might use it one day.'

Esther had a paint-stained sink in one corner and Lucy peered at the notice pinned above it. It was bizarre – a painting of a letter, with the Ford Mill logo rendered in meticulous, realistic detail. Esther saw her looking and said, 'It's my final warning from Perry. No more white spirit to go down the drain. I threw the original away and had to paint that as a reminder to myself. He didn't say anything about tea leaves, though.'

With that, Esther emptied a multicoloured teapot into the sink and rinsed out the loose leaves. She kept her back to Lucy while she made tea, and while she did, Lucy realised that there was only one seat in the room – a stool in front of the easel. She planted her feet apart and stood up straight. This was not a moment for slouching.

Esther left the tea to brew and turned round to fire her opening shot. 'I still don't see why you and Ms Gorrigan have got involved in this business. I'm as grateful as anyone that Millie Easterby wasn't buried unavenged, but Tony Carson deserved what he got.'

Whoa, that's radical, thought Lucy. She tilted her head. 'Why don't you tell me what you really think, Esther.'

'I assume that was sarcasm. It doesn't become you. Unlike that shade of red in your shirt. I can see why you chose the colour: it makes you look both paler and more exotic at the same time.'

Lucy hadn't felt this bamboozled since they'd had a guest lecturer at university in Milan. He was talking about the ethics of business from a post-Marxist perspective and it was then that Lucia Maria Berardi realised her Italian wasn't as deep as she'd thought. She'd survived that lecture by muttering *Whatever* under her breath and getting her brother to write the paper, and that brought her back to Tony Carson.

'Jonathan Carson has lost a brother, Esther – I'm sure you know that I did, too. Mrs Carson has lost a son, like Mama did. If Hayley is innocent, Laura will lose a sister and Shannon a friend. Donna's already lost one business partner and might lose another. In a murder case, the dead body is only the first victim, never the last.'

'Was your brother a scheming, vicious little boy given too much power, Lucy? For your sake, I hope not, because then you'll have been a victim *before* he died and not just after the fact, like Shannon, Donna, Hayley and, yes, me, were all Tony's victims, and that's only the people I know personally. If Anthony Carson didn't pull the wings off flies when he was little, I'd be shocked, because that's what he specialised in as an adult. Metaphorically speaking.'

Such hate. Such contempt for a life lost. Lucy had barely met the man and had no opinion about him. That was Bridget's case to argue, and in the face of Esther's hostility, Lucy stuck to the facts.

'I was talking to Kat this morning, and she said that you live just upstream from Water Cottage, on the other side of the little wood, so even though your drive is miles away, you don't live far from the Mill.'

'That's correct.'

'Did you see or hear anything on Sunday night?'

'No. I was too busy shooting Tony Carson.'

Lucy didn't flinch. 'Were you at home all evening?'

'I've just told you. I was out. Breaking into Water Cottage and stealing Joseph's shotgun.'

As a strategy, Lucy couldn't fault it. Much better than a *No comment*. She tried a different approach. 'You said there might be victims you don't know personally. Did you have anyone in mind? Would you include Jonathan Carson on that list?'

'That depends on how sentimental he is.'

'Oh yes?'

Esther finally poured her tea – something she had in common with Tom. If you can't stand a spoon up, it's not strong enough. She added a drop of milk and stirred with the end of a paint brush. Now, Tom would never do *that*. 'When the police searched Hayley's house, I presume they were looking for the gun. I believe they were also looking for a model engine.'

'The *City of Lancaster*. Yes. Tony inherited it from his grandfather.'

'Mmm. Well, whatever was stolen from that empty case in the studio, it wasn't the *City of Lancaster*. It didn't exist, and hasn't existed for a quarter of a century.'

Esther leaned back on the sink and brought her mug up to her mouth, keeping her eyes on Lucy, a Lucy who suddenly knew why Tom always took a break when interviews threw up new questions. She struggled to put them in order. *How did you know about the empty case? What happened to the locomotive twenty-five years ago? How well did you know Tony in London?*

What Lucy hadn't counted on was the thudding of large feet across the wooden floors of the craft village and a knock on the door. 'Coach? You in there?' said a breathless Kat. 'You're needed. Incoming tourists.'

Damn. Damn and double damn. 'Coming.'

'Off you go then,' said the artist.

'Thanks, Esther,' Lucy responded automatically. *Sometimes I wish I hadn't been brought up to be so polite,* she thought. Across the studio, Esther Thornfield was clutching her mug of tea to her chest and giving Lucy her best Cheshire Cat impersonation.

Forty-Six

No one had yet moved into the flat over the Cairndale shop, so the rear parking space was empty, and Bridget slipped into the building via the propped-open rear door. Inside the café, Lilianna was working flat out on her own, and the pile of cups next to the machine was getting dangerously low.

'You are Saint Bridget,' declared Lili. 'You take over here, and I start sort. Yes?'

'Is there a spare apron?'

Lili grabbed a tray in one hand and chucked Bridget an apron with the other. Bridget started tying the cord and smiled at the next customer. 'What can I get you?'

Twenty minutes later, they were just about holding their own when the other barista returned from his break. Twenty minutes after that, Lili decided it was safe enough for her to take a few minutes.

Bridget was still driving the espresso machine when the open door wafted some of Lili's cigarette smoke through the kitchen. Yeuch. 'Raymond, close the back door, will you?' she shouted, but the smell had triggered something in Bridget's brain. It promised nothing good, but there was a thought in there somewhere, trying to get out. She paused, one portafilter in each hand and tried to excavate the idea. Nope. She knocked the grounds into the bin and carried on.

When the lunchtime trade thinned out, Lili declared that she and Raymond could cope on their own and that Bridget could go. When Bridget passed her the apron, Lili didn't move out of the way. Instead, she slapped the apron on the counter and said, 'This is what happens when big girls are not doing their job.'

Lilianna's English was calibrated to the inverse rate of her heartbeat

– the more stressed she was, the worse it got. Bridget didn't mind being referred to as a *big girl* when Lili was speaking. Not only was there a language issue, even Lucy looked well-padded next to the ninja barista from Wroclaw. As for the rest of the sentence …

'You've got me there, Lili. What was that again?'

Lilianna risked a broken wrist by prodding a finger towards Bridget's chest, drawing it back at the last moment. 'We need you here, Brid-get. And in Byford. You are the Boss. I am not. You cannot leave me with only Raymond and lazy Katarina.'

No one could match Lili's work rate. No one. Not even Lucy with the Chemical Brothers in her earphones worked at Lili's pace. That didn't give her the right to disrespect Bridget's duckling though. Bridget eased Lili out of the way using her chest and a smile. 'Kat's a hard worker, Lili. So long as you give her the right incentives. And my place is in Southport. With the ice cream.'

'You will see,' said Lili, cryptically. Or maybe literally. It was hard to tell, which was kinda cryptic in its own right. Bridget made it back to the van and still had no idea who she needed to see next. What would a real detective do? They would be proactive, that's what they'd do, and that's what Bridget would have done if Mina Desai hadn't called at that moment.

'Lucy has a message for you,' announced Mina. 'And so do I.'

'Great. Why can't Luce give me the message herself?'

'Because she is coping with a coach party and your assistant has threatened to walk out if Lucy uses her phone in the café when she is not allowed.'

'Does she want me back there? That's Lucy, not Kat.'

'No. Lucy says she has things under control. She also said something very garbled about an engine not existing? A model train?'

Bridget was stumped for a second. 'Was that the *City of Lancaster*?'

'Yes. Someone called Esmeralda said that it hasn't existed for twenty-five years. I have no idea what this means.'

'I do. Well, I understand the message. Thanks.'

'A pleasure. Now for my message. Do you understand rights issues?'

'Women's rights? I've got a good grip on them. Not so hot on animal rights.'

There was an audible sigh. 'Are you sitting comfortably?'

'No. It's hotter than Mumbai in here.'

'Given that it is monsoon season in Bombay right now, you could be right. Open a window and I'll begin.'

When Mina had finished her lesson in corporate finance, Bridget couldn't wait any longer. She started the engine, closed the window and put her face by the air vents. She took a minute until the compressors were at full blast then switched the engine off. She flicked through her phone and placed a call. It was answered straight away, and by a real person, not a menu of options.

'Carson Metrics, how can I help you?'

'I'm sorry to bother you, but could you put me through to Mr Carson's office?'

Bridget heard the sniff down the line. 'Who shall I say is calling? We're not taking press calls.'

'Of course not. I know this is a really difficult time, but I'm a friend of Tony Carson's from before. From Leyland Films, and I wanted to send my condolences and ask about the funeral. I wouldn't *dream* of asking for Jonathan's contact details, but I wondered if he was up to having a quick word.'

The voice on the line was still guarded. 'I've got your number on the screen. What did you say your name was?'

'I didn't, and it's Bridget Gorrigan.'

'Then I'm sorry, Bridget, but Mr Carson's taken the week off. I send him an email at the end of every day, so I'll put your details in it, okay?'

'That would be very kind. Thank you.'

That settled it. Jonathan Carson would be very annoyed when he saw that she'd pretended to be from Leyland Films, but it wouldn't matter by then. If he wasn't at work, in the Mill or with the police, then he'd be at home. Two minutes later she'd made her first, tentative trade with the Devil. In return for a promise of free coffee, Jed Holmes messaged her Jonathan Carson's home address.

The road to Aldhaven leaves Market Square, dips down and passes under the railway bridge before skirting the Ashes Estate, where many of Abi Tennant's clients lived. Once past the expanse of houses, you're in another world and getting closer to the sea. To Bridget's right, the softer ground of Cowan Sands stretched away, presumably now concealing Hayley's half-burned shoes.

Ahead of the van, woods clung to the firmer south shore and hid the village of Aldhaven, named by Vikings. When they'd first arrived, it had been *Newhaven*, but time and commerce took them upstream to found the harbour at Cairndale, leaving Aldhaven to be neglected until the fishermen's cottages became *quaint* and the land became *desirable*. The housing here was even more expensive than Byford when it had a sea view.

The satnav directed Bridget away from the village centre and up a steep road lined with pre-WWI villas, then round a bend and down a track. She slowed to a stop. 'Wow,' she announced. 'Now that I was *not* expecting. If it's got a sea view and the roof doesn't leak, then it's an extra zero on the price.'

Tucked in behind the Victorian and Edwardian villas, someone had carved a plot out of the hill during the 1960s and built a Modernist's dream house, all exposed glass, concrete pillars and (yes) a flat roof. Who puts a flat roof on a house in the dampest corner of a wet county? Maybe it was the father of the architect who Tom Morton was always going on about – the Spanish guy who did the nick.

She drove slowly along a track with rock on one side and a steep drop on the other, and then into an open space which sloped alarmingly and which she wouldn't have trusted her last car with. That handbrake would never have held. She carefully executed a seven-point turn, ready for a quick getaway, and by the time she'd finished, Jonathan Carson was standing at his front door, arms folded and a thunderous scowl on his face.

She killed the engine, and the aircon died with it. How long would it be before people wore diving suits with personal aircon attached, she wondered. She grabbed her phone and opened the door.

Jonathan waited until she was in hailing distance before he spoke. 'What do you want?'

Short, blunt and shorn of unnecessary curiosity. No questions about how she knew where he'd be or how she'd found him. Bridget returned the favour. 'I wanna talk about Sunday night. Your second visit. I've seen the CCTV, Jonathan.'

'Good for you.'

The rumpled suit from the other day was gone, replaced by dad chinos and a linen shirt. He hadn't changed out of his grief, though. He still wore that as heavily as a winter greatcoat. Bridget glanced around for some shade to stand in. No chance. Jonathan was protected by a canopy, but she was in full sun. She played her least favourite card. 'I'm not gonna go away, Jon, and if you make me stand here much longer, I'm gonna faint, and you don't wanna be carrying me anywhere.'

He jerked his head backwards in a gesture which might have meant *Follow me* or might have meant he had a neck problem. He turned and went inside, leaving the door open. Bridget followed him, closing it behind her.

Forty-Seven

The interior of Carson Halt was as pared back as the exterior, and she tried not to dwell on the implications of the house name. None of the architecture existed but to carry out its job: holding up a roof, dividing a space or giving access to the first floor. Bridget quite liked it. Because of the house being cut into the slope, it had been built long and thin, only one room deep in most places, but what rooms. Bridget was quick-marched through an impressive double-height hallway and into a living room whose appreciation needed serious time. And light. Both were in short supply.

Out there, Morecambe Bay would be glistening in the sunlight. In here, Bridget's eyes could see almost nothing because metal shutters were keeping the space cool and dark. Very Mediterranean. She nearly bumped into a sofa, avoided a sideboard and almost ran to get through a door to the right which glowed with artificial light.

'No view!' she said when she entered the man cave.

There was a window in here, at the back, showing around ten feet of clear ground and then the retaining wall which was stopping Aldhaven Hill from crushing the house under thousands of tonnes of rock ... *No. Don't go there. He's an engineer, and so was his grandfather. You'll be fine.*

The study wasn't huge. The left and far walls were hidden behind bookcases crammed with a mixture of old technical manuals, paperback fiction and a special extra-deep section given over to railway books. Jonathan was standing behind a pale oak desk which must have been original to the house, so sleek was the design. He waved her to a chair and sat down.

'No, there's no view,' he began. 'My grandfather thought it would be a distraction. He also thought you should get out there and walk if you want a view.' A reflex smile flickered. 'I'm sure it had nothing to do with my grandmother telling him he should be grateful for having any space in the house at all.'

Bridget looked at the fourth wall, the one with the door. To the left were family pictures covering four generations of Carsons, with Jonathan's immediate family in pride of place: wedding, holiday, his parents, her parents, and then a line of awards pictures. Mr and Mrs Carson were in evening dress holding the Queen's Award for Enterprise, and the image was flanked by photographs of their daughter's graduation and Mrs Carson in a nurse's uniform being handed a certificate. On the other side of the door was just one painting, and it wasn't by Esther Thornfield.

With dramatic fells in the background, the City of Lancaster steamed up some hill in its crimson lake livery, pulling a train of matching carriages. She could see brushwork, so it was either an original or a superb print.

'I've got an older brother,' Bridget began. 'Quite a bit older. I put him through hell sometimes, when I was a kid, but he still loved me. Still does, and I loved seeing him last weekend, even though it feels like a lifetime ago. I don't have a younger brother or sister, so I don't know what it's like from your side of the fence.' She glanced right. 'There's no picture of Tony as an adult.'

'So therefore I must have killed him? It doesn't work like that.'

'I liked him. Not everybody did, but I liked him. In some weird alternative universe, maybe I might have loved him one day. We'll never know. You had no choice did you?'

'No, I didn't, and when I've stopped being in shock, I'll be grateful for the time we had together after he moved back to Cairndale.'

Bridget paused to honour the memory, and to get what Mina had told her straight in her head before she shared it with Jonathan. 'You loved him despite Tony not taking up his rights offer two years ago, when you needed his investment to save the business, and when he certainly had the money?'

Jonathan didn't move a muscle other than the ones needed to turn his sad smile into a grimace. 'You're good. Better than the police.'

'Nah. They just haven't put an expert on it yet. They will. Sooner or later.'

Bridget had discovered that if you go to the Carson Metrics website, you'll see that the home page describes the business as *A NapaTech Company*, and the Silicon Valley firm had been the owners for two years, ever since Carson Metrics had been badly let down by their Chinese partners. The Guangzhou company was supposed to be supplying an integration system that would tie Carson's sensors to their Wi-Fi and Bluetooth equipment, only they were late and the equipment was incompatible.

According to Mina, that failure might have been a deliberate act by the Chinese Communist Party. Either way, Carson Metrics had needed a *lot* of extra capital, and Jonathan had already re-mortgaged this house once. When Jonathan had asked Tony to invest in proportion to his shareholding (the rights issue), Tony had declined the offer. In real, human terms, his brother had begged him to help save the family firm, and Tony had refused. Cain had got it in the neck from Abel for far less than that.

Jonathan reached for something on the desk, like a smoker looking for something to do with their hands (and why had that image come into her head?). He settled on a brass trinket, a model of Stephenson's Rocket, which Bridget recognised because of the famous Liverpool pub.

He tossed the locomotive from hand to hand and thought about his answer. 'My daughter has no interest in taking over after me. Don't blame her. Tony was incapable of running any form of business, despite his talents. The night he made me sell out to the Americans, I could have throttled him. I might have done if we'd been alone.'

He put the engine down with the boiler pointing towards Bridget. 'Since then, Carson Metrics has thrived. We're number one again, and I have a team who are as passionate as me about staying ahead.' His smile seemed genuine this time. 'My chief researcher says they'll wait until I retire to change the name. He's joking – they could change it tomorrow for all I care, and they know it. If your source is as good as he seems, you'll know that I have a stake in NapaTech which is worth more than Carson Metrics on its own would have been.'

'She. My source is very much a she, not a he, and she had to be quick when she told me. I'll double check with her.'

'And when you have, you'll see that I had no motive to kill my only brother now, even if I did then.'

Bridget disagreed. If there had been a business in her family – Gorrigan's Brewery, for example – then losing the name would mean a lot to her, and many junior doctors burn out. If there was a nice tech company to run, Jon's daughter, the young Dr Carson, might prefer it to endless nights on the wards for no thanks and little reward.

'Thank you, Jon,' she said, and part of her meant it. 'So what were you doing in the Mill on Sunday night, and why did you leave via the fire escape?'

'We'd had a row. About the *City of Lancaster*. For some reason, Tony wouldn't show it to me when Geoff and Darren were there, and I couldn't see why not. I went back on Sunday evening to find out why and I went then because my wife was called in for an unexpected end of life shift. You can check with the RLI.'

Bridget had no idea what an *end of life* shift might be, and she had no intention of finding out from the hospital. Mrs Carson was welcome to her privacy on that score. 'I see. And what happened at the Mill?'

'You know what that service lift is like, don't you?' Bridget nodded, and he continued, 'Tony knew that *someone* was coming because for once he didn't have music blaring around him. By the time the lift had got up to the studio, he'd covered up his workbench with a dust sheet. I'm fairly sure that the *City* was under it.'

'Was he sitting down when you came in?'

'Yes. On a swivel chair, rotated to face the lift. Why? Is that important?'

Jonathan seemed genuinely puzzled, so Bridget didn't lie. 'I don't know. I'm just checking. Sorry.'

'If you've seen the CCTV, you'll have seen the bag. I'm surprised you haven't asked about it already.' Bridget smiled and said nothing. 'Well, you've seen the pictures of the locomotive. Tony took that with him when he went to art school. He left the rest of the train with me – the carriages and the guard's van. I took them to the Mill in the hope of getting a bit of quality man time. You know – well, I suppose you don't. I said, "Let's set up a bit of O Gauge and put it together. Just to see it running." He said no.'

'How did that make you feel?'

Jonathan waved away the question, as if his feelings weren't important. 'He said that it was the wrong night. He had to prep for the launch of this channel. He was worried about it.' The sad smile was back. 'I'd brought a couple of beers, and he took one. We clinked bottles and drank to grandfather, and to Tony's new venture. I took a couple of swigs and said that I'd go and see mother. I left the rest of my beer behind, and that was the last time I saw him.'

'Really? The other day you told me that no one went to see your mum.'

He blushed. For the first time. 'Funny what you feel guilty about.

The other day, I was in shock and I told you the truth. Now I've had time to think of it, the only lie I choose to tell you is that I visited my mother.' He grunted. 'Rather than be thought of as a murderer than a man who came home and drank scotch instead of visiting his mother. Guilty.'

Bridget thought about it. The way that Hayley had told the brothers they couldn't go for a drink in the afternoon. This house being empty on a Sunday night. Jonathan not being able to face the nursing home. It all made sense. She had one ace to play – Esther Thornfield's assertion that there was no locomotive. Something made her keep that ace in the hole for now, and she asked a different question instead. 'Why did you leave via the fire escape?'

'The lift had gone back down of its own accord. The fire escape door was propped open for ventilation, so I just walked out.'

'Was it now?'

'Yes. That's how I knew he was up there when I drove in: light coming out of the door.'

That was news to Bridget. Hayley had said she opened the door, so either Tony or the killer had closed it behind them. Unless Hayley was lying. Bridget had one more item to tick off.

'What did the police say?'

'They came round at breakfast on Monday. It was a late breakfast because we'd both been up late and I was in no rush to get to the office. They were quite a double act, actually. One officer made tea while the other one asked if he could look in my car and check the house, with the clear implication that failure to co-operate would mean immediate arrest.'

That sounded like Liz: iron fist in a leather glove. 'And what did they find, Jon?'

'They found the holdall still in the boot, and my clothes in the washing basket. The shoes were by the front door. They took them all away and asked me to come in for an interview later that day.'

Bridget knew how she'd have done it. Jonathan owned a precision engineering company. There would be a clean room in there, with protective clothing. She'd have walked in the service entrance, donned the clothing out of sight of the CCTV camera and then gone up in the lift. Once back in the car park, she'd have put the protective suit in the holdall and driven off. The railway models, stashed in an identical holdall, would never have left the car.

With Mrs Carson at work, Bridget would have waited until the tide was in and chucked the evidence into the sea to let the sand and water take it. Or buried it in the woods until the heat was off.

Forty-Eight

Bridget stopped thinking about how Jonathan might be Cain in disguise, just in case it showed on her face. Without the mask of white make-up, who knows what people could see? 'Thank you for talking to me, Jon. What made you change your mind?'

'At first, it was the thought of lifting your limp body into the house, because you seem like a woman who carries out her threats.'

'True. And after that?'

'I remembered that Tony said you were one of a kind.' He leaned forwards. 'And if I didn't do it – and I know I didn't – then one of the others did. Hayley, Donna, Shannon. Even that rude mad-artist woman who lives on the other side of Water Cottage.'

Bridget felt the heat rising up her back, heading for her face. The door was open. Jonathan was firmly stuck behind his desk, so why did she feel trapped? Because he was a man, and she wasn't. That's why. She closed her eyes, just for a second, and the house was completely silent. No whisper of air conditioning, just the roar of blood in her ears. When she opened her eyes, Jonathan was still looking straight at her, and not a muscle had moved in his face.

She tried to swallow the sudden mouthful of saliva, and had to cough to clear her throat. She latched on to something unexpected. 'You know Water Cottage, then?'

'Yes. I knew it from visits to Byford as a kid, and Geoff Barton told me all about it, and who lives there, which I also told the police. I know who Joseph Hayton is, including his appointment as rook-scarer-in-chief to Lady Felicia. She doesn't like them roosting in the trees on her side of the millpond.'

'Right.'

Jonathan wasn't finished with his campaign of information (or disinformation). 'Tony didn't talk much about his life in Leyland. He did tell me about Donna, and how they split up when Andy Staton was ill. Donna was not generous about it. He also reckoned that Andy had a fling with Hayley.' There was a pause. 'He might have made that up, though. Mostly he blamed Shannon.'

'I see.'

Jonathan moved some papers and picked up an antique pocket

watch. He carefully opened it and checked the time. When he saw Bridget staring, he said, 'Grandfather's. It's the only clock I have in here, because it takes so much effort to open it and I try not to be ruled by time. Now I *have* looked, it's telling me that my wife is due home soon, and you're in her parking space.'

Bridget got up and stepped towards the door before Jonathan could block her exit, then felt absurdly guilty for doubting him. Then she remembered that *one* of the people she was talking to was a killer. 'I'd better get going then.'

He walked her to the door. 'Carsondale doesn't need the *City of Lancaster*,' he said. 'Despite what Darren says. We'll finish it for Granddad and Tony. Let me know if there's anything I can do to help, Bridget, and I'll no doubt see you soon.'

When she was back in the van, she breathed out and muttered, 'You might see me soon, Jonno, but until I know otherwise, it won't be on my own. What *was* I thinking going in there alone?'

She started the engine and worked her way back along the track, or tried to. Her exit to the public road was blocked, and not by Mrs Carson coming home from work. 'Bloody ferret,' she muttered. 'What on earth is he doing here?'

Jed Holmes waved, waited until she had stopped, and then approached the driver's window. Reluctantly, Bridget lowered it. 'Give me strength, Jed. I don't need a stalker as well as everything else I've got goin' on. What the frigging hell are you doing here?'

'Hi, Bridget,' he said, as usual unperturbed. 'I came out to have a look round. Any chance of a lift back? I had to catch the bus, and there's not another one for an hour now the schools have finished.'

'Gerrin.'

'Cheers.'

He scuttled round the back, and she was *so* tempted to drive off and leave him. *I'm too kind for me own good*, she thought. Once he'd got in, she emerged carefully, waited until a cyclist had sped down the hill, then turned right. 'I am not telling you what Jon Carson had to say. Let's get that clear, okay?'

'Loud and clear. Look, are you in a rush to get back?'

Bridget wasn't in a rush to do anything. She knew a lot more than she did an hour ago, which was good, or would be if only she understood what it meant. She didn't even know where to go next.

'Not particularly.'

'Why don't we stop on the front and get an ice cream? There's something you might be interested in, and I can't show you while you're driving.'

She got to the bottom of the hill and debated. Turn right and back to Cairndale, or go left and be confronted with what Tara Doyle was taking away from her in the shape of a cold ice cream? Oh yes, and spend time with Jed. How enticing. Not.

The rumble of a badly muffled exhaust behind her made her look in the mirrors, where she saw a convertible being driven by a midlife crisis who looked like he wanted to race. He was also signalling right. Bridget turned left.

Aldhaven is not overflowing with car parking, but the tide was in and it wasn't yet the school holidays. Bridget squeezed into a spot facing away from the promenade and slipways. What it lacked in prospect, it made up for with proximity to the café and ice cream parlour. She passed Jed a fiver and said, 'Mine's a vanilla 99. You can get them. I'm gonna enjoy the aircon until you get back, then we'll go for a paddle, shall we? Roll up our trousers and stick our toes in the water.'

'Erm, right. Yeah. Great.'

'Don't be stupid. I was winding you up. There's less chance of you seeing me toes than there is of me taking me top off and running round the Mill, but we will sit on that bench, okay? Now scoot.'

It was only when he'd gone that she remembered having a bet with Perry about moving into the village, and losing. 'No chance of losing this one,' she muttered, then called Lucy. 'Coach party finished?'

'Yeah, but Kat forgot to write down that one of the nursery babies is having his first birthday in here! Can I stay with you again tonight? Pleeease?'

'Yeah. Course. Can you cope?'

'Should do. Might need a hand cleaning up after we've closed.'

'No probs. Catch you later.'

Bridget leaned back and rested her eyes for a moment, until Jed knocked on the window. She got out and let him carry the ice creams to a bench which had just been vacated by two girls in the Cairndale Grammar uniform. 'Cheers,' said Bridget. 'Ice cream first.'

Jed had either chosen or had no choice in buying a small tub rather than a cone. On the whole, Bridget approved. Less messy. It did have the flake, though. And a little wooden spoon. 'Which part of this spoon did you touch?' she demanded.

'Just the end sticking out. And I used a serviette. Kat told me you liked that sort of thing.'

'No filter, that girl. Like mother like daughter. But thanks for thinking of me.'

She curled away a sliver of ice cream and popped it in her mouth. The melt was smooth and steady. No vegetable fats here, and the lingering hint of vanilla was just right. She should have given him a tenner, because this was not cheap seaside rubbish. She took another mouthful, trailing the spoon around the part-melted surface of the scoop and enjoying the rich, soothing tracks it made down her throat, like having your insides massaged in a spa. Mmm.

She stared at the water lapping gently against the sea wall beyond the railings, and then out to the bay, the dunes of Cowan Sands to the right and the hazy fells of the Lake District in the distance. Another laden spoon went down, and she couldn't avoid the cliché. It really was beautiful here. In the summer. She sighed. Bridget was not a big one for Shakespeare, unlike her first-year tutor, who'd taken her to one of those little parks in central London that lurk between the billion-pound houses.

He'd bought her an overpriced can of Diet Pepsi and told her that she'd aced her exams and that she should try a more challenging module next year. 'I'm just enjoying myself,' she'd told him, still trying to iron out the Scouse accent occasionally.

'But Bridget "Summer's lease hath all too short a let." As they say.'

'Do they? Not where I come from they don't.'

She'd looked up the quotation later, in an actual book of quotations, and she'd never forgotten it. By the time she'd got back to Liverpool for the long vacation, it was raining. She had taken his advice, though, and look where that had led her.

'Are you a first year?' she asked Jed, who was trying to eat his ice cream and scroll his phone at the same time.

He closed the screen and shifted to look at her. 'Second.'

'And what is it you're doing again?'

'Digital media creation. There's all sorts of options and modules. Last year I did mostly editing and techy stuff. This year I wanted to get out a bit more, so I did the new podcasting unit.'

Her ice cream was at the tipping point between too cold and melted. She twirled her flake and took a bite. 'What was it you wanted to show me?'

'I rang my dad last night and asked him for advice.'

'Is he an old school journalist?'

Jed laughed. 'No. He's an old school copper. Sergeant in Solihull.'

The spoon stopped halfway to Bridget's mouth. Apart from her academic achievements, there was almost no trace of Bridget on the public internet. The same was not true about the Police National Computer. Surely he hadn't got his dad to look her up. 'Oh yes?'

'Yeah. I told him about the case and about no one wanting to talk to me.' Jed waggled his eyebrows. 'He told me I should stick close to you for one thing.'

'I don't know whether to be flattered or take out a restraining order.'

He made a face. 'He was right, too. Being with Ciara got me diddly squat but you've shown me where all the interesting stuff is.'

'That's the trouble with parents. They have an annoying habit of being right. What else did he do for you?'

'Dog walkers. He said that when the murder happened, all the dog walkers would have been out. Cooler then. He told me that without dog walkers, the conviction rates would plummet.'

That was very sensible. If Bridget didn't have a profound dislike of dogs, she'd have thought of it herself. 'So are you going out to see who's about tonight?'

He took a big slurp of ice cream and grinned. 'Twice a day minimum. I was actually out this morning, just after the sun came up.'

Bridget narrowed her eyes. 'You didn't go to bed last night, did you?'

'Didn't seem any point.'

She sighed. She could have done that once. Not any more. 'And did you get anything?'

'I did,' he answered smugly. He put his tub down and held up his phone. 'Listen to this.'

Forty-Nine

The sound from his phone was tinny but clear, and it began with Jed speaking. 'I'm standing on the footbridge over the River Cowan, upstream from Ford Mill, where Anthony Carson was murdered. I'm with Julie and Dylan, her dog. Were you here on Sunday night, Julie?'

'I was,' said an older woman. 'We always come this way, don't we, Dylan? He's a rescue dog and he likes routine.'

'What did you see, Julie?'

'I didn't see the murder or anything like that. I told the police the same.'

'But you did see some people out and about, didn't you?'

'Heard them. You can't miss that motorbike, for one thing?'

'Shannon Turner rides a Moto Guzzi. Do you think it was her?'

'I know it was her. It came out of her cottage and went down the hill and into the gingerbread house.'

'From where we're standing, you can see several properties. The Mill, of course, and the grand mansion of Byford Lodge, but also some of the smaller places. Which one is the gingerbread house, Julie, and why?'

'Where the witch lives. Esther Thornfield. We don't like her, do we Dylan?'

'How long was Shannon Turner there?'

'I don't know. Not long. We were still out and about when she roared off. She went down the hill, then I couldn't hear her any more.'

'She went towards the Mill. Did she go in?'

'Don't know. Sorry. I did see her for a second, between the hedges, and she had a pillion passenger. I reckon it was Esther.'

'What makes you think that, Julie?'

'The hair. She wasn't wearing a helmet.'

'What did the police say?'

'That nice detective, Smith? The other one called him *Barney*. He said it was very useful, though he was a bit disappointed when I couldn't tell him what time it was. It was after nine o'clock, because that horrible programme came on the telly. We don't like the shouting, do we, Dylan?'

'Thank you, Julie.' There was a slight crackle, and a slight change in the acoustics of Jed's voice. 'It seems that the police were thorough. They spoke to everyone they could find who was out and about on the fatal evening. But what did they do with the information?'

Jed ended the playback and raised his eyebrows. 'Useful?'

It was useful. Very useful. If Lucy had known this when she went to see Esther, she might have done a lot better. 'It is, Jed. Thank you. Why did you share it now?'

'Kat. After I saw you at Hayley's place this morning, I hopped on the train back to Byford. Thought I might get a better chance with you not there.' He grinned. 'I ambushed Kat when she went for her break and got talking.'

'Oh yes?'

'Yes. I asked her about Millie Easterby. She told me you were good, but I knew that already. When I played her the tape, she said you needed to hear it.' He shrugged. 'When you asked for Jonathan Carson's address, I knew I'd find you here. And I got some great footage of his house.'

'I told you to go to lectures, not chat up my staff.'

He shrugged again. 'No point. The lectures are all online later, and the lecture theatre is like a bedroom right now – dark, warm and comfortable. I fall asleep after ten minutes.'

Bridget had finished her ice cream, and so had Jed. She stacked her carton in his and took out the wet wipes from her bag. She plucked one for herself and offered him the packet. He took one and said, 'She told me a bit more about you, too. Much happier to talk about you than herself. She told me all about the ice cream and why you're leaving.'

'I wish she hadn't, Jed. That's none of her business. I shall be having words with my duckling.'

'Your what?'

'Never mind.'

'I think it's a great idea. You enjoyed it, didn't you?'

Bridget frowned. What on earth was the ferret on about now? 'You've lost me again, Jed. Must be me age.'

He pointed to the ice cream tubs. 'This raw milk ice cream is great. Really creamy. Too expens—'

She lurched up and her stomach heaved. She took two steps to the railing and gripped it, trying not to gag. *How could he! The bastard!* She closed her eyes and shivered with nausea. *I've eaten raw milk. Unpasteurised. Deadly. Got to breathe. In and out.*

She did breathe. She got a grip on her breathing and … nothing. The automatic reaction to what she'd been told didn't provoke her stomach into a full rebellion. It stayed quite happy. As soon as the panic had left her, she found herself hot, sweaty and seeing little lights in front of her eyes. But not sick.

She blinked, and the lights turned into glints off the water below her. She breathed in and out and turned around. Jed was standing up, still clutching his wet wipe.

'You okay, Boss?'

'How could you? How could you do that to me, you little shit.'

'Do what?'

'Feed me that muck and take advantage.'

He trembled and twisted the tissue to shreds. 'B-but you saw it!'

'Saw what?'

He turned and pointed to the café. 'There. On the board. *Natural Lakes Raw Organic Ice Cream.* I wouldn't have bought it if you hadn't seen it.'

'I was parking the van, soft lad! I didn't have time to read the bloody sign!'

'Sorry. I'm really sorry.'

'Not good enough, Jed. Put that lot in the bin and get in the van. If you speak one more word to me before we get to Cairndale, I won't be held accountable.'

His nose twitched. He really did look like a ferret. 'Thanks. I thought you were going to leave me here.'

'You're only coming in case I pass out. Not one more word. Got that?'

He zipped his lip and cleared up. Bridget clicked the doors open and drove way too quickly out of the village and back to civilisation. Someone would pay for this.

Fifty

Bridget dropped Jed in Cairndale – he said, 'Thanks. And sorry,' once he was safely out of the car. Then she drove to Byford on autopilot. Most of the time she was thinking about what was happening inside her, where the raw milk was sitting and the bacteria were multiplying. One of the things she'd learned in therapy was to treat physical symptoms as real, even if the cause was psychological.

The nausea that swept over her at the traffic lights wasn't caused by food poisoning. That was biologically impossible. It wouldn't stop her vomiting all over the van, though. She didn't grip the steering wheel. She tried to relax and focus on her breathing, letting the rhythm of the road work into her system. When she got to St Peter's Church, she turned left and headed to the sanctuary of Midland Terrace.

She lay on the bed and looked at her phone. Jed had sent a link to the interview with Julie, and she played it again, letting the implications sink in. She now knew that all of the possible suspects were out and about that night. None of them had a truly secure alibi except Wendy, and she had no motive anyway. The only ones who hadn't accounted for their movements to Bridget yet were Shannon and Esther. Before she knew what she was doing, she was stripping off and heading to the bathroom for a wash and change.

When she'd put clean clothes on, she went to repair her make-up, especially the SPF primer. She took a good look at herself and told her reflection, 'Well, girl, you've got two days before E. coli or campylobacter make an appearance. If they're going to. Use them wisely.' She left the house and got in the van. She messaged Lucy where she was going and headed off.

The drive to Shannon Turner's cottage was more suited to motorcycles than vans, and Bridget took the lesser risk of slowly reversing through the gates rather than the greater risk of a close encounter with the milk tanker while reversing out. And talking of motorcycles …

She passed the gleaming Moto Guzzi and Shannon watched her from the standalone garage/workshop; Bridget smiled at Shannon and didn't get a smile back. The chaos in the print studio was mirrored in

Shannon's workshop. A tool board on the wall was completely empty, its residents scattered among the socket sets, parts and detritus covering two benches. In between the benches was a substantial ramp with a stripped bike held in place at the top by clamps. Another bike rested on a stand with the fuel tank and seat removed. Bridget thought the one on the floor might be some sort of off-road machine and the one up the ramp looked vintage, but what did she know?

'Not working today?' said Shannon, gesturing with a socket wrench towards Bridget's outfit, which no longer featured a Caffè Milano shirt.

'It *is* me day off, but yeah, I won't be serving again today.'

Shannon herself was wearing shorts and a vest, and her knees were black with dirt or grease, as was her forehead. She seemed totally oblivious of this and said, 'But you are still sticking your nose into things.' She lifted the wrench and pointed it at Bridget. 'Esther called me after Lucy went to see her.'

There was no hiding Shannon's age, but she was a striking woman, tallest of the ones on Bridget's suspect list, and with that wiry strength which comes from an active lifestyle, unlike Donna who was quite petite, or Hayley who clearly went to the gym. Bridget thought carefully before she responded to Shannon's blunt challenge.

'I know a lot more than the last time I came, Shannon. Just hear me out, okay? That's all. There's one thing I can promise you: nothing you say today will go any further without your permission.'

'Esther says you've been hanging around with that cub reporter from ULIST.'

'Kit. He's a kit reporter, not a cub. Mini ferret, our Jed. Sometimes you keep your enemies close. I'm saying nothing to him that he can't find out for himself. You and me could chew him up and spit him out for breakfast.'

'True.' Shannon sighed and chucked the wrench onto the bench, not caring where it landed. 'I could do with a break. Changing dampers is not my favourite job.' She returned from wherever she'd been in her head and sniffed. 'Have I got oil on me?'

'Just a bit. On your forehead.'

'Shit. You know where the lounger is, don't you? I'll get some lemonade.'

Bridget was beginning to pray for a citrus fruit shortage, and the thought of downing more squeezed Lieutenant Lemons did nothing for her stomach. 'Any chance of a cuppa? I haven't had caffeine since lunchtime.'

Shannon took another look at her. 'Good call. We all have our addictions, don't we? Won't be long.'

Since Bridget's last visit, Shannon had added two chairs to her sunlounger haven. Bridget moved one into the shade and tried to relax. No chance. The bacteria in her stomach wouldn't let her. She got out her phone and messaged Kat. *You are in so much trouble.*

The first-birthday party must have been in full swing, because she didn't get an immediate response. Who has a child's party in a café anyway? What were they going to do? There was no soft play or ball pit in the Spinning Room, so perhaps this was only stage one of a birthday marathon, like the racecourse had been stage one of Mina's hen party. Just before Shannon emerged with a clean face and a tea tray, Kat messaged back. *Jed told me what happened. So sorry.* And then some emojis that Bridget couldn't make out.

Shannon put down the tray and passed Bridget a mug of decent-looking tea. They took a moment to enjoy it, then Shannon spoke. 'I called Esther. She offered to come up and get rid of you, then told me not to say anything.'

'We could talk about the weather?' suggested Bridget.

'It's hot. End of story. Look, Bridget, Esther is only trying to protect me, okay? Do you want the honest truth?'

Bridget had her own internal table of truth. Any suggestion beginning *Do you want the honest truth* meant that she was going to get *some* truth but no way would she get all of it. Beggars can't be choosers, though. 'I want to find out what happened to Tony,' she told Shannon, 'and we won't get there without the truth.'

Shannon shifted in her chair – she had eschewed the lounger, presumably because it would put her at a disadvantage. 'Is that what you want? To find out what happened to Tony? Is that more important than clearing Hayley?'

'It is now. Maybe it wasn't to start with.'

Shannon considered this. 'The thing about Esther is that she truly doesn't care about Tony. She doesn't want anyone charged with his murder or to go to prison, but if the police scale back their enquiry with Hayley as prime suspect, she won't shed any tears.'

'That's harsh. Why not?'

'Because she blames Hayley for bringing Tony here. If they'd set up their business anywhere else, none of this would have happened.'

It was an interesting thought, and Shannon's repetition of Esther's opinion suggested that she agreed with it. Bridget tested the theory by asking, 'What about you, Shannon? Would you be happy with that outcome? Given that Hayley had an affair with your husband.'

Shannon was not happy. A flash of anger made her face sharper. More feral. 'He wasn't my husband by then. He was a man with an addiction. Possibly several. I don't think sleeping with Hayley helped him deal with them.'

Bridget didn't feel threatened. Not here in this garden with everyone knowing where she was. She pushed a bit harder. 'That's not what Tony thought, though, is it? Look, I wasn't there. I don't know. But I heard about what he said to you on Sunday. He blames *you*, Shannon. Or he did. And he didn't want anything to do with you. Didn't want you involved in 3M3 in any way.'

'I ain't gonna lie – it hurt, Bridget. You've seen the CCTV. I was in tears, and not just because of what that dickhead had said to me. It brought it all back, too. All the insinuations, the backstabbing. And watching the man you love fall apart. Tony was a complete wanker. Total arsehole. He shafted me and Donna and Hayley, and he'd have done it to you soon enough.'

Bridget blinked, trying to think of a response, but Shannon wasn't finished.

'I loved Andy Staton. If we'd had kids when we wanted them, I think he'd have been a *great* dad. Coming up to Leyland Films and meeting Tony Carson was the worst thing that could have happened to Andy. Talk about bringing out the worst in people. Whoever killed Tony was not the first person with blood on their hands. That would be Tony himself.'

Her eyes burned with hatred now that she'd opened up, and Bridget knew she had to choose: to be a proxy for the reviled Anthony Carson or join the club trying to bury his memory along with the body. What the hell. She was leaving soon anyway.

'And what about you, Shann? I know you were out and about on Sunday night – there was an eyewitness. Did you go back to Ford Mill and get blood on your hands? You haven't denied killing him yet.'

Shannon looked away, pretending to adjust her chair, and Bridget knew that she was about to be lied to. 'No. I didn't kill Tony. I was wound up, so I went to see Esther. She said we should go and get some weed, so I took her with me.'

Damn. Too much story and no way of telling which part was the lie. Or all of it. 'Weed? Are you joking? The witness said you drove down the hill with Esther on the back wearing no helmet, and you're telling me you were going to find a dealer? Come on, Shannon.'

'It's true! He's not just a dealer, he's a grower. We didn't get as far as Cairndale, and I'm a *very* good rider, so no helmet needed.'

'Who?'

'No chance. I'm not gonna grass him up.'

'Not even if Liz arrests you and he's your alibi?'

'Nope.'

'Why did you take Esther anyway?'

Shannon's smile seemed genuinely struck with the utter unlikeliness of what she was saying. 'Because I had no idea who or where the guy was, and I needed an introduction from Esther.'

'Then what?'

'We came back, smoked a joint and I crashed out. Not used to it any more. Esther made sure I got to bed and walked home by herself. It's downhill from here.'

Bridget finished her tea and got up to put the mug on the tray. When she sat back down, she perched on the edge of the chair. 'What time, Shannon? When did you go, and what time did she leave?'

'Not sure. Some time after nine. Esther told me not to take my phone where we were going, so I didn't, and I'd had enough of the outside world by then, to be honest. I didn't look at it again until Monday morning.'

Bridget didn't spell it out. The police would have done that already – *you were out committing a crime and you won't say what time.* Based on what Julie and Dylan saw, Shannon could have come home, faked being stoned and then gone out again, or Esther could have walked down to Coffin Joe's house and killed Tony.

There was one part of the story that didn't fit with Shannon or Esther being the killer, though. 'What do you know about the *City of Lancaster*?'

'Until this afternoon, I thought it was just a train in a box. Sorry, a *locomotive* in a box, then Esther told me it didn't exist, so your guess is as good as mine.'

'What did Esther tell you about it?'

'That it didn't exist any more, and given that I didn't kill him, I have no idea what was stolen, do I?'

It fitted with Shannon being innocent. If Esther were telling some sort of truth, then Shannon wouldn't know what was going on. On the other hand, this would be the easiest part to lie about, and Shannon's motive was looking stronger the more Bridget discovered. The heartache from losing her child, the pain of seeing Andy Staton disintegrate and the many betrayals she'd suffered. When Tony had capped it off with his vicious insults, who'd blame her for finally cracking? If Bridget had been in her shoes, the thought of working downstairs from Anthony Carson every day might have tipped her over the edge, too.

Bridget sighed and got up. She was going to have to see Esther at some point, so why not today? But not on her own. No way. 'Thanks for talking to me, Shannon. I'm sorry for what you've been through. I really am.'

'I made my bed. I get to re-make it, too. Good luck going back to your old one in Southport.'

'I think you're stretching that a bit, but thanks. I'd hoped to leave without anyone knowing, but two days later and the whole village has an opinion.'

'Welcome to Byford.'

Fifty-One

Bridget was very glad she'd reversed into Shannon's drive earlier. When she inched the van forwards into the narrow lane, it wasn't the milk tanker that nearly gave her heart failure, it was a convertible. In fact, it was the *same* convertible which had prompted her to go for an ice cream, and as the driver nearly swerved into the opposite hedge, she realised that this wasn't the first or second time she'd seen it. The driver was the mysterious man from Station House – balding and full of ego, judging by the car. 'Hardly worth being curious about,' she muttered. 'If he is Count Dracula, he can keep his fangs to himself.' She double checked for cyclists and drove down the lane to Ford Mill.

The café and craft village were closed now, and only a couple of cars sat in the yard – Perry's and … yes, Laura's, presumably back from collecting her children. And there she was. Oh, and there was Perry.

They came out of the estate office after Bridget had already parked, and they didn't look in her direction. Perry said something to Laura, then put his hand on her back and walked the few steps to her car. He leaned in as if he was going for a kiss and said something else. Laura laughed and blushed and then got in her car. Bridget stayed stock still and waited until Perry had gone back inside.

'Face it, girl, Laura might be the same age as you, but she's slimmer and way prettier. And she doesn't smell of coffee. You're leaving soon, and it was never gonna happen anyway.' She got out of the van and headed to the Spinning Room. She stopped in the archway and shouted, 'Where's Kat? I wanna word!'

'Gone home,' said Wendy. 'She was traumatised by having to feed a baby.'

'You what?'

Their new worker looked as washed out as Bridget felt after the close encounter with the raw milk ice cream. Wendy stood up from polishing a table and looked askance at Bridget's outfit. 'Alright for some. I didn't realise how physical this job could get. Still, it's this or take in lodgers. Where've you been, Boss?'

'I am not your Boss. Lucy is the Boss round here, talking of which … I mean talking of who … Or is that *whom*? Whatever. Where is she?

No, hang on. What were you on about, Wendy? What happened to Kat?'

'Amanda? Ananda? Amienda? You know the one?'

'Arabella. Has a small girl she dresses like a boy. A girl who's old enough to feed herself but doesn't. That one?'

'Yes. Arabella begged Kat to feed her little girl and then took a picture and put it on Instagram with some noxious caption about taking a village to raise a child. She doesn't even live in Byford. She lives on the Rivers Estate.'

Bridget shook her head to clear the nonsense. Sometimes, running a café with high margins attracts high maintenance customers. 'Nah, Wendy. I don't think it was that. Katarina Chester is avoiding me. I'm surprised Lucy let her go.'

'There was a promise of Kat bringing in a new starter for the weekend. Lucy's off to York tomorrow afternoon. Oops. I think she wanted to tell you that herself. She's in the back, listening to that awful music and finishing the deep clean.'

'Cheers, Wendy. You okay for the weekend?'

'So long as I get my day off tomorrow. I'm shattered, and I've promised to run some of Donna's stuff down to Penwortham.' Wendy frowned. 'Her car wouldn't start after we loaded it this morning – I think you'd gone to Hayley's by then. Well, it started okay, but it wouldn't move. The AA said it was something in the transmission. We had to unload it, and they've taken it to a place in Cairndale and dropped her at the station.'

'You get off, Wendy. I'll finish sorting.'

'Are you sure?'

'No problem. I haven't had to face a coach party or a birthday party.'

'Then I'll see you on Saturday. Oh, where did you get to after Hayley's?'

Bridget hadn't wanted to tell her, but she couldn't change the subject twice. 'Jon Carson's place, then Shannon's. The more I hear about Tony Carson, the less I know for certain.'

Wendy finished the table she was working on and moved the cleaning caddy to the next in line. She took off her apron and said, 'Tony was always nice to me unless the subject was doll's houses. He didn't have much time for them, and as that's my hobby, we didn't have a lot in common. I don't like trains. Right. See you on Saturday, unless I pop in to get a coffee for the road tomorrow.'

Bridget set to on the tables and almost walked into Lucy when she went to get the mop. They stood on either side of the kitchen doorway for a moment, and Lucy looked down rather than meet Bridget's eye. 'I'm sorry, Bridge,' she said.

'Shift out the way,' said Bridget.

Lucy backtracked, and Bridget went through to dump the caddy. 'Sorry for what?' she asked Lucy. 'Did you tell Kat something that was none of her business?'

'Not here, Bridget. I'll apologise over a bottle of beer at Midland Terrace, then you can shout at me properly.'

Bridget weighed up her options. That actually sounded quite good, because she could get the punishment in first. 'I'll mop the floor and you can get changed.'

'Why?'

'We're off to the gingerbread house, that's why.'

'Gingerbread house?'

'Where do you think witches live?'

'In my experience, they tend to live in sacred groves or mansions.'

It was Bridget's turn to be stumped. 'Whatever you say, Coach. Witches in mansions. I'm gonna mop the floor, then we're off to see Esther Thornfield.'

Whatever it was that Esther had against Julie the dog walker and Dylan the walked dog, only someone as short-sighted as Bridget without her glasses would describe Fern Cottage as a gingerbread house. 'Ugly thing. A bit like her paintings,' she observed.

'No,' said Lucy. 'It's a highly desirable agricultural cottage in superb location, perfect as a second home, holiday cottage or retirement property. Needs some modernisation.'

'Including an inside toilet, unless I'm mistaken. You're right about the location, though.' She looked at Lucy, and the faraway look was back. 'Do you actually dream in estate agent speak these days, Lucy? When you're in bed with—'

'Stop right there. Look at the back, just past the old chimney there's a wire vent cowl.'

Bridget peered. She could just make out the black balloon shaped wire mesh structure. She knew they meant something, but had no idea what. 'So?'

'It's a soil pipe terminal. She must have at least one inside toilet.'

Bridget stared at Lucy. 'How in the name of Jesus do you know that's what they're called and what they're for? Who actually cares?'

Lucy went redder than she had when Bridget mentioned being in bed with Tom. 'You pick things up when you're house hunting.'

'How come the only one hunting is you? Tom has no idea where he's even gonna work, never mind where he's gonna live. You keep looking at the Lodge and the Old Rectory, so I assume your plans include him.'

'Doesn't hurt to get a feel for the market. Let's stop wasting time. The sooner we get this over with, the sooner I can get a shower and open a beer.'

'Right you are, Coach.'

'Stop calling me that!'

'Why? You made the team call me *Boss*. And who's wasting time, eh?'

'It is a lovely view.'

It was. Fern Cottage was just upstream from a footbridge which crossed the Cowan at the top end of the millpond. It didn't have a river frontage, but it did have views down to the Mill and across to where Laura lived in Grange Farm Croft. Bridget guessed that parcel deliveries might be a little hit and miss here – the lane did not have a name, and the track down was longer than most drivers had time for. And if that footbridge was a public right of way, she could imagine that intrusive dog walkers might be an issue.

They descended the last forty yards to the cottage, went round a bend and found a scrapheap of superannuated domestic appliances, a sofa, and a mattress. 'Fly tipping?' said Lucy. 'All the way down here?'

'Doubt it,' said Bridget. 'I'm guessing she can't get anyone to pick them up for nothing, and she won't pay proper disposal charges. See? They're piled against a blank wall, so she can't see them.'

'Sad,' said Lucy ambiguously. 'You insisted, so you knock.'

'Fine.'

Esther didn't keep them waiting, although Bridget almost asked the woman who answered the door if Esther were in, because she looked nothing like the artist. For one thing she was wearing a clean, floral dress, and for another she had her hair up. And make-up. The eyes were Esther's though, and they weren't radiating a warm welcome. Bridget felt almost scorched from the anger.

'Are you ganging up on me now? Not content with disturbing Shannon, you've actually come to my *home*, have you? Shannon's too polite for her own good. I'm disappointed in you, Bridget. Someone with your sensitivity shouldn't be mixing themselves up in this. You are better than that.'

The speech was not delivered with sympathy, it was delivered with the acerbic superiority and condescension of Bridget's convent school art teacher and it was designed to belittle rather than challenge her. Bridget didn't quail, but she did shrink, right back to school size, and just like then, she couldn't find anything to say back. Good job she'd brought a friend.

Lucy slipped round Bridget, right to the edge of Esther's personal space. 'Just tell us about the *City of Lancaster*,' Lucy said, with an edge of weariness in her voice that ever so slightly hinted at an end to patience. Esther did not get the message.

'It's none of your business. Any of it. It's not your business, it's not that creature from the polytechnic's business and it's not Laura Paige's business either.'

'What about the police?' said Lucy. 'Is it their business?'

Now that she was spectating, Bridget saw the tell – a double blink which told her that Esther had not shared her secret with the cops. If there actually was a secret. Lucy hated involving Tom in any way, but would she use him as a bluff?

Esther avoided the question. She just stared and said nothing. Then she folded her arms and raised her eyebrows.

Bridget stepped back, allowing Lucy to do the same if she wanted. She didn't want. She was happy getting in Esther's face. 'I'll ask Barney Rubble about it – that's DC Smith. If it's in the public domain, he'll tell me, but I don't think it is, because this afternoon Bridget went to see Jonathan Carson, and he knew nothing. As far as he knows, the *City* is missing. After all, he's the sole beneficiary of Tony's will. Then again, he might have murdered his brother and stolen it. Either way, the police haven't told him it might not actually exist. Isn't that right, Bridget?'

'Sure is. Jon has no idea what you're on about, Esther.'

Esther's wall cracked a little. Jonathan Carson wasn't on her mental map of the crime and she hadn't expected this. Her lips pursed. Her shoulders jerked with tension, then her eyes flicked to her left and her posture changed completely, and it was Esther who took the step backwards as if *she* were the one afraid. You can't fake that, so Bridget turned around.

'Is everything okay?' asked the vicar. *Where did she spring from?* wondered Bridget.

Esther wasn't the only one to have donned her glad rags. Deborah Giddings had also dressed up, and there was no sign of the dog collar. Bridget's mouth twitched reflexively. Every time she thought of Debs and dog collars, she also thought of the three assorted ones she had in her bottom drawer. Especially the handmade leather one with studs and a D ring.

'I thought I recognised your car, Lucy,' said Deborah with a disarming smile. 'I had to park at the top of the lane. Good job I had my driving sandals on.'

Debs' sandals were at odds with the dress, so that probably meant a pair of heels in the car. They must be going out somewhere, something Lucy also worked out. 'Hi, Debs. Esther was just telling us what she told the police about the *City of Lancaster*.'

Talk about going *all in*. Lucy would now either get what they wanted or a thump on the nose. Bridget cringed as Esther unfolded her arms and struggled to decide whether to upset her friend or give in to Lucy.

Friendship won in the end. Esther forced a smile and said, 'Yes I was just going to do that, Lucinda. Anthony Carson destroyed the model train in his first year at Thames School of Fine Art. He did it as part of a pathetic and mistaken attempt to impress the judge in the annual competition. You do not destroy family heirlooms to make art. Incorporate, yes, dismantle and dispose of, no, a fact which I made very clear in the judging. I believe he left the school at the end of the year and went off to make toys.'

'Thank you, Esther,' said Lucy. 'We'll leave you and Debs in peace to enjoy your night out, and we're sorry to have troubled you.'

Fifty-Two

'Where does that leave us?' asked Bridget, passing Lucy a beer and the bottle opener. It was too hot in the sitting room, so they were crammed into the tiny space between the kitchen and the side wall at Midland Terrace. As long as they kept their voices down, they should be okay.

Lucy adjusted her dressing gown before opening the bottle. Neither of them had wanted to talk until they'd scrubbed the heat off their bodies, and Lucy said she didn't want to get any more clothes dirty. Bridget never wore her dressing gown in company unless she was answering the door to firemen, and that hadn't happened since she was an undergraduate. Happy days.

'I don't get it,' said Lucy. 'I'm sure that no one I've spoken to knew Esther's story about the *City of Lancaster*, and you're sure as well?'

'Hundred per cent. Everyone I've seen believes that the locomotive was in the case on Sunday morning, and I'm including Shannon in that group because Esther didn't tell her until today, I'm sure of it.'

Bridget had delivered the last line with confidence, then doubt crept in. 'The one thing that bugs me is Donna Ramsey. She actually lived with Tony. I'm gonna call her.'

'Now?'

'Yes. Hang on.'

Donna took the call, though she didn't sound happy about it. Bridget tried to be supportive, asking, 'I'm sorry to hear about your car, Donna. What did the garage say?'

'That the variable twister has done the hokey cokey.'

'Of course they did. You're not a petrolhead then?'

'No. I thought about Googling it while I was on the train. Couldn't be bothered. They did say I needed a part for the automatic gearbox to fix it, though.'

'Ouch. Sounds expensive.'

'It is. They quoted me two hundred less than the original dealer, so I'm car-less for a week. That's all I need.'

'I'm sorry to hear that. I really am.'

'But it wasn't why you called, was it?'

'No. Look, I'm with Lucy, and we've just been to see Esther Thornfield. She told us this weird story about the *City of Lancaster*.'

'Yes. I've had Shannon on the phone as well. I can't believe it.'

'Neither can we. I don't want to intrude on your relationship with Tony, but did you ever see it while you were together.'

'No. I saw an old cardboard box in the loft with *City of Lancaster* written on the side. It was covered in parcel tape, and don't forget, Tony was a born-again railway modeller. All through the time we were together he was all about the fruit. And the other stuff Leyland Films were working on. The posh instrument case was new. Last week was the first time I'd seen it as well.'

'It doesn't make sense, Donna, especially when you think that it was empty on Monday morning.'

Donna gave a dark laugh. 'That struck me and Shannon as well. If the locomotive wasn't in the case, what was? Drugs? Sandwiches? Your guess is as good as mine.'

'Thanks, Donna.'

'Look, Bridget, I've not had a good day. I'm talking to you out of respect for Hayley, but this is taking a toll. I admire you and what you're doing, but without the police resources, this is just gossip.'

'I understand, Donna.'

'Thanks.'

'Good luck with the car, and thanks for talking.'

Bridget disconnected and put the phone down. She'd had Donna on speaker, so Lucy had heard everything. Bridget took a swig of beer and said, 'What about the trolling? Who put that picture on Esther's Facebook page? Surely only the killer could have done that?'

'I don't agree,' said Lucy. 'Unfortunately, I *can* see Esther doing it to herself. You didn't see her this afternoon, casually letting slip that the *City* didn't exist any more. She did that deliberately, to throw mud around, and tonight, when the vicar turned up, she went from mad witch to sad spinster in a heartbeat. She could have faked the outrage in the café.'

Bridget thought about it. 'True. What about the others? What about Jonathan Carson?'

'From what you've told me, he might have been closer to his brother than he's letting on. If he's innocent, he could have posted it to make us look at Esther more closely, to stir up trouble. Same if he's guilty –

spreading the blame around.'

That made sense. 'And the same goes for Donna, Shannon or Hayley. Innocent or guilty, they could be trying to muddy the waters.'

'So what does that mean?' asked Lucy 'Have we got it wrong? Is the killer someone else?'

'I can't see that,' said Bridget after a moment's thought. 'Only Hayley, Donna, Shannon, Esther and Jonathan had all the necessary knowledge and access, though I'm guessing that a key wasn't needed if the fire escape door was propped open. I simply cannot see someone like Edwin or Perry or Mike Mason killing Tony Carson in such a premeditated way. I can't see them killing him at all, never mind after breaking into Coffin Joe's house and then walking off with a random artefact from the studio. Only our suspects would have done that.'

'Then what did the killer steal? If it wasn't the *City of Lancaster* in that box, I suppose they'd have kept quiet and worked out their story. I can't believe that a chuffing toy train is all we've got to go on.'

They drank in silence for a moment. 'I don't think we'll get anywhere like this,' said Bridget. 'We need to sleep on it, I reckon.'

'Good idea.'

'So why don't we talk about raw milk ice cream instead?' asked Bridget in a bad impersonation of Lucy at her most Pollyannish.

The emotional temperature in the corner of the yard plummeted. Lucy tucked her feet under herself and looked like she was trying to climb out her chair over the back. She seemed hurt, guilty and defiant in a radioactive soup of emotion, a bit like the soup of bacteria which Bridget had unwittingly consumed that afternoon.

'Go on then,' Bridget said. 'What happened? How come Jed the ferret fed me that stuff?'

'It's that door to the kitchen. You know how Kat likes to lurk in there on her phone and listen to see if anyone's coming.'

Bridget did know, and she was wise to it. Hopefully this would be a lesson to Lucy, but what had she been talking about that Kat overheard? She lifted her bottle to her lips and raised her eyebrows in enquiry.

Lucy was having some inner struggle. She twisted in the chair again, adjusted her dressing gown and then stood up. For a second, Bridget thought her friend was going to take a toilet break and change the subject. No. Lucy retied the gown and almost collapsed in her seat.

'I'm sorry, Bridge. I really am. Kat heard me talking to Mike Mason, then Jed Holmes turned up and – don't ask me how – he made a positive impression on her. She told him everything, and he thought you knew about the café in Aldhaven. It was an honest mistake.'

Bridget pointed her bottle at Lucy. 'I get that. Jed looked genuinely upset. Doesn't change the fact that he poisoned me, though.'

'You'll be fine.'

'You hope, and you're missing something out. Tell me, Lucy, what was it Kat overheard, eh? How come she got from eavesdropping to pillow talk with Jed Holmes?'

'Pillow talk! They were only gone half an hour. The closest they got to pillow talk was swapping phone numbers.'

'Changing the subject again. What did she overhear?'

Lucy surrendered. 'I was talking to Mike about getting a milk separator. You know, to get the cream out of his Magic Milk so you can set up the Cowandale Creamery in the back room.'

'Pardon?'

Lucy said nothing, and Bridget knew she had heard correctly. Her best friend – her only friend outside the business – was conspiring behind her back. She'd have to change that. And quickly. 'You were so out of order there, Luce. I can't believe you've done that. What did you tell Mike, eh?'

'I told him the truth. I told him we were losing the Giuseppi's contract and I wanted an option to try and replace it, given that I have an ice cream wizard to go with his Magic Milk.' She looked thoroughly miserable, as she should, and she added, 'I don't want to lose you, Bridge. Not from the business and not from my life. I'm so sorry you got blindsided like that.'

'Sorry for what? For talking to Mike or for poisoning me? Neither of those is gonna be easy to forgive, Lucy.'

'I know, and there's nothing I can do to make it up, is there?'

'No.' Bridget put her empty bottle on the tiny patio table. 'I don't want to lose you as a friend, either, but you're not gonna keep me as one by acting like that. How about you get off to York tomorrow afternoon? If I haven't been rushed to intensive care by Monday, we'll start again. Who knows, one of us might have a blinding flash of insight into Tony's murder over the weekend.'

Lucy nodded mutely. They sat in silence for a moment, then Lucy stood up. 'I am totally doing the bakery run tomorrow morning, aren't I?'

'Yes.'

'Then I'll go and tell Tom I'm coming over in the afternoon and go to bed.' She picked up her phone and shuffled out of the corner where she'd been sitting. 'I really am sorry, Bridge.'

'Yeah, I know. Love to Tom and all that.'

Lucy couldn't resist it. Despite all she knew about Bridget, and despite the warning look on Bridget's face, she came over and put her arms round her. 'You're wasted in Southport. G'night.'

Bridget sat back and shivered. She had caught more of the sun today than she'd have liked. Definitely feeling a tad burnt. Unless it was the food poisoning kicking in. The nerve of the girl. Lucy was wrong to have spoken to Mike, and she was wrong about Southport. Bridget would show her exactly that. She had two reasons for sending Lucy away: one was to let them have some space from each other, but the other was to give Bridget some freedom to move. She stood up and went back inside. Now where was that medical thermometer, and should she Google the symptoms of food poisoning again, just to be sure?

Fifty-Three

It had been a long time since Bridget had had to work with a friend she'd fallen out with. At least she hadn't had to share breakfast. When she walked into Caffè Milano at nine o'clock, Lucy had been to Cairndale, unpacked the bakery order and even started prepping the lunches.

'Is that your way of saying sorry?' Bridget asked her.

'No, it's my way of keeping busy so that I don't have to worry about things. Did you sleep okay?'

'Not really. I keep thinking the sunburn on the back of me neck is sepsis, and it's too effing hot. While I waited for the rush hour to finish, I checked every weather app and website going. None of them think this heatwave is gonna pass any time soon. How far away is the Lake District?'

'About ten miles as the raven flies. Why?'

'Raven? What, is the crow on holiday or something? Anyway, we're due a water shortage at the end of the month, despite being connected to England's largest reservoir. I give up with this lot.'

Lucy passed some cucumbers, a knife and a question. 'What did you mean *rush hour*? Even when the M6 is closed, there's zero traffic between here and your house.'

Bridget got a chopping board. 'The school bus. It can delay me by up to ninety seconds. And while I was checking the weather, I remembered about Kat. Not only did she run away yesterday, Wendy said something about a new starter. What's that all about?'

'It's the last maths GCSE exam this morning. Only biology and religious studies to go.'

'Jazz! Why didn't I think of that?'

It was true. Kat's little sister, a good six years younger, had been in purdah since the GCSE exams started in earnest and had only been allowed out to work that one day in the café because she'd clocked up enough hours of revision. Kat being Kat had moaned a lot about Jazz always getting her own way, but these exams were a very stressful time. Jasmine's future would look very different if she didn't get the right grades.

On the other hand, did they want her? 'Why is she coming up here? What's wrong with the shop?'

Lucy gave her the side-eye. 'Didn't you ask Kat the same question?'

'Yeah, I did. Refuses to work for her mother.'

'Correct. I found out yesterday that Jackie told Jasmine that she had to work in the shop or somewhere else, starting next Monday. Jazz popped in for ten minutes to drop off her CV while you were away. She says she won't work at the same time as Kat, because that would be cruel.'

Bridget had to break off slicing to laugh. 'I can see that. Totally. What was on her CV? She's still at school, for God's sake.'

'Oh, they all have to do them. Part of the curriculum. It was pretty bare, though, because she knows I'd check it with Kat, so no porkies. She put down her commitment to St Peter's Choir, her duties as May Queen and about five hundred words she's copied and pasted off the internet. I told her that if she wants to be a nurse, she should apply to nursing college, because that's where she'd nicked it from.'

'Sounds about right. Was she embarrassed.'

'Nope. Totally unbothered. Said no one reads these things. I did tell Jackie about it, though. Don't want her doing the same on her university application. Time to open, I think.'

Bridget checked her phone. They had two minutes – long enough for what she had to say.

'Look, Luce, I've been thinking. There's no bakery run on Sunday. I'm gonna go to Southport after work tomorrow and see if there's a job going at Giuseppi's.'

Lucy took off the food prep apron and replaced it with the barista's. 'I think you're making a big mistake, Bridge, I really do. I also hope you get the job, okay?'

For the first time since she could remember, Bridget initiated a hug. It felt good.

Wendy Sadler and her reusable coffee cup made an appearance around half past eleven. 'I'm off to Donna's,' she announced. 'I think I can risk an extra shot cappuccino.'

'It's good of you to help her out,' said Bridget.

Wendy shrugged. 'My car is nowhere near as big as Donna's. I've put her toolbox and a couple of her branded products in, but I've had to leave the rest. At least she can get working again. And the professional crime scene cleaners are booked for Monday, so maybe they'll come up with something.'

Bridget doubted that very much, but she wasn't going to burst Wendy's bubble. 'It all helps put things into perspective,' she said to Wendy. To herself, she thought, *Since when did I start quoting TV therapists?*

Wendy smiled around at the café, which was getting busy. 'I know I said it was hard work yesterday, but I've fallen in love with the place. Thank you for taking me on, Bridget. I know I'm a fair bit older, but I reckon I've got something to offer.'

Bridget set the milk to heat. 'You have. There's going to be a few unhappy toastie customers today.'

'I've enrolled on the food hygiene course. Kat told me all about the online option.'

Bridget shook her head. 'If you learn anything, let me know. When you've passed, I'll give you the real version. If I'm not struck down by food poisoning and carried off for one of Mrs Carson's *end of life* shifts at the hospital.'

'I shall miss your glass-half-empty approach to life, Bridget, even though I've only just met you. I'd better go because that Tickle Trout roundabout can get very busy on Fridays.'

Bridget watched her go, and watched Laura Paige walk through the main entrance with Perry. Whatever he said made her smile, and she touched his arm as they parted ways, Perry heading for the stairs and Laura coming into the Spinning Room.

She went over to another of the regulars and said hello. She dropped her bag on an empty chair, took her purse out and came to the counter. 'Hi, Bridget. I'm glad I've caught you.'

'Likewise, Laura. What can I get you?'

The bookbinder placed her order, and Bridget asked, 'How's Hayley today? Have you been in touch?'

'I've just come from there. I went round after dropping the kids at school and nursery. She's not good, Bridget. Abi Tennant is doing her best to find out what the police are up to, but they're not giving much away. I think they're still waiting on some forensic tests and for the digital team to finish analysing Tony's laptop. Abi did tell Hayley one thing, though. She said that when she arrived at the station, Esther

Thornfield was in the witness room.'

'Have you spoken to Shannon?'

'Briefly. We're not even thinking of reopening until after the weekend.'

'You should call her and ask her about Esther's theory concerning the *City of Lancaster*. And then you should tell Hayley about it. There you go.'

Laura looked at Bridget and blinked. She hadn't been crying today. Not yet. 'Abi also told Hayley the true meaning of *released under investigation*. There is absolutely no legal requirement for the police to tell her anything. Ever. It could go on for the rest of her life in theory.'

'That's … I didn't realise it was that bad, Laura. I'm sorry. Have they taken her passport or anything?'

Laura humphed. 'The other side of the coin is that there are no legal restrictions on Hayley, either. Abi said that it means rapists can – and do – make contact with their victims.'

The panic which clutched at Bridget's insides was back. *Think of Hayley,* she told herself. 'For once, I'm gonna focus on the positive, Laura. Tell her to stick two fingers up to them.'

'I'll try. If you could go and see her over the weekend, that might help, too.'

Bridget sighed. 'I'll see what I can manage. I'm hoping to be away on Saturday night, but I won't bail out on her, Laura.'

'I know. Thanks. See you later.'

Bridget knew that the vast majority of coppers were good people. She'd come into contact with enough of them over the years. She also knew that they were human, overworked and pulled in as many directions as a mother with quads at an amusement park. The next major enquiry that landed in Commander Ross's lap would edge Tony Carson's murder down the priority list, just like the need to negotiate her exit from Caffè Milano would mean that Bridget had other things to worry about. She shook her head and served the next customer.

Bridget waved Lucy off in the middle of the afternoon, and they parted as friends, which told Bridget everything she needed to know. Actual friends just say goodbye and wish each other a nice weekend. Only when a friendship is strained to breaking point do they make a fuss.

She and Kat dealt with the Friday afternoon rush of after-schoolers, then it went quiet, as it usually did. Bridget sent Kat off to get ready for a Chester family night out, celebrating the end of Jazz's GCSE exams, and Kat cheered her up no end with her parting soliloquy.

'I don't know why she gets a meal at Alfredo's just for turning up to her exams. I didn't. I didn't even get one for passing my A levels because we were on holiday. It's better than her going into town with her mates and necking cider. I'm telling you, Boss, you don't know what you're letting yourself in for hiring her. She's trouble, that one.'

'I blame the parents. Now scoot.'

When Bridget was absolutely sure she had five minutes, she got out her phone and started to put Operation Southport into action. She checked her emails – still no reply – so she sighed and dialled his number.

The footballer Owain Marshall did not oversee his investments himself. Too busy training for that, and if Bridget's first-hand observations were right, he'd lost a fair few brain cells from years of defensive headers. Or he never had them to start with. In his place, a management company ran things (for a generous fee), and Bridget waited for Jack Tidy to answer the phone.

Bridget had never run the branch in Southport. She had worked there part-time as a barista and focused on the ice cream. It had been Jack Tidy who recruited Lucy, and Jack was now dealing with the fallout from Lucy's decision to sever ties with Tara Doyle. Jack knew exactly who Bridget was, so why hadn't he responded to her email and why wasn't he answering his phone? She tried him again and was cut off with no option of voicemail. This was not good.

She was staring into space and considering her options when Perry walked in, for once looking less than chilled. 'Hiya,' she said. 'I'm afraid we don't do discounts at the end of the day if you're after cheap cake. Allan has already tried that one.'

It was lame. She knew that. He knew that. He made an effort to take her remark as she'd intended – a bit of harmless banter.

'Good job, too. Feargal tried his best, but your cakes are almost as addictive as your coffee.'

'Ready for the weekend?' she asked.

'I'm ready for a break in the weather. Are you working both days?'

'Someone has to – Lucy's gone away.' She tried for a brighter smile. 'I'm hoping to get to Southport tomorrow night. If I haven't come down with food poisoning.'

He looked genuinely concerned. 'What's up? Should you be telling me this, given that you run a food outlet?'

She waved a hand. 'Accidental ingestion of raw milk ice cream. I should have another twenty-four hours before I succumb.'

'Lisa used to say the same on nights like this. The disappearance of the mint choc chip tub was entirely accidental.'

She could think of nothing to say to that, and the conversation hung as heavy as the waves of heat outside. Time to be professional. 'Is there anything I can get you? Nice cooling pot of tea?'

'No thanks. I just came to see if you were okay after the week you've had. I was going to say that I still haven't processed your notice to quit, but if you're off to Southport, it sounds like you mean it.'

She tried to brighten things up. 'Yep. A night of debauchery and karaoke is just what I need. Not necessarily in that order, though. I find that debauchery does nothing for my high C.'

'Shame I'll never get to hear it. I'll put your notice through on Tuesday, Bridget. I hope you enjoy yourself.'

'You too.'

He left, and Bridget headed into the privacy of the kitchen, leaning against the wall at the exact spot where she could see if there was a real paying customer on the way in. She opened her contacts again and scrolled to C. Two names leapt out at her – Connor Holden and Conrad Bloody Clarke. Maybe she should put Clarke's name in quarantine. She made sure that Connor's name was selected and placed the call.

Connor Holden was the self-described *Oldest Swinger in Southport.* He wasn't that old – mid-forties – but he had been a lot older than Natalie. His marriage was in trouble when his long-suffering wife kicked him out, and in Natalie, Connor had found a refuge.

It worked both ways, of course. Natalie had latched on to Connor like a rock in a stormy sea, and they had both been good for each other. Say what you like about the age difference, but while they were together, Natalie had been truly happy. Whether it would have lasted is another matter. Like Bridget's "relationship" with Tony Carson, death had given the question an unexpected answer.

In her visits to Southport to finish emptying the flat she'd once shared with Nat, Bridget had avoided Layla's Piano Bar, where Natalie had worked and where Connor ran the entertainment, because she didn't want to be reminded of the past. Right now she had no choice but talk to him. Unlike Jack Tidy, Connor Holden answered on the second ring.

'Hiya, Bridget, long time no speak to.'

'Hiya, Connor. How's things?'

'Good, yeah. How're you?'

'Have you heard that Lucy's been kicked out of Giuseppi's?'

Connor took a breath. 'I had, yeah. What's going on?'

'Search me. Seriously, I have no clue. Look, Connor, I'm leaving Caffè Milano and coming back. Well, I was trying to. I can't get hold of Jack Tidy.'

'Is that right?'

'I was hoping to come down tomorrow night and have a chat.'

Connor hesitated. 'Look, tomorrow's not good. I'll tell you what, I'll ask around and FaceTime you tomorrow afternoon. How's that?'

It was better than nothing. 'Can you do it after we've closed. Say six o'clock?'

'No probs. Leave it with me. Catch you later.'

Bridget stared at the phone. This was not what she'd been expecting. She put it in her apron and walked out of the kitchen. Through the window, the creaking mill wheel slowed down and stopped under the command of Coffin Joe, the ghost of Ford Mill.

The absolute silence of an empty building on a hot day settled around her. She caught the smell of roasted beans on some invisible current, and that smell took her back to the top floor on Monday morning. She shuddered and went to collect the *Closed* sign. The ghost of Ford Mill was not the mysterious Joseph Hayton. No, it was Tony Carson.

She started packing up and getting ready to face the traffic chaos of Cairndale. At this time on a Friday night, it might take her a whole extra five minutes to get to Hayley's house. Not worth it. A bath first.

Apart from wanting to clean up, there was another reason for going home – Bridget had left the medical thermometer behind, to stop herself constantly checking for a fever. She took off her apron and went to lock the outside door.

Fifty-Four

When she finally answered the door, Hayley looked worse than yesterday. Her face was going puffy all over, and her eyes blinked through tears. There were white stains down her hoodie and a slight tremble in her hands. 'You'd better come in' was all the welcome Bridget received.

Hayley led her back to the patio, where an ashtray had joined an open bottle of white wine. 'Drink?' said Hayley.

'No thanks. I'm driving.'

Hayley slumped into the patio chair and took a gulp of wine. She picked up a packet of cigarettes, realised she wasn't alone, and dropped them back on the table. Bridget moved the other chair to face Hayley and saw the reason for the white stains – a bowl of cereal on the floor was dried out with flakes stuck to the sides. That would be a bugger to clean off and no mistake.

'Laura came to see me this morning,' said Bridget. 'This "released under investigation" thing is a right bitch, Hayley.'

'It's even worse on the inside,' Hayley replied, leaving it open as to whether she meant that she was feeling it more than Bridget or whether imprisonment was worse than the limbo of uncertainty she faced now.

'I know,' said Bridget. 'And I really am sorry. Is there nothing that Abi can do?'

'I'm not supposed to tell you.'

'But you will anyway.'

'Given that you're running off, yeah I will.'

'I'm going nowhere yet.'

Hayley took more wine and this time she opened the cigarettes and lit one. 'Forensic tests can take a month to complete. Abi says they've rushed the important ones, but they won't finish the rest for a while. If they've got no physical evidence by then, they'll scale back the investigation. They already have, really.'

Hayley made an effort to stop the smoke blowing towards Bridget and continued, 'Abi says that if they draw a blank, she's going to put pressure on the top man – Commander Ross, is it?'

'He's the one.'

'Well, she says that he's actually very fair. Not sure whether I believe her. Allegedly, in a couple of months, if she gets the right people to have a word in Ross's ear – not herself, obviously – then Ross will tell them to drop me off the list. Completely free. I was hoping you'd be one of the people to have a word in his ear.'

'Me!'

'You, or get Lucy on the case. Anyone. But you're leaving. So that's a bust. Like my life generally. And that wasn't the only bad news. The insurance company won't pay out on Tony's death while the case is open.'

'That's not fair.'

'Since when were insurance companies fair? Donna's decamped to Penwortham, and Laura's busy with the kids and getting her business going again.' She let out an enormous sigh. 'Thanks for coming, Bridget.'

'Is there anything else I can do?'

Hayley stubbed out her cigarette, half smoked. 'Can you negotiate the return of the leased cameras and find a market for the lights? No? Then leave me to wallow for a bit if you can't clear my name.'

Bridget didn't want to be on the wrong side of Hayley's temper, which was surely the next stop on her self-pity train. She stood up and said, 'I haven't given up yet, and I know you haven't either.'

Hayley topped up her glass and liberally watered the patio when her hand swerved. 'Shit! What a waste. Good job I've got more. Cheers, Bridget. You know the way out.'

Bridget left and got back in the van. She drove off on autopilot and found herself heading up the wide and leafy boulevard of Byford Old Road instead of Midland Street, so presumably she was now passing the childhood home of Hayley and Laura. She was also heading into the dead end created when the roads were revised in the sixties. 'Shit,' she muttered and got ready for a three-point turn. 'Oh no,' she added. 'Seriously?'

She could see through the bollards to the junction, and a workman was pinning up a *Road Closed* sign across the entrance to the Rivers Estate. 'On a Friday night? You're kidding me.'

Still, forewarned is forearmed, and when Bridget had got back to Midland Square, she had an idea. Instead of taking the official route to

Byford, she headed back into town and turned left at Millhouse and skirted the ULIST campus. 'It's round here somewhere,' she said. 'I'm sure I saw it yesterday … there we go!'

Not far from where she'd dropped Ciara Davenport at the physiotherapy clinic, she found first the back of the Red Rose Hotel and then Spice Ireland, the pub where Kat had said the local Goths hang out. It was worth a look.

The 1950s building, cloned from some brewery master plan, had been painted green like plastic Irish bars the world over. The difference here was that the mural on the gable end showed a shamrock surrounded by exotic-looking foliage and spices, including a flourishing cannabis plant, all embraced by the Irish tricolour and something in red, white and blue horizontal stripes that she'd never seen before. She chuckled. A giant pot plant, and how far was it to Divisional HQ? Two minutes? She drove into the almost empty car park and got out of the van.

Around the corner, away from sight, half a dozen students were vaping and laughing. She walked into the pub and stopped dead. *When did I get so old?*

She shouldn't have been surprised. After all, the university was just over the road. Apart from a couple of men around her age, all the customers were students – of one sort or another. In the corner, three girls were huddled round bottles of alcoholic pop. They were too busy talking and looking at their phones to notice Bridget, and she walked up to the bar in a daze.

'Food's through the other room,' came a voice from below the bar. The owner straightened up and smiled. He looked a bit like a sumo wrestler in build, and his black hair and olive skin showed ancestry somewhere in Asia. The voice, though, had come from North Dublin, probably round the corner from Grandma Gorrigan. 'Sorry, I assumed you were after the Friday special on account of you looking a bit lost on this side.' He peered at her and grinned. 'Unless you're a lecturer looking for one of your students to tell them their essay's overdue. You wouldn't be the first.'

Bridget laughed, flattered to be taken for a lecturer. And why not play up to it? 'Not tonight. I'm allowed a weekend an' all. Now you've mentioned food, what's on the special?'

'Same as every week – turbo-charged green curry, like me mammy used to make, her being a Thai chef.' He was quick, this guy, because he said, 'If you didn't know about the food, and you're not after a wayward scholar, what *are* you doing in here? You know the mural's just a laugh, right? We don't actually sell weed.'

'Could I not just have come for a drink?'

His answer was a raised eyebrow. 'If you're after a man, I wouldn't bother. They're all callow youths.'

'Not all of us.'

'Jesus!' exclaimed Bridget. 'Where did you spring from, Jed?'

The barman looked from Bridget to Jed Holmes and back again. 'Things just got very interesting here.' He leaned on the bar. 'How do you two know each other? And are you gonna take pity on Jed and buy him a proper drink? And yourself as well, of course. I've a gorgeous gin from Donegal in the other room.'

Bridget's head was spinning. This was a big mistake. Unless …

'Pint and a half of Guinness. The half's for me.'

'I don't like Guinness,' said Jed. 'Can I—'

'No,' chorused Bridget and the barman together.

'Sit yourselves down,' said the barman. 'I'll bring it over.' He winked. 'As a special favour.'

Jed retreated, and Bridget leaned over the counter to whisper, 'There's one for yourself if you tell me whether I'm being wound up.'

The barman put the drinks to settle and said, 'Oh yeah?'

'I was told this is where the dark tribe hangs out.'

He smiled an Irish smile, with added twinkle. 'You were not being wound up, but your informant only gave you half the story. Come back on Thursday night. Was it someone specific you were after, 'cos I still can't figure you out. Missing person? Anthropological research?'

'Sort of,' replied Bridget. Anywhere else, the combined nosiness and flirting would have put her back up. Not here, and not from the guy in front of her. It seemed fitting somehow. 'My name is Bridget and I am a Goth. I have worn black for twenty-five years.'

The barman's eyes glinted with mischief. 'Welcome, Bridget. My name is Declan and you are safe here.' He tilted his head and went to finish the drinks. 'You look a bit out of practice, mind.'

'You're probably right. Keep the change.'

'Cheers. I'll bring them over.'

Bridget joined Jed in a dark corner and Declan deposited the drinks without any further comments. As he got back to the bar, a young woman appeared and they swapped over. Declan headed for the better paying customers in the lounge leaving the barmaid to wring what she could from the students.

'How are you feeling?' asked Jed. 'I spent all last night researching the dangers of raw milk. There haven't been any cases I can find that are linked to ice cream.'

'No one had been hit by a car until they developed the internal combustion engine.'

Jed digested this thought with a swig of Guinness. He made a face. 'That's nasty.'

Bridget joined him. Perfect. Not too chilled and as creamy as … No. Don't go there. 'It is not nasty, Jed. It is rich and slightly bitter. This is a free pint, so drink it and savour the taste of Dublin.'

'You're worse than Declan.' He took another long swallow. 'I think my tongue's gone numb.'

He pronounced *tongue* to rhyme with *wrong*. It sounded weird. He put his drink aside. 'Are you okay, though. I really am sorry.'

'I know, I know. Touch wood, no symptoms yet.'

He looked very relieved. 'Great. Have you found out anything else?'

She took another large pull on her half. Where had that gone? She put the half-empty glass down and an idea came to her. 'You know what, Jed, you did good work with Julie the dog walker. If you volunteer to do a little mission for me, I'll tell you what Esther and Shannon's alibi is.'

He sat up straight, nose twitching. Literally twitching. He grabbed for a handkerchief and sneezed, turning away from Bridget at the last moment.

'If you infect me, I will boil you alive and serve the juices in small Japanese teacups,' she told him.

'Sorry. It's the Guinness. I must be allergic. Go on. What was their alibi?'

'Mission?'

'Whatever.'

Bridget couldn't help it. She checked to see if anyone was listening and leaned in. 'Esther says they were off to score weed from a guy in Byford who grows his own. Can you find him?'

Jed suddenly looked very worried. 'I might, yeah, but I'll need to show willing.'

She took a moment. Money. Of course. Tight git. She passed two twenty-pound notes under the table. 'Good luck.'

'Thanks.'

She drained her Guinness and rolled the glass in her hand. She was so tempted to have another, it was that good. However, unless she fancied leaving the van here and getting the train back, she'd have to go. Then again, she could seduce Jed and crash at his place.

'Why are you laughing?' he asked.

'I need to stop talking to meself. See you later, Jed.'

Fifty-Five

There was a surprise waiting for Bridget on Saturday morning when she parked outside the Market Square branch. Along with the Tabor's order, Lilianna had a large, soft package addressed to Lucy.

'This came yesterday. Coach Lucy says to give it to you.'

This was getting out of hand. *'Coach?'*

'Yes. Here.'

Bridget tore at the wrapping and several slippery polythene packets cascaded out, most landing on the cobbles. Inside each packet was a sports top in Caffè Milano red. That was both encouraging and terrifying at the same time.

'Also message,' added Lili. 'There is one for each at Byford, including Yasmeen. You are to wear them. I say it is not fair because if you have lightweight shirts, it will rain soon.'

'I think you're settling in nicely, Lili, if you think that. Cheers.'

In the privacy of the Spinning Room kitchen, Bridget swapped shirts. The new uniforms were samples, as yet unbranded. They were definitely cooler.

'Morning,' said Wendy. 'That looks nice. What colour bra are you wearing?'

'Black. Can you see it?'

'No.'

'Good. You okay? You're early.'

'Still can't sleep. If I had a bigger car or your van, I'd do the bakery run. I go past the Market Square on my way in.'

'If you keep up this excellent start, you might inherit the van when I go.'

Wendy made a face. 'I'd rather you stayed. Is there one in my size?'

'Here. There's one for Lucy, Kat and even Jazz. If she turns up.'

Jasmine Chester did not turn up. At nine fifty, Jackie breezed into the Spinning Room with Kat following behind. 'My fault,' said their mother. 'Chris didn't want Jazz to drink anything last night, but I said it was about time she learned responsible drinking. Turns out you can have too much of a good thing.'

'Too much responsibility?' said Bridget.

'No. Too much house Chianti,' said Jackie. 'And she may be salami-intolerant.'

'She just didn't want to get out of bed,' said Kat. 'This is my day off. I don't see why I have to come in.'

'Well *I* can't do it, can I?' said Jackie. 'Someone has to work in the shop.'

'What about Dad?'

'He volunteered to make sure Jazz didn't die in her sleep. The man's suffered enough.'

'It's not my problem,' huffed Kat.

Jackie put her arm into the small of Kat's back. 'The Chesters have said that they will provide a worker today, and that's you. Besides, if you hadn't wound her up so much, she might not have stolen that extra glass of wine, so it's your fault really.'

'I'm changing my name. I don't like being a Chester any more.'

'Well it's better than my maiden name, so count yourself lucky.' She propelled her daughter forwards. 'See you later, love. Bye, Bridget, bye Wendy.'

Bridget raised her eyebrows at her grumpy duckling. 'How bad was she really?'

'Bad enough.'

'Do you have anything on today? I appreciate you volunteering, but I wouldn't want you missing out.'

Kat shrugged and wandered into the kitchen.

'Wendy, you take over for a minute.'

Bridget intercepted Kat and said, 'Look! New uniforms, and they really are cooler.'

'Oh. Is that what you're wearing?'

'Hadn't you noticed?'

'It's five to ten. I don't notice anything until ten o'clock. I'll start work in five minutes.'

Kat's phone was in her hand before Bridget had left the kitchen.

By two o'clock, Bridget had messaged Lucy that the new shirts were a hit. She didn't feel nearly as washed out, even though the weather was, if anything, even hotter. Kat had woken up and been her usual efficiently grumpy self. Apart from needing to cover each other's breaks, they could have coped with two staff. Until the Cowan Valley Horticultural Society came in.

A line of well-dressed seniors had formed, and Bridget asked the second customer if they were a coach party.

'Oh no. Wouldn't be seen dead on a coach,' the woman declared, then added. 'We're the Ho Soc. That's what my grandson calls us and he thinks I don't know what he means. No, the Hackthwaite Garden Centre turned us away because they said they were too busy. Their loss is your gain, I suppose. Do you offer group discounts?'

'Yes, but only if you book in advance,' replied Bridget. 'Sorry.'

Kat wheeled by. 'And that's difficult, because we don't take advance bookings.'

'Oh! Hello,' said the woman. 'Don't I know you?'

Bridget rolled her eyes and went to chop more salad. When the group had been served, she messaged Lucy again. *Just picked up custom from Hackthwaite Garden Centre. You should check it out.*

On my list, came the reply.

Bridget was just starting to relax when Jed Holmes came in wearing his most mournful face. 'Can I have a pot of tea and a word?'

Bridget surveyed the Spinning Room. 'Yeah, but we'll have to sit in the foyer. No empty tables. Go and lurk out there and I'll be along in a sec.'

She put some iced water on the tray for herself and slipped through the archway when the tea had brewed. Jed looked up from his phone. 'I thought you'd forgotten me,' he said accusingly. 'And that tea will be like treacle.'

'Wrong, Jed. I could never forget you, and this tea is as ripe as one of Magic Mike's strawberries. How did you get on?'

'There was no point looking this morning, so I rang my dad and asked what to do.'

Bridget couldn't believe her ears. 'You're a student! You don't need lessons in tracking down a drug dealer! Still less do you need to call a retired copper and ask him how to break the law!'

'He's not retired. He can't afford to.' Jed grinned. 'Serves him right for marrying a younger woman and starting a second family.'

'Whatever. I mean, seriously, Jed?'

'This is the country out here. I stick out like a sore thumb. I asked him about it and he laughed at me. Told me to subcontract it to a local, but the only local I know is Kat. Why didn't you ask her?'

'Why didn't *you*?'

He sipped his tea and made a face. 'How can you drink this?' He waited and took another sip. 'You've met Jackie, right?'

'Duh.'

'I don't want Kat to get in trouble with her mom.'

That was both considerate and wimpish. A bit like Bridget. She smiled ruefully. 'And that was my thought process, too. Probably for the best. I'm sure the actual police know who he is.'

He contorted his hands into his jeans pocket and fished out the two banknotes. 'Here. How are you feeling? You look okay.'

'Fingers crossed. No symptoms so far that can't be put down to the heat. And these new shirts are much better.'

He looked relieved. 'Is there anything else I can do? I can't think of where to go next.'

Bridget took the money. 'You and me both, Jed. Hang on.'

She looked at the message which had just come in. Connor Holden. *Am seeing someone later. Can I call at 8?*

She gave the message a quick thumbs-up and put her phone away.

'What happens now?' asked Jed in an open question. He really didn't seem to have a clue. Bridget, on the other hand, had too many clues and too many suspects.

'Any one of five people could have done it, Jed. They are all unaccounted for on Sunday night and all could have had the knowledge to break in and steal the shotgun. I'm not Liz Swindlehurst—'

'Thank God,' broke in Jed. 'Much nicer.'

Bridget was flattered. Bound to be. 'Yeah. She's older than me. She's also a good detective and has minions at her beck and call. If *she* can't find any evidence that puts the case beyond reasonable doubt, what chance have we got?'

She'd done it deliberately: *we*. Jed was as flattered as Bridget had been, and his nose twitched again. Thankfully, this time he didn't sneeze. Then his ferret brows wrinkled. 'You didn't come into Spice Ireland last night looking for me, so what *were* you doing there?'

She was past caring now. 'I'd been told it was the Goth hangout. Wrong night. Don't know why I bothered.'

Jed finished his tea. 'My auntie's a Goth. Well, she's me

stepmother's sister. She's really sound. Kindest person I've met. She says it's two fingers to the mainstream without wanting to destroy it. It's where she can be who she is.'

'I used to think that, when I knew who I was.'

They smiled at each other, until Jed's eyes flicked behind Bridget to the Spinning Room. She turned reflexively to see what was going on, but all she saw was Kat's back. 'Did I miss something?' she asked Jed.

He went bright red. 'Kat came to say something. I think. Then she saw me and turned round.'

Bridget folded her arms. 'What have you done to upset her? I did warn you.'

He was outraged. 'Me! Nothing! It was *her*. I asked her out and she said I was too short, only she dressed it up. I was nice back to her because I didn't want to upset you.'

Poor kid. She unfolded her arms and braced them on the chair, ready to stand up. 'I know how you feel. I felt the same when I saw Perry with Laura. Young, thin and pretty.'

'She's the same age as you,' said Jed with some conviction. 'I looked her up.'

'Thanks for the vote of confidence, and for the record, I think Katarina needs to get real about her dating options. Thanks for everything, Jed.'

She picked up the tray and went back to her proper job.

'There you are,' said Wendy. 'I sent Kat looking for you because there's an issue.'

Bridget did a three-sixty on her heel. The Spinning Room was bustling and busy, but that was as it should be. No sign of drama.

'Go into the kitchen,' said Wendy.

Bridget strode up to the doorway and found Kat furiously working her phone. 'What's up, kid?'

'Stay there and don't move,' ordered Kat. She put her phone down and hoiked up her new top. 'See?'

Bridget did see. Kat had opted for a white sports bra this morning. It was now pink, as were her armpits. Oh dear.

'Let me take a picture,' said Bridget innocently. 'For the claim form.'

Kat thrust down her shirt. 'Only if you want to die.'

Bridget did take a picture. Of herself. When she got home. She sent it to Lucy with several exclamation marks then ran a bath.

OMG! SO SORRY! My fault for ordering a custom colour. Apart from that, how were they?

Bridget sent a couple of suitable emojis and climbed into the tub. When she discovered that the dye washed off skin quite easily, she felt almost human again, especially as she was still free of food poisoning. As for Kat, Jackie would no doubt have something at the back of the shop to restore her *favourite new bra* to pristine whiteness.

She poured herself a glass of wine at ten to eight and Connor messaged her a few minutes later. *Whenever you're ready.* She propped the phone on the table and FaceTimed him.

He was in his bedroom. His old bedroom at the family home. She'd heard his wife had taken him back. 'Are you hiding up there?' she asked him.

'Sort of. The girls are watching some rubbish on the telly. Something with shouting and lots of blood.'

'Not working tonight?'

Connor was a fixer in the entertainment business. Part talent scout, part booking agent, part coach and part promoter. The night was his element.

'I'm going out later. How's things in the Shire?'

'Full of hobbits, as you'd expect.'

He looked down and spoke to his jeans. 'You're the only one I can say this to, Bridget. I miss her, you know. Not like you do, of course. And I'm happy back here now I've been put in me place, but I miss her.'

'Yeah. I know.' She drew a breath to change the subject before she started crying. 'Have you got some good news for me?'

He looked up and gave her a sympathetic smile. 'Sorry. I really am. I had to twist a few arms to find out what was going on, but it's a done deal. Jack Tidy has franchised the coffee shop to one of the national chains and that girl you trained up on the ice cream is taking over the gelateria part of the operation.'

'Shit, Connor.'

He grimaced. 'I know. I pushed him, I really did, but he was under orders. No one from Caffè Milano to have any place in Southport. I told him to go shaft himself and told him that if you want to come and work for Laycross Entertainments, I'll roll out the red carpet. Or black carpet in your case. You know that.'

Bridget couldn't speak. She shifted on the sofa and cleared her throat. 'I … er … thanks, Connor. That's great. I'll need to think about it.'

'Of course. Whenever you like and whatever job you like. Except mine, of course. We'd go bust.' He grinned at an old joke about Bridget's choice of bands for the piano bar.

Her world shifted on its axis again, just like it had when she'd found Tony in the Mill. She grasped at a straw. 'How are the girls doing at school?'

'Good, yeah. No thanks to me. They get their brains from their mother. They get their looks from me, of course.'

'No they don't. That would be a tragedy.'

'You're not wrong there.'

As with Lucy and with Perry. As with Hayley and with Jed, there was nothing to say any more. She had nothing to offer. The tears were coming any second now. 'Take care, Connor, and I'll be in touch.'

'Too late for me to take care. Not for you, though. Look after yourself, Bridget, and mind out for those hobbits.'

He ended the call and the screen went back to her contacts page, with Connor's name highlighted. She picked up her phone and something moved internally. Maybe it was the imminent tears, maybe it was her determination to stick two fingers up to the world. Whatever it was at work inside her, it made her stab the number after Connor's and quickly put the phone to her ear so she couldn't change her mind and cancel the call.

To paraphrase Liz Swindlehurst, when your problems are really, really bad, maybe Conrad Bloody Clarke is the *only* answer.

Fifty-Six

He took the call almost straight away, and a wash of beery noise flooded out of the speaker.

'Bridget? Is that you?'

'Yeah. I'm sorry—'

'What? I can't hear you. Don't panic. I'll call you back in two ticks.'

'There's no need, Conrad, I misdialled you and it's …'

Too late. He was gone, but he'd be coming back. She topped up her wine and propped up the phone again because she'd heard that he preferred video calls. It took two minutes longer than she'd expected. Gone to the toilet probably. Like she should have done. No, don't think about Conrad in the toilet. At least the shock of the noise had stopped her crying. No, don't think about that either. *So what am I gonna think about … saved by the bell.*

She accepted the video call and the chaos was replaced by distant chatter. For a second, the screen showed a pub's beer garden with fields in the distance. The Inkwell, she supposed. He adjusted the phone and sat back. 'Hello, Bridget. Is everything okay? Is Lucy okay?'

'Course she is. She's with Tom.'

'Sorry? Let me adjust the volume. Did Lucy tell you I'm losing my hearing? That's better. What's the problem?'

'I just fancied saying hello.'

'Yes, and I'm an Olympic gymnast … Oh, no, he's heard your voice.'

Conrad's dog jumped onto the bench next to him and leaned forwards, the mismatched blue and brown eyes boring into the screen. Brilliant white fangs appeared and were washed with a long pink tongue. 'Arff!' declared Scout, then he turned round and jumped down.

'Sorry about that. He's bloody incorrigible when he hears a voice. Just be thankful he doesn't really know you. He tends to lick the screen.'

Was dog saliva worse than raw milk? Bridget shuddered. 'I'm really sorry, Conrad. I didn't know it was a party.'

'It's a double party, Bridget. Both the Wizards and the Witches won today. It was the girls' first league match, and Mina held three catches.

We're going to party like it may never happen again, because it probably won't.'

Bloody cricket. Bloody sport. Bloody dogs. Conrad Bloody Clarke's version of life in the country was another reason Bridget was leaving, only she had nowhere to go now, did she?

He leaned forwards. 'But you don't give a flying fig about that, do you? What's up? And don't try to bullshit a bullshitter.'

She sighed. Lucy once said that Conrad didn't forgive people, nor did he bear grudges. He exacted revenge and forgot about it. And he could keep a secret. 'It's this murder at the Mill. You must have heard of it.'

'I have. Mina told me you'd gone into bat for one of the suspects.'

'Not my choice of metaphor, but yeah, sort of. It's the victim. There's a lot of people trying to say we're better off without him. Even his brother's keeping quiet because he might be a suspect.'

Conrad nodded sympathetically. He lit a cigarette and lifted a substantial tankard to his mouth. From the gleam in his eyes, this was a long way from being his first pint. 'That's not good, is it? How can I help?'

'I've run out of ideas, Conrad. What would you do? How would you go about things?'

He laughed so much that Scout's ears appeared above the table edge, keen to join in the fun.

'Oh dear, Bridget. You don't want to copy me.' He leaned forwards. 'When I go into the field looking for something, my method is to first upset everyone, then threaten them until the guilty party tries to kill me. I wouldn't recommend it as an approach to crime solving.'

'Put like that, I can see why Mina worries so much. And why Lucy worries about Tom when he's with you.'

He grinned and took another drink. 'It's fast and it gets results. Now, what does the crime tell you?'

'That someone didn't like Tony Carson.'

He waved that away as if disappointed. 'No, I mean the actual act of taking a life. Up close and personal. What does that specific event tell you?'

'I … I don't think I've thought of it like that.'

He turned serious for a moment. His hand dropped out of sight and his arm shook. Giving Scout a scratch behind the ears, no doubt. Then

Bridget tried to keep the *yeuch* off her face as the same hand that had scratched the flea-ridden hound pulled at his lip in sign of deep thought.

'Can you face it, Bridget?' he finally asked.

'I'm not sure I can face anything in this heat,' she said, deflecting the question.

He leaned closer to the screen; Bridget forced herself not to lean back. She could now see every day of his life written in the lines on his face, and his eyes told her of the lives lost. And the lives taken. His expression softened, but he didn't blink. 'The jet stream moved south last night and strengthened.'

'None of the weather forecasts have a break in the heatwave, Conrad. Just because meteorology has *-ology* at the end, that doesn't make it a science. Like astrology and theology, for example.'

'Now we've got the weather out of the way, I'll ask again. Can you face it?'

Bridget *did* blink, and in that moment she knew he was right. About her, about the crime and about the threshold she needed to step over.

'I owe it to Tony.'

He leaned back and lit another cigarette and poured a pint of beer from a glass into his tankard. He stared at the foam running down the sides of the glass. 'Do you think I could do divination from this? People do it from tea leaves, don't they?' He put the glass down. 'Tell me about him.'

So she did, including everything except his hands. Those were hers to treasure. She did say that she fancied him, though. Best to get that out in the open.

He didn't ask any questions, but he did frown a couple of times and shook his head when she repeated what he'd said to Shannon. Tale told, she folded her hands on her lap.

He took another drink and put down his tankard. 'It won't be easy. You'll need your A Game for this.'

'If I knew what me A Game was, I'd be on it.'

'No time for doubts, you know, and I will do what I can.' He pulled his lip again. 'Be outside the Mill at – say half past eight tomorrow? Have one of your excellent extra shot cappuccinos ready, oh and a packet of dog-friendly chocolate treats.'

'Yeah, right. I am not feeding your bleeding dog, Conrad.'

'They're not for Scout, and it's not me who'll be coming to see you. Text me if you change your mind.'

Her hackles rose. He always had that effect on her in the end. 'No chance. I will be there and I will be on my A Game.'

Like a ninja accountant, Mina darted into view and frowned at the screen. 'Oh. Bridget. Is everything okay?'

She put her palm on her new husband's shoulder. He reached up and his huge fingers took her whole hand in a digital hug. He glanced round. 'All good, love. Bridge was just asking for help with something. I'll tell you later.' He looked back at the screen. 'Good luck, Bridget, and don't, whatever you do, plan any outdoor events for the second half of June. Or date an Aries. Neither is going to end well. Good night.'

They closed early on the Sunday. They closed early every Sunday because who wants to buy coffee after four o'clock on a Sunday afternoon? Quite a lot of people, it seemed. Bridget had to be firm and shut down the line. By then, the crew were all flagging, especially as they'd had to revert to the old uniform shirts. Wendy had been only half joking when she said that she was going to join a union and threaten to strike unless Lucy could sort out a colourfast lightweight top.

'You do that, Wendy. It'll serve Lucy right,' Bridget told her. 'Come on, Kat, I'll give you a lift home.'

'Thanks, Boss. It's still boiling out there and I don't want to faint on the way home.'

'Don't be dramatic. It doesn't suit you, and besides, I need you to run in and get something from the shop.'

Kat rolled her eyes. 'One day you'll be nice to me without an ulterior motive.'

'I have news, Kat. Not even your mother is nice to you without an ulterior motive.'

There was a time lag. Just half a second while she parsed the insult. 'Yes she is!' said the outraged duckling.

'You're cruel to that girl,' said Wendy. 'But don't stop on my account.'

'Wouldn't dream of it. Just wait until her sister starts working here.'

'Be careful what you wish for,' said Kat. It was one of her favourite sayings, and Bridget wondered if the girl ever wished for anything for herself.

The trouble with finishing early, and with having to stay sober, was that by half past five, Bridget was clean, refreshed and waiting. She paced up and down. She refastened her dressing gown. She picked up her phone and put it down again. She sat down and looked into space until her eye fastened on the snow globe, now restored to pride of place on the mantelpiece. 'Come on, Tony,' she said to no one. 'What *is* my A Game? What in the name of Hades am I doing going to meet some random guy outside the Mill? And their effing dog.'

If Anthony Carson had become a ghost, he wasn't haunting Midland Terrace, or his own snow globe. The blackbird arrived on her roof with a *chuck* and a *choochoochoo* that marked its territory but had nothing to offer Bridget on what she should do.

She pushed up the sleeve of the fluffy robe, which was supposed to be keeping her cool. Maybe she'd put pyjamas on for an hour. Underneath the sleeve, her arm glistened with post-bath moisturiser, and the petals of her rose tattoo looked like they had water on them. Funny how you can look at something every waking hour and not really *see* it.

She flexed her arm, and the thorns rippled. Bridget knew what her A Game was.

Fifty-Seven

At eight twenty-five, Bridget pressed down the lid on the takeout cup containing her mystery guest's cappuccino. She carefully removed the yellow rubber Marigolds which had been protecting her fingerless lace gloves and smoothed them up her arms. These were her best gloves, the ones where you could see her tattoos winking through the fine yarn which disappeared underneath the puffed sleeves of her best dress, the purple silk one with the black trimming and the pinched waist.

She put the cup next to a cookie and the packet of dog treats. She took as deep a breath as she could in this outfit and carried the tray out of the Spinning Room. She moved round the side of the Mill, away from the direct sunlight and stood holding the goods like the statue of a Victorian hostess.

Conrad Clarke was clearly mad to have suggested this – the standing around part. She only had herself to blame for the outfit, the hour and a half she'd spent on the make-up, and the sweat running out from underneath her corset.

Further down the valley, a tractor was pulling some sort of machine across a green field, the colour and texture of the grass changing as it passed. *Who works at this time on a Sunday night?* A cow in the river meadow protested loudly at something, and then a car engine shattered the peace of the Shire.

It was a boy racer's vehicle, low, loud and lairy, and it executed the turn into the grounds of Ford Mill like there was a rally driver behind the wheel, churning up dust along the track. It shot past the Mill, bass notes thumping over the engine, roared round the large car park and came back, screeching to a halt. What sort of knobhead hooligan had Clarke sent to help her?

'God help me,' she muttered in counterpoint. Oh. 'That I was *not* expecting,' she added when the door opened and she saw who it was.

The driver got out and settled her ponytail. She grabbed an overstuffed manila folder and jogged across the grass. *Scarywoman*, as Lucy called her. Detective Constable Elaine Fraser to everyone else. She was as thin as Abi Tennant, but her chosen relaxation was –

allegedly – free climbing, not running. Bridget glanced at the hand holding the folder. Yep. Those fingers looked strong enough to lift her bodyweight. Elaine's bodyweight, that is, not Bridget's. If Bridget were that way inclined, she'd be very interested to discover just how strong those fingers were. She tore her eyes away from her new object of desire and looked up at the scrubbed-clean, healthy face.

DC Fraser had come to Cairndale as a package with Tom Morton, which is why Lucy knew Elaine well enough to give her the *Scarywoman* nickname. Since Tom's secondment, Elaine had disappeared from the gossip and, as far as Bridget knew, she had had nothing to do with the investigation of Tony's murder.

Elaine was wearing her usual ironic smile. 'Hi, Bridget. You look spectacular. Very on-trend for Goth detectives.' She waved the folder. 'Got something for you. And please tell me that drink is mine. I *need* caffeine. *So* badly.'

'Do you want to go inside?' asked Bridget.

'Thanks, but I'm off back to Manchester. Got to finish packing. Actually, I've got to start. Anyway, shall we swap?' she asked, offering the folder as a trade.

'Put it down there,' said Bridget.

Elaine stooped gracefully, laid the folder carefully on the grass and stood up to look at the tray. 'What on earth are they for?' she asked, pointing to the choccy dog treats.

'You. Conrad said I had to give them to whoever turned up, along with the coffee. The cookie was my idea.'

Elaine took the cookie off the plate and folded it into the paper napkin. She accepted the coffee, removed the lid and sniffed with pleasure. 'Mmhmm. Oh yes. Thank you.' She eyed the dog treats warily, then shoved them in a back pocket. 'Man's a bloody wind-up merchant.'

'I think he'd had a few when he told me to get them.' She put the tray down with great relief and asked, 'What have you been up to? You've not been seen in the Market Square for a while, according to Lilianna.'

Elaine patted the pocket with the dog treats. 'I'm Conrad's police minder now. Tom couldn't handle the pace any more. Like his dog, the Chief needs to be kept on a tight lead.' She snorted. 'And if you've met Scout then you'll know that he *hates* being kept on a lead unless bribed.' She pointed to the folder on the floor. 'Exhibit one.'

'Sorry?'

'There's all sorts of reports and statements in there that no civilian should be looking at. The pictures even more so. There was hell on when they found out what I was doing this afternoon.'

Bridget shivered in the heat. 'Are you in trouble? Am I in trouble?'

'Nah. The Commander said that any input would be gratefully received. Liz had a problem, though.' She grinned. 'Wouldn't let me take them away unless I charged the photocopying to MI7. All that colour printing costs a fortune.'

'Did Conrad say anything else?'

Like her boss – her *Chief*, apparently – Elaine turned serious for a moment. 'Yeah. He said that you should walk in the murderer's footsteps and start reading the file from the moment you enter the studio.'

They stood for a moment, both looking at the unexploded bomb of the innocuous folder.

'I'd better get going,' said Elaine. 'Cheers for the coffee and cookie. Take care, Bridget.'

'Thanks for giving up your Sunday.'

Elaine was walking towards her car. 'Rob's at training camp ahead of the trip to South Africa, and unlike Tom, I'm only a detective constable. I get overtime for this. See you later.'

Bridget watched as Elaine took an empty cup out of the holder and threw it in the back of her car, along with the doggy chocolate. She replaced the old cup with the new one and took an enormous bite of her cookie. A wave, the roar of an engine, and she was gone, leaving Bridget alone with the folder.

'I'll need more than me A game for this,' she muttered. 'Come on, girl. Let's make a start.'

'I'm not going up there,' Bridget announced when she saw just how much the brambles had encroached onto the public footpath at the side of the estate office. 'Not wearing a dress that cost more than a month's rent.'

She turned on her heel – and it really was a heel tonight: flat shoes are not worn in the A Game leagues. She crossed the yard to the Mill and picked her way down the slope to the lower car park. She stopped and looked around, just as the killer had done exactly a week ago. Maybe an hour later, but otherwise Bridget was standing in her version of the killer's shoes, although heels had probably not been worn on the night of Tony's murder.

'Get a grip,' she told herself, then she looked around *properly*. And the first question that popped into her head was one she should have thought of before: just how premeditated was this murder?

Obviously, the killer had broken into Coffin Joe's gun cupboard and walked up the fire escape with a shotgun. You can't get much more premeditated than *that*. But what about when they arrived at the Mill and stood here? Did they know what they were going to do at that moment, or did they decide after they'd been upstairs first? Had Tony done or said something which tipped them over the edge, sending them back down the stairs to get the gun?

Possibly was the answer. Unless you were talking about Jonathan Carson, because he had driven in and taken the lift. He was happy to be seen on the way in, and for him to have a rush of blood to the head and charge over to Water Cottage was just *wrong*. Jonathan Carson didn't have rushes of blood to the head. She let the image try to form in her mind: an outraged Jonno running down the fire escape, over the car park and into Coffin Joe's garden to grab an axe. She stopped there. He was not Cain. His shoes had not rested where Bridget now stood. Score one for Conrad Clarke. Do you score ones in cricket? Whatever.

That left the women. Bridget shuffled the four suspects across her mind's eye: Shannon, Donna, Hayley and Esther. She could see no reason to rule any of them out. Yet. If only they didn't all have a motive.

Shannon's grief for her lost child and lost husband, coupled with her public humiliation was bad enough for a spate of murders in Bridget's opinion. Less so for Donna, unless there had been things going on in their relationship that Donna was keeping to herself. Bridget now knew that Tony had had a petty side, but had he also been a domestic abuser?

Hayley's motive was less clear cut, and entirely dependent on someone else being convicted of the killing: so far, she had lost everything, and unless the insurance paid out, she would hit rock bottom. Could Tony's refusal to allow the third prong be enough? Hayley certainly had little solidarity with the others. And that left

Esther Thornfield.

The diorama Tony had created was nasty. No question. And yes, it was probably a harbinger of more to come. Bridget had failed to discover why Esther had once been arrested for assault, and she certainly knew more about Coffin Joe's habits than anyone. Bridget considered the woman who'd dressed up to go out with the vicar – the eccentric Artist persona was just that. A mask. Esther also cared a lot for Shannon.

Bridget sighed. This was getting her nowhere. She moved on, rounding the corner and swishing her way to the fire escape, forcing herself to think about how to score runs in cricket, and that mental shift gave her a second answer. Whoever killed Tony *had* gone to see him first, because if they'd come here with murder on their mind, they would have brought something with them, not grabbed the first weapon they could find which would allow them to kill him at a safe distance.

Bridget retraced her steps to the estate office and wracked her brains. She'd walked up the footpath days ago. What was at the other end? Nothing but the lane and Meadow Farm. 'Of course!' she declared. 'Pure blind luck.'

Out on the lane, there was nowhere to park that wouldn't have been spotted by *someone*. The killer really had driven into the Mill. Yes, they'd parked out of sight of the Dukes' house over the millpond, but it had been pure blind luck that Perry was out on a date leaving his boys on their games consoles and that Louis and Amos had gone for a drink. She went back to the car park, and this time she sailed straight up to the fire escape.

Or tried to. 'Bloody boots,' she muttered. 'Why in Satan's name did I not think of the gaps in the treads? Bloody Z Game, that's all I'm up to.'

She stepped back down and took a breath. The sun seemed even brighter beyond the shadows, and the shadows were Bridget's happy place once more. 'You can do this, girls,' she told her feet. She opened her bag (the black one with the embossed skulls) and took out the spare cleaning cloth, then used it to protect her lace glove from the handrails. Thus prepared, she began climbing the fire escape on the balls of her feet, only resting her heels on the solid landings.

Halfway up, she had to stop and curse herself. She cursed herself for choosing the dress with the under-corset rather than the red, on-display version. She cursed herself for giving the strings the extra tug which meant she could get into the dress at the cost of deep breathing. She cursed the extra layer of moisturiser that was turning her face into a greenhouse and she cursed her boots roundly. 'What for, eh? Why am I trussed up like a chicken and painted like a doll and standing on a fire escape in the middle of nowhere?'

A pair of ducks flapped up the valley and landed on the millpond without answering Bridget's question. 'See if I care,' she told them, then swapped climbing hands and started on the next level. 'I wonder if Elaine could climb the bricks,' she mused. 'Nah. She's Scarywoman, not Spider-Woman.' She *whoofed*. 'Another level. Did you see that Mr and Mrs Duck? Only two more to go. At least I'm high enough to die if I fall off. No embarrassing broken bones, just a corpse, eh?'

Fifty-Eight

Bridget stood three steps from the top. Three steps from safety. Three steps from having a rest. Sweat was getting into layers of her outfit that should never see liquid, never mind the drenching her skin was giving them tonight. She was also swaying. Alarmingly.

She dropped her bag and the folder on the top landing and gripped the handrail even more tightly. *Corset breathing. You've done the hard yards plenty of times before,* she told herself. She relaxed her grip on the rail and closed her eyes, moving her focus to the side of her chest and the intercostal muscles. Not *in-out,* you need *up-down* she reminded herself.

She forced the muscles into action, bypassing her diaphragm and getting her lungs to open by just moving her rib cage. 'Still got it,' she whispered as the muscle memory of a thousand nights on parade came back. 'Here we go.'

Thump. Thump. Thump. *Clang*. 'Made it. Now don't look down, girl.'

Which was fine in theory. If only she hadn't dropped her bag and the key with it. She braced her feet, squeezed her damp knees together and forced her hips into a Z, swooping down her arm and just catching the strap of her bag. *Gotcha.*

On the way up, momentum swung her round, and the solid tarmac of the car park filled her vision. *Ooh no. Not now.* She straightened up, moved her feet apart and closed her eyes. Points of light danced in the darkness. She held her breath, and they flickered out. Another breath and she opened first her eyes, then her bag. She found the key and jammed it into the lock. Made it.

Inside the studio, she forced her steps towards a clean set of shelves, dumped her baggage and turned to lean against the metal supports. When her pulse was no longer mixing techno bass in her ears, she carefully opened the folder.

'For God's sake,' she muttered. 'Can't see a bleeding thing.' She fumbled for her phone and activated the torch function. 'Better.' The first page of the package was titled *Locations with only victim's fingerprints and no evidence of cleaning*. And top of the list were the light switches. 'Sounds like a plan.'

Once she'd spotted the glaringly obvious, getting the studio well lit was easy. She'd fiddled fruitlessly with knobs, buttons and dials until she put herself in Tracey Kenyon's disposable booties and checked the power supply: all the lights had been switched off and unplugged at the mains.

Power restored, the studio lights ignited, blinding her and sending her blinking back to the safety of the shelves. Once her eyes had adapted, she flicked the switches for general lighting (*And why didn't I think of them first, eh?*). She looked around the room and realised that Tony had only turned on the studio lights for his workstation; both Donna's bench and Hayley's sales table were in relative darkness. What next?

She turned the page and gagged. '*Bleuch.* Oh shit.' She fumbled to close the folder and tried to unsee the image. Instead, she dropped it and the photograph slipped out, shiny, heavy paper gliding across the floor.

The crime scene techie had been standing exactly where she was now, and they'd taken a framing shot to set the scene, the studio lights picking out every detail. It was horrible and it was lying at her feet. If she walked away now, she'd be turning her back on Tony and leaving him alone for a second time.

She carefully lowered herself to put the folder back together, and in doing so she saw that Elaine had annotated the back of the glossy A4 print.

General view from likely distance weapon discharged.

'Well what do you know. I am literally standing where the killer did. You can't get more A Game than that.'

She stood up, fished out her black diamanté glasses and studied the picture, forcing herself to begin with the sight of Anthony Carson's body, tangled in the overturned legs of his stool. Tony was lying mostly on his front, and for the first time Bridget realised that he'd been shot in the back. Or shot in the back *as well*. When she'd found him on Monday, she'd seen what was left of his head and turned away. This time she spent long enough looking to realise that she had learned all she could from an image of his lifeless body.

The technician's camera had been angled slightly down, and though she could barely see the top of the bench, it was plain that something was missing – a cleared area about two foot by three was surrounded by tools in the photograph. She let her eyes roam over the image and got nothing more. With some trepidation, she turned to the next picture, offering a prayer to her guardian angel that it wasn't a close-up of Tony's face.

It wasn't. It was a 3D drawing of the pellet scatter proving that she was standing in the key place. She stepped back and looked down. Wow. Her generous, part-stiffened skirts had been hiding a cross made from gaffer tape – her subconscious must have picked it up and led her to it. Bridget did not think the universe held a benevolent deity, but she was a firm believer in the power of the unconscious. And guardian angels. 'Thanks,' she told the stagnant air. 'I owe you one.'

She looked back at the CGI picture and saw that Tony's body had been drawn in twice – once sitting on the stool at his bench and then again on the floor. Lines had been drawn back to a stick figure with a gun, and Elaine had scrawled *PTO* next to the shooter. Bridget flicked over the printout and observed, 'She should have been a doctor with writing like that.'

Screwing her eyes closed she made out the likely height of the gunman based on pellet trajectory. No wonder they had eliminated Jonno: unless he'd fired from the hip, he was way too tall to be the killer. Unfortunately, all the women were within the margin of error. Great.

She looked at the outline drawing of Tony again, finding it easier to focus on the drawing than the HD image of the real person. The second shot had been fired with him full stretch on the floor and a good two steps away from the bench. What had happened? Had the killer dragged him away before finishing the job? That was horrific. When she turned to the next page, she discovered that the truth was much, much worse, and she bit her knuckle through the lace to stop herself whimpering.

The printout was a heavily redacted extract from the autopsy.

The first discharge would have proved fatal within an hour unless emergency medical help was received. However, it did not damage the heart, nor did it sever the spinal cord. It is likely that the victim collapsed onto the bench at first before standing up and turning round. The pain and disorientation meant that they tripped over the stool and that the second shot was fired from less than three metres. It would have been instantly fatal.

Fifty-Nine

'You poor man,' she said. 'I can't imagine that.' She could try, though.

She closed her eyes and thought of the deepest hurt she'd suffered. She projected it onto how she imagined Tony would feel – flinching away from the impact, then turning around to realise he'd been shot and that someone he knew was holding a shotgun. When he jerked forwards and fell, did he see the gun being raised for a second time? She hoped not.

'Tony, if you're here, if your spirit is in this room, then I am so, so sorry.'

A tiny breath of wind from the open door caressed her face, and she tried not to wonder whether it was a coincidence or a sign. Best not to know.

She opened her eyes and turned to the next page. Pages. There were four annotated photographs of bloodstains and blood spatter, including one with a big ring around Hayley Horst's footprint. The rest of the results told her only one thing: the fatal head shot had left a shadow on the floor where the killer had stood, a shadow caused by droplets hitting their clothes. *Her* clothes. So where were they? Burned on Cowan Sands? Buried on a blasted heath? Or stuffed behind a bath panel somewhere, perhaps?

The blood spatter pictures had another of Elaine's annotations, drawn in vibrant orange. Who has a pen that colour? Whatever. Her eyes followed the line traced by Scarywoman's scary ink and it led round the workbench to a tiny *PTO* at the top. She flipped the page and read, *Likely route around bench to give access to possible theft of model.* Typical coppers – the missing locomotive, the beautiful *City of Lancaster* was a *possible theft*. It showed that the killer had been *very* careful of most things, and if Hayley had done it, then the footprint must be a double bluff.

'What the hell?' said Bridget when she realised that most of the rest of the folder was an inventory of objects in the room, starting with the ones they'd removed and then going on to every item they'd fingerprinted, sampled or tested, and every entry was cross-referenced to the HOLMES2 index for the results of tests or for the evidence log number. 'What am I supposed to do with *that*?'

She knew what she needed to do first, though, and that was to sit down. She crossed to the table where she'd sat on Thursday and opened the windows. Whether or not Tony's spirit had touched her a moment ago, there was certainly more of a mundane breeze tonight, and about bloody time, too. She lowered her immobile back into the chair and tried to cross her legs. Euw. Instead, she spread them wide and made a large lap from her skirts.

There *was* more after the database printouts – four wide-angle pictures of the whole room, taken from the centre and forming a panorama. She allowed herself a smile as she imagined Tracey Kenyon and her team shuffling around like a reality film crew to stay out of the shot.

She put the evidential printouts to one side and laid out as many of the photographs as she could on the coffee table. Her hand was halfway to her lip in an unconscious echo of Conrad Clarke when she remembered how much make-up she'd put on and how difficult it was to get lipstick out of her gloves.

'So why did I nearly do it?' she asked herself. 'I don't know about *him*, but I'm definitely missing something here.'

There was only one thing to do. On Monday, she'd taken in nothing but Tony's blasted face and the smell of blood mixed with chicken tikka masala. She laid the evidential printouts on her lap and tried to add back in to her mental picture everything Tracey had ordered to be taken away.

Tony's tools on the bench. The stool. The case allegedly containing the locomotive. Two panels from the backdrop. Mugs. Coffee cups. Food waste and containers. Two pre-packed and two unpacked model railway kits from the central bench.

'The backdrop,' she said. 'Why wasn't Tony sitting facing the room? Why did he have his back to the cameras?' She looked up at the scene and whispered, 'He's moved it. His backdrop is two feet closer to the bench. He's rearranged it so they'd be filming his back. Hayley would *not* have liked that!'

Yes, there were cameras overhead and to the side, for close-up work, but there were two main cameras pointed at Hayley's table and Tony's bench. At some point last Sunday, Tony had rearranged the set, presumably after he saw videos of himself from the front. That act of defiance had allowed the killer to get very close without him noticing. But only if he'd been as deaf as Conrad Clarke – this floor was like a drum when it came to footsteps.

He turned his back on her, she realised. *He argued, she went away, and when she came back, he didn't look up.*

It was there, just out of reach. She knew what had happened, but not who or why, or how they'd covered it up. She slapped her thighs in frustration, lace on silk making no noise, so she stood up and stamped her foot. *Better.* She adjusted her skirts and gave them a swish, stepping back into the first part of a waltz to even them out.

A waltz.

Bridget knew who had killed Tony Carson, and she knew why.

She got out her phone, crossing her touchscreen friendly lace fingers and praying that the only useful witness took her call.

Sixty

'What?' whispered Jonno Carson. There was a rustle in the background. 'I'm visiting my mother.'

'Please,' said Bridget. 'Just one question. It's really important.'

'Hang on.' There was more rustling and the ambient noise changed. 'This had better be good.'

'When you went to see Tony on … on that night, was the big doll's house open or closed?'

Silence. Hopefully the silence of thought not contempt for Bridget's mad idea.

An intake of breath, way more than Bridget could manage. 'When I got out of the lift, he was closing the door.'

Yesss!

'One sec.' Bridget shuffled through the papers, right back to the beginning. 'Thanks, Jon. I'll let you get back, and I'm really sorry to have disturbed you.'

'She's asleep, as it happens. What does this mean, Bridget?'

But she had already ended the call. She stared at the doll's house. Could Tony really have been murdered over *that*? It seemed he could, because the meticulous forensic technicians, under Tracey's merciless gaze, had been very clear: there were *no* fingerprints on the doll's house. It had been wiped, only no one had spotted the significance of that or wondered why the featured scene for Tuesday's show was empty and naked when every other room was filled with beautiful miniature characters. Where were the waltzing couples?

They were nowhere, and in their place Bridget could guess what Donna Ramsey had seen when she walked in on Tony Carson. Bridget knew who and why, so how in Tony's name was she going to prove it to Liz Swindlehurst?

Bridget sat down again and let her mind wander now that she only had one story to unpick, and when it came to her, the answer had been staring her in the face all night. She launched herself out of the chair and strode across the studio, leather soles beating out a triumphant tattoo. She bent from the waist and dragged the two giant carriers she'd packed the other day under the studio lights, then she squatted down and spread out her skirts. Somewhere in those packages from Whistles, Hush, Boden and Jigsaw were the clothes Donna had worn when she shot Tony.

The police had no doubt looked at every plastic packet, box and environmentally friendly paper sack, but they hadn't opened them, had they? Donna had, and she'd resealed them with the same precision and illusion she brought to her miniature work. Bridget picked up the first box and checked the seal. She'd got about a quarter of the way through when a voice froze her in place.

'They're in the Popsy box,' said Donna.

Bridget stood up, her heart trying to burst out of the corset. Her knees could barely take her weight, they were shaking so much, and her throat was dry. That wasn't the worst thing, though. Her phone was on the other side of the studio. Why the *hell* hadn't she worn a dress with bigger pockets?

She couldn't see a thing beyond the floodlights except shadows. She wanted to move left, towards her phone, but that's where the voice had come from (and how had Donna crossed the floor without making any noise?). She moved right instead, and the blazing lights were replaced by sparkling stars. It was going to take a while before she could see properly. Play for time.

She coughed and croaked, 'Why, Donna? Just because Tony swapped out a few of your figures for *Space Fruit* characters?'

'It was more than that,' spat Donna. 'I was going to run the console for the launch, you know. Hayley was going to open the front of the house in the introduction segment, to show what I'd be working on, and our future customers would have seen a ballroom full of copulating pigs. In full HD glory.'

'Even so, Donna. Come on, you found out in time, didn't you?'

'It wouldn't have stopped there. He was on a mission to ruin *everything*. He'd already treated Shannon like a piece of dirt and gone back on his promise to support Hayley's third prong. After we'd left, he moved the set so he could be filmed from behind. This was only the start, Bridget.'

Shadows and blackness were turning into walls and windows. Colours were going from splodgy to defined shapes. Keep going. 'What was in it for him? He was an equal partner with you and Hayley. He'd be just as bust as you two.'

'He could afford it. He'd lose a lot, but he wouldn't lose everything. Not like me. Not like Hayley. And with her in prison, I could claim on the insurance.'

Bridget was getting lightheaded. The shock was taking oxygen out of her system that shallow breaths weren't replacing. She centred herself again and focused on her ribs. *Up and down.* Better. 'You were trying to frame her. What had Hayley done to deserve that?'

'You weren't there. You didn't see the way she made *Space Fruit* all about her and Andy and Tony.'

Bridget's eyes were locked on Donna's face, and the years of hatred were written in every clenched muscle. Donna met her gaze and almost shouted, *'They were supposed to be toys for Shannon's baby!'* Donna took a deep breath that made Bridget jealous, then added, 'And when Hayley had squeezed the goodness out of Andy's ideas, she squeezed the goodness out of the man. She deserves everything she gets.'

Donna looked down, and Bridget's eyes dropped, too. *In the name of all the goddesses, what is she doing?*

Donna was wearing a forensic paper suit, including the hood, over … nothing. Completely naked underneath. Scratch that. You can't walk up a fire escape with only booties on your feet, and her silent approach was down to light feet and a pair of dance slippers. It had taken half a second to work out how Donna had surprised her; it took much less to realise that the forensic suit was bad news. Very bad news. And then it got worse.

She had thought that Donna was carrying a wooden watch case or something in her latex-gloved hand and ignored it. When Donna pulled the case apart, Bridget saw first a series of kanji characters on the box and then a long-bladed knife, and Bridget knew why Donna had told her about Tony: because Bridget was going to take the secret to the grave with her.

Donna stepped forwards, and Bridget tried to loosen herself, to turn her body into the water which would flow over her opponent. *That's not gonna work,* she realised. When she'd slammed Abi Tennant into Hayley's front door, she'd drawn on reactions honed in a dojo where she'd learned how to stop people – men – from assaulting her. Her sensei had somehow never covered attack by someone who wants to kill you.

Bridget was about to make a run for the outside door when it moved of its own accord, swinging first closed, then open, and the doorway was filled with Jed Holmes, phone held out in front of him. 'Don't worry, Bridget, I've got it,' he shouted.

Donna stopped, flicking her eyes from one to the other.

'Are the cops coming?' demanded Bridget. 'Have you called them?'

'No, I was recording …'

The stupid, stupid kid. As soon as Donna had registered what he'd said, she flew at him, and Bridget had to choose between getting her own phone or trying to rescue Jed, but that wasn't a real choice, was it? She grabbed her dress and tried to run towards the door.

Sixty-One

Jed saw the knife. He fumbled backwards onto the fire escape landing, dropping his phone in the process. He tried to close the door but hit his own leg with it. He desperately dodged to avoid the knife, then tumbled out of sight, a scream covering the sound of fragile bones rolling down the iron stairs.

Bridget wasn't running. Not in those heels, but she was moving at a pace, and Donna whirled round just before Bridget could cannon into her. Bridget's vision shrank to nothing, nothing but the blade. She could change course or she could plough on. She spread her arms and tried to launch herself as Donna took a great roundhouse slash at her.

Bridget felt the knife strike her with all the force in Donna's arm. It wasn't enough, though. It wasn't enough to stop Bridget hitting Donna like a runaway train and slamming both of them into the wall.

They collapsed into a heap, with Donna's arm trapped between them. Donna open-handed Bridget in the chest with her left hand and was extricating her right when Bridget realised she had one chance to save herself. One chance to stop Donna getting away with it. One chance to bleed out in peace, alone in the studio. She took it.

She rolled right, allowing Donna to lift her right arm, but freeing Bridget's left. Before Donna could wield the knife, Bridget grabbed her forearm and leaned in. Then she collapsed all of her weight onto Donna's arm and sank her teeth into the biceps. Deep into the muscle. And she didn't let go.

Donna grunted. Then she screamed and thrashed, freeing Bridget's right arm. When Donna screamed a second time, Bridget placed all her chips on red. She let go with her teeth, leaned back and brought her elbow up to smash into Donna's jaw. And again. Finally, she heard the knife drop onto the floor.

Bridget pressed down on Donna's chest and scooted the knife across the floor with her boot, then she lifted herself onto her knees. Donna was down; she was not out. She tried to sit up, but Bridget had only lifted herself to get a swing in with her fist, and she jabbed it into Donna's diaphragm.

Donna tried to curl into a ball, so Bridget rolled her onto her front and sat on her. There. 'Get out of *that*, you bitch,' she muttered, then she tried to work out how long she had to live. 'Oh,' she said. It was all she could manage, because she wasn't going to die. Not tonight.

The reason she hadn't felt the knife rip through her flesh was that it hadn't. It had cut the most amazingly clean line through her dress, its lining, and the cover of her corset. Then it had skidded over the steel boning and left not a mark on her.

Bridget stared at the ruined dress until Donna started to groan and gasp for air in a way that sounded like *she* was the one dying. Bridget put her hand on Donna's neck, pressing down *hard*, then shuffling back to sit on Donna's bum.

Bridget was no longer in danger, but she was stuck with both phones out of reach and a potentially dead ferret somewhere down the stairs. She'd smack Donna's face into the floor if she had to, so long as there was no better option …

'Jed! Can you hear me? Are you okay?'

'I don't know.' His voice was weak and strangled. He was alive, though. 'I don't want to move because everything hurts. Owww!'

Now that she wasn't being attacked and now she knew that Jed was alive, the thought of deliberately assaulting Donna, just to knock her out, was more than Bridget could stomach. She sighed and looked at her dress with a view to tearing strips out of it and tying Donna's hands.

Heavy footsteps clanged up the steps, getting closer, and Bridget pressed down on Donna's back, just in case. She'd not thought about of an accomplice, and it would serve her right if her heroics were for nothing.

The footsteps stopped below the top floor, presumably where Jed had landed. Silence. A groan, then a scream. Bridget started to stand up, ready to try and grab the knife, then she heard Jed muttering something and a louder, 'Thank you. Oww.'

She froze. Another man's voice said, 'Hello? Yes, you …' but Bridget couldn't hear the rest because the speaker set off down the stairs again. So, Jed was alive and it sounded like someone was getting help.

'My arm,' groaned Donna. 'It's bleeding.'

It was. The blood had soaked the paper suit. 'Tough shit,' said Bridget. 'I missed the artery, so you won't bleed to death.'

'What if I catch something?'

Bridget leaned forwards and pulled the hood down, releasing Donna's hair. Once she had a target, she slapped her ear. 'It's me that needs to worry about catching something, you complete bitch. Right, start talking. Where's the *City of Lancaster*?'

'Sod off.'

Bridget slapped harder.

'Oww! It's in the garden shed of Hayley's next-door neighbour.'

'You what?'

'I miscounted the gardens when I climbed over the back wall. Snotty cow never invited me into her house, so I wasn't sure which one it was.'

'What's it doing there? Why in God's name did you take it, Donna?'

'To throw the blame on Hayley. To get back at Tony for what he'd done.'

Bridget opened her mouth to say that shooting him in the back was pretty much the definition of revenge when more footsteps outside shut her right up. She tensed again. The footsteps paused, there was muttering, then they flew up the last flight, and Perry appeared in the doorway, panic in his eyes. He stepped into the studio and said, 'Bridget! Are you okay?'

The concern in his face was more than that of a landlord. She was sure of it. He really cared. Then again, he was a thoroughly nice bloke. Of course he cared.

'Yeah. No damage to me. Can we swap places?'

Perry ran over was going to put his foot on Donna's arm until he saw the blood flowing from the biceps. He barely hesitated, just changing his target limb. Once Donna was secured, he held out his hands to help Bridget up. She took the hands and heaved, but she was much heavier than he was expecting, and he had to press down to take the strain. Donna screamed as his foot bit into her arm, but the screams were drowned out by sirens.

Bridget rose up and Perry drew her towards him. For a millisecond, her heart thought he was going to pull her in for a kiss. No such luck. She did get a hug, though, and she could have melted into it and surrendered. Bridget crossed her fingers behind his back. *I hope there's a next time,* she told herself, then pulled back. She had to check on her livestock.

She tried to walk to the door, but her legs were none too steady. She weaved a little, arrived in the doorway and grabbed the jamb for support. *Do I really want to go out there and risk fainting and falling over the railing? No. Do I have a choice? Also, no.*

'Where are you going?' Perry asked with almost a squeak.

She raised her left hand in acknowledgement and gripped the door frame hard. She took a step outside and peered down. Jed was sitting on the next landing, stretched out and his whole upper body bent over as he cuddled himself. 'You okay, kid?' she asked.

He looked up and smiled with relief. 'Hurts, Bridget. My arm really hurts, and my chest. Did you get her?'

'Yeah. I got her. No thanks to you, soft lad.'

He looked like his breathing was even shallower than hers. 'I … I distracted her!' he managed.

'And if you'd called the bizzies like a normal person, you wouldn't be lying there in agony. Look, do you mind if I don't come down?'

'No, so long as you tell me what happened while it's fresh in your mind.'

Wow. The little ferret rolls down an iron staircase, probably breaks several bones and his first thought is *still* getting the story. He'll either win the Pulitzer Prize one day or die trying.

A rapid response police car drove into the car park, blue lights flashing. 'Sorry, Jed, but there are bigger priorities.'

She was feeling a bit better now. She went back into the studio and crossed the floor, patting Perry on the shoulder as she passed, saying, 'Thanks,' and then she got to her bag and took out her anti-bac wipes and her emergency make-up kit. Donna's blood down her face was not a good look when the bizzies were on the way up the stairs.

Sixty-Two

'Here we go again,' said Bridget to the pile of soft toys. Since Monday morning, they must have had a customer in the family room, because the toys had been carefully stacked into a pyramid with a bright green plush crocodile perched on top. 'Who are you staring at?' she told him. 'Never seen a Goth before?'

She was still waiting for a reply from the reptile when the door was knocked and opened by Abi Tennant. 'Sorry, Bridget. I thought you were talking to someone.'

'I was.' She pointed at the toys. 'I was talking to Swampy over there.'

'Eh? Swampy?'

'Swampy the Crocodile. Talking to river dwelling predators is probably the least bonkers thing I've done tonight.' She turned to look at the human in the room and gave her a hard stare. 'Have you come here for Donna?'

Abi was outraged. 'No chance! I have a client already, and I will be pushing for Hayley to be formally cleared as soon as possible.' She closed the door and stepped closer to Bridget. 'But I didnae come here for that. I came because I thought you might like a friend, and if not a friend, then at least a friendly face. They'll leave you here for hours given half a chance.'

'Don't I know it.' Bridget patted the other end of the sofa. 'Barney Rubble has a friendlier face than yours. Much friendlier. So I guess you'll have to count as a friend. What's going on, apart from offers of tea?'

Abi was wearing baggy sweats tonight, branded with a logo that put them at a x20 premium over Bridget's supermarket version. The lawyer took a step and landed lightly on the institutional couch. 'Are you okay, Bridget? Given that you've just survived a deadly assault, I mean. You know.'

'Yeah, Abi. I know. I'm fine right now. Still having difficulty breathing, but that's me own fault.'

Abi frowned. 'Were you hurt? Should they have called the doc?'

Bridget shifted to show the gaping wound in her dress. 'Lucky escape, but this corset wasn't designed for heatwaves.'

'Your dress! That's …' She grinned. 'That's a miracle, that's what it is. It looks spectacular, by the way. The whole of you does. Were you going somewhere?'

'Thanks. No. I was told I needed me A Game to catch the killer, so that's what I wore. Any news on Jed Holmes? Last I heard was that the paramedics thought he was safe to move and he was moaning that Sergeant Marsh wouldn't give him his phone to take to hospital.'

'Aye, that's another reason I came down. I knew you'd be worried, and they've just had an update.'

She held out a hand, then withdrew it, and Bridget recognised the gesture: Abigail Tennant was lonely. Bridget shifted her centre of gravity and leaned out an arm. How had her lace gloves survived all *that* tonight? Well, they had. Abi took her hand and squeezed. Nope. Those fingers did nothing for Bridget. 'How is the little kit?' she asked.

'Suspected broken arm and suspected broken rib, plus bruising. As well as the broken bones, they've admitted him for concussion monitoring.' She gave a feral grin. 'And you're no wrong about his phone. Apparently he refused to go unless Ryan gave it to him, and Ryan couldnae be bothered to seize it officially. Not once Jed had sent him the recording.'

'He really got Donna confessing on tape?'

'Mmm. He certainly recorded *something*. Liz took me to one side when I got here. Well, she could see I was about to kick up a stink.' Abi grew a couple of inches as she donned her professional armour, which must include a gorget, because her chin tilted alarmingly as she prepared to look down her nose. 'Donna settled for the duty solicitor from Morecambe, and well, what do you expect? The wee munchkin went pale when Liz told him about the evidence. He scuttled into the interview room and told his client to confess because it would go easier on her.' She sighed. 'I'd *never* ha' done that. *No comment* and *Not guilty* until the day of the trial. You'd be amazed how many cases collapse. I mean, there's all sorts of pleas …'

Abi seemed to realise that suggesting *self-defence* for the attack on Bridget would not be a shortcut to friendship and shifted uncomfortably, touching her face to feel the sudden heat.

Bridget let her suffer for a moment, then said firmly, 'Not this one. Liz would not mess this up.'

'Aye. Mebbe.' It was as close as Abi was going to come to complimenting the police. She swiftly changed the subject. 'Jed is of course itching to tell his story to the highest bidder. Or he was until the A & E nurse cornered him. Ryan said she's much scarier than him, and Jed's phone is now behind the nursing station until he's discharged.'

Bridget chuckled. 'I only want to know one thing. How did she get out of the Red Rose Hotel without appearing on CCTV?'

Abi's armour was off again. She looked troubled, and more than that, she looked like she didn't know *why* she was troubled, as if some previously unexperienced emotion was gnawing at her insides, trying to get out. 'When I told Liz I was coming to see you, she asked me to pass on a message. She said that they've only just finished getting the CCTV from Spice Ireland's car park and from two doorbell cameras on the Millhouse estate. Donna parked her car in a corner of the car park and used the back exit. She knew the hotel camera covering it was broken because they told her when she checked in. *Don't leave your car there because it might get nicked*. They looked at the tapes urgently tonight, but they were already pursuing it.'

Abi had got carried away with the story and with the chase. She'd forgotten why it was important. Bridget hadn't. 'You mean I could have died tonight and they'd have caught her anyway?'

Abi shivered. 'Cold in here. Aye. You could.' She paused. 'But they wouldnae have had the evidence – the bloodstained clothes. The confession. The attempt on your life.'

There was an awkward silence. Awkward on Abi's part, anyway. Bridget was busy offering prayers of thanks.

Liz knocked on the door and walked in. 'Sorry to keep you, Bridget. Look, we could be hours sorting this out. We've got your statement to Ryan on his bodycam and the pictures of your dress. Why not come in tomorrow and do the formalities then? Unless you're planning to go to work, of course.'

Bridget stood up. 'You must be joking. My new friend here is going to give me a lift home and I am going to get out of this corset and start making phone calls. I'll bet Lucy already knows.'

'Not from us,' said Liz sternly. 'The Sheriff is no longer a Cairndale detective.' Then she laughed. 'Lucy *does* know, as it happens. Jackie Chester, Kat Chester, Lady Felicia Duke, Perry Lockwood, Louis Young and of course Jed Holmes have all called or messaged her with the news or to ask questions. Off you go, Bridget. And thanks.'

Abi went to the soft toys and picked up Swampy the Crocodile. 'Fancy a souvenir?'

'Are you mad?' said Bridget. 'That's been sucked and mauled by every child in Cairndale, I'll bet.'

Abi looked the crocodile in the eye. 'Lucky Swampy. Fair point.'

As they were signed out of the station, Abi said, 'Good job I brought my car. I usually jog up here.'

Bridget gave her a dark look. 'Each to their own.' They entered the car park, and she continued, 'Do you want to know what happened. All the gory details?'

Her new "friend" did something Bridget hated: she bumped Bridget's well-padded hip with her bony one. 'Why the hell d'you think I really came to see you?'

It was nearly midnight when Abi drove slowly up Church Road and Bridget brought the story to an end. 'Do you want me to stay over?' asked Abi. 'You've had a terrible, terrible shock, Bridget.'

It was tempting. 'That's really kind, Abi. Thanks, but I think I need to find out how I feel. If that makes sense? Until then, I reckon I need to be on me own.'

They'd arrived in Station Square, and Abi had started to say something about *knowing what you mean* (unlikely), and then she stopped. 'You've a visitor, Bridget, and it's no the press. Who's that?'

A feminine figure was sitting on Bridget's doorstep, resting her head on the front door and staring at Abi's car. Abi turned a little further and her headlights picked out the form of Wendy Sadler.

'It's Donna's number one fan. Wendy Sadler. Would you mind coming with me.'

'Shouldn't I call the polis?'

'I don't think so.'

'Well, I've got my can of pepper spray.'

Abi more or less dumped her little car and got out first while Bridget was still struggling with her skirts and the fact that she was utterly shattered. Abi moved to the right and put her hand in her bag as Wendy got up, the aches from sitting on the step clear in her stiff leg. As soon as Bridget was nearer, Wendy took a step forwards and drew her waterfall cardigan round her like a shield.

'I am so sorry, Bridget. I knew nothing. Honestly. I am so, so sorry.'

'Oh aye?' said Abi.

'Yes. You have to believe me, Bridget. As soon as Lucy told me what had happened, I knew.'

'Knew what?' snapped Abi. Bridget let her – she was quite enjoying having her own personal Rottweiler.

Wendy looked too scared to be puzzled about what Abi was doing there and answered the question. 'On Friday, when I took Donna's toolkit down, she asked me why I'd left the clothes behind. I just thought she was stressed. That's why she came back tonight, wasn't it? Because I didn't have a bigger car.'

Bridget took a step closer. 'No, Wendy. She came back tonight because she was losing the plot. I don't know where she got the courage to shoot Tony from. I really don't, but that act tipped her over the edge. She's been stewing for days now, waiting to be found out. None of this is your fault.'

'You're … you're very kind.'

'And you didn't need to come here to tell me that.'

'That's not why I came. Lucy ordered me to collect the van off you and do the bakery run in the morning.'

That was Lucy all over. No wonder she was so good at first aid with crisis management skills like that. 'It's at the Mill. Where's your car?'

'I came by taxi. About an hour ago.'

Bridget angled her bag to the streetlight and found the van keys. 'Here you are. This is Abigail Tennant, Hayley's lawyer. If you ask nicely, I'm sure she'll give you a lift up there.'

Wendy was already shaking her head. 'Oh no. I've been too much trouble already. And I need the walk. That step is colder than I expected.'

Abi stood watchfully at the side as Wendy came and collected the keys. To Bridget's relief, there was no attempt at a hug, but Wendy did say, 'Are you okay?'

'I'll send a status update,' replied Bridget. 'Just as soon as I've got changed, but yes, considering what's happened, I'm good.'

Wendy went back, picked up her tote and dropped the keys in. 'Then I'll see you later. Much later. When you're ready.' She put the bag on her shoulder. 'Take care, and I'm so sorry.'

Abi waited until Wendy had disappeared down Church Road before saying, 'Last chance for a sleepover?'

Bridget frowned, then smiled. 'Was that your way of asking whether I'm okay without actually saying the words "Are you okay?"'

'Something like that.'

'I promise that the next time I have a black silk and leather pyjama party, you'll be top of the guest list.'

'Have you *ever* had one of those?'

Bridget got out her door keys and put on her most enigmatic smile. 'I'll leave that to your imagination, Abi. Thanks for being there. It made a real difference.'

'Aye. Nae bother. See you later, Dark Angel.'

Corset removed and make-up carefully cleansed, Bridget donned her economy sweats and poured a large glass of wine. She went into the back room and put the glass on the table, then crossed to the mantel and picked up the snow globe. She stared at the likeness of herself and Captain Berry. *So much talent,* she thought. She tipped up the scene and looked at the blank where her face should be. *I guess he just didn't understand people like most of us do.* Tony might not have grasped the surface emotions of others, but something told Bridget he knew their essence. How else would he have been able to wind people up so easily? And more than that, how could he have caught her tattoo so perfectly unless he knew who Bridget *really* was.

She put the globe back and sat down. She took her wine and raised it at the snow globe. 'You can rest in peace now, Tony.'

She drank to his memory and picked up her phone. The last time she'd looked, there had been twenty-four missed calls. Up to thirty now, and the poor operating system had lost count of the number of messages. This was going to be a long night.

Sixty-Three

Sunday was a *very* long night, and Monday wasn't much better. After an afternoon making statements at Divisional HQ (and handing over her dress), Bridget had worried all evening about whether she'd sleep, especially as it was now borderline impossible to think because of the humidity.

She did sleep in the end, and there were no nightmares. She got up on Tuesday morning and booked a return train ticket to Liverpool. Why not? It was right on her doorstep. Among all the messages that filtered in during the day, there was one which made her sit up on the train home. It was from Jonathan Carson, and it was as meticulous as you'd expect from a precision engineer.

Donna Ramsey has been charged and remanded in custody. I have just finished with the police and I would really like to talk to you (so long as we don't discuss Sunday night). Is there any chance you could come out to Aldhaven tomorrow? Any time to suit you.

She already knew about the long charge sheet Donna was facing – including attempted murder of Bridget – because Barney Smith had left a voicemail, and Bridget had already decided to go back to work on Wednesday. After thinking about Jon's message, she sent one of her own to Wendy. *Drop the van round at my house after Kat gets in tomorrow. I'll do the afternoon shift but I need to see someone first. And before you ask, yes, I'm fine.* She also replied to Jon, then settled back and closed her eyes.

She slept no better – or worse – on the Tuesday night, and Wednesday morning found Bridget sitting in her yard with a cup of tea well before she would have needed to get up for work. It was six o'clock and the sun was already up, just like it had been on the day she drove back from Liverpool and took Tony his extra shot Americano. Ten days ago. And three days since Donna had tried to eviscerate her. Good word, that. *Eviscerate.* Much better than *disembowel,* a point she'd made to her therapist (ex-therapist?) yesterday.

It was why she'd gone to Liverpool – "Sarah" would always see a client if there was an emergency, and it was worth the journey to see the only Goth psychotherapist Bridget had ever found. Not that her therapist dressed up for sessions. Apart from the piercings and the ink.

When Bridget walked out of the consulting room, she was no more cured than the last time she'd left, but Sarah had given her the perspective she needed. Bridget would talk to Lucy and others about what had happened in Byford, but there's something special about seeing the only person who knew Bridget's *whole* story, and who could take jokes about verb choices in attempted murder. Sarah had even asked how to spell *eviscerate* for future reference.

Bridget sipped her tea and closed her eyes. She tried to differentiate the crowded back row of the dawn chorus. Nope. Still couldn't tell a chaffinch from a chough. The resident blackbird hopped onto her fence from the field beyond, gave her a chirrup, then headed up to the chimney pots to properly mark his territory.

Wendy Sadler didn't knock on the door when she dropped off the van; she just put the keys through the letterbox and sent a message. Good job, too, because Bridget was still trying to decide between a reproduction Victorian mourning gown and something more predatory from Midnight Veil's Transylvania range. It was the lack of corset that made her choose the mourning gown in the end, and she gave the unrelieved black some colour by getting out some of the swag she'd picked up in Liverpool after she'd finished with her therapist – a bright red sash round the waist, matching lipstick and a faux emerald brooch.

She paused in the hall and cursed Perry Lockwood for not having put a mirror there. It should be part of building regulations that all properties had a mirror by the final exit door for a last check before facing the world. She was putting her bag together when the doorbell rang.

'Who the hell?' she groaned.

The figure on the doorstep looked truly pathetic. Jed Holmes had his left arm strapped up and he was leaning over to avoid the pain in his ribs. And his face was black and blue. She peered over his shoulder and there was no sign of a taxi or an Uber.

'Please tell me you didn't come on the train, Jed.'

'Can I come in? I think I might have overdone it.'

'No.'

He looked like she'd just kicked him, and his face puckered up in a brave attempt not to cry. She took the keys and clicked open the van. 'You can get in there. I've got to go out and I'll give you a lift. Go on. In you get.'

He turned and limped to the van. Bridget grabbed the rest of her stuff and locked the door, then glided to her chariot and quickly got the engine and aircon going before she melted.

'Thank you for Sunday night, Bridget,' said Jed formally. 'Oww!' he added in a more natural whimper.

He'd already thanked her profusely by message, and she'd been sparing in her replies. Not because she didn't like him. She just didn't have the headspace. 'You didn't risk a punctured lung just to say that in person, did you?'

'Dad said I had to. And yeah, I also wanted to interview you. I think that might have to wait.'

'No kidding.'

She put the van in gear and reversed out of her spot.

'Who are you going to see?' he asked. *Persistent little ferret, aren't you?*

'None of your business.'

'Then it must be connected to the murder because if it wasn't, you'd just tell me the truth to shut me up. And you're not dressed for work unless Lucy's changed the uniform again.'

Persistent *and* perceptive. She sighed and started driving down Church Road. 'I'm going to see Jonathan Carson. He wants to talk. Still none of your business, though.'

'Oh good. I need to see him, too.'

'You what! You've got a bleeding nerve, Jed.'

'Not really. I'll wait patiently in the van while you speak to him then get a taxi back if you can't wait, not that I'll be long. I'm just preparing the ground for later.'

Human beings can have mixed motives. It was a lesson she'd learned late in life. Jed was both genuinely grateful and up to something. Something he was itching to tell her. She turned onto the main road and picked up speed. 'Preparing the ground for what?'

The grin wiped out all the pain in his face. 'I've been commissioned to make a serial to go out after the trial. You'll be my star guest, of course.'

She was speechless. There was just so much so wrong in what he'd said that she was stumped. Was *stumped* a cricket metaphor? Probably. 'I don't know where to start,' she told him.

They were bouncing along the road into Cairndale. Way too many blind corners for a serious conversation. Something Jed had figured out, because he said nothing further until she pulled up at the traffic lights to join the A6.

He twisted in his seat, groaned in pain and failed to take a deep breath. He swallowed, grimaced and said, 'I know I was a dick. I should have dialled nine-nine-nine straight away, but you haven't asked me what I was doing up there, have you?'

It was something that Sarah had latched on to as well. Bridget stared straight ahead at the traffic. 'No.'

'I was giving it one more go. Like you. I was out looking for more dog walkers. Maybe someone who works away during the week and was only home on Sunday nights. I was going to give up when I saw the lights on in the Mill, so I went over and crept up the stairs. I was watching you and then I heard Donna's car come in. When she got out I couldn't believe my eyes. She stripped off and put that suit on. I thought I was seeing things, Bridget.'

'Have a thing for older women, do you?'

'You wish. I hid behind the open door where there was just enough space next to the railings. And I could see through the gap into the room.'

So that's where he'd sprung from.

'I recorded it because I didn't know what she was going to do. As soon as I saw the knife, I showed myself.'

A car horn blared behind them. Bridget ignored it because she'd been led to the same place by her therapist yesterday. She turned her head. 'Thank you, Jed. I should have said it before, but I didn't want to encourage any more stunts. You saved *my* life by being there just as much as I saved yours. More so. Thank you.'

A delivery van roared round them with an extra blast of his horn and the lights went back to red. Bridget looked forwards again and said, 'Yes, I'll take you to Aldhaven, and yes, I'll do your effing podcast. Now shut up.'

'Mmm,' said Jed.

Sixty-Four

Bridget repeated her reversing manoeuvre at the Carson house, and Jed said, 'Surprised you didn't park up the lane. The outfit doesn't go with the van.'

She killed the engine. 'You would think that, because you're a man. You obviously haven't noticed that this hand-dyed Chinese silk sash and custom lipstick are in the *exact* shade of Caffè Milano red. My outfit matches perfectly.' Point made, she opened the door. 'If it looks like I'm going to be a while, I'll take pity on you and get Jonathan to put you in the utility room rather than bake out here.'

She got out and swished towards the house, where the front door was standing ajar. Jonathan was halfway across the darkened living room and said, 'Do you mind if we talk in the study? All the stuff's in there.'

Stuff? What stuff?

'Of course not,' she replied and followed him into the little man cave.

'I'll go and get the tea. It's made because you strike me as a woman who's always on time.'

'On business, yes. Otherwise it can go either way.'

He looked both more relaxed and more exhausted today – a bit like Bridget felt, despite the uniform and the A Game warpaint. He smiled and left her alone for a moment, and she had another look round the room. 'I thought so,' she murmured.

Since last week, the wall of family photos had been rearranged. The row of three awards pictures had been shuffled to accommodate a fourth – Anthony holding some animation industry gong for *Space Fruit* and wearing the same limited edition Captain Berry T-shirt he'd sported when he and Bridget first met.

Jonathan bustled in with the tea tray and put it on a side table. 'Milk? Sugar?'

'No sugar, thanks.' While he poured, she said, 'Glad to see Tony up on the wall.'

He put her tea down and went behind the desk. He picked up another picture and held it in front of Tony's image. It was from the same night, and showed all the Leyland Films crew – Hayley, Shannon, Donna and others she didn't recognise. Shannon had her arm intimately around a tall guy who was holding the trophy in this picture. Must be Andy Staton. Good-looking bloke. Older than Shannon.

Tony was on the end, the only one not in evening dress. He looked *so* out of place until you remembered that this was an award for intergalactic talking fruit, not the Nobel Peace Prize.

Jonathan lowered the other picture. 'My PA is good, but not the best decision maker. I asked her to get the awards picture printed and framed, but she was too timid to ask which one and got them both. Obviously I don't want Tony's killer staring at me, but I've kept the group shot. It'll go somewhere as a … a something.'

'A *Memento Mori*,' said Bridget. 'His best life and his death in one picture.' She hesitated. 'Look, can I have access to that one, the one on the wall. I'd quite like to have a picture to go with the gift he made me.'

Jonathan put the group shot down and picked up an identically framed copy of the solo shot. 'My PA got this for our mother not knowing she already has too many. I was going to offer it to you anyway, but it means a lot that you asked for it.'

He handed it over and Bridget took a closer look. The award was a big golden star, so big that Tony had to hold it in two hands, and all his fingers, as well as his right wrist, were on view. She smiled to herself. This was going somewhere only she could see it.

'Thanks, Jonathan.' She put the award down and picked up her tea – served in a vintage china cup, no less.

He drank his own tea and looked at the papers spread around the desk. 'I've been in to see the family liaison officer. She's very no-nonsense when it comes to practicalities.'

Bridget had run her ruler over many a family liaison officer and police victim support worker over the years. If she was any judge, the woman he'd seen today recognised that Jonathan needed practical help more than he needed tea and sympathy. 'How are you getting on?'

'It should be me asking that question.' He slumped for a second, then picked himself up. 'Tony wanted a cremation, not a burial, but as this is homicide they won't allow that until after the trial, and if

Ramsey changes her mind and pleads not guilty. She might even appeal.' He looked at Bridget. 'I don't think Mum could cope with that. The FLO said I should just do it, so he's going to be interred next to Dad and Granddad in Aldhaven. I hope you'll come.'

'Of course I will.'

Tony would have made a comment about Bridget being already dressed for a funeral; Jonathan did not. Either he hadn't noticed, he'd had more practice, or he was just more empathetic.

'That's not why I asked you to come,' he said. He picked up a multi-page document on heavy cream paper. 'Tony's will. He made a new one two years ago. His shares in NapaTech go to me and most of the residue to his niece – my daughter, obviously. It's the other bequests that are causing a problem, especially the one to Donna Ramsey.'

That *was* awkward. 'Ouch,' said Bridget.

'I said something much worse, believe me. She can't have it, obviously, neither morally nor legally. No question about *that*. It's very complicated, but she was going to get a share of his IPR. To cut a long story short, I'd like to offer you an equivalent cash sum.'

'I can't take any money.' The words were out of her mouth before she could think. When she'd spoken, a tiny sliver of her regretted it.

'I thought you might say that, Bridget. I don't need it and my daughter won't take it. Not because she thinks it's wrong but because she thinks *you* should have it.'

'She's never met me!'

'You deserve it, Bridget.' He held up his hand to forestall her. 'You'll get a letter in a few days offering you one hundred and twenty-five thousand pounds or asking you to nominate a charity.'

She rocked back. *A hundred and twenty-five grand. Bloody hell.*

Jonathan put the will to one side. 'I really hope you take the money. It wasn't a "good cause" risking everything for Tony's memory in that room, Bridget, it was *you*. You nearly lost your life. Let us give you something which will change it for the better. You can't decide now, because you haven't got the letter. Think it over.'

She didn't answer him because that sliver of regret was growing, and so was the outraged guilt on behalf of the other women it might help. 'Was Donna's share really worth that much?'

'Back of an envelope, yes. Spread over ten years.'

'Thank you, Jon. I don't know what to say.'

'You've already said *thank you*. Not a lot to add.'

'There is. I wasn't alone up there. Jed Holmes risked just as much, and he came off a lot worse.'

'I know. I also know that it was you who figured everything out. I will make him an offer when I see him, but it will be nothing like yours.'

'Then it's your lucky day. He's in the van.'

'Oh.'

'Can I ask you a real favour? As well as offering him money – which he'll definitely accept – can you give him five minutes on something else?'

'Of course.'

She finished her tea and stood up. Can I use your loo and what's the mobile signal like out here?'

'Cloakroom's last but one on the way out. Hang on.' He opened a drawer and took out a double-sized business card. 'Wi-Fi password's on the back. There's a base station outside, too.'

She took the card and smiled. 'Of course there is. Can I walk round the garden? It's boiling in the van.'

'Please do. In fact, if you go round the other side, there's a lovely shady seat. Mum's pride and joy.'

There was a silence while they both thought of the elder Mrs Carson sitting there on the day of her son's funeral, and that it might be the last time she did.

'I'll get Jed,' said Bridget.'

'Tell him to come in here.'

'Be nice to him.'

'Depends on whether he comes straight in here or goes poking around and pretending to be lost.' There was a mischievous grin on his face, and Bridget's heart surged with regret. It was the look that Tony should have grown into but never did.

'Thanks for the tea.'

She went back to the van and held the passenger door open for Jed to get out. There was sweat trickling down his temple from the heat or pain. She picked up on Jonathan's sense of humour and decided not to tell Jed it was his lucky day.

'In you go,' she told him. 'Go directly to the study at the back. Do not search the rooms. Do not take pictures. And you can take as long as you want. If I'm not here, I'll be in the garden. Message me.'

She went back indoors ahead of him, used the loo and repaired her lipstick. It might be a custom shade, but it didn't have the staying power of premium products. She walked outside and went in search of Mrs Carson's special place.

Sixty-Five

Most of the garden was built in terraces below the level of the house. It looked almost institutional in its neatness, with different sections given over to strawberries, to shrubs and to flowers for cutting. Bridget knew a lot about plant extracts but almost nothing about gardens. Not surprising given that she'd grown up in a house with concrete front and rear. A bit like No 4 Midland Terrace, really.

She passed the shutters protecting the living rooms, noted the expensive patio furniture and imagined the Carsons having drinks on the terrace looking out at Morecambe Bay. If Lucy ever saw this house, she'd go weak at the knees.

Round the other side, the hand of an expert gardener was evident, and it had to have been Jonno and Tony's mother. Tony had said she thought that Aldhaven was too steep and too close to the sea, so Mrs Carson had created her own little patch of Byford on the only flat ground. *Someone* was keeping it up these days, but it was clear that the guiding spirit was fading. Between the heavily flowering – and heavily scented – rose bushes, there were gaps: something taken away and not replaced. A small patch of lawn stood in front of a picture-book bower of climbing roses over a rustic bench with cushions. The whole thing was utterly at odds with the modernist house in Bridget's opinion, but what did she know?

She knew it was shady and she made herself comfortable, accessing the Wi-Fi and putting her phone on the little side table. After that, she let the good angel and bad angel on her shoulders slug it out. The only trouble was, she couldn't tell which was which.

Perhaps if she'd done her thinking somewhere else, under the railway arches for example, she'd have made a different decision, but once her mind was made up, she acted straight away. She picked up her phone and called Perry on video WhatsApp, crossing her fingers that he'd answer. He did, and he looked cool as the AC in the estate office.

'Hello, Bridget. How are you?'

'I'm fine. Well, as good as can be expected. Listen, Perry, have you processed my letter quitting the tenancy?'

'Why do you ask?' he said mildly, putting it right back on her.

'Because I want to stay. If you'll still have me.'

'Just stay in Byford or stay in Caffè Milano as well?'

'Both. Lucy has no choice but to keep me.'

By way of an answer, he disappeared off screen for a second, then reappeared with her letter. He tore it up in front of the camera and smiled. 'Good,' he announced. 'Best news I've heard since the police told me you were uninjured.'

She glanced away, hoping the foundation would cover the blush rising up her cheek.

He leaned closer to the camera and said, 'What's up?'

'Oh, nothing. Is there still a place for me on the quiz team as well?'

'Absolutely. You're still responsible for the fourth member, though.'

She couldn't help it. The rejection she'd felt when she saw Perry with his arm around another woman burst out of her lips. 'I thought you'd already got Laura Paige lined up.'

He frowned. 'What makes you think that?'

Damn him. Why didn't he just admit it and go public with their relationship? Bridget suddenly felt thirteen again, and not in a good way – she'd had exactly the same experience with her first boyfriend. It was one of the things that had made her turn to the dark side and join the two Goth pioneers who lurked in the corner of the chemistry lab.

Bridget gave her inner child a biscuit and tried to look innocent. 'I thought you were discussing team tactics with her the other day.'

He scratched his head. 'And there was me thinking that Jackie Chester was the Queen of Randomness. I'd love to get a quiz team together, but I doubt I'll ever be spending time on tactics.' He paused to let that sink in, and to let Bridget know that he knew what she was really asking. 'No, Laura came to ask me for advice on dealing with the enemy.'

'Does Laura even have any enemies? Apart from her ex-husband?'

'They're still married. I don't normally gossip, but I think Laura's hoping he'll grow out of the other woman and come home.'

That was a bombshell and a half. On her visit to Laura's house, she'd noticed that the family pictures still featured both the children's parents, something that had quickly changed in her own home. 'So who's her enemy?'

Perry raised his eyebrows. 'The Angels. Who else? Something to do with the effects in Millie Easterby's estate.'

'Oh right. I'll let you get on and I'll get back to you on the fourth team member.'

He laughed. 'I can't wait.' He turned serious again. 'I'm really, really pleased you're staying. See you soon.'

'Yep. I'll be back in the Old Spinning Room this afternoon.'

'I look forward to it. Bye for now.'

Lucy would be flat out prepping the lunches right now. Bridget got her thumbs busy and typed *Am staying. I want to withdraw my notice. I'm afraid you're stuck with me. Don't tell anyone else yet and I'll get Peroni in for tonight. We might be inviting Mike Mason over as well.*

She pressed Send and went to see how Jed was getting on. Knowing her little kit, he'd have collapsed and Jonno Carson would be doing CPR and breaking more ribs.

She blinked at the darkness inside the house and ran her hands along the wall until she could see the study, and she wasn't far wrong about Jed.

He was hunched over the desk clutching a glass of water, and there was a strip of pills in front of him. 'You okay, kid?'

'He's really overdone it,' said Jonathan. 'He jerked in shock and pulled something.'

'You should have warned me about the surprise,' said Jed.

'Wouldn't have been a surprise then, would it? Are you sure you're okay?'

'I'll be fine when the morphine kicks in.'

'I had a friend who used to say that,' said Bridget.

The friend had been Natalie, and those were probably the last words she'd spoken before she overdosed. Bridget shook her head to clear the image.

'Do you want help to get outside?' asked Jonathan.

'Actually, I wanted another quick word with you,' said Bridget. 'If you don't mind.'

'Can I lie on the settee for a bit?' asked Jed.

'Of course,' said Jonathan.

'Only if you take your shoes off,' added Bridget.

'See?' said Jed. 'I told you she reminds me of me auntie.'

Jonathan got up and offered an arm to support Jed, who hesitated, then took it. When the budding investigative journalist had been settled in the living room, Jonathan came back and shut the door, patting the wood when it was closed. 'Don't worry. It's soundproof. My grandfather liked Wagner. Trains mostly, but Wagner also.'

They sat down and Bridget leaned on the desk, pushing Jed's water and codeine tablets aside. 'I've decided to accept the money.' She let that sink in for a second. 'Don't ask me why, I just have, okay?'

'Good. I really am pleased.' He glanced at the door. 'Young Mr Holmes didn't even *think* about it. He just gasped out a *yes* and doubled up in pain. It does you great credit, Bridget.'

'Yeah, well. We'll see. Look, Jon, there is one other thing. When I had Donna Ramsey at my mercy, she told me that the *City of Lancaster* was in some shed. Did Liz say anything about it?'

He looked down, and the self-effacing mask slipped. 'She did. She told me about Esther Thornfield, too. The woman was right: Anthony destroyed it to make some teenage artwork. He's been trying to rebuild it. Or make a new one from scratch. Hard to tell without seeing it for myself.'

'You'll get it back, won't you?'

'Eventually.'

'And will you finish the job? Tony would want you to, I know that much.'

He looked up. 'You're right. He would.'

'And CARM want to carry on with Carsondale, don't they? They can't do it without you.'

'Yes they could, but they wouldn't. Darren has a thing about Carlisle, but he can wait his turn. I'll be back at the Mill soon enough.'

'Perfect. You can also join our quiz team. Me, Perry Lockwood, Fliss Duke and you. Tuesday nights at the White Hart.'

'That sounds like an offer I can't refuse. I haven't quizzed for ages. I don't know. It depends on my wife's shift patterns and her book club evenings.'

Bridget stood up to leave, and this time she offered Jonathan her hand to shake.

When she turned to the door, she said, 'If Jed's not fit to travel, you can keep him for a bit, can't you?'

'No I cannot. My wife knows the number of a private ambulance service. I'll deduct the fee from his share of the estate.'

Sixty-Six

Jed looked a little more human when Jonathan helped him off the sofa. There were more thanks and they left the cool of the Carson house to face the heat. Bridget unlocked the van and said, 'Let's leave the doors for a bit before we get in. Let the heat out. If you can stand up.'

'Yeah. Good idea.' He opened his door and leaned on the roof with his good arm. 'How much did you get?'

The nerve! Was it how all the kids behave these days, or was it just Jed? She thought of Katarina. Nope. Definitely Jed. 'That is a question whose answer you will never know, and if you try to find out, I will use my psychic powers to haunt your dreams.'

'I just wondered, that's all.'

'*All!* You just don't ask questions like that, Jed.' She paused. 'Yeah, I guess you do, actually. Still not gonna answer. How did you get on with asking for an interview?'

'He hasn't said no. Once I told him that you were on board, I think he was leaning towards a *yes*.'

'Good. Let's go.' They got in the van and she started the engine. 'Are you in a rush?'

'No.'

She drove down the hill and turned left onto the prom. There were plenty of spaces today, and she pulled up with the van facing the bay. 'You need something to go with those painkillers. Sit here or on the bench if you can make it, but put the windows up and take the keys out of the ignition first.'

'Yes, Auntie Bridget.'

She looked down her nose at him for a second then sniffed with disdain. She got out, crossed the road and checked her phone. Lucy had messaged back, and Bridget opened the app with a little trepidation.

'What on earth?' she said. The message was almost completely emojis, too small to read, but they seemed to be mostly hearts and stars, so good news. She peered at the end. A pint of beer and a champagne bottle. Fair enough.

She locked her phone and went into the ice cream shop, the one selling unpasteurised raw milk. There was a girl behind the counter who had *student* written all over her, including the Chinese characters snaking up her arm.

Bridget shuddered and looked away. Far too similar to the kanji on Donna's knife. It was funny how horrors got you when you least expected them. 'I want two large tubs, one strawberry and one vanilla, both with flakes, please. I also want to know if it's safe to eat.'

'Erm …'

The girl was probably local – it wasn't just the accent and the pale skin, it was the inherent niceness of most of the kids round here. Bridget wondered how she'd cope with a stroppy Goth.

'Yes?'

'All our ice cream's safe,' the girl pleaded.

'How do you know?'

Her eyes flicked around the corner of the tiny café. No one was coming to rescue her. In desperation, she grabbed the five-litre tub out of the freezer and read the label. *'Made from certified tested organic raw milk.'*

'What for?'

'So we know it's safe. That's what for.'

'No, I mean what is it *tested* for? Which bacteria? How frequently? Every batch or just samples?'

The tub slammed back into the cabinet. 'I'm sure it's on the website.' The girl pointed to a poster. 'The address is there.'

'I'll take your word for it. Two tubs, please.'

The ice cream was scooped and served in a silence frostier than the product. Bridget took three wooden spoons, gave the girl a generous tip and took the tubs to the bench. 'There you go, Jed. Hold it steady for a sec.'

She took the third spoon and dug into his strawberry. 'Hey! That's mine!' he protested, channelling his inner child. Not that he had to dig very deep to find it.

The strawberry was badly made. No question. Whoever had done this had no real idea about depth of flavour or holding back on the enhancer. She could do better in her sleep. The vanilla was good, but with quality ingredients and the right machine, anyone could make it. Vanilla was the espresso of ice cream, yes, and the same applied to coffee: right machine, right beans and anyone could make it. The mark of a true barista was what you did afterwards.

'What the hell!' said Jed, holding the tub at eye level and radiating outrage. 'This is raw milk! After what you put me through last week? What are you doing, Bridget?'

'Being a grown-up and changing my mind. As you no doubt discovered, there have been no actual cases of food poisoning from raw milk ice cream. Now shut up and tell me about your injuries. I know you're dying to.'

'Shut up *and* tell you something?'

'Auntie's prerogative.'

His arm had not fared well, apparently. They hadn't even operated properly yet: Jed had that to look forward to on Friday. 'My mum's coming up to take me home afterwards. For a few days.'

'You'll be out of action for a while, won't you? Not just a few days?'

'Yeah, but she'll soon get fed up and send me back to Dad's.'

He took it stoically enough, but Bridget could see the hurt. Before she could comment, he went slightly red and turned to face her. 'Look, there's something I should have said, and even with this money from the Carsons, I can't change it. When I do the serial, it won't be me interviewing you. It'll be Ciara Davenport?'

'Whatever for? That piece of fluff couldn't figure out the killer in a game of Cluedo.'

'I know that. I'm writing the script and interview questions, and I'll direct the recordings, but it was a condition of the contract that I had no more than twenty per cent of the air time.'

Bridget was outraged on his behalf. 'What on earth for? You earned this!'

He shrugged. 'I know. It's Ciara's dad's company behind it, which is fair enough, but that's not why I got throttled.' His voice shifted. 'It's me accent. Rates very badly, unlike yours. Until I get to see a voice coach, I'm gonna struggle.'

'But it's who you are! It's part of what makes you into Jed Holmes, Ace Reporter.'

He took another scoop and bit his flake. 'No it isn't. I wasn't born with a Brummie accent any more than you was born with them tattoos or jet black hair.'

She opened her mouth to argue, then she realised he was right. 'Did you come up with that one on your own?'

'No. It was one of the lecturers. He used to be an actor and he came to give us some inside tips from the business. The others thought he was too old and knew nothing about new media. I reckon some things don't change.'

He was right about that. Bridget looked out to the west, towards the Irish Sea. 'Wow.'

'What?'

'Clouds. Real clouds. Black ones. It's gonna rain.'

He tried to crane his neck round and gave up.

'What star sign are you, Jed?'

'Aries.'

'Good. That means we're incompatible, so you can stop trying to flirt with me.'

'Fine. So long as that goes both ways.'

'We'll see. Remember, I have auntie's prerogative. Now shut up and eat your ice cream. We've both earned it.'

* * *

The Adventures of Caffè Milano will continue in

Murder in the Cloud

Available from Paw Press sometime in 2025. Probably.

Coming in 2025 from Paw Press

Murder in the Cloud

The Third Caffè Milano English Village Mystery

By
Ruth Ward

It's hard to mind your own business…
When your business is murder

Bridget is doing what she does best – serving coffee and making ice cream.

She's also a woman who pays her debts, and one of those is to her pet ferret, Jed Holmes.

When she turns up to be interviewed for Jed's podcast at the university, all that's on her mind is going for a drink afterwards.

And then she hears a scream.

Soon, Bridget is hired by her new best friend/annoying lawyer Abi Tennant to investigate the crime.

Can Bridget fight her way through the maze of lies and alibis to solve the murder of an unloved IT investor? Find out, in *Murder in the Cloud*.

If you're enjoying the Byford stories, why not join Ruth's elite group of supporters:

The Friends of Ford Mill

Visit the Paw Press website and sign up for the mailing list, or search **Facebook** for the Friends of Ford Mill Group.

Either way, you're guaranteed to be kept up with news from Paw Press.

Author's Note

A Note from Ruth.

Thank you for reading my second book, and I hope you enjoyed it.

I wrote this book because I wanted to and because people asked me to. A lot of the readers of the original (Advent calendar) version of *Murder Within Tent* said that they'd like to read more about Bridget. I hope I've lived up to your expectations.

If the gods are smiling, there *will* be a third book, too – look out for *Murder in the Cloud* at some point in 2025. Hopefully. Fingers crossed. Probably. You get the picture.

This book would not be in your hand without the help of many people – first and foremost are Katie Birks and Kirsty Parkinson.

Katie has been Mark's website designer, graphic designer and mailing list maestro for some time. When the awesome Rachel Lawston passed on the baton of cover design work, she picked it up and ran with it, and I'm very grateful she did.

Also crucial is Kirsty Parkinson, who bravely took on the editing and hammered out all sorts of bugs, errors and infelicities. All remaining imperfections are entirely my fault.

Thanks to Lucy Campbell, Paula Berman, Lore Deus and Sheila Joss, all of whom read the first draft and gave me feedback.

And finally, thanks go to Mrs Hayden. Not only did she read the first draft for me, she allowed Mark time off to work on the project. Greater love hath no woman…

When it comes to writing *Murder in the Cloud,* I hope to hark back to the charity dimension and sell off some of the naming rights for characters, so if you fancy putting yourself or your spouse in my next book, make sure to join the Friends of Ford Mill and watch out for announcements.

Until then,

Thanks again,

Ruth Ward.

Printed in Dunstable, United Kingdom

65918377R00190